# GOLD RUSH

BLACKWOOD SECURITY
BOOK 4

ELISE NOBLE

True strength is in the soul and spirit, not in muscles.

— UNKNOWN

# 1

## LARA

There it was. That prickle at the back of my neck as somebody watched me.

I glanced at my reflection in store windows as I passed, trying to get a glimpse of who or what might be behind. There! What was that? A shadow flitting across the sidewalk? I whipped around, holding my breath, one hand on the can of pepper spray I carried in my jacket pocket.

My eyes darted from left to right, my gaze as jittery as a coffee addict looking for their mid-afternoon fix, then I sagged in relief. It was just a loose shop awning, flapping in the weak breeze that managed to find its way amongst the tightly packed jumble of crumbling apartments and the few stores that clung to life. The locals had christened this part of town "NoHo."

No Hope.

As if by giving it a hip-sounding name they could stave off the need for a wrecking ball, which was the only way left of improving things. A solitary soul roamed the sidewalk—a woman on the corner, shoulders stooped as life weighed her down. Her harsh make-up and lack of clothing on an unseasonably chilly night told me what she was waiting for. I exhaled a thin stream of air then forced myself to breathe in and out, slowly, telling myself I was once again being ridiculous.

Paranoid.

Crazy.

*Breathe in and out.*

*Breathe in and out.*

*Put one foot in front of the other, Lara.* I started towards my apartment, just another girl returning home after a night out, trying to act casual. But my feet didn't get the message and moved faster and faster, seemingly of their own accord.

More than once over the past couple of weeks, I'd given in to the urge to run and ended up pounding along the street. I must have looked like an escapee from the asylum as I was chased by an army of monsters invisible to everybody except me.

Tonight that wouldn't happen. No, tonight I was going to stay calm. Except when I reached the bottom of the rickety stairs leading to the shabby walk-up I called home, I almost sobbed with relief. I abandoned my attempts to look unruffled and raced up the steps two at a time, feeling them wobble beneath my weight.

The key was already in my hand, and I stabbed it at the lock.

Missed.

Missed again.

*Will you get in the freaking keyhole!* I forced myself to pause and used my shaking left hand to help my equally tremulous right one to aim carefully. Twisted the key. Ran inside.

The slam of the door echoed in the hallway, and I quickly shot home the two bolts I'd begged the landlord for weeks to install. He hadn't, of course. In the end, I'd given up and asked the creep who lived two doors down to do it with the promise of a six-pack and thirty minutes in which to stare at my cleavage.

But for now, I was home.

*Home.*

I'd made it for another night, and I leaned against the door and slid slowly to the floor. How much longer could I keep this up?

Believe it or not, I hadn't always been a lunatic. In fact, until a couple of months ago, I'd considered myself relatively normal. Although in the little slice of heaven I called home, normal could be considered abnormal. I was probably the only person on the block who didn't indulge, either recreationally or professionally, in some sort of illegal activity.

I'd lived in my one-room apartment for almost a year. A tiny kitchenette occupied the corner nearest the door, opposite a small, screened-off shower room that had seen better days. The place sat above Randy's Grocery Store, or at least that was what the fading sign claimed. I'd ventured in there once when I ran out of milk and found a distinct lack of groceries on the dusty shelves. Everything I picked up was well past its sell-by date. Still, Randy had a steady trickle of visitors throughout the day and most of the night, silent shadows with hoods drawn up to hide their faces. I didn't know what they were in the market for, but I suspected it wasn't ramen noodles or a Snickers bar.

I'll be the first to admit the apartment had a lot of negatives. But all of those were cancelled out by one huge, big, wonderful positive; I could afford it. And until two months ago, I'd never felt unsafe living there. Depressed, maybe, but not out-and-out scared like I was now.

Things changed not long after I was mugged. I say after, because in the grand scheme of things, the mugging itself wasn't really that bad. Living where I did, it had been about due.

I'd been on my way home that night. Three blocks away, a scrawny kid stepped out of a doorway, his expensive sneakers and designer jeans at odds with his unwashed odour. Wild eyes peered out at me from beneath a tangle of hair, and from the way they rolled, I guessed the reason he'd turned to crime was to fund his pharmaceutical habit.

"Gimme your money."

The demand wasn't original, but when he thrust a gleaming knife in my face, it worked. I handed over my wallet and the week's wages it contained, then clutched at a nearby lamp post because my legs refused to hold me up.

As his footsteps receded into the night, little did I know that he'd stolen my sanity as well.

The cops had been sympathetic, and the detective who came out to take my statement spent enough time listening to almost make me believe I mattered. He'd bought me coffee, feigned sympathy, and only looked at his watch once while I told my story.

At the end of it, he'd given me his card and said, "If you're worried about anything, call me."

What was the point? I was realistic enough to know the high the kid spent my money on had worn off by now. I was just another statistic. And at first, I thought the jitters I felt afterwards were a reaction to the theft. That was perfectly normal, right? Surely I couldn't be the only girl who got a bit nervous walking home at night?

*Be logical, Lara.*

I'd lived in Baysville all my life, and this was the first time I'd ever been mugged. Well, apart from the moment Joey Rogers pushed me over in third grade and stole my lunch money, but I couldn't really count that.

I told myself that I hadn't been hurt, that by the law of

averages it wouldn't be my turn again for a while. Sure, I hadn't been able to pay my rent on time, and I ended up living on oatmeal for two weeks, but that was just the way my life seemed to be lately.

Unlucky.

In another lifetime, when I was a child, my pop used to call me Lucky Lara. Each Thursday, the guys came over to play poker, and he'd sit me on his lap and let me hold his cards because he said he always won that way. Back then, we'd lived in a proper house, and I had toys and friends and nice clothes and birthday parties and everything else a child dreamed of.

Then a week before my tenth birthday, my luck ran out. As did my father. When he left for work, he'd kissed me on the cheek and said, "Be good at school, Lucky." I hadn't seen him since. Gone were the house and the toys and birthday parties.

My friends went too, once I no longer wore the latest sneakers or played with whatever toy happened to be in fashion that week. Until that day, I hadn't realised how nasty little girls could be. I came home crying most days, and when I walked in the door, my momma would dry her own eyes and comfort me.

She tried to hide her tears, but there's no way one person could be unlucky enough to get grit in their eye almost every day. Still, I couldn't complain. Momma did her best to look after me, even if she was never the same after Pop left. At first, I used to ask when he was coming back, but that only made her sadder, so I stopped. Once, I'd asked if it was my fault he left, and she swore it wasn't, that he'd disappeared because he simply didn't love her anymore.

Then she'd cried again, and that was the last time I mentioned him.

I went from being Lucky Lara to Lara the Loser, or occasionally Lousy Lara for variety. Grades four through ten were spent hiding in the library, avoiding the outside world in general and people in particular. The bullies couldn't get to me in the library. Mrs. Weiss, the dragon of a librarian in high school, wouldn't stand any nonsense in her domain. Books were my best friends—math, science, economics—I drank them in. I kept my head down and my GPA a smidgen under 4.0, so my teachers liked me even if nobody else did. But the loneliness? Yes, the loneliness got to me.

People say your school days are the best of your life, but at the time they didn't feel like it. If only I'd known back then it was true, I might have smiled more. Either that or given up altogether. I put in all that work for a bar job and a dingy apartment with water that ran cold five days out of seven.

I tried to tell myself things would get better, that happiness lurked just around the corner, but it always remained a few steps ahead of me. And what was behind me? Well, I'd acquired either a genuine stalker or a deep-seated sense of crazy.

## 2

---

## LARA

I couldn't sit on the floor all night. Besides the draught creeping under the door, my behind was slowly going numb, and the rest of me ached from being on my feet the whole day.

Just thinking about work brought on a yawn. I needed to get some sleep, because in five hours, I'd have to get up for my morning job cleaning Buck's Bar of the detritus left by fifty or so men who treated drinking as a sport. Believe me, I knew all about that—in the evenings, I worked the late shift as a waitress-slash-barmaid-slash-general-dogsbody.

Living the dream, right?

I hauled myself to my feet and breathed in deeply, cringing at the familiar scent. The faint trace of cigarette smoke and cheap men's cologne that meant an unwelcome visitor had been in my apartment. Again.

The first time I noticed the strange aroma, I'd convinced myself I was imagining it. The second time too, although doubt started to creep in. The third time, when I saw the TV remote on the fold-out bed, I knew I'd had an uninvited visitor. My apartment may have been tiny, but everything had its proper place, and the remote always lived on the crate that doubled up as a television stand.

Twice more over the next week, the odour of stale cigarettes seeped through the mustiness that came with thrift store furniture. Paranoia set in. Had I forgotten to put my favourite mug back in the cupboard? Did I move that pen from its home on the nightstand?

Was I losing my mind?

The day I came home to find my underwear drawer cracked open and the contents in disarray, I threw up. What kind of sick freak chose to rummage through my panties? Actually, I wasn't sure I wanted to know the answer to that question.

But I suspected he was following me. The next evening, I was almost certain I heard soft footsteps trailing behind as I walked home from Buck's, but when I spun around, there was only darkness. A paper bag blew past, end over end. Had I been mistaken?

Another week passed, and my nerves stretched thinner with every waking hour. A rustle here, a shadow there. Was I going insane or had I acquired an unwanted companion?

My friend Missy thought the former. She didn't say that, of course, but when I confessed all over coffee, her frown told me she doubted my story. I remembered that day well. We'd met in our regular spot, a diner midway between us that served food that was edible and, more importantly, cheap, and she dumped three spoonfuls of sugar into her cappuccino before she spoke.

"Have you actually seen anyone following you?" she asked.

"Well, no. He could have hidden behind a tree or something."

"You see many trees in NoHo?"

"I guess not."

The place was a concrete jungle. The only greenery was the

occasional cannabis leaf that popped up in the graffiti that adorned every building.

"So maybe there isn't anyone? What if the smell in your apartment drifted in through a vent or something?"

Was Missy right? Did I just have an overactive imagination?

That afternoon, I taped a plastic bag over the air conditioning duct. The AC hadn't worked since I'd moved in, so it was no great loss. But the day after, the whiff of cheap cologne and tobacco smoke once again lay in my apartment like a slumbering monster.

A knock at the door a few hours later made me jump out of my skin.

"It's me," Missy yelled. "I've come to check you're okay."

Bless her, even though she thought I'd lost my marbles, she'd come to help me gather them up again.

We'd first met two years ago, in the hospital. Her brother was having chemo at the same time as Momma, except his was for bowel cancer. Someone up there smiled down on him, and he pulled through, but although I lost Momma, I gained Missy. We bonded in the cafeteria over a shared love of stale sandwiches and lukewarm coffee, and she helped me through the most awful time of my life. What would I do without her?

I cracked the door open. "He was here again."

She pushed her way in and hugged me. "Oh, honey, you should call someone."

Like who? Did she mean the police or a psychiatrist? "My phone's got no credit."

She reached into her purse and pulled out a crumpled ten-dollar bill. "Take this."

My eyes prickled with tears at her generosity. She was saving up for her wedding, and money was tight. "I can't."

She tucked it into my pocket. "You can and you will."

After another rummage, she held out a can. "I brought you a gift."

"Pepper spray?"

"A girl needs to be prepared. You should take a self-defence class. The one I did last year kicked ass."

I didn't want to kick ass. I just wanted to sleep in my own bed at night without some freak staking out my apartment.

"I'll think about it."

"Call me if you change your mind. The instructor was hot."

I loved that girl. Even when she thought I'd gone insane, she still tried to make my padded cell a happier place.

Tried and failed.

Feeling slowly returned to my bottom as I went into the bathroom to put my pyjamas on. Once, I'd have changed next to my bed, but now the madness had set in, I locked myself away before I peeled off my jeans.

In bed, I wrapped the blankets around me like a shield, regressing to my childhood belief that if the bogeyman couldn't see me, he couldn't get me. Even so, I barely closed my eyes. The prospect of being murdered in my sleep kept me awake better than a double dose of caffeine.

The next day, I was wiping down the bar at Buck's when my phone rang. My heart skipped as "Unknown caller" flashed up on the screen. Only a handful of people had my number, and my hand shook as I answered.

"Lara Reynolds?"

"That's me." I hated the quaver that crept into my voice.

"I'm the detective who took your statement a couple of

weeks ago. The mugging? I thought I'd check up to see if everything was okay."

Oh shoot, should I tell him about my fears? Momma always said a problem shared was a problem halved, but if Missy didn't believe me, why would a complete stranger? I had no proof, just instances of untidiness and an intangible scent problem. I may as well tell him I was being haunted. Hey, maybe I had a poltergeist? Did ghosts smoke?

"Hello?" His voice crackled out of the speaker.

"Yes, I'm here." I hesitated. "I'm not sure... Sometimes I think..."

"You sound nervous, and that's perfectly normal. A lot of people get jumpy after an assault. If you want, I could refer you to a..." I heard the rustling of paper in the background. "To a therapist. Now, where did I put the card with the number?"

Therapy? He thought it was all in my head, didn't he? "No need for that. Everything's fine, really."

"You're sure?"

"Never been better."

"Glad to hear it. You know where to find me if you ever want to talk."

As the line went dead, a ball of dread rolled around in my stomach. Perhaps I should have said something? Well, it was too late now.

Things only got worse the week after. I had four teabags left, enough to last until my next visit to the grocery store. Tragic that I should have to count them, but every cent counted when you lived on the breadline. When I got in from cleaning at lunchtime on Wednesday, four had turned into three. Had my math skills deserted me as well as my sanity? I thought they had until I touched the kettle and found it warm.

Heart pounding, I tried phoning Missy. I needed a hug,

her positive words, and a hot self-defence instructor. No answer. A single tear escaped, and I wiped it away with the edge of my T-shirt. Now what? I checked my watch, did the math in my head, and calculated it was 8 a.m. in England. Tori would be awake—her kids never let her sleep past seven.

I'd known Victoria since I started elementary school. She was the one person who stuck by me after Pop left, and even though we attended different junior highs, we'd stayed close. When she moved to England at fourteen, that was the greatest loss I'd experienced up until Momma's death. Now she lived in a London suburb, happily married to a cab driver, with two young sons and a cockapoo named Gordon. I'd snorted coffee when she told me the dog's breed, but apparently cocker spaniels crossed with poodles were all the rage over there.

I trembled so much it took me three goes to dial her number, but the effort was worth it when I heard her voice.

"Lara! It's been ages! How are you?"

I tried to keep my sobs to a minimum as I poured my heart out, detailing everything from the mugging to the unshakeable feeling that someone was stalking me.

Her gasps, followed by a stunned silence when I finished, helped to strengthen my tenuous grasp on reality.

"That's awful. You need to go to the police."

"And tell them what? That my apartment smells odd? A pen isn't where I left it? They'd have me committed."

Although that might not be so bad. Compared to my apartment, a padded cell would actually be quite comfortable.

"Okay, so it sounds a bit farfetched, but I still think you should consider it. Maybe they'd put your apartment under surveillance?"

I couldn't help laughing. "Last month, a kid got murdered on the next block, and it took the cops three days to interview anyone. My issue's hardly going to be a priority. When I put it into words, I can barely believe it myself."

"Just think about it, okay? Do you have any idea who it might be?"

I'd racked my brains in that regard, staring at my neighbours with suspicion and trembling every time I saw a stranger.

"Not a clue. But when the mugger took my wallet, my address was in it, so maybe it's connected somehow? What I don't understand is why someone would follow me. I'm the least interesting person I know. I might as well be invisible."

"You're only invisible because you want to be. Billy did that to you."

At the mention of his name, fear trickled through me. I'd tried so hard to forget him. "Don't talk about Billy."

"Just because he was an asshole doesn't mean you need to hide away for the rest of your life."

"I don't hide away."

"You go to work; you go home. What else do you do?"

"I need the money," I mumbled.

"You need to live."

What was I supposed to say to that? Deep down, I knew she was right. I just didn't want to admit it.

"When are you coming to visit?" Tori asked.

"When I win the lotto."

Since I couldn't afford to play the lotto, it would be a long wait.

"I've offered to pay for your plane ticket."

"I know, and I appreciate it, I really do. But I can't accept something so expensive. I'm saving up." And at the rate I was saving, I'd be able to fly to England about the same time as mankind colonised Mars.

"Well, the offer's always there." Her voice softened. "Take care of yourself, okay?"

"I will," I lied.

I flopped back onto the bed, thunking my head on the

wall as I misjudged the distance. Despite the early hour, I was tired. So tired. My body craved rest, but I made myself get up and change instead. If I didn't hurry up with the chores, I'd be late for work, and I didn't have the energy to run all the way there.

That evening, I wore a chocolate-brown knee-length skirt with a cream blouse, topped off with a pair of sneakers—ugly but practical. I couldn't sprint in high heels. When I first started working at the bar, one of the waitresses, a twenty-year veteran, had explained that tips were directly proportional to skirt length, and careful experimentation had proven her absolutely right. The shorter the skirt and the higher the heels, the more money I made.

Not only was my income suffering with my new outfits, Buck wasn't impressed either. A pervert at best and an asshole at worst, the first day I turned up in jeans and a sweater, he'd hauled me through to the kitchen.

"What the fuck are you wearing?"

"Uh, jeans?"

"Did you forget that this is a bar, not some mom and pop grocery store?"

I withered under his stare. "I'm sorry. It's just that I'm a little nervous after the mugging, and I can walk faster in pants."

He folded his arms. "Well, I suggest you get un-nervous before I lose clientele to bars where the girls make an effort. If that happens, I'll have to start losing staff as well."

And work was scarce in Baysville. I wasn't sure whether Buck was genuinely concerned about his customers or peeved that I'd spoiled his viewing pleasure—because I couldn't recall having a conversation with him where his eyes got higher than my chest—but it didn't matter. Without that job, I couldn't pay the rent, so I switched back to skirts and carried my pumps in my purse as a compromise. If everything else failed, I could always smack any would-be attacker with a shoe.

On my half-run, half-walk to work that evening, I thought back to my conversation with Tori. Even with her encouragement, I felt too embarrassed to report what was happening. It was bad enough that Billy thought I was an idiot without proving to everybody else that he was right.

No, I could cope. After all, the person hadn't hurt me, right? I'd be an adult about this and ignore the problem.

I repeated that to myself all evening while I served up beer and got my ass groped by a drunken regular. Every time a customer looked at me for a second too long, or smiled a touch too readily, I wondered... Was it him? I even caught myself sniffing a man before I scolded myself for being ridiculous.

My mantra continued the whole way home, while I climbed the stairs, unlocked my apartment door, and stepped inside. I could cope. I could *cope*. The books I'd carefully stacked hadn't moved, and the mug I'd left perched on the edge of the counter was exactly where I placed it. If not for the now-familiar aroma, stronger than usual, I could have steadied my pulse. I sniffed again, and a faint memory flickered in the recesses of my mind. *Had* I smelled that before somewhere outside of home? I tried to cling onto the thread, but it skittered away like a child's balloon, farther, farther, until it floated out of reach.

My gaze darted around the room, then stopped on the bed. Why was the bedspread wrinkled? Running late or not, I always smoothed out the covers before I left home. *Always*. I tiptoed over and ran my hand over the spot. Could I have sat down without remembering it? I paused, touched it again. Why was it warm? Warm like someone had been lying there?

My breath came in pants as I realised what that meant.

Someone had been in my apartment again, and they'd been there recently. And not only that, this time they'd been in my bed.

## 3

## LARA

How long did it take for a mattress to go cold? Ten minutes? Twenty? Surely no longer? I shuddered because that meant my intruder had left just before I got there. Was he still nearby?

I never normally swore—Momma had brought me up to be politer than that—but a string of expletives left my mouth.

Oh gosh, what to do? I scrabbled for my phone as I came to a decision—I'd call the detective who took my statement after the mugging. He'd said to contact him any time, right? And even if he thought I was mad, at least my fears would be on record somewhere if I turned up dead. Now, where did I put his card? I thought I'd tucked it into the front of *To Kill a Mockingbird*. Or was it *Far from the Madding Crowd*? I flicked through my meagre stack of books. Dammit! Where was it?

Perhaps I should call the station? What was the officer's name? Jones? Johnson? Something like that—I couldn't quite remember. I tugged at my hair so hard I must have loosened the roots.

For a brief moment, I considered calling 911 instead, but I

soon discounted that. This was hardly an emergency. What would I say? *Er, I think someone's been sitting on my bed. Could you send a car out?* They'd laugh at me for drinking too much wine and reading too much Goldilocks.

In the end, I jammed my dining chair under the door handle, and just for good measure, pushed the rickety table and chest of drawers up behind it. Would that hold? It would have to—apart from the bed and a tiny nightstand, that was all the furniture I had. I'd take a walk to the police station first thing in the morning. At least if I went in person, they couldn't hang up on me.

When daylight dawned, I almost got cold feet. Venturing outside where *he* could be waiting was the last thing I wanted to do, but I forced myself to go. As I explained my story to the officer at the front desk, even I knew how crazy it sounded. He nodded and said "mmm-hmm" in all the right places, but he glanced at the big clock on the wall four times and didn't bother writing down a word I said. His mind was probably on his next donut instead.

"So, let me get this straight," he said when I'd run out of words. "You want to file a report that says you think you might have been followed on occasion, but you're unable to give us a description. And last night your bed looked wrinkled and your apartment smelled funny?"

I nodded, already backing out the door.

"Without wanting to trivialise any of this, Ms. Reynolds, have you considered using Febreze?"

He definitely thought I was a few olives short of a pizza. And maybe I was? I was beginning to wonder myself, so I didn't bother to continue with the report. Why put my mental breakdown on record?

After I left, a bad day only got worse. A detour to avoid a narrow alley that gave me the creeps made me fifteen minutes late for work, and my tardiness didn't escape Buck's notice. He made a show of looking at the clock as I hastily changed my shoes.

Then Becky arrived. Five feet eight of fake tan and push-up bra with another three inches of blonde hair piled on top of her head. Although she was pretty in a vacant sort of way, she struggled with the beer pump, and her nails were so long she couldn't write the orders properly. By the time I'd done my work and half of hers, I was exhausted.

"Are you working here permanently?" I asked her.

She giggled. "Dunno. Buck said to have a chat with him after closing."

A chat? Yeah, right.

A stranger came in and took a seat. Was that a pack of cigarettes on the table next to him? Dammit, he caught me looking. All I could do was nod as he mimed drinking from a bottle.

"You want me to take that over?" Becky asked. Another giggle. "That guy's hot."

"I'll do it." Was he wearing cologne?

I'd barely taken two steps in his direction when Buck yelled at me. "Lara, the barrel needs changing. Give that to Becky."

I handed the drink to my unwanted sidekick, but I still felt the prickle of the man's eyes on me as she teetered towards him. At the end of the shift, he was still there, drawing out a second beer that must have gone lukewarm by now. Could he be my stalker? Should I try talking to him?

I got out a cloth and started wiping things down. Closer

and closer I got, until I was two tables away. I inhaled, and...
Nothing. I needed to get nearer.

But Buck interrupted with a tap on my shoulder. "Here."

He handed me an envelope.

"What's this? Payday isn't until Friday?"

He shifted on his feet and leaned back against the bar, which creaked ominously under his weight. "Yeah, about that. I can't give you any shifts for a while. You haven't been the picture of happiness lately, so I decided to try Becky instead."

"You're firing me? Just like that?"

Buck looked down at his feet like a toddler who knew he'd done wrong. "Not exactly. It's more that I'm giving you a break for a while. You look as if you need it."

Which translated as, "I'll see how the younger, prettier girl does, and if she messes up completely, I'll give you a call."

I bit my lip to keep from crying in front of Buck and the few patrons still finishing their drinks. Almost a year I'd worked there without missing a shift, and this was what he did?

Thanks for nothing.

And worse, I glanced over at the stranger's table and found an empty seat.

My eyes stung as I tugged on my coat. I needed to get out of there, and quickly. Buck could have fun cleaning up and explaining to Becky, for the tenth time, how to work the darn register.

As soon as my feet hit the pavement, I started running. Why try to act normally anymore? I obviously wasn't fooling anybody. I sprinted all the way home, ignoring the *slap, slap, slap* of shoes on the sidewalk I swore I heard echoing along behind me.

Back in my apartment, I took in the scene. The zip of the laundry bag was open, a T-shirt poking out, and the book I'd left open at page fifty had skipped a couple of chapters.

"Why me?" I yelled at empty air.

The upstairs neighbour pounded on the ceiling, banging the final nail in the coffin for my sanity. Sheesh, couldn't I even have a breakdown without upsetting someone?

Dragging the chest of drawers in front of the door took the last of my strength, and when I'd piled the chair and table behind it, I crawled into bed and fell into a restless sleep.

If only I didn't have to wake up in the morning.

When the sun showed its face through a haze of clouds, I took a long, hard look at my life. I was closer to thirty than twenty, and what had I accomplished? I'd lost my job, and if I didn't find another one fast, I'd lose my home. I needed a hug, but Missy would be working, and the only other friend I could count on lived in another country.

A hysterical bubble of laughter escaped. Maybe I could ask my stalker for help? What would he do if I left a note begging for spare cash? I thumped my head against the pillow, because that was hardly a solution, was it?

No, things needed to change.

Heck, *everything* needed to change.

Until now, change was something that happened *to* me. I'd never tried to effect it for myself. Where should I start? Apart from Tori and Missy, there wasn't a single thing I liked about my life. If I never saw my apartment, or NoHo, or even Baysville again, it would be a blessing.

In a moment of clarity, it came to me. What was keeping me here other than memories of Momma and a fear of the unknown?

I may have called Baysville home my whole life, but the town hadn't been kind to me. If I stayed, what would I be doing in ten years' time? Working to stay alive but not to live?

And those memories of my momma, they weren't all good. She'd spent years battling cancer and even thought she'd beaten it once, but as I'd been packing for my return to college, a return that was long overdue after an unwelcome break, we got the news that the tumour was back.

"You should still go to Brown," Momma said. "I'll manage."

Yeah, right. How could I leave her? She'd aged a decade since we got home from the hospital.

We fought together, one round of chemo after another, radiotherapy, and even a double mastectomy. When her hair fell out, she was devastated, and I learned how to pencil in her eyebrows and glue on false eyelashes so she could hold her head high at her weekly book club.

Staying positive was hard. I'd plaster on a smile every morning then cry alone at night, and I knew she did too. I heard her quiet sobs and felt the dampness on her pillow. I'd been so desperate for her to try a new experimental drug treatment, I borrowed everything I could to fund it, only it didn't work. Before my eyes, she wasted away to a shadow, and a week before my twenty-fifth birthday, she slipped away in the hospital.

I'd never forget her last words to me, whispered so softly I had to put my ear to her lips to make them out.

"Be happy, Lara. Promise me you won't waste your life. We only get one try each, and it's far too short."

"I will, Momma. I promise."

Well, so far I'd done a sterling job of keeping that promise, hadn't I? Alone and unemployed, residing in the worst part of town—how could I be happy? I didn't hold out much hope for the future, either. The last time I dared to open the statement, the total I owed for Momma's medical bills stood at $153,278.27.

In the year since she passed, I'd managed to pay off just over two thousand dollars. At that rate, it would take me another seventy-six years to be debt free, which basically meant never.

As I lay there, staring up at the cracks in the ceiling, I came to the realisation that I didn't want to spend the time I had left in Baysville. Yesterday, I'd thought my life was ending, but at the dawn of a new day, it began again. Buck had gifted me with freedom. *Nothing* was keeping me here except my own fears.

I'd never been impulsive, but years of planning and organising hadn't gotten me very far, had they? It was time to open myself up to new possibilities. And as an added bonus, perhaps I could leave my stalker behind too?

Before I changed my mind, I levered myself out of bed and grabbed my suitcase, the one I'd bought years ago in preparation for my return to Brown. A thick layer of dust covered the fabric, and I blew it away. It took me just over an hour to pack up my life. More than two-and-a-half decades on this planet, and everything of value that I owned fitted into a thirty by twenty-inch space.

Looking down at my possessions, my feet felt decidedly chilly. Was I doing the right thing? Baysville was all I'd ever known, and what about Missy? What would she say?

I slumped onto my chair and dialled her number.

"What's up? Are you crying?" she asked.

"No," I sniffed. "I'm worried I'm about to do something really crazy."

"Are you finally gonna tell Buck he's an asshole?"

A laugh escaped through my tears. "No, but I wish I could. He fired me. I'm thinking of leaving Baysville for a while."

"Wait, wait. Back up a bit. He fired you? Why the heck would he do that?"

I told her the whole sorry story, ending with my stalker sleeping in my bed, and it sounded even worse out loud. "So that's why I want to leave. These walls are closing in on me."

Not to mention some sick freak.

Missy paused for a few seconds. "You know what? Go. When I was nineteen, I did the same thing. That year I spent in Florida was an impulse move, although I'll admit too many cosmopolitans had something to do with it." She giggled. "I learned a lot about myself and life while I was away."

"You really think I should?"

"A break would do you good. After...you know, everything. You'd sure as heck better come back for my wedding though."

"Nothing would keep me away from that." Except maybe the thought of the bridesmaid dress she'd choose. Missy and fashion made an interesting mix.

"Wherever you go, you'll have a great time," she said, sounding more confident than I felt.

"I'll call you, I promise."

A flicker of fear ran through me. I was really going! Into the unknown, whatever it may bring.

I stuffed some money and a note into an envelope for the landlord and dropped it through his mailbox on the first floor before I left. Baysville was coming to life as I walked along my street for the last time. Normally a creature of habit, I rarely saw this side of the town since I slept late after work, and in the daylight, it wasn't so scary. As I reached downtown at 8 a.m., the sun burned through the clouds, bathing me in bright light. Was it an omen? Would it shine on my new life?

At the bus station on Main Street, I stood in front of a confusing array of screens. Years had passed since I'd been past the town limits, but now the world was my oyster. Or at least the bus network was—my finances wouldn't stretch overseas.

Where should I go? New York? I could disappear among the thousands of other lost souls who flocked to the city in search of a new life. But I wouldn't even be able to afford the rent on a closet. The West Coast? Land of surf, sun, and beautiful people? No, I wouldn't fit in there. What about Minnesota? Snow was pretty, but also cold. Texas? Atlanta? Florida?

Scientific reasoning wasn't helping here. If I thought about this logically, I'd spend so long weighing up the pros and cons that I'd never leave. Instead, I closed my eyes then spun around and pointed, ignoring the crowd of strangers staring at me as if I'd gone mad.

My heartbeat sped up as I followed my finger. Where would life take me?

The block letters on the front of the bus jumped out in all their neon glory. *Virginia*.

I was going to Virginia.

## 4

### LARA

A month later, I lay back on the shabby bed in my new apartment, studying a water stain on the ceiling. If I tilted my head and squinted, it looked like North Dakota. So, how had things changed? Not a lot, in all honesty. The place in Richmond wasn't much different from my old home, apart from being in a different state and having pale blue walls instead of cream. And it had a separate bedroom, albeit one I could touch both sides of if I stretched my arms out, plus the hot water seemed reliable if not a little sludge-coloured. As a bonus, it came with a grumpy landlady who lived on the floor below and treated complaining as a hobby.

"You came home too late last night," she'd told me soon after I moved in.

"Eight o'clock?"

"A lady needs her beauty sleep."

She'd missed a couple of decades of hers. "I'll try to be quieter."

"And don't forget to lock the communal door. You left it open the other day."

No way. My unwanted visitor had made me paranoid with regard to security, but I didn't want to argue.

"I'll make sure I do."

I'd make sure to keep out of her way too.

But the place had its good points as well as the bad. I hadn't seen any signs of the stalker since I left—although I still broke out in a sweat every time I smelled tobacco smoke—and my mind, which I'd temporarily misplaced, was slowly returning.

The alarm on my phone trilled, informing me it was time to get ready for work. I'd picked up a waitressing job for two days a week. The café was nicer than Buck's—the tips were better, and the clientele didn't try to grope my butt—but it barely covered my rent.

"You're first on the list if more shifts come up," my new boss told me, but I knew the prospect was unlikely. She worked most of them herself, and the other girls showed no signs of quitting.

And that meant I needed to look elsewhere for extra income.

Luckily, the public library was within walking distance of my apartment. I spent a morning there updating my résumé, what little of it there was, and printed a hundred copies. My hopes were high as I started to deliver them to local businesses, but with every rejection, my spirits sank lower. After two days, the only offer I'd had was waitressing Monday to Wednesday in a gentlemen's club. Topless. I'd sleep in a cardboard box before that happened.

Shoulders hunched, I traipsed home at the end of the afternoon, running through the food I had left in the cupboard. Could I eke it out for another day or two? *Think positive, Lara—at least you've lost a few pounds.*

Of course, the landlady popped out as I tiptoed past. How did she always do that?

"You keep playing your TV too loud."

"I don't have a TV."

"Don't give me that. Young people these days, they've got no respect."

"But I really don't own a television. I haven't even got a radio."

"Kids were honest back in my day too."

That was it! I'd had it up to here with that woman. I clenched my fists as I tried to stop my tears from escaping. "Look, I swear I don't..."

I clammed up at the touch of a hand on my shoulder.

"Just ignore her," a blonde girl who looked to be my age whispered. "She's like that with everyone."

The landlady glared at the newcomer, backed into her apartment, and slammed the door. My ally giggled. "Cantankerous old biddy. Don't let her upset you. She's not worth it."

"It's not just that." I sniffed and resisted the urge to wipe my nose on my sleeve.

"What, then? Man trouble?"

I shook my head. "Right now, money trouble."

She nodded sagely. "If it's not one, it's the other. Do you feel like grabbing a coffee? My treat—you look as if you need one."

I wasn't sure whether to be pleased or depressed by that statement, but I found myself nodding. "That's very kind of you."

"I'm Sylvia, by the way."

"Lara."

In the imitation Starbucks on the next corner, I told Sylvia a sanitised version of my recent move.

"You're braver than me," she said. "Before I came here, I planned for a year, and now I can't ever see myself moving away."

Brave? I couldn't believe that. Stupid? Definitely.

"I'm beginning to regret leaving Baysville. At least I had contacts there. Job hunting's so much harder when you don't know anyone."

She took another sip of her mocha. "It may not be something you'd enjoy, but would you consider cleaning? That's what I do, and the lady at the agency I work through may have something available."

I could clean. Heck, I'd had enough practice when I was with Billy. "A cleaning job would be perfect."

Sylvia gave me Michelle's number and promised to call her in the morning to put in a good word for me. Could this be the answer to my problems?

Meeting Sylvia turned out to be my lucky break. Over the next month, Michelle offered me a few days a week of housekeeping work in various hotels, covering for staff sickness and vacation. Some were nice, some not so much, but they all paid money and that meant I could afford to eat.

"They love you," Michelle told me when I stopped by to pick up my pay cheque. "The manager from the hotel yesterday called me personally to say what a good job you did."

That would be the slimeball who'd squeezed my bottom while I was dusting. I forced a smile.

"That's good. I don't suppose there's any chance of extra hours?"

"Things are slow at the moment, but if more work comes in, you'll be at the top of my list."

Where had I heard that before?

I kept my fingers crossed as I walked home, because while I was off the breadline, it still came down to a choice between heating and eating. With my new-found sense of optimism and the sun shining from above, I searched for the silver lining in the dark cloud hanging over my life. Hmm... At least the lack of work meant I had free time to explore the city I now called home. There we go.

Over the next few weeks, I did the tourist thing and visited Maymont Mansion and its beautiful gardens, Monument Avenue, and Agecroft Hall. Apart from a single horrid trip abroad with Billy, I'd never had a vacation, so I pretended I was on one now. The number of Kodak moments made me wish I could take some photos, but I'd pawned my camera to pay for Momma's medication. *Think positive, Lara.* Maybe I could learn to draw instead?

On rainy days, I huddled under my umbrella and walked to the library. While the world outside glistened in shades of grey, I transported myself to far-off places through second-hand romance. I'd given up hope of finding my own Prince Charming, but I still loved to dream. In between those adventures, I flicked through math textbooks to give my mind a workout. College may have turned into a nightmare, but I'd always be a geek at heart.

While I loved the books, the building itself brought back unwelcome memories because it was in the school library that I'd first spoken to Billy. As I'd done every day for the last ten years, I rued ever meeting him. Back then, I'd thought it was a magical moment, but I soon learned not all spells were good.

And Billy Cooper was no wizard.

Teenage me hadn't had the benefit of hindsight on that fateful day. It was mid-afternoon on a rainy Thursday when Billy Cooper, the wide receiver on the high school football team—

some said the best wide receiver *ever*—strutted into the library and asked me to help him with his math homework.

Me!

Lara the Loser!

What was I going to do? Say no? Of course not—I'd read those stories about the nerd ending up with the football star, and they gave me hope, okay?

I spent an hour working through all the problems with him and explaining two or three times what I'd done, and when we were in class three days later, he passed me a Post-it with a few scribbled words.

*Full marks! Your a genius!*

I kept that note stuck carefully in the back of my math textbook, and every time I looked at it, a smile crept across my face. Looking back, the fact that he didn't know the difference between *you're* and *your* should have given me a hint we weren't compatible, but when you're sixteen years old, you tend to turn a blind eye to these things.

The next week, Billy came into the library again and slid into the seat beside me.

"Hey, Einstein, gimme some help with the new math assignment?"

Mesmerised by Billy's grin, I refrained from pointing out that Einstein was a physicist rather than a mathematician.

"Sure."

Our weekly library sessions became somewhat of a fixture, and I counted down the hours, minutes, and seconds until he walked through the door. Back then, he'd been sweet to me—he'd bring me a soda one week, a bar of chocolate the next.

For a girl with few friends, the attention was flattering. I wasn't Lara the Loser anymore. I was Lara-who-Billy-liked.

People began to notice me, to see me in a different light. Now, I understood it was the attention that had attracted me rather than Billy himself, but as a teenager, I was blinded by his rudimentary charms.

After one particularly gruelling algebra session, he slammed his textbook shut and sat back in the chair, fingers laced behind his head. "I've got a game on Saturday. Wanna come? We could go get a burger after."

Like I was going to decline that offer. My pulse sped out of control as I willed my voice to stay steady. "I'd like that."

A burger led to a trip to the cinema, and before I knew it, we were making out every night in the back of Billy's car. He changed me, and I didn't realise at the time it was for the worse.

With him, I was in the popular crowd again, and with that came a sense of euphoria I hadn't felt since my pop left. The feeling of acceptance overrode any niggling doubts I may have had over whether Billy was the right boy for me. Not only did I get access to his social circle, he also had money, and he liked to buy me things—snacks, dinner, even clothes.

"The way you look reflects on me, sweetheart. I want you to look good," he told me one evening before we went to a party.

"Are you sure this top suits me?" I turned back and forth in front of the mirror. "It's awful tight." I gave the skirt another tug down. It didn't cover much.

"It makes your tits look awesome. I want everyone else to know what's mine."

I kept the outfit on. I was seventeen, all right?

Mom saw the warning signs I'd missed. "It's better to have your own style," she told me. "Wear what's comfortable."

"I'll wear whatever I want," I snapped back, because like any teenager, I hated being lectured.

Oh, if only I'd listened.

When the opportunity came to follow Billy to college, I jumped at it. The day our acceptance letters for Brown arrived, we threw a party so wild I woke up on the kitchen floor, minus my underwear and my dignity. Even that didn't bring me to my senses.

Billy won a football scholarship, and mine was in math. At first, I loved college. As a natural bookworm, studying was fun for me, and surrounded by like-minded people, my knowledge grew. Plus there were the perks of dating a football player.

For the first year, I lived in the dorms while Billy moved into a frat house, but I spent more time in his room than I did in my own. My roommate was nice enough, but we had nothing in common. Life was good, and I thought we'd stay in that arrangement for the whole of college, but a misunderstanding with a goat and a professor's car led to Billy getting kicked out of Sigma Kappa Phi.

"Assholes," he said as he shoved his belongings into a suitcase. "They were too tame for me, anyway."

At first, I snuck him into my room, but the girl I shared with soon got annoyed with him hogging the bathroom. The hair. It was always the hair. He wore it slicked back, stiff with so much gel it felt crispy when you touched it. Plastic. Billy was a Ken doll but without the charisma—I saw that now.

"Maybe we could get a place of our own," nineteen-year-old me suggested, blinded by what I thought was love.

"Already sorted. Pop's buying me an apartment. We can move in next week."

Why wasn't I surprised? Mr. Cooper thought the sun shone out of his only son's ass. He was wrong, though. It was the fires of hell glimmering through.

But back then, I'd still had my sunglasses on, and within seconds, I was mentally decorating the living room.

"Ooh, our own place! I can't wait."

Mistakes? My life was full of them.

# 5

## LARA

After three months in Richmond, I was keeping my head above water, albeit with a bit of kicking and the odd splutter. My chequebook balanced to the cent, and I was considering writing a cookbook called *50 Ways to Jazz Up Your Ramen Noodles*. Apart from the lack of money and missing Missy terribly, my new life surpassed the old. My boss at the café let me take home leftovers on the two days I worked, and so far, Michelle had only asked me to clean at hotels where the managers treated me okay. I was on first-name terms with the librarian, and I'd even found time to catch up for coffee with Sylvia on a couple of occasions.

Tomorrow I only had work in the morning, and in the afternoon, I planned to take a long walk in the park if the weather was good. I was contemplating whether I could afford an ice cream when the landlady popped out of her door.

"I need a word with you."

"If it's about the hamster, I've already told you I don't have one."

"I know. It was mice. I got the exterminator in."

Well, wonders would never cease—she'd admitted she'd gotten something wrong. Although ick, mice.

"So why do you want to speak to me?"

"Rent's going up next month. Fifty dollars."

"What?" Even to my own ears, my voice sounded weak.

"Fifty dollars. I need to buy medication for Muffy." She reversed into her apartment with the incontinent poodle trailing behind her. *Slam.*

The elevator was broken again, and by the time I climbed up to the third floor, what little energy I'd had left had deserted me. I fumbled the key into the lock, then sagged onto the bed.

Where was I supposed to magic up fifty dollars from? It might not sound like much, but when you don't even have fifty spare cents, it might as well be a million bucks.

My first thought was to move, but where to? I already lived in the cheapest place I could find. Perhaps I could buy a tent? I paced my tiny room, trying to come up with a plan. How about trying another city? Another state? But I liked Richmond. A vision popped into my head of me sitting on a street corner with a begging bowl, and a bubble of laughter escaped my lips. No, I couldn't do that. I'd try speaking to Michelle at the cleaning agency again before I resorted to anything desperate.

"Cup of coffee, hun?" Michelle asked the next morning.

I'd been waiting outside the door when she arrived.

"Yes, please. I've run out at home."

"No time to go to the store?"

More like no money. I explained the difficulties with my rent while Michelle poured me a mug of caffeinated heaven from her drip machine. "So I was wondering if you might have any extra work going? I'll even go to that place with the cockroaches Sandy walked out of last month."

"No can do, hun. The cockroach place got closed down by the health department."

"How about private cleaning? Don't you do homes as well as hotels?" A note of desperation crept into my voice, and I hated it. Hated that my survival depended on begging to clean up other people's filth.

"The standards are higher for those clients. They tend to be more demanding." She rolled her eyes. "Sometimes impossible."

"I can deal with picky."

Heck, I'd had enough practice in my years with Billy. The apartment his father bought him was spacious and comfortable, by far the nicest place I'd ever lived, at least in terms of bricks and mortar and fancy floor-to-ceiling windows. With no rent to pay, I felt I should earn my keep by helping around the place, which roughly translated as doing everything—cooking, cleaning, laundry, the lot—while Billy watched TV or drank beer with his buddies. I asked him to take the trash out once, and he gave me such a scathing look I did it myself.

He liked the place to look immaculate, though I doubt his friends would have noticed if the living room was knee-deep in pizza boxes. The mess would surely have reminded them of home. And although his nagging never let up, the buzz I got going to football games with him every Saturday cancelled it out.

Then there was Momma. I visited her every month, and her face glowed with pride when I updated her on my studies. I didn't want to tarnish the illusion by telling her Billy was awful to live with.

So I coped. At least, until the beginning of the second semester. The front row was packed with screaming girls as the Brown Bears played Harvard, and I was one of them. Then, just ten minutes into the game, my shouts of joy were drowned out by Billy's howls of agony as he landed awkwardly from a tackle.

I perched nervously beside his bed in the hospital as the doctor walked in. He pushed his glasses up and took a quick glance at his notes before breaking the news.

"Well, Mr. Cooper, you've torn your anterior cruciate ligament." His mouth twitched. "Right the way through."

"What does that mean?" Billy snapped. "In English."

The doctor sucked in a breath, clearly not used to being spoken to in that manner. Me? I was dead to it by then.

"We can perform surgery to help you walk again, but your football career's over." He arranged his features into canned sympathy and shrugged. "I'm sorry."

Billy didn't take it well. The doctor barely had time to duck before the pitcher of water whistled past his ear and smashed against the wall behind him.

"Send a different doctor. One who knows what he's talking about."

The poor man ran out of the room. With hindsight, I should have been hot on his heels, but I stayed. Stupid me.

Doctors two and three gave the same diagnosis, and life with Billy became unbearable. With no outlet for his pent-up anger on the football field, the beast that slumbered inside him came out at home. Playing in the NFL was all Billy had ever wanted to do, and now that he couldn't, he took it out on me.

When the consequences of a stray speck of dirt were liable to hurt, a person became real good at cleaning, believe me. I was prepared for anything Michelle's clients could throw at me. Literally.

She fished a package of cookies out of her drawer and offered me one before replying. They were the good kind with chocolate on them. Would it be greedy if I took two? Probably.

"Yeah, I reckon you'd be able to cope. Problem is, I haven't got so much on the books at the moment. Kids are home from college for the summer, and they'll work the low-end hotel jobs more cheaply than our staff. I've had to push more people over to the private side temporarily." She smiled and pushed the cookies towards me again. "Things'll pick up in a month or two."

"I'll be homeless before then." I bit into a second cookie, holding a hand up to catch the crumbs.

Michelle tapped away at her computer for a few seconds. "There's one possibility, but I'll be honest. You've got a slim chance of landing the job. Still, you might as well have a shot at it, hun—you've got nothing to lose."

A sliver of hope was better than none, and I grabbed at it. "What is it?"

"A full-time housekeeping job. Sounds straightforward, but I've sent twelve of my best people over so far, and none of them has gotten past the first interview." She shook her head. "I've never had so much trouble filling a position before."

"Why? Is the boss a complete ogre?"

She shook her head. "The company's hired domestic staff for their executives from me in the past, and they've all raved about what a great place it is to work. It's just difficult to get a foot in the door."

"Could I put in an application? Like you said, I've got nothing to lose."

"I'll send off your details, hun. Keep your fingers crossed."

Two days later, I was vacuuming up what appeared to be an entire package of chips from a motel room floor when my phone vibrated in my pocket. I stiffened as the screen announced Michelle was calling. Would it be good news or bad?

"Well, hun, you've got an interview."

I let out a squeal, then clapped a hand over my mouth.

She chuckled. "You're the thirteenth candidate."

Gee, thanks for reminding me. "When? Where do I need to go?"

"Can you do tomorrow? You'll be meeting the client's assistant."

"I'm free in the afternoon."

"I'll set it up."

"Uh, I've never had a proper interview before—do you have any tips?"

All my jobs had come through word of mouth or popping into a bar or agency for an informal chat. What should I expect?

"Oh, just be yourself."

Well, that was super advice. Being myself hadn't gotten me very far yet, had it?

"Do you have any more details of the job?"

"My contact was a bit cagey with those. Apparently, you'll discuss it during the interview." Another phone rang in the background. "Good luck. I'll text you later with the time and place."

Having the interview so soon gave me little chance to prepare, but at least I had less time to get nervous. Actually, scratch that. I wasn't nervous; I was terrified.

My hands trembled as I opened the door to the swanky office building downtown. The plaque outside listed an insurance company, a law firm, and a software business. Which of those would I be visiting? Michelle's message just said to go to the desk in the lobby and ask for Bradley.

The perfectly groomed receptionist with her razor-sharp blonde bob made me feel like an impostor as I fidgeted in front of her.

"Uh, I'm looking for Bradley?"

"Lara Reynolds?"

"That's right."

"Take a seat, please." She waved at a bank of cream leather chairs by the window.

I shuffled over and sank into one. What was I doing here? I didn't belong. Not in my cheap white blouse and the thrift shop pants I'd worn to Momma's funeral. They didn't even fit properly now—I'd lost too much weight on my unwelcome diet, and they sagged around the middle. I peered at my reflection in the floor-to-ceiling glass. My hair desperately needed a cut, and a bunch of brown strands had escaped from my ponytail again. I tucked them behind my ear. Last night, I'd considered taking the scissors to it, but I'd chickened out.

"Can I offer you a glass of water while you're waiting, Miss Reynolds?" the receptionist asked.

"No, thank you, I'm fine." My mouth was dry, but I was too nervous to drink.

"Bradley will be down soon."

My right foot tapped of its own accord, the heel clicking on the polished floor. *Stay still, Lara.* Squirming in my seat wouldn't create a good impression.

A blur of movement caught my eye as a small man bounced through the door to the stairwell. Was he lost? Between the turquoise skinny jeans and the pink streaks in his hair, he looked even more out of place than me. And why was he wearing a Christmas sweater in July?

The receptionist pointed at me, and he bounded over.

"Hi, I'm Bradley. Sorry to keep you waiting."

"It's no problem." I put my hand into his, and he nearly shook my arm off.

"Follow me. We're on the fourth floor."

I was puffing like an out-of-shape asthmatic when we reached the computer company. The plaque beside the door said HC Systems, and Bradley pushed it open.

"I borrowed a meeting room. Hope this place was convenient for you to get to."

An hour's walk. "Perfect."

"You want coffee? I'll send someone to Starbucks."

"A cappuccino would be lovely."

He called out to a nervous-looking girl, who grabbed a notepad and pen on her way over.

"Can you get me a cappuccino and a venti iced skinny hazelnut macchiato, sugar-free syrup, extra shot, light ice, no whip."

Ah, now I understood the need for the notepad. She scribbled as he spoke, then dashed off.

He gave me a wink. "I like to keep the interns on their toes," he said as he led the way into a conference room. "Have a seat."

I perched on the edge of the leather chair opposite him, carefully folding my hands in my lap.

"So, Lara, can you tell me about your cleaning experience?"

That question was easy enough for me to relax a little. "I've been cleaning hotels through an agency for the last two months, and before that, I cleaned a bar every day."

"And have you worked in private homes?"

"Only my own," I said quietly.

"How about shopping? Do you like shopping?"

Shopping? What did that have to do with anything?

"What girl doesn't love shopping? I'm limited to the window variety for the moment, though."

"Good. Nick needs someone to shop for him from time to time as well as cleaning his house."

"Nick?"

"Nick Goldman. That's who you'd be working for. Initially, he wants someone to sort out his house, do some cooking and cleaning and the like, but later it could turn into more of a PA role. We're looking for flexibility."

"I'm definitely flexible. I could put my foot behind my head when I was little."

Oh cheese and rice! Why did I say that? An interview was hardly the time for joking. My cheeks heated, and I wanted to sink into the floor.

"Good, good." Bradley pulled out a sparkly pen and matching notepad, and wrote down "flexible" with three exclamation marks after it. His lips twitched as if he was trying not to smirk. "The successful candidate will also need to pitch in and cover vacations for the other assistants."

"I wouldn't be working on my own?"

"When you're at the house you would be, for the most part, but there's a whole team of staff."

"Oh, that's lovely. I wouldn't be quite so lonely with other people to talk to. Not that I talk much. I mean I do, but only after I've done all the work." Shoot, this was going from bad to worse.

Bradley jotted something else on his pad. I tried to read it, but his hand got in the way.

"And what do you like to do in your spare time?"

"I go for walks and read. Not at the same time, obviously. That'd be dangerous."

"Anything else?"

"I used to watch TV back when I had one. I don't have a lot of money."

Put into words, my life sounded even duller than it was.

"Nothing like an episode of *Project Runway* to cheer me up," Bradley said. "I've got a monster TV; I just don't have time to watch it."

"*Project Runway*? I love that show. I used to drool over the outfits and especially the shoes."

"Who's your favourite designer?"

"Jimmy Choo. I've never owned a pair, though."

"They don't fit me. Too narrow. I'm more of a Louboutin guy. What else do you watch?"

"Oh gosh, all the stuff I shouldn't—*Dancing with the Stars*, *My Super Sweet Sixteen*, *Hoarders*." Billy had always told me off for my choice of viewing. I used to flick over to a documentary whenever I heard the front door slam.

"They're on my list, too. Although *Hoarders* gives me the creeps."

"It makes me want to rush in there with a pair of rubber gloves and a dumpster."

Bradley laughed, but it sounded kind of forced. "Better you than me. So, how about travelling? Do you enjoy that?"

"I've only been out of the country once. My ex took me to Bermuda for Christmas a few years back."

And I'd spent the whole vacation in a kaftan to hide the bruises.

"If you could go anywhere in the world, where would you choose?"

"That's easy. England." Because I could visit Tori as well as see Buckingham Palace and shop on Oxford Street.

Bradley, it seemed, had travelled the globe—England, France, Italy, the Caribbean, Brazil, India, Germany, Egypt... I soon lost track of all the places he'd explored. He pulled out his phone and took me on a virtual tour of Windsor Castle—quirky, but the decor needed updating, apparently—and I found myself telling him about my life too. Even what happened with Momma and my impulsive move to Richmond, leaving out the stalker, of course. Time flew, and I'd been in there almost an hour when Bradley pushed his seat back.

"It's been lovely meeting you, Lara."

That was it? "Uh, you too."

"Do you have any questions for me?"

I should have been thinking some up rather than gossiping about cocktails in Paris, and now that I'd been put on the spot, my brain froze. All I could do was shake my head and inwardly curse my incompetence. As I gathered up our coffee cups and dropped them into the trash on my way out the door, I swallowed a groan. I'd messed up, hadn't I? If there was a prize for the least professional interviewee ever, I'd win it hands down.

Out on the street, all the questions I should have asked popped into my head. Where was the job based? What were the hours? The salary? Why had the previous housekeeper left?

Of course, that was irrelevant if I didn't land the job. And what chance did I have? I wanted to slap myself for that foot-behind-my-head comment. Stupid me, once again.

Back in the sanctuary of my apartment, I stared at my naked reflection in the cracked mirror and sucked in my stomach. Did I have what it took for the topless waitressing job? I turned sideways and pressed on the poochy bit at the bottom that always stuck out. Maybe if I wore a high-waisted skirt, I'd be okay? Then nobody would see the way my thighs rubbed together either.

I felt sick at the thought of working in that place, but I was running out of options if I was going to pay this month's rent. What else could I do? With a knot of nerves growing ever bigger in my belly, I decided to visit the man at the gentlemen's club tomorrow.

## 6

## LARA

Three days later I stood sweating in a dingy basement, and the ferrety man in front of me leaned forward in his seat.

"Come on, let's see 'em."

I reached for the bottom of my T-shirt. Could I do this? If I felt this scared undressing in front of one man, how would I parade around a club full of them?

His eyes raked up and down my body as I hesitated. "I haven't got all day."

I peeled my top off and dropped it on the chair next to me. Cool air washed over my skin. Goosebumps popped up, and my nipples hardened involuntarily.

"And the bra."

I closed my eyes, forcing down the bile that rose in my throat, and reached for the clasp. Then the phone in my purse vibrated, and the tinny sound of Lakmé's "Flower Duet" filled the room. Who was it?

"Can I take this?" I asked.

"Hurry up."

Michelle's name flashed on the screen, and my heart lurched. *Please, say it's not bad news.*

"You did it!" she squealed when I answered.

"What? I got the job?"

"You got a second interview which is better than anyone else so far. I was beginning to lose hope."

That made two of us. "What do you think my chances are?"

"Honestly? No idea."

Oh, that was helpful. The creep tapped his watch and gave me a dirty look.

What should I do? Carry on with this horrible process or take a chance on a job I might not get? His eyes roamed over me again, making my skin crawl. That made the decision a little easier.

"Can you hold on a sec?" I asked Michelle.

I dragged my shirt back on, squeaked, "Sorry," and tore out of the room, feeling relief flood through me with every step I took. In the daylight, I put the phone back to my ear.

"So what do I do next?"

"The second interview's tomorrow at four. Can you make that? If not, Bradley's boss won't be back in town for another week."

"Tomorrow at four's fine." At least, it was now I wouldn't be serving drinks in a thong.

"I'll call back with the details."

By the time Michelle rang again, I'd gotten home and taken a shower to scrub the feeling of the man's eyes off of me. Dressed in clean clothes, I still felt dirty, and I knew I'd made the right decision. Even if I didn't get the job working for Mr. Goldman, I'd need to find something else. Thoughts of Baysville flitted through my mind. Maybe I could go back and see whether Becky had brought Buck to his knees? Surely my stalker would have lost interest by now?

When the phone trilled, I snatched it up.

"All arranged," Michelle told me, sounding far too cheerful.

"Am I going to the same place as last time?"

"No, to a restaurant. French. Although I'll warn you now, a friend went there once, and after three courses, she had to remortgage her house."

A shiver of fear ran through me. That sounded worse than the office building.

"What am I supposed to wear?"

"Do you have a cocktail dress?"

I'd thrown everything Billy gave me away, not that it would have been suitable for a fine dining establishment in any case.

"I have a skirt."

"I'd go with that."

I tossed and turned all night, wondering how I'd get through the next interview. I had my doubts it would be as easy as the first. Mr. Goldman was obviously successful if he could afford a housekeeper, and I'd never had coffee or anything else with a wealthy businessman before. Those sorts of men didn't frequent the places I worked.

When my alarm went off, I'd gotten two broken hours of sleep, my eyes had black circles under them, and I'd turned into a gibbering wreck. I'd once read a book on the power of positive thought, but every time I convinced myself I'd ace the interview and swan into an amazing job, my subconscious overruled me, and I sank into the doldrums again. Part of me wanted 4 p.m. to never arrive so I couldn't screw up, while the other half wanted the clock to race ahead so I could get the interview over with. Of course, neither happened, and time ticked by in its steadfast manner.

At noon, I jumped into the shower and used every toiletry product I owned, most of which were half-empty bottles I'd gathered up while cleaning hotels. Make-up was out because I didn't own any. The dark smudges under my eyes would have to stay.

At three, I scuttled out of the apartment in a black knee-length skirt, mid-height heels, and the same white blouse I'd worn to see Bradley. Maybe it would be my lucky charm? The bus pulled up to the stop as I arrived, and I hopped on. So far, so good. According to the route map, it would take me within a quarter mile of the restaurant, and I could walk the rest in five minutes. I tried to calm my breathing as I stared out the window. Everything was going according to plan, so I should stop worrying.

Then the rain started. Huge, fat drops that splattered against the window as the bus splashed through the fast-forming puddles. And where was my umbrella? Ah yes, on a hook next to the door at home.

Great, just great.

A quick glance at my watch confirmed what I already knew—I didn't have time to go back and get it. I said a silent prayer for the rain to stop, but nobody up there listened, and if anything, the torrent was falling harder by the time the bus deposited me at my stop.

I half walked, half ran through the storm, ignoring the pain from my ankle as I twisted it on the kerb. Where was the restaurant? I caught sight of it ahead of me—a shiny black marble facade with *Claude's* written at the top in elegant gold script. Thank goodness, I was in the right place.

The roar of an engine from behind made me turn, just in time for an SUV to hurtle past, splashing me all over with dirty water. My skirt was left dripping, and my blouse, already see-through from the rain, was streaked with brown from collar to waist.

A tear leaked down my cheek, mingling with the water. What had I done to deserve this kind of karma? I longed to run back to my apartment, bury myself under my quilt, and never face the world again, but Momma had brought me up better than to leave Mr. Goldman waiting with no explanation. I'd have to go and apologise before I went home.

As I opened the glass door, I caught sight of my reflection. Eek. If nothing else, I could get a job as a scarecrow. Inside, a greeter in a tuxedo looked on in horror as a puddle spread over the polished wood floor towards his fancy lectern.

"I'm here to meet Mr. Goldman," I said before he could escort me out again.

"Mr. Goldman is not expected today."

What? I'd worried about standing him up, and he'd done it to me instead? How rude! Then a faint hope sprung forth. If he wasn't here, perhaps we could reschedule? I needed to call Michelle.

The besuited man quickly dashed that hope, though, his accent French and haughty. "Perhaps you are due to meet Ms. Black. She's a friend of Mr. Goldman, and she is 'ere waiting for a guest."

I ran through my conversation with Michelle. All she'd said was that I'd be meeting Bradley's boss, so maybe Ms. Black was a senior personal assistant? A sigh escaped my lips. I'd better explain to her what happened.

The man led me through the restaurant, past tables full of people who looked up in disgust at the tramp-like woman leaving trails of water as she hobbled along. I knew what was going through their minds: "She doesn't belong here," or possibly "Who let her in?" I couldn't blame them. If I'd been in their position, I'd have been thinking the same thing.

We halted in a quiet corner, next to a table partially hidden beside a large, exotic-looking plant. My heart sank lower. It must be in the devil's hands by now, surely?

The woman staring at me was impeccably dressed, with blonde hair tied back into a chignon and make-up that wouldn't have been out of place on the red carpet. Her short-sleeved top looked like cashmere, and fastened above it was an exquisite necklace, diamonds and rubies sparkling in an abstract pattern of swirls. If they were real, it must have cost hundreds of thousands of dollars. Nobody would wear that out to lunch, surely?

And her sophisticated attire only emphasised how awful I looked. The beast to her beauty. If I'd had a genie and a lamp, my one wish would have been to disappear through the floor I was currently dripping all over.

# 7

## LARA

Talk about feeling intimidated.

When she saw me, the woman's lips opened slightly as her eyes widened. Lips so impeccably outlined in a shade of red that matched the necklace exactly. And although she tried to hide it, I knew what must be going through her mind.

She recovered before I did and stepped forward, perfectly balanced on a pair of red-soled pumps.

"I'm Emerson Black, and you must be Lara?" Her accent seemed out of place—upper-class English in a French restaurant in an American city.

I reached out for the hand she extended and grasped it timidly. It came complete with perfectly manicured nails, also ruby red, and I was surprised she didn't grimace when my grubby skin touched hers.

"Pleased to meet you, Ms. Black. I'm so sorry about...well, this." I indicated my soggy attire.

She waved her hand dismissively. "Call me Emmy. 'Ms. Black' makes me sound like some fancy divorcee. And don't worry about the unexpected shower, these things happen to all of us."

I bet they didn't happen to her.

She picked up a menu and flipped it over to me. "I hope you'll join me for food. I'm bloody starving. I got stuck in one of those lunch meetings where you end up spending more time talking than eating. Three hours, it went on for, and two and a half of those were taken up with bullshit."

She wanted me to stay? Was she crazy? Why would she want to have dinner with someone who looked as if she'd just been through the spin cycle of a washing machine? Did she have a problem with her eyesight?

Possibly not, since she snapped her fingers at a man hovering beyond the potted plant. "Claude, could you get a towel or something for Lara to sit on, please?"

Claude hustled off and returned almost immediately with a pristine white towel clutched in his outstretched fingers. He carefully draped it over the cream leather chair that he pulled out for me. But how could I sit on that? I'd ruin it.

Emmy saw my hesitation and pointed at the seat. "Don't worry. Just sit on it. The amount they charge for dinner, they can afford to buy a new towel."

I sat.

The menu came bound in leather, rich and intimidating. The prices on the first page made me gasp. A meal here cost more than I earned in a week, and I didn't even understand the ingredients. I tried to recall my high-school French. What were *champignons*?

"Is everything all right, madame?" Claude asked.

"Uh, fine."

Emmy broke in. "Claude, there's a pashmina on the passenger seat of my car. Would you be a darling and bring it?" She dangled a set of car keys from her finger. Obviously "no" wasn't an acceptable answer.

She fell silent but her eyes stayed alert, watching me and occasionally flicking over to the other diners. Now I knew what a lab specimen felt like. Movement caught my attention, and I saw one of the country club set point at me then whisper to her companion and laugh.

"Bitch," Emmy muttered under her breath.

"Pardon?"

"That woman staring at you. She's a bitch. Ignore her."

"Uh, okay." Of all the words I might have imagined coming out of Emmy's mouth, that wasn't among them.

A low vibration sounded, and she rummaged around in her purse.

"You'll have to excuse me a second."

She pulled out a small jar of pickled eggs and set it on the table before fishing out a phone. As she tapped away on the screen, the silence grated on my nerves, and the women at the next table kept glancing at me. *Stay calm, Lara.* This was only a restaurant, and I'd be leaving soon enough, then I'd never have to see any of them again. I stifled a laugh—it wasn't as if our paths would ever cross accidentally.

Claude returned, placed the car keys on the table, and held out a black pashmina to Emmy.

"It's not for me. It's for Lara." She looked up at me. "You've gone a bit see-through, I'm afraid, and you must be freezing."

Claude draped the shawl over my shoulders, and I pulled it around me, trying not to wince at how much it undoubtedly cost. Emmy was right—with the powerful AC blasting out cold air, my teeth were on the verge of chattering.

"So," Emmy said, putting her phone face down on the table. "We could make small talk about the weather, but I think we both already know it's raining. Let's talk about you instead. Why do you want to work for Nick?"

"I've been working in hotels, but I'm looking to make a

move into private cleaning. I want to concentrate on doing one job and doing it well." I mustered up a smile. Did I sound convincing? It had to be better than the truth—that working for Mr. Goldman was the only thing standing between me and a homeless shelter.

"But why do you want to work for Nick in particular?"

Oh, heck. Michelle had barely mentioned the man himself. The fact was, I'd have worked for Harvey Weinstein if it paid money.

Emmy's gaze held steady, and for an instant, I had an uncanny feeling she could read my mind. Something told me honesty would be the best policy here.

"I don't really know much about Mr. Goldman. The agency suggested the job because I was looking for something full-time and permanent."

"They didn't tell you anything about the house at all?"

"No, nothing."

"Shit."

"Sorry?"

Instead of replying, she gestured at the menu. "What do you want to eat?"

"Uh..." Should I just pick the cheapest option and hope for the best?

"Or shall I order for both of us?"

"Yes, please."

Claude was at her elbow in an instant.

"Two English afternoon teas, and be generous with the cakes, would you?"

He pursed his lips briefly but nodded before gliding off.

English afternoon tea? "I didn't see that on the menu."

She grinned. "It isn't, but I convinced them to come round to my way of thinking a while back."

That didn't surprise me. I imagined they'd fly to the UK to pick up special dishes if she asked nicely.

"So, you started talking about the house earlier?"

Her full lips twisted into a grimace. "Here's the thing. It's a tip. No, that's being generous. Nick's house is such a mess there's probably a lost indigenous tribe living in there." She rubbed her temples. "Fuck, I'm not selling it, am I? He needs someone to come in and sort out the whole bloody mess, and when it's tidy, he needs help to keep it that way."

"Oh." She didn't mince her words, did she? "Well, I do like a challenge."

"We'll see if you're still saying that after you've seen the place. Let's eat, then we can take a drive over there."

My ears perked up. "So you mean there's still a chance I could get the job?"

"Of course. You've already got the job if you want it. Bradley likes you, and you had enough balls to walk in here looking like you travelled by tornado rather than going home. Nick needs someone tough enough to put up with him."

Tough? I wasn't tough. I wasn't about to tell Emmy that, though. Not when she'd offered me a job. Why on earth would she think I wouldn't want it? As long as it paid my rent, I'd take anything. Surely the house couldn't be that bad? I mean, I'd had to pick a man's toenail clippings out of shag pile carpet the other day, the same man whose aim was a little off when it came to the toilet.

I blocked out that memory as Claude walked towards us carrying a tray full of gourmet delights—crustless sandwiches, scones, and tiny cakes. As I dug in, the taste was enough to make me want to renounce my citizenship and move to England.

"The pastries are good, huh?" Emmy said as she helped herself to a second plateful.

I nodded and snuck another scone onto my own plate, catching the look of disgust on the face of the woman at the next table. Emmy and I were the only people in the restaurant actually eating food—the others were just pushing it around with their forks while they gossiped.

"You want me to order more?" Emmy asked.

"No, this is plenty."

"Stick this on the tab, would you?" she said to Claude, who'd materialised at her elbow.

A tab? Who had a tab in a place like this? I barely had time to marvel before she pushed her seat back and got to her feet, then air-kissed Claude on both cheeks. Guess we were leaving.

"Uh, you forgot your eggs." I spotted the jar on the table, hiding behind a vase of white orchids.

"That's intentional." She carried on walking.

I gave up on the idea of making sense of today. I felt like Alice, fallen down the rabbit hole. That experience only continued as I followed Emmy through the kitchen and out to the staff parking lot where a Corvette was backed up next to the steps.

"This is us." She bleeped the doors open.

I'd just clicked my seatbelt closed when Emmy mashed her foot on the gas and sped out of the lot. My fingers gripped the edges of the dark purple leather seat all of their own accord as she hurtled past the speed limit and overtook a minivan, then screeched back onto the right side of the road with inches to spare as a truck came the other way. Did she have a death wish?

I risked a glance in her direction. She seemed perfectly relaxed, tapping the steering wheel in time with the rock blaring from the stereo. She had a Bluetooth earpiece in, and occasionally she paused the music to speak in code for a few seconds before returning to her imaginary Grand Prix.

With the speed she was driving, it wasn't long before we left the city limits, and half an hour later, we flew past a sign for Rybridge. I did a double take. Sylvia worked in Rybridge, and she said it was so exclusive potential homeowners got vetted by a committee before they were allowed to purchase a property. The minimum income was seven figures. Even her maid's uniform was designed by Tom Ford.

Emmy braked sharply and swung the wheel to the right, screeching to a halt in front of a pair of imposing iron gates. She wound down her window, tapped a code into a keypad, and the gates slowly swung open.

Around a kink in the driveway, a huge house came into view—peach coloured and Mediterranean in style, with four white columns rising the full two storeys on either side of the front door. The smell of fragrant blossoms drifted in through the open car window, reminding me of the flowers my pop used to buy Momma when I was small. Stunning was an understatement. I felt as if I should be paying to cross the threshold, not earning money for doing so.

Emmy hopped out of the car and glided to the front door. I scurried behind her, so busy watching the tiny birds hopping from tree to tree that I tripped over the step. *Klutz*. I grabbed a pillar for support as Emmy fitted a key in the lock. Would the inside be as spectacular as the outside?

The answer was yes, but for all the wrong reasons. I gasped and covered my mouth as Emmy threw the door open.

"Holy freaking fudge."

Emmy gave me a lopsided grin. "Yeah, something like that. I've got desensitised to it over the years."

"What? How?" I had no other words.

Every available surface had something dumped on it, and the floor had to be two feet deep in junk. A narrow path led through the hallway to the horrors beyond. I trailed behind Emmy as she picked her way through with the care of someone crossing a minefield.

The kitchen sink held a pile of washing up, and from the look of the mummified remains, it had been there since the last century. Pizza boxes were piled three deep on the coffee table in the living room, and the number of assorted takeout containers indicated a culinary tour of the world.

The master bedroom was just as bad.

"What's that pile in the corner?" I asked.

"I think there's a laundry hamper under there somewhere. That's just the start of it—when the pile got as high as him, Nick started throwing things into the room next door. And the one beside that. And the one after."

I held up my hands. "Okay, okay, I get the picture." I took another look around, just in case my brain had malfunctioned and misrepresented the piles of chaos. It hadn't. "How does he live like this?"

She sat on the edge of the bed, the only visible piece of furniture in the room. "He doesn't, not really. Occasionally he sleeps here or grabs takeout and sort of...picnics, but mostly he's away working or he stays at my place."

*Her* place? Maybe she wasn't his assistant then? Ah. She must be his girlfriend. I made a mental note not to let any derogatory comments slip out, although Emmy seemed less than impressed with the house herself.

Even so, I couldn't help asking, "B-b-but how... How could he let it get so bad?"

Emmy pursed her lips and stared past me for a moment, considering her answer. "There was an incident a few years back. He lost interest in the house, and tidying fell off his to-do list."

That must have been some incident. "What about clothes? How does he find anything to wear?"

"If he's in a hotel, they do his laundry. Sometimes it gets done over at mine." She shrugged. "Otherwise he just buys new stuff."

Wow. *He buys new stuff*. Just like that. "Oh my gosh. I'm not sure I'd even know where to start."

I had visions of me driving around in one of those trucks

you see at garbage dumps, shovelling everything out of the way. A bubble of laughter threatened to escape, and I quickly smothered it with my hand.

Emmy grimaced. "I was afraid that you might say that."

I know she warned me it was awful, but nothing could have prepared me for how bad it was. Even watching *Hoarders*. And this house was huge—I'd be like an ant trying to move a mountain.

But I really, really needed a job, and this dumpster fire of a mansion would guarantee employment for a very, very long time.

"I suppose I could tackle one room to start with, then work my way through."

Emmy arched a perfectly plucked eyebrow. "You'll do it?"

"How much would I get paid?" Not that it mattered. I couldn't afford to be picky.

"How about seventy?"

Seventy dollars a day. If I worked six days a week, that made four hundred and twenty dollars, so seventeen hundred dollars a month. That would definitely pay the rent, food, and utilities, but there wouldn't be a lot left over towards all the medical bills. Dare I try my luck?

"I'll do it for eighty."

"Done. When can you start?"

Huh? She didn't even come back with a counter offer? I'd only been hoping for seventy-five. Still, Momma always told me not to look a gift horse in the mouth, and that was two hundred dollars a month extra for me.

"Uh, anytime? Tomorrow?" I didn't have any shifts scheduled at the café until next week, and the boss had a pile of résumés behind the register from people looking for work. She'd understand.

"Great. I'll have someone meet you here with the keys and paperwork. Nine o'clock okay?"

"I'll make sure I'm here." I'd ask Sylvia which bus would get me closest, then walk the rest.

"You'll be on a three-month probation period with a pay review at the end. That's standard for all employees." She ran her eyes over a stack of boxes. "I'll get a dumpster ordered."

"Only one?" I couldn't help myself—the words just popped out.

Luckily, Emmy laughed. "You're right. Multiple dumpsters are needed. Come on, let's get out of here. I can't stand the sight of this place for another second."

I took one last glance before she closed the door behind us, burning the image into my retinas. No doubt it would fuel my nightmares for weeks to come.

# 8

## LARA

At first light the next morning, my sense of euphoria at having a job was soon tempered by realism.

When I told Emmy yesterday I'd start with one room and work through, it had sounded so easy. But which room? They were all horrendous.

I hit my first challenge before I even left my apartment. What should I wear? I'd seen Sylvia in her perfectly pressed shift dress, and I didn't have so much as an iron. My only short black dress may have been suitable for hotels, but it wouldn't look the part in Rybridge. Still, I didn't have much choice. I picked a couple of bits of lint off my apron and slipped it into my bag, and as an afterthought, I added a pair of jeans and a T-shirt, just in case I was allowed to wear them. Climbing over Mr. Goldman's piles of debris in my regular outfit wouldn't be particularly practical.

I hadn't thought the food situation through either. Microwave noodles had become my staple, but cooking in Mr. Goldman's kitchen was out of the question for the foreseeable future. It would have to be plain peanut butter sandwiches since I'd run out of jelly.

The bus Sylvia suggested trundled along and got me within a mile of the house. While the drive with Emmy had roared by, my new commute was just shy of two hours. Thank goodness for library books.

At least it didn't rain, probably because I'd remembered my umbrella, and I couldn't deny the walk was pleasant. As I passed each driveway, I tried to catch a glimpse of what lay beyond the gates. Sports cars, tennis courts, and fountains abounded.

I arrived five minutes early, but I still felt late. As I hovered outside, a blonde lady leaning against a black Mercedes inside glanced at her watch before buzzing the gates open. She didn't have the same air of intimidation as Emmy, but there was a hard edge to her, even when she smiled.

"I'm Nadia, Nick's PA. You must be Lara?"

Another assistant? How many did he have? "That's me."

I followed her to the door and stood back as she flung it open. Her nose crinkled as she took in the scene beyond.

"Hell, it's worse than I remember. At least he's finally admitted he needs help."

My lucky day. I'd been hoping that if I wished hard enough, the house wouldn't look as bad as it did yesterday, but if anything, it was worse. The sunbeams shining through the grubby windows made the thick layer of dust covering everything all the more obvious. And was that the remains of a palm tree festering in the corner?

"I've brought a contract for you to sign," Nadia continued. "And there's a truck full of cleaning products on its way. The dumpsters should be delivered by lunchtime."

"Thank you."

She handed me a leather document folder and a pen. "I'm going to go check the mail. I'll be back in a few minutes."

Inside the folder, I found two copies of the contract, both marked up with little sticky tabs where I needed to sign.

Someone must have been working late last night—Emmy hadn't dropped me home until after seven.

Clause 3.2... My place of work was listed as this house and "other locations by agreement." What did that mean? I read further, hoping to find out what my working hours would be, but it wasn't mentioned. Hold on, I got twenty days of vacation a year. Four weeks! Never in my life had I held a job that included paid vacation. The three-month trial period Emmy mentioned was noted in Clause 17.1, to be "assessed on performance." I looked nervously at the clutter awaiting me. Seemed I'd have some long days to get that lot cleared by the end of my probation.

When I flipped to the fifth page, I found a chink in Nadia's efficiency. She'd gotten the salary wrong. No way should it be eighty thousand dollars. Nobody in their right mind would pay a housekeeper that. Not with health insurance on top. Much as I'd have loved to sign for that amount, the honest girl in me felt compelled to point it out.

Next, my untrained eye came to rest on a confidentiality clause, which forbade me from saying a word to anyone about anything. Surely that was overkill? It wasn't as if the man was a celebrity, was it? I'd certainly never heard of him. Oh, what did it matter? I barely had anybody to talk to in any case.

The front door swung open as Nadia came back, clutching a small pile of papers.

"Got the weekly quota of junk mail." She rolled her eyes. "Usually I just grab it and run. Fortunately, Nick has the important things sent straight to the office."

I cleared my throat. "Can I ask some questions?"

"I thought you might want to. Shoot."

"I can't see anything about working hours. What are they?"

My colleagues at the agency were full of tales about being

made to work sixteen-hour days, and I sure hoped it wouldn't come to that.

"There aren't any set times. We all tend to be flexible."

*Flexible.* There was that word again. I bit my tongue, managing not to make a ridiculous comment like I did with Bradley. Nadia wouldn't care that I could do the splits.

"What about days?"

Nadia leaned back against the door, the only accessible surface in the room. "If Nick's around, he'll expect you to be here. If he's away, not so much."

How often was he here? Was I expected to be at his beck and call? My face must have shown my doubts because Nadia expounded.

"Last month, Nick was around, so I worked seven days a week. This month, he's been travelling overseas, and I spent two weeks answering emails for an hour a day from the beach in Antigua."

That didn't sound so bad. "I can't vacuum from the beach, but a few easy days would be lovely." I flipped back to the start of the contract. "This paragraph mentions other locations?"

And I figured it wasn't talking about Antigua.

"Emmy didn't tell you?"

I shook my head.

"Nick's got two more houses, one in LA and another in Italy. Lake Como. They'll need attention at some point."

"Are they..." My voice dropped to a whisper. "Are they as bad as this one?"

"I haven't been to either of them. Probably."

I didn't swear much, but the only word that sprang to mind had four letters and rhymed with duck.

"How does one person create so much mess?"

"Years and years of practice, I think." Nadia flashed me a

grin. "But you haven't run screaming, which is a good sign. Anything else?"

I pointed out the end paragraph. "The salary's wrong."

She stepped forward and peered down. "No, eighty thousand dollars is right. That's what Emmy told me."

"I thought it was eighty dollars a day?"

"Who would take on this car crash for eighty dollars a day?"

Er, me? When people got desperate, they'd do anything. Could eighty thousand really be right? I went a little lightheaded and my legs threatened to give way, so I perched on the edge of a box that apparently contained a coffee table. Oh gosh, Emmy must have thought I was ridiculously greedy when I turned down her offer of seventy. But I parked that embarrassment at the back of my mind as I did some quick calculations. At eighty thousand, even after tax, I could clear Momma's medical bills in only five or six years. For that, I'd clean all three of Mr. Goldman's houses, on my knees with a toothbrush if necessary.

Nadia's tapping foot snapped me out of my stupor.

"Are you ready to sign now?" she asked. "I need to get back to the office."

I grabbed the pen and scribbled on both copies, fearful they'd vanish if I hesitated. Nadia stuffed one back into the folder and handed the other to me, along with several pages of typed notes, her business card, and a bunch of keys.

"Here are the security codes, my number, and a sheet of information. Give me a call if you need anything."

"I will."

She took one last look around before she backed out the door. "Good luck."

I'd need it. As the lock clicked, my heart sped up as the enormity of the task hit me. One woman against a lifetime of garbage.

I was on my own in the closest thing to hell on earth.

# 9

## LARA

The music blaring from Nadia's car stereo had only just faded into the distance when the entry phone by the front door buzzed, making me jump.

I picked my way over and pressed the button. "Who is it?"

"Delivery from Ee-Zee Clean."

Wow, that was quick. "I'll get the gates."

Nadia hadn't been kidding about the truck. It took the man four trips to carry everything into the house, and he choked a little the first time he walked through the door.

"It's my first day on the job," I hurried to point out, just in case he thought I was in any way responsible for the mess.

"Better you than me, ma'am."

By the time he'd stacked a vacuum cleaner, floor polisher, carpet washer, gloves, dusters, mops, buckets, paper towels, an iron and ironing board plus every type of cleaning liquid, powder, and spray imaginable on top of the other junk in the hall, I had a tiny space of about two feet square to stand in.

"That sure is a lot of stuff," I said.

"Lady called up and ordered one of everything." He shook

his head, eyes wide. "That's never happened before. Looks as if you'll need it, though. Good luck."

After a brief moment where I considered asking the delivery driver to drop me at the nearest airport, I decided to start with the kitchen. At least if I cleared that, I'd be able to use the sink. And surely there had to be a washing machine in the house somewhere? I'd need one for the mountain of dirty clothes—there had to be years' worth of laundry.

I rummaged through the boxes in the hallway and found dish soap plus a pile of tea towels, then tiptoed back to the kitchen. The glasses could go in the dishwasher, but I'd have to scrub the plates by hand. The food had probably dried on them when dinosaurs came out of the sea. Some of it was practically fossilised. Good thing I didn't have long, perfectly manicured nails like Emmy, because they'd have been in a sorry state once I'd finished.

Three hours later, I had neatly stacked piles of china and rows of glasses. I counted up forty-two dinner plates. Forty-two! Either Mr. Goldman was a real big entertainer or Emmy was right when she said he kept buying more of everything. I'd been worried about where to put all the dishes, but when I got the cupboards open, they were empty. It seemed Mr. Goldman wasn't so much of a hoarder—he simply took everything out, used it, and didn't put it away again. Ever.

Another buzz of the entry phone heralded the arrival of a row of dumpsters. The man left them lined up along the edge of the drive, their garish red clashing with the pale peach of the detached four-car garage.

In the afternoon, I set about transferring the contents of the pantry to the trash. It was full of dried goods, but the only things that hadn't expired were a can of hotdog sausages and a half-empty jar of manuka honey. It took me a dozen trips to get rid of it all, and my arms ached by the time I'd finished.

Outside, sun shone from a clear blue sky, and a gentle

breeze rustled through the trees. The garden, with its neatly mown lawn and colourful flowers, hadn't suffered the same fate as the house in terms of care, and I sat out on the patio to eat my lunch. As I watched small birds flitting from tree to tree, I could almost believe life was good.

But all too soon, my break was over, and it was time to tackle the giant refrigerator. The silver monster had been staring at me the entire morning, striking fear into my heart. What would be inside? I had visions of previously undiscovered life forms lurking, green and furry.

I crept over and reached out a hand, heart pounding. *Oh Lara, just get on with it*! I closed my eyes and pulled it open, holding my breath. Only the tick of the clock kept me company, and the near-silence stretched my nerves as I risked an inhale. No stench—that was good, right? I cracked one eyelid open, then the other. Was that it? Two six packs of beer sat on a shelf, next to a pizza box containing a couple of dried-up slices. Something small and shrivelled sat in the egg-holder. I peered closer. Had that once been a lemon?

Feeling slightly braver, I tried the freezer and found a similar picture. I'd steeled myself for a horror story, and the reality of six elderly TV dinners and a thick layer of ice was almost disappointing. As afternoon stretched into evening, I set about defrosting it.

Time flew by, and when I next looked at my watch, it was almost nine o'clock. A groan escaped my lips as I realised I still had to trek to the bus stop. With one last glance at the dent I'd made in the mess, I set the security system according to the instructions Nadia had left and began my journey home.

At least the exhaustion from cleaning gave me a good night's sleep, my first in months. I could have done with another year in bed, but I needed to finish the kitchen. The bus driver who picked me up was the same one as yesterday, and my smile was met with a grimace as I hopped on board. I guess not everyone was a morning person.

As I spent the time before lunch digging through the remaining junk in the kitchen, the things I expected to be filthy were spotless. Under a layer of dust, the stove gleamed, and the dishwasher still had that plasticky-new smell. When I opened the oven door, I found the operating manual inside, still shrink-wrapped. Mr. Goldman had never used any of these appliances, had he?

By the end of the day, I'd tidied everything into its proper place to reveal a state-of-the-art kitchen. Any budding chef would fall in love with it. How could Mr. Goldman live here and not cook? The marble countertops and slate floor must have cost a small fortune, and the wrought iron chandelier hanging over the central island twinkled now that I'd dusted it. Who had designed this place? I bet it wasn't the house's owner.

Behind a pair of surfboards stacked haphazardly in a corner, one turquoise, one neon-green, I found the door to a utility room. A quick peek revealed it was just as full as the rest of the house. That would be tomorrow's job—I hoped to find a washer and dryer.

I'd planned to leave before it got dark today, but time had run away from me again. This community may have been rich, but that didn't make the shadows any less scary, so I decided to celebrate my achievement with the kitchen and my ridiculous new salary by getting a cab to the bus stop. Extravagant, but better than unravelling my frayed nerves any further. As I waited by the gates, I even considered buying a car. Just a cheap run-around, something economical and definitely not flashy, because I certainly didn't want to draw attention to myself after my experience in Baysville. Then I did the math and quickly put the idea out of my mind—I needed to make a dent in my debts before I made any big purchases.

From that day on, I got into a routine. The place was more messy than dirty, and I set myself a target of clearing one room per day. For the most part, I managed it. I was used to working among a team of hotel staff, and it was oddly liberating to be my own boss, seeing as Mr. Goldman still hadn't shown up. Where was he, anyway?

Day six came without me seeing a soul, and when I heard the front door slam unexpectedly, I jumped so violently I almost knocked myself out on the piano I was crawling underneath.

"Lara?" a man's voice called.

I got to my knees, rubbing my head. "In the living room."

Bradley swanned in, clutching a bakery bag. "I was in the neighbourhood, so I brought donuts." He held out the bag and grinned. "This looks like a different house already."

I smiled back, proud of my achievements. "This floor's half done, but I haven't started upstairs. I'm going to need more dumpsters."

"Consider it done. Nick'll hardly recognise this place."

I only hoped he'd be happy. I'd had to take a few liberties as I guessed where to put things, but I could soon rearrange them to his tastes.

"When's he due back?"

Bradley shrugged, and his mint-green off-the-shoulder sweater slipped down farther. "Don't know yet. Probably a week or two."

At least that bought me more time. "That's good."

"Why's it good?" He leaned in close enough that I caught a whiff of his shampoo. Something floral. Violets, maybe. "Don't tell me you're nervous about meeting him?"

"Is it that obvious?"

"He'll love you, don't worry. Do you want the jam-filled or the cream?"

My mouth watered as he opened the bag. "Jam-filled?" I liked this job more and more.

He passed my treat over. "Do you need anything else? Bleach? Laundry detergent? A dump truck?"

"The truck's tempting, but I've still got enough cleaning products. I do have a question, though."

"Go for it."

"I found a pile of boxes full of women's clothes and trinkets in the room next to the living room. Should I unpack them?"

Big brown boxes, sealed with shiny brown tape that had gone dry under the edges. Unable to contain my curiosity, I'd opened a couple. A china eagle was wrapped in pages from a German newspaper dated seven years ago. Was that when Mr. Goldman moved in? Seven freaking years and he hadn't touched half of his stuff?

Bradley's eyes widened for a second, but he quickly flashed a smile. "No, no, leave them. Uh, just stack them in one of the spare bedrooms."

"Do you know who the stuff belongs to?" Emmy perhaps?

"Shut the door and forget about it. No point in stirring up the past."

*What past?* I was dying to ask, but Bradley got up and headed to the front door. He gave me a finger wave, but I didn't have time to return it before he disappeared.

*Time to get back to work.* I returned to my chores, licking the last traces of sugar off of my lips. Really, I needed to start on the laundry if I was to have any chance of getting it done before Mr. Goldman got back.

Investigation on the second floor revealed six bedrooms, although only one looked like it had ever been slept in. As well as the mammoth pile in the master, the other five were full, and I mean *full*, of dirty clothes. I grabbed an armful and put on what would be the first load of many, then headed back to the living room.

By the end of the second week, I'd begun to get just a tiny bit lonely. Rybridge was the quietest neighbourhood I'd ever been in. No door-to-door salesmen, no street sounds, and no loud music, at least until Bradley stopped by with Disney tunes blaring from the speakers in his Lamborghini. He even brought me treats—macarons on one day, and a birthday cake on another.

"Uh, my birthday's not until January."

"I know that. It was on your application. But the cake's pink, and every girl needs a pink cake."

How could I argue with that logic? "I'll get some matches for the candles."

I scurried off, wiping a tear from my cheek. Why? Because it was the first time since Momma died that anyone had thought of my birthday, even if it was six months early.

My only other company was the gardener, who nearly gave me a heart attack when he started the lawnmower outside the window one overcast Tuesday morning. By the time I'd picked myself up off the floor, he was at the far end of the lawn, head bobbing away in time to music I couldn't hear. He turned out to be a man of few words. Apart from a grunt of thanks when I took him a cup of coffee, I didn't get much out of him.

Sick of my own company, not to mention my dubious singing as I tidied, I gave Sylvia a call. I'd checked the map, and she was only a ten-minute walk away.

"Feel like getting a coffee?" I asked. After the kindness she'd shown me, I owed her a treat.

"I can meet you at lunch, but I won't have long. I know a place with amazing muffins."

That suited me—even though I'd added cheese and ham to my sandwich repertoire, I could do with a bit of variety. I set out with time to spare, enjoying the walk along quiet streets. Living here must be a surreal experience. Until I started working for Mr. Goldman, the biggest home I'd been in was Billy's father's mansion, but these places made his look like a doll's house.

I snagged a table next to the sidewalk at the café Sylvia suggested, earning a suspicious look from the waitress. Maybe I shouldn't have come in jeans? I'd decided that until Mr. Goldman came back, I might as well wear something comfortable even if I didn't fit in with the Rybridge set.

Sylvia did, though. She turned up five minutes later, dragging a pocket-sized dog on a sparkly pink leash.

"Sorry I'm late. Mitzi insisted on sniffing everything."

What was she? A chihuahua? I bent to pet her, but when she growled, I snatched my hand back.

"It's no problem. I haven't been here long."

Sylvia raised an eyebrow at my attire. "Jeans?"

Next time, I was definitely going to change before I set foot in this place. "My boss is away. Actually, I haven't seen him once yet."

"Figures. The people around here fork out millions for a palace then spend their time skiing in winter and kicking back at the beach in summer."

"I think he's away on business."

"They all say that. He's on a yacht with his mistress."

"You know him, then?"

She laughed and shook her head. "Just a guess, but I bet you a cupcake I'm right. The likes of you and me don't get to 'know' the people who own these houses. If you're lucky, they might learn your name eventually, but only because that makes it easier to shout orders at you."

"Does your boss shout a lot?"

"If I do absolutely everything perfectly, only ten times a day."

"How do you cope?"

"The family has another home in Florida, so they're only here for half the year. The rest of the time it's just me, the housekeeper, and the gardener. Very quiet."

"I could keep you company sometimes, if you want?"

"We're not allowed visitors at the house, but I'm always up for coffee."

I doubted I'd be allowed guests either. "Same. It's a crazy world here, isn't it? Like living in a bubble?"

She giggled. "A velvet-lined, gold-plated bubble filled with diamonds and caviar."

I dissolved into laughter with her, and Mitzi yapped along. "Don't forget the Ferraris."

# 10

## LARA

Spending day after day on my own started to wear me down. I threw my sandwich crusts out onto the back lawn for the birds just to have some company. After my fourth morning in a row spent without seeing a human soul, I phoned Missy as I hung out yet another load of laundry that was too delicate to tumble dry.

"How's the wedding planning going?"

My eardrums protested as she squealed down the line. "I've been meaning to call you! How's your new life?"

I told her about my job at Adler House, glossing over the gory details of the inside. "It's hard work, but at least I've left my stalker behind."

"Sounds amazing! And you're far enough away that you can't hear my soon-to-be mother-in-law screeching, either."

"She's giving you a hard time?"

"You'd think it was her getting married, not us. She's trying to get me and Clyde to take ballroom dancing lessons."

"For your first dance? That could make it memorable."

"Honey, if I'm paying for the alcohol, then I'm damn well

drinking it. If I'm still standing by the first dance, I'll be disappointed."

When she put it like that, dancing lessons did seem a bit of a waste. "When Mr. Goldman comes back, how about I see if I can get a weekend off? I could come and give you some moral support."

"I'd love that! You're still gonna be a bridesmaid, right?"

"Nothing could stop me being there with you on your wedding day."

Apart from perhaps the mustard-coloured dress she'd threatened me with before I left.

It was too late to call Tori by the time I finished clearing the conservatory, so I saved that for my walk from the bus stop the next morning.

"You're getting paid how much?" she yelled when I told her my new salary. "Eighty thousand bucks a year just for cleaning?"

"Well, yes."

"Are you sure 'extras' aren't required?"

"What do you mean, 'extras'?"

"Oh, you know. Like *Pretty Woman*-style extras."

"Yeuww! No! At least, I don't think so. Oh gosh, do you think he might expect that?"

Was that something that went with the territory of being an overpaid housekeeper?

"I hope not, for your sake. No amount of money's worth losing your dignity over."

I thought of Emmy. Surely *she* kept him happy in that department? "He's got a girlfriend, and she looks like a supermodel except not so skinny. Probably he won't even notice me."

Hopefully.

"I'm sure it'll be fine." Tori didn't sound convinced. "When will you meet him?"

"I don't know. He's still away on business." Bradley had told me yesterday that Mr. Goldman's return was delayed, something about negotiations that had gotten a little complex.

"He could be some old pervert."

"I don't think so. I found a picture, and he looks quite normal."

Although the house was oddly devoid of personal touches, I'd come across a newspaper clipping on a shelf in the living room. The caption under it said *Nicholas Goldman at the opening of the new marina at Colonial Beach*. I guessed his age at early fifties, and the woman he had his arm around a decade younger. Was she his wife? Ex-wife? Had he gotten divorced? No woman lived in Adler House, that was for sure, and then there was Emmy.

"It's always the quiet ones who have the strangest tastes. Did I tell you about the guy I dated a couple of times before I met Paul? The one who wanted me to wear a diaper?"

"What? No!"

"It's true. Until he turned up with that, plus a rattle and baby powder, he seemed kinda boring."

"Freaking heck. Did you try it?"

"I said I was going to the bathroom and snuck out the back door."

My uncontrollable giggles earned me an alarmed glance from a jogger on the other side of the road. "I've been through most of the house now, and there's no baby wear, thank goodness. But judging by the surfboards and the scuba gear, I think Mr. Goldman might be having a midlife crisis."

"He'll probably turn up with a ponytail and a trashy blonde in the passenger seat of his sports car."

I'd seen men of that type at Buck's. They were poor tippers as well. "His girlfriend isn't trashy, and I haven't seen his car yet."

None of the keys I had fitted the garage. Was it filled with vehicles? Or more junk?

"I'll keep my fingers crossed he's not a freak. Make sure you look after yourself and remember I'm always here if you need someone to talk to."

"Love you, Tori." She'd always look out for me.

"Love you too, Lara."

As well as the garage, there was one room in the house I couldn't get into. I asked Bradley about it that evening when he turned up with pizza.

"Should I be cleaning it?" I gave a nervous laugh. "He doesn't have a body in there, does he?"

"It's his study. He hates anyone going in."

I couldn't complain—that was one less room to tidy. "No problem."

Bradley leaned back on the sofa and put his feet up on the coffee table. "Don't worry, my shoes are clean," he said when he caught my sharp look.

"What would Mr. Goldman say if he caught you doing that?" I may not have met my boss, but I felt an irrational need to stick up for him.

Bradley shrugged. "He wouldn't care. Trust me."

I wasn't sure about that, but nerves forbade me from saying anything else. After all, Bradley was my boss too, even if he did act more like a friend most of the time. I just made sure to give the table an extra polish after he'd left.

Four weeks passed with no sign of my mysterious employer. I was beginning to wonder if he existed at all when Emmy paid a surprise visit. I heard the front door close while I was tackling Mr. Goldman's en-suite bathroom, followed by her distinctive voice.

"You here, Lara?"

"Upstairs."

Almost ten minutes passed before she appeared, and when she did, she was grinning.

"I knew you could do it. You're a miracle worker."

"Huh?"

"The house. Nick's not gonna believe his eyes. The place hasn't been this tidy since he moved in. Actually before that, because the day he got the keys, we all came round for dinner and beer, and I'm pretty sure those pizza boxes were still in here."

"When *did* he move in?"

"Seven years ago." So my guess was right. "He was renting before that, and I think it's safe to say he lost his security deposit." She made a face. "Although he didn't used to be this bad."

"You've known him a long time, then?"

"Yes."

She didn't elaborate, and I wasn't about to pry.

"Is he easy to work for?"

"He likes things to be done properly, but he's fair. Anyhow, you'll meet him soon. He's due to fly back on Sunday."

Sunday was five days away, and I quickly ran through the list of outstanding jobs in my head. "I think I'll have the place finished by then."

Emmy's grin got wider. "Glad to hear it. I'll arrange a credit card for you—can you buy in some groceries?"

I nodded. "And maybe a few plants, too? It's those touches that turn a house into a home."

"Whatever you think's appropriate." Her phone pinged, and she scrolled through a message. "Gotta dash. See you soon."

As she roared down the drive, I scurried back upstairs. I had a time limit now, and I was determined to make everything perfect by the weekend.

# 11

## NICK

Nick yawned, not bothering to cover his mouth with his hand. Raising his arm would have taken energy he didn't possess.

When a buddy in the CIA offered him a ride back on the C-130 military transport plane on Saturday afternoon, it had seemed like a great idea because it meant getting the hell out of Somalia a day earlier than planned. What he hadn't bargained on was having to fly the fucking thing himself. But then again, it wasn't as if his former colleague had known the pilot was going to get sick and spew over the cockpit, was it?

Still, having to forego his nap and sit in a small space stinking of vomit for the last six hours wasn't something that left Nick in the best of moods, and by the time he landed at the military airbase near Washington, DC, all he wanted to do was get home, take a shower, and find pizza and beer, in that order. Then sleep for a week.

Once the plane was safely stowed in its hangar, Nick bid goodbye to his buddies of the past few weeks. "See you in a few days, okay?"

"At least the Pentagon's more civilised than the Gulf of Aden," Jed said as he swung his bag over his shoulder.

"Couldn't complain about the outcome, though."

"No, or the suntan."

The job had been a tough one—what started as a straightforward mission to take down some pirates had turned into a tense standoff when the little fuckers managed to capture a cruise ship that had strayed off-course in a storm. A month of negotiations culminated in a seat-of-the-pants operation to retake the ship, led by Nick and Jed. The final score was Blackwood Security and the CIA twenty-three, pirates nil.

A job well done, but there was no escaping the paperwork.

Nick was part-owner of Blackwood, heading up the Protection Division. Two of his friends had started small sixteen years ago, and between the pair of them, plus Nick and Emmy, they'd grown it into one of the largest security firms in the world. But while Nick could certainly afford to sit back and enjoy the spoils, he preferred to be at the centre of the action—after all, he'd once been a Navy SEAL—and when the opportunity came to take a break from his regular role and spend a month on a boat, he couldn't pass it up.

A vacation, military-style.

But despite the fun in the sun, he'd missed his creature comforts. Maybe he was getting old? His bones never used to ache this much after a job. The lack of washroom facilities had left him smelling ripe, and most of his meals for the past month had consisted of unidentifiable meat or fish, made edible only by the liberal addition of chilli powder.

Dammit. He remembered too late that he'd forgotten to reschedule his car ride home from Sunday morning to tonight. Emmy wouldn't appreciate a last-minute call, so he grabbed his bag and hopped in a cab.

"Where to, sir?" the driver asked.

Good question. Should he go to Emmy's place or his own? He weighed up the options. Emmy's home came with an abundance of clean towels and food in the fridge, but last time he arrived there unexpectedly, he'd walked in on her husband nailing her over the billiard table. Although she'd grinned and invited him to join in, the black look on her husband's face meant Nick would rather avoid a repeat of the experience. They may have shared an occasional woman for the night in their wilder days, but not Emmy. Never Emmy.

"Head for Rybridge," he told the driver.

Had Bradley bought him more towels? Nick couldn't remember whether he'd asked him to or not. So long had passed since he'd been home, he was surprised he recalled his own address. As the driver trundled out to the main road, Nick sent a quick email to stop Emmy from coming to the airbase tomorrow because if she arrived and he wasn't there, she'd probably shave off his eyebrows as he slept.

A soft glow glimmered from the living room windows, welcoming Nick back as he walked up the drive. That was an added feature of his custom security system—it switched the lights on and off at random times as well as opening and closing the drapes.

The first hint that something wasn't right came when he turned to the alarm panel next to the front door. It blinked green. Why was the system unarmed? More to the point, where was the stack of boxes he usually had to lean over to reach it?

Who the hell had been in his house?

One of Nick's new clients had gotten his house invaded by fraudsters while he was overseas recently, and the bastards had the gall to pass the property off as their own while trying to sell it cut-price. Nick pressed his lips together, trying to fight off the headache that had been threatening all evening. If his house had been broken into, the team paid to monitor his state-of-the-art system was getting fired first thing tomorrow morning.

As he crept through the hallways, his senses were on high alert, and it wasn't long before he found what he was looking for. An intruder. When he saw the strange woman asleep on his couch, he did what came as naturally to him as breathing—drew his gun and pointed it at the T-line, that small area between the upper lip and the bottom of the nose. One round through there would hit the medulla oblongata—or the apricot, as his sniper colleagues called it—and turn the lights out instantly.

"Who the hell are you?"

She blinked a couple of times as she woke, then her eyes went wide as she focused on the semi-automatic. The scream she let out made his head pound, and he screwed his eyes up as fireworks exploded behind them.

"P-p-please don't shoot!" Seemingly as an afterthought, she flung her arms above her head.

"Who the fuck are you, and what are you doing here?"

She straightened, pulled back her shoulders, and narrowed her eyes, even though she was trembling worse than San Francisco during a 7.0 on the Richter scale. "I could ask you the same question, mister."

"It's my house, so back at you."

"It's not your house. It belongs to Mr. Goldman, and I'm his housekeeper."

If he didn't know better, he'd have believed her. "Try again."

"What do you mean?"

"I don't have a housekeeper."

"You're not Mr. Goldman either."

Huh? "Yes, I am."

"No way. I've seen a picture of him, and he's much older."

"What picture?" He took a step forwards, and her mouth opened. "For fuck's sake, don't scream again. You could wake the dead."

"Then stay back."

"Fine. What picture?" he asked again.

"It's on the shelf over there." She gestured towards the corner of the room.

Without taking the gun off her, Nick walked over to where she pointed and picked up the newspaper clipping.

"That's my father."

She pursed her lips together. Cute.

"I'm not sure I believe you. You look like a burglar."

Nick sighed and fished in his pocket for his wallet, then flipped his driver's licence over to her. She looked down at it, then back at him. Her pretty face crumpled, and she sagged back in the seat.

"I'm so sorry I fell asleep. I only meant to rest for a few minutes."

He was still hung up on her earlier comment. "How do I look like a burglar?"

"Well, you're wearing black and pointing a gun at me."

"What's wrong with wearing black? It goes with everything." He'd lost count of the number of times Bradley had told him that. "And I'm pointing a gun at you because you're in my house, and I don't know who you are."

"I told you, I'm your housekeeper."

"And I told *you*, I didn't hire a housekeeper."

"I had two interviews, and then your assistant met me here with the keys."

"Who were the interviews with?" He held up a hand. Actually, a name wouldn't help—his acquaintances changed theirs more often than Nick changed his boxers. "On second thought, that doesn't matter. Was it a blonde, a brunette, or a redhead?"

"Blonde, really pretty, and there was a man too."

"Small guy, very colourful?"

"Yes, that's him."

"Fucking Emerson." What the hell did she think she was playing at?

Nick reached into his pocket again, this time for his phone. He stabbed at the screen and waited for the call to connect.

"Uh, would you mind not aiming the gun at me?"

"What? Oh, sorry."

Nick put the gun back in its holster. The poor woman wasn't a threat, and it was hardly her fault Emmy had been meddling. He meandered into the hallway as the phone rang.

And rang, and rang. He was about to try another line when Emmy picked up.

"What do you want?"

"It's ten in the evening, and you sound slightly breathless. I do hope I didn't interrupt anything."

"This'd better be good, Nick. I'm fucking busy."

"Other way around, more like. I've just had the flight from hell, then I arrived home to find a woman asleep on my couch."

"I'm not surprised. The poor girl's probably exhausted. I was going to tell you about her tomorrow."

"Who the fuck is she?"

"Your housekeeper. Her name's Lara. Hasn't she done a great job? I mean, a month ago you wouldn't even have known you had a couch."

"Where on earth did you get it into your crazy little head to hire me a housekeeper?"

"You agreed to it," Emmy said.

"No, I didn't."

"Yes, you did."

"When?"

"The day after the Blackwood Foundation Heroes and Villains Ball. Remember? We were sitting in the kitchen, just before Miriam the Bitch turned up, and you were complaining about your lack of socks. I suggested getting a housekeeper, and you said 'I guess.'"

"That doesn't count as agreeing. I was half asleep and hungover."

"The words still came out of your mouth."

"You never play fair. I don't want a housekeeper."

"Well, you can't fire her, because technically she's on my payroll at the moment." Nick could hear Emmy's smile over the damn phone.

"You're impossible, you know that?"

"Not impossible, Nick, just difficult, and you wouldn't have me any other way. Besides, Lara's awesome. Did you know you actually have six bedrooms? As opposed to one bedroom and five rooms full of shit? You'd better not be mean to her."

Before Nick could answer, there was a rustling sound from the other end of the line, then Emmy's husband spoke.

"Amusing though this conversation is, my wife's got better things to do this evening than argue about the state of your house. She'll speak to you tomorrow. And trust me, buddy— you need the housekeeper."

There was a click as he hung up, and Nick groaned to himself as he recalled the conversation Emmy referred to. Never for one moment had he dreamed she'd act on her absurd suggestion. He tugged at his hair in frustration, wrinkling his nose as grime coated his fingers. If Emmy said the housekeeper was staying, she was staying, at least until he could come up with a convincing reason to get rid of her.

Nick tucked his phone back into his pocket and sighed, half wishing he'd stayed in Somalia. Now he needed to introduce himself to the poor woman caught up in the middle of this. After all, they'd have to put up with each other for a few more weeks at least.

## 12

### NICK

Nick plastered on a smile as he pushed open the door to the living room. Where was the woman? The couch sat empty, a dented cushion the only evidence that she'd been there. Too late, he realised the security lights outside the house had come on again, two thousand watts illuminating the driveway. She must have set off the motion sensors as she left. Nick ran outside, but the gates were already closed. The damn girl had a head start, and he didn't know what car she drove or whether she'd gone right or left.

He trudged back to the house, cursing the woman under his breath. Her taking off like that meant he'd have to face the wrath of Emmy. Tomorrow. He'd call Emmy tomorrow. His headache was bad enough already without speaking to her again tonight. No, he'd go back to his original plan of pizza and beer, then confess in the morning after he'd gotten some sleep.

Only there was a flaw in his pizza plan. Where were his takeout menus? Over the years, he'd collected a whole pile of them, which he kept stuffed down the side of the microwave, but they were nowhere to be found. He ground his teeth together, trying to stay calm. Tell him the woman hadn't taken his beer as well? He pulled open the fridge door, finding not only three kinds of beer but shelves full of food. Had she done all this? He used the edge of the counter to pop the top off a bottle, then stepped back to peruse the contents.

Steak, salad, pizza, vegetables, chicken, a selection of condiments—everything Nick should be eating and normally didn't. At the bottom, he spied a couple of covered dishes. He poked at one and found a lasagne. Was that for him? He hoped so, because he was going to eat it. At least, he was if he could figure out how to work the oven.

By twiddling the knobs on the front, he got a light to turn on, and a fan whirred. He gave it a minute, and sure enough, it got warm. This was progress. He slid the dish in, then checked his watch. How long did a lasagne take to heat? Fifteen minutes? Twenty? Enough time to take a shower in any case.

In his bedroom, he found his festering pile of dirty clothes had disappeared, the only remaining evidence of its existence being the empty laundry hamper next to the bathroom door. The bathroom itself was clean and stocked with toiletries, and fresh towels hung on the rail rather than lounging in their usual spot on the floor.

When he'd scrubbed the remains of his Somalian escapade away, he opened his walk-in closet. How long since he'd been in there? Years. It must have been years. The shelves were stacked with hundreds of shirts, more than he'd ever imagined he owned. It must have taken hours for the woman to wash this lot. A tiny knot of guilt formed in the pit of his stomach when he thought of how he'd scared her earlier.

Once he'd pulled on jeans and a T-shirt, he poked his head into the other rooms. Emmy was right—they were all clear. The place looked like the house he remembered buying years ago, not long after he'd joined Blackwood. The house that had never been a home.

He'd once hoped it would be, and that thought opened the floodgates. He lay back on the bed in what should have been the master bedroom, the one he'd never slept in, as memories of the girl he'd once dreamed of sharing his life with hit him.

Jana.

They'd chosen the house together, yet she'd never been here. The real estate agent had made them videos of several properties, and Jana had fallen in love with this one as they sat together in her kitchen in Germany. As soon as the video ended, he'd called and bought it. He'd have bought her the moon if it would have made her happy, but she claimed she only needed one thing.

And she had him.

For five short months, she had him and he had her.

Without Jana at his side, Nick had lost interest in Adler House. She was the one who'd named the place—as a historian, she'd wanted a reminder of her German roots when she moved to the other side of the world to be with him. He'd thought of changing the name, even selling it, but he'd never been able to sever that final connection. Instead, the place had turned into a ruin as he'd lost interest in life and love.

But now it had risen from the ashes, and Nick wasn't sure how to feel about that.

As he walked back to the kitchen, he saw the house with fresh eyes. He'd all but forgotten the love seat Jana had picked out in Berlin and that hideous vase her colleagues gave her as a going away gift.

"We have to keep it for a few months," she'd said. "Roland threatened to pay us a visit."

Her ex-boss may have had terrible taste in ornaments, but she'd had a soft spot for the old professor, so the vase stayed.

Only now it was dust-free and filled with flowers.

Back in the kitchen, the lasagne was piping hot. Nick ate it with salad and bread he found in the fridge, and after the rations he'd been surviving on for the past month, it was heaven on a plate. Had the housekeeper made it?

He could get used to coming home to this.

Despite Emmy's nagging and Bradley's endless badgering, Nick had always resisted employing domestic staff. Not due to the cost, but rather because he'd never liked the idea of virtual strangers poking through his life. But deep down, he knew he couldn't carry on living the way he had been. Adler House should be more than a place to sleep when he couldn't cadge another bed for the night. Hell, he could name several hotels he'd spent more time in.

And today, the place felt different. Like it could be somewhere he looked forward to returning after a long day at work. Maybe having staff wouldn't be so bad after all.

He had to laugh at the absurdity of it—he owned a house that cost him over three million dollars, and he never stayed in it because he'd been too stubborn to admit he needed a housekeeper whose wages were no doubt a fraction of that. Emmy could be an interfering bitch at times, but she meant well, and although he hated to admit it, she was probably right when she hired that woman.

What had Emmy said her name was?

Laura?

Shit, and he'd held her at gunpoint. Emmy would be furious when he explained that one. He'd have to find Laura and apologise, but first, he needed to get her address from Emmy. He wasn't looking forward to either of those conversations.

Once he'd finished eating, he almost abandoned the dishes in the sink as usual, but then he thought about all the work Laura had put into clearing the place up. He had a dishwasher somewhere, surely? Nope, that was a cupboard. He opened one door after another until he found what he was looking for and loaded the plate and cutlery in. Turning it on presented a whole other problem, but he'd sort that out tomorrow.

Right now, he needed to sleep.

# 13

## LARA

The muffled sound of my phone interrupted my broken sleep, the ringtone entirely too cheerful for my mood. When I managed to drag an eyelid open, a glance at the clock on my lopsided nightstand told me it wasn't quite seven. Who would be calling at that time? Missy worked late and never got up before eight, so my money, if I had any, was on Tori.

Or what if it was Michelle? Had she heard about the incident last night? As the phone continued to ring, the full horror of what happened hit me like an army battalion, complete with horses and one of those giant catapult things they used in medieval times. Mr. Goldman had pointed a gun at me!

As if the man I worked for—or rather, used to work for—trying to kill me wasn't bad enough, now I was jobless again. Not that he'd truly been my employer. Up until he aimed the gun at me, all black and lethal, he hadn't even had a clue I existed. When I got home, I'd checked my contract and found I'd been employed by Riverley Associates, which I'd assumed was Mr. Goldman's company, but perhaps I'd been wrong on that. Sylvia certainly hadn't heard of it when I'd mentioned the name to her.

I buried my face in the pillow, resisting the urge to drop my phone out of the window. How could things have gone so badly wrong? I was beginning to wish I'd stayed in Baysville. My stalker may have been scary, but at least he'd never threatened me with a freaking pistol.

The phone stopped ringing, and I relaxed a smidgen, but not even ten seconds passed before it started again. At least when I pulled the quilt around me and stuffed the pillow over my head, it blocked out the sound. I didn't feel like speaking to anybody today. What I wanted to do was curl up on the couch with a good book and a pint of double chocolate chip ice cream and eat until I felt sick.

The only problem was, I didn't have any chocolate ice cream.

Or a couch.

Four hours passed before I woke up again. My head wanted to stay buried under the covers, but my back protested at spending more time on the lumpy mattress. Whenever I turned over, a broken spring jabbed me in the side, and that spurred me into action. Worry over finding work weighed heavy as I sat up and stuffed my feet into well-worn slippers, but thankfully, I'd already received my first pay cheque from Riverley. They couldn't take that off me. After tax, I'd deposited just over four thousand dollars into my bank account—more money than I'd ever seen in my life. I could stretch that to cover a couple of months.

The phone began ringing again, jarring my already frazzled nerves. I felt a sudden temptation to jump on the flipping thing until it broke, but I made myself take slow, calming breaths until the urge passed. Had I lost my mind? Violence never solved anything. Billy taught me that lesson.

Not a day had gone by without him yelling, and if we

made it to ten o'clock in the morning without him telling me nothing I ever did was good enough, it was because he was still passed out drunk from the night before.

*The house is filthy, what have you been doing all day? You look like a heifer in those clothes. Get your fat ass on Jenny Craig... What was dinner supposed to be? Roadkill? How the fuck could you let us run out of beer? The TV remote's not working. You need to buy more batteries.*

Or my particular favourite, *It's pouring outside. How are me and the boys supposed to grill steaks in that?* Yes, I even got that once. Somehow, the bad weather became my fault. If only it were true, I'd have struck Billy with lightning and ended my misery.

In the months that followed his accident, our joint friends stopped visiting, partly because Billy lost the kudos of being on the football team, but mostly because he was an asshole. Not to be deterred, he found a new set of buddies, losers who liked nothing more than sitting around drinking, smoking, and zoning out in front of the TV. As well as waiting on them every hour of every day, I was expected to put up with their lewd suggestions and occasional groping without comment.

My social life took a further nosedive when Billy forbade me from seeing my girlfriends, his reasoning being that if he wasn't going out, then neither was I.

"I'll miss you, babe," he said. "Friday nights wouldn't be the same without my girl."

Without his girl to fetch his beer and dial for his pizza, more like. I stewed over his orders until one evening I decided to hell with it, I was going out anyway.

That was the first time he hit me.

Just an open-handed slap when I tried to get past him to the front door. As the crack of skin on skin echoed in the hallway, he looked almost as shocked as I felt.

"Sweetheart, I didn't mean it. I'm so sorry."

He gripped my hands, his knuckles as white as his face. Words wouldn't come as he bundled me up in a hug and cradled me against him.

"I'm so sorry," he mumbled over and over again. "Please forgive me."

Eventually, he wore me down with his constant begging. Anyone could make a mistake, right? That's what Momma always said.

"Okay, I forgive you, but promise you won't do it again."

He didn't hesitate. "I promise, sweetheart. I promise."

The truth rarely passed Billy's lips and, of course, that was no exception. I should have known, but he had a way of making me doubt my own sanity. The slaps became punches, the punches turned into kicks, and occasionally, he'd slam me into the wall for variety. My visits home to Momma became an exercise in hiding bruises and putting a brave face on things.

"Are you all right, Lara?" she'd ask. "Is everything okay with Billy?"

"Everything's fine. I'm just tired."

The second part was true. I lay awake most nights plotting my escape.

Pride stopped me from admitting how Billy hurt me. He'd conditioned me to shoulder the blame, to believe I drove him to it. The dumb part of me remembered the good times and kept waiting for the old Billy to return.

Not only that, I couldn't bear to let Momma down. She'd sacrificed so much for me growing up—working two jobs, dressing from the thrift store, skipping meals—all so I could have a roof over my head, eat well, and do things I loved like going to math camp in the summer. When I got accepted to Brown, her grin made the Cheshire Cat look so-so.

"All those years were worth it," she said, grabbing my hand and dancing around the apartment. "My daughter, the college student."

She told everyone the good news—her friends, the neighbours, the cashier at the supermarket, the man who came to read the electricity meter. I wouldn't have been surprised to pick up the local paper and find a half-page announcement. How would she feel if I dropped out?

Because if I left Billy, staying in Providence would be impossible. He'd make my life a waking nightmare. I ticked off each passing day on the calendar in my head, counting down until graduation and the day I could finally run from him.

Whenever I heard people talk about domestic violence, their first question was always, "Why didn't she leave at the beginning? Why stick around to be used as a punching bag?"

Once upon a time, I'd asked the same thing, except when I ended up in the situation, I realised words were so much easier than actions. Billy's cruelty crept up on me like a high tide. My self-esteem got washed away with every drop of my blood he spilled until I became an empty shell, battered and dulled around the edges. Devoid of colour. Incapable of feeling.

I was the ghost to Billy's monster.

I tried to block out those memories as the phone rang yet again. It was no good—I'd have to answer it to have any hope of peace. I nearly tripped as I stumbled over to the jacket I'd worn yesterday and fished the phone out of the left-hand pocket.

*Tori calling*, the screen announced. Thank goodness for small mercies—at least it wasn't Emmy, or worse, Mr. Goldman. Not that I expected him to call. After all, he'd only met me for two minutes and neither of them was pleasant.

"Hi, Tori."

"What's up? You sound glum."

"How can you tell that from two words?"

"I know you, remember? Now, tell Auntie Victoria what happened."

It was good to finally have someone to talk to, and I told

Tori the whole story, starting with the interview, moving on to accidentally falling asleep on Mr. Goldman's couch, and finishing with me running away after he tried to shoot me.

At the end of it, Tori started laughing.

"Hey, it's not funny!"

"It sort of is. Last year, you were complaining you had no excitement in your life. Now you've had a stalker, moved clean across the country, gotten a new job working for a mysterious millionaire, and survived nearly being shot, all in the space of a few months."

I guessed she had a point, and I couldn't help giggling with her. "When you put it like that, my life does look quite thrilling, doesn't it?" I straightened my face. "What am I supposed to do now, though?"

"I'll tell you what you're going to do. You're going to go out and buy the biggest tub of chocolate ice cream you can find and scoff the lot." Tori knew ice cream was my go-to comfort food. "Then you need to get yourself an even better job, one that doesn't come with a horrible boss, and after that, you're going out to have some fun."

"One step at a time. Fun is something that happens to other people. At the moment, I'd settle for being able to pay the rent. And maybe buying a couch."

"You need to think big. How about a couch and a pair of armchairs?"

I laughed again. Two minutes talking to Tori always cheered me up.

"Okay, my new goal for this year: a three-piece suite. Why are you calling, anyway? I'm sure it wasn't just to hear about my car crash of a life."

"I have a teeny tiny piece of news."

"What's that?"

"I'm pregnant!"

I squealed loud enough to make the man next door bang

on the wall. "Ooh, that's fantastic." Especially since they'd been trying for so long. "When's it due? Do you know if it's a boy or a girl?"

"I'm only a month and a bit gone. My first doctor's appointment isn't until the day after tomorrow."

"I'm so happy for you both! And I've got a new goal now —I'm going to find a job so I can buy myself a ticket to come and visit."

"I keep telling you I'll pay for your flight."

"No, I need to do this myself. Besides, you'll need every penny for when the baby comes."

"They are expensive little blighters, aren't they? In this one shop in Soho, they want twenty quid for a T-shirt. Twenty quid! Even *my* T-shirts don't cost that much, and the baby'll probably outgrow them in a fortnight."

"Well, that's settled. I'm getting a job, and then I'm coming to visit."

"In that case, I'll be your one-woman cheerleading squad while you're looking for the right position. We're gonna find you a kickass job in a place where you can find the floor without having to dig for it and without a nutso, gun-toting boss!"

"Yes! But first I'm going out to buy ice cream."

Tori's pep talk left me psyched up for the search. The problem was, nearly everywhere was shut on a Sunday, so job-hunting would have to wait until tomorrow. Today was ice cream day. Yeah!

Feeling much more positive, I grabbed my purse and skipped out of the door, only to trip over Emmy, who was sitting on the floor right beside it, her legs stretched out across the hallway in front of her.

"Yow!" I squealed as I struggled to keep my balance. My purse flew from my hands and promptly ejected its contents everywhere.

Emmy sprang to her feet before I could blink. "Shit. Sorry, I wasn't expecting you to come out quite that fast."

"What are you doing here?" I asked, shoving coins and assorted pieces of paper back into my purse and checking that my phone still functioned.

She stared down at the lit screen. "Does that work? If it was me, it would've broken for sure."

"Yes, thankfully. Why are you here?" I asked again.

"I've come to apologise. Nick and I have both been complete arses."

"I can't disagree with that."

"I should have told him about you, but I wanted to surprise him when he got back. I'd arranged to pick him up at the airport this morning, and I was planning to bring him over and introduce you, but the stupid sod came back last night without telling anybody."

"He nearly shot me!"

"No, he pointed a gun at you. He wouldn't have fired it."

I glared at her. "How do you know?"

"Because I know Nick." She took a step back. "I don't suppose that's much consolation, is it?"

"No, it isn't. I was terrified! Do you have any idea what it's like having a gun aimed at your head?"

"Unfortunately, yes."

That was an answer I hadn't expected. Little Miss Perfect had actually been threatened? Why? Mind you, if she was always this persistent, I could understand it.

"Really?"

"More times than I care to think about. Anyhow, I've come to take you out to lunch so you can meet Nick in a slightly more civilised manner. He needs to apologise as well."

"Hold on—I quit."

"No, you didn't. You just left without a word."

"Well, I quit now."

"Resignation not accepted."

"You can't do that."

"Just did. Come on, the car's downstairs."

"I can't go back. I heard Mr. Goldman say on the phone he didn't want a housekeeper."

"No, he didn't *know* he wanted a housekeeper. That's a completely different thing. We've had a little chat, and now he understands the benefits. He said your lasagne was delicious, by the way. Oh, and you don't need to call him Mr. Goldman. He's Nick."

Emmy wasn't going to leave, was she? She clearly wasn't a woman used to ever being told no. Her air of authority made me want to nod in agreement even as my brain screamed not to.

"Fine, he can apologise if it makes him feel better." And after that, I could tell him it simply wasn't acceptable to go around pointing guns at people.

Her lips quirked up. "He can't wait."

"But I still quit, and I'm not going out for lunch. I've got things to do this afternoon."

Important things, like eating a whole pint of chocolate ice cream. Perhaps two.

"We'll see."

# 14

## LARA

Like in Baysville, I didn't live in the best area, and as Emmy jogged past a vagrant sleeping in the stairwell, I wanted to sink into the floor. What must she think of me? She didn't give any clues as she hustled to her Corvette, which she'd parked in a tow-away zone. Oh, crap. Two men were hanging around next to it, wearing the light blue do-rags Sylvia told me signified membership of a local gang. Was my week going to get even worse?

Emmy paused, fishing through her purse until she came up with her car keys.

"What about those guys?" I hissed.

They wore their pants hanging low, almost at mid-thigh. Maybe if we ran away, they'd trip over them?

"Tyrone's watching the car for me."

She walked up to the larger man and bumped fists with him before climbing into the driver's seat.

I wrenched open the passenger door and leapt in after her. "You know them?"

"Sure."

Who was this woman? She looked like a princess but hung out with gang members?

I didn't have time to consider the question further before the car shot forward. On the plus side, riding with her was faster than taking the bus, but I did run the risk of having a heart attack before we arrived at our destination. She made a dubious call at a traffic light, and I closed my eyes and sucked in air.

"Don't worry, I won't crash," she said, glancing my way.

*Look at the road!* I forced a laugh, trying not to show fear, and attempted a joke. "So this is what they mean when they say 'drive it like you stole it,' huh?"

"Oh, no. If I'd stolen it, I'd be sticking to the speed limit," she replied in complete seriousness. "Less chance of getting pulled over."

That was it. Next time, I'd walk.

No. No! There wasn't going to *be* a next time.

Twenty minutes later, she smoked out the tyres as she pulled up outside Franco's Italian. Before my heart rate had dropped back into double figures, Emmy hopped out of the car and beckoned me to follow her. Legs shaking, I trailed her through the near-empty restaurant to a small room at the rear where a table was set for lunch. A man already occupied one of the seats, his broad back to us as we walked through the door. Emphasis on broad. As Emmy's heels clicked on the wooden floor, he rose and turned.

See, now here's the thing. When I first saw Nick, it was in the dim glow of the little lamp on the side table in his living room. Also I was, understandably I think, concentrating on the gun in his hand rather than his face. Or his body.

Which was why I'd somehow missed that he was the genetically blessed offspring of a Greek god and a Hollywood screen siren. But I could see that now. Oh boy, could I see it. My pulse still raced from Emmy's chauffeuring skills, and now it sped out of control as I willed my legs to stop shaking. Nick took a step towards me, and I tilted my head up to get a better look at him. He had to be over six feet tall. My eyes paused mid-chest as his shirt stretched over pecs that spoke of a gold-plated gym membership, then I forced myself to focus on his face. Chestnut eyes looked lazily back at me from under messy dark brown hair. He used a hand to sweep it away from his forehead and smiled.

Oh wow. Dimples. He had dimples.

I smiled back, an automatic reflex, then caught myself. What was I thinking? I hated this man! He'd tried to kill me less than twenty-four hours ago. Sadly, nobody had told my body that though, and heat flooded south in a way I'd never quite felt before.

Fortunately, Emmy chose that moment to step forward, and Nick pulled her into a hug, leaning down to kiss her hair.

"Missed you, baby," he murmured.

"Missed you too."

*Well, this was awkward*. I didn't know where to look during their special moment, and I was studiously pretending to gaze out of the window when Emmy pulled back and poked Mr. Goldman in the chest.

"Right, now you can apologise to Lara."

He flashed another grin, sheepish this time. "Lara, I'm sorrier than I can say for scaring you last night. I was half asleep, and I got a shock seeing you there when the house was supposed to be empty." He paused to glare at Emmy. "I promise I'll never do anything like that again. Can we start over?"

My brain screamed no! No! NO! This is *not* a good idea! But my inner harlot must have been standing above me like a puppet master because my head started bobbing all of its own accord.

He held his hand towards me to shake. Did I dare to touch

it? A hand in no way connected to my sanity reached out by itself and gripped his tightly.

"I'm Lara Reynolds."

Somehow I forgot to let go, and after a few seconds, I felt a gentle tug as Nick tried to free himself. I came to my senses and stumbled back a couple of steps, at which point I fell over the chair a waiter had helpfully pulled out behind me.

Nick leapt over and caught me before I hit the floor, hauling me up by my sweaty armpits and depositing me upright next to the table. Wow, he was strong. Emmy stifled a giggle, heat flashed up my cheeks, and quite honestly, if dying had been an option at that point, I'd have taken it.

What was wrong with me? This was the second time I'd been for lunch with Emmy and completely embarrassed myself, and I was hardly creating a good impression for the man who would be my employer now that it seemed I might have gone back on my decision to quit.

Emmy, meanwhile, stood perfectly composed and upright on a pair of four-inch designer heels that I could only dream of owning, and now she broke into my thoughts.

"Well, since you two are acquainted, I'll head off. See you later, Nicky."

Wait, she was leaving? I belatedly noticed the two place settings at the table, complete with shiny silver cutlery. Was I expected to have lunch with Mr. Goldman by myself? How on earth would I survive that? In his presence, I could barely string a sentence together.

He raised his eyebrows at me, and I realised he'd sat down while I was still standing there like an idiot. I hastily lowered myself, but not without carefully checking that there was actually a chair under my bottom. I didn't want to land on the floor and look even stupider than I already did.

Once I was seated, I had no idea what to say. Thankfully, I was saved by the waiter who draped a napkin across my lap with a flourish, then presented me with a menu. Oh fudge, what did all these words mean? Was this Italian? What on earth was an *insalata mista verde*?

"Mixed green salad," came Nick's voice, deep but velvety smooth.

Oh flip, I must have said that out loud. "You speak Italian?" I asked stupidly, belatedly kicking myself. Of course he spoke Italian. He'd just translated what I'd said, hadn't he? I also had a vague recollection of Nadia telling me he owned a house in Italy. He must think I was the dumbest of the dumb, and he'd be right.

"I do. Want me to translate? Or I can order for both of us if you'd prefer?"

"Uh, could you just order?" The less I said the better.

"Sure. Is there anything you don't like?"

"Mushrooms, and I'm not very keen on sushi."

"It's okay, I'm pretty sure they don't serve sushi here." He tried to keep a straight face as he gestured at the decorative bottles of olive oil arranged on a shelf. Tried and failed.

*Stop talking, Lara.* I wanted to slap myself. Or crawl into a cave. Or curl up and wither away quietly. Was it possible for me to say one thing, just *one* thing, that didn't make me sound like a complete moron?

I stared at the table, developing a fascination for the ornate detail on my knife and fork as the waiter returned. Nick rattled off a string of Italian at him, and he replied, also in Italian. I understood none of it, but I did catch the waiter glance at me and smile. Nick was probably telling him how much of a klutz I was.

Once the waiter left, silence reigned again. I sat there twiddling my napkin in my fingers until Nick spoke up.

"You want to fill me in on what's been happening while I've been away? I got a condensed version from Emmy on the phone earlier, but mostly she was busy chewing my ass out."

I forced myself to look up at him. "She hired me to clean up your house, and she said you needed someone to keep things tidy going forward. I thought you knew about it. I honestly didn't realise you didn't."

"Yeah, I know that. Believe me, I gave as good as I got in my little chat with her this morning. Well, maybe not quite, but as close to it as anyone will ever get with Emmy. What I need to know now is whether you're sticking around?"

"Honestly? I don't know." Yes, he'd apologised, and he seemed sincere, but I hated the thought of staying somewhere I wasn't wanted. Then there was the small matter of me turning into a complete ditz in his presence.

"What can I do to convince you to stay?"

Did that mean he really wanted me to?

"I guess I don't want to feel like I'm in the way. I understand that you didn't even want a housekeeper?"

"I'd never seriously entertained the idea before. As you can probably tell, I haven't spent much time in that house. More than a few times, I've wondered why I even kept it."

"Couldn't you just sell it?"

His eyes changed, going from a rich brown to something darker as he stared past me to the window. In the mirror behind him, I saw a bird soar past the clouds, wings outstretched.

"I can't," he said finally. "I loved it once."

I had a strange feeling he wasn't only talking about Adler House when he spoke those words.

"What about your other properties?" I asked softly. "Nadia said you had two."

His sadness melted away as he turned back to me. "I only use the place in Italy for vacations. The LA house is habitable, but the designer Bradley hired made it into a museum of modern art. I'm scared to set foot in it in case I break something. Mostly I stay in a hotel because it feels more hospitable." He laughed, but not because he was amused. "I'm a thirty-five-year-old hobo."

"Surely the decor can't be that bad?"

"The living room has three couches consisting entirely of right-angles that are less comfortable than a bed of nails. All the furniture's white, except for a rug that looks like a cat threw up on it, and there's a clock with no numbers that plays excerpts of Holst's Planet Suite on the hour, every hour. I tried accidentally dropping it, but the fucking thing was covered by a lifetime guarantee, so the designer got me another one. And Bradley told me I couldn't have a TV because it wasn't good Feng Shui."

I laughed. "Okay, it does sound kinda sucky, I'll give you that." Sucky? My vocabulary had regressed to that of an eight-year-old.

Nick picked up a breadstick and bit into it, silent until he'd finished chewing. "The Richmond house is the only one I've ever liked. Maybe I'll try living in it for a while, see how it feels." He reached for his glass of water and took a sip. "I'll need your help to keep it tidy. Will you stay? Please?"

When he put it like that, I knew what my answer would be. Then he smiled and my heart just about melted.

"Yes, I'll stay."

He leaned back in his chair, relaxed at last. "I promise I'll behave. Just tell me if I do anything irritating."

Like heck I would. The guy could make more mess than a toddler on Red Bull, and as long as he gave me that panty-dropping smile afterwards, I'd clear it up and probably enjoy doing so. Not to mention the fact that he was paying me eighty thousand dollars a year.

Food arrived, and the waiter placed the dishes in the middle of the table. Bruschetta, mozzarella, tomatoes, and a platter of thinly sliced meats. *Don't drool, Lara.*

"I thought I'd order a selection to share," Nick said.

Share? Now that was a novel concept. Billy hadn't understood the meaning of the word.

The appetiser, or antipasti, as Nick told me it was called in Italian, tasted delicious. Melt-in-your-mouth salami and crunchy bread exploded with flavour, ruining me for all other food. Or so I thought until the main course arrived.

A small plate of dainty little ravioli parcels filled with venison was followed by a baked fillet of sea bass with fresh tomato and basil and a selection of sautéed vegetables, and together, they made up the most delicious meal I'd ever eaten. The waiter was generous with the wine, pouring from a bottle I suspected cost more than I earned in a week. Sweet with a hint of fruit, it slipped down far too easily. As the waiter twisted the cork from a second bottle, I motioned at Nick's glass, still half full from the first.

"Aren't you drinking?"

"Only one glass for me. I'm driving." His smile was kind of fuzzy. "But you carry on if you're enjoying yourself."

Just as I wondered whether I could discreetly open the top button of my jeans without Nick noticing, the waiter came out with tiramisu. I was done for. Tiramisu was my absolute favourite dessert. Probably my button wouldn't pop off if I sucked my stomach in, would it?

I kept my fingers crossed, and after I'd eaten the whole bowlful, the danger of falling into a food coma became very real.

"Satisfied?" Nick asked.

Oh boy, was I ever. Here I sat, in this amazing restaurant, eating the most fantastic food ever cooked, accompanied by a man who looked like he should be on the cover of GQ magazine even if he was my boss and his girlfriend had forced him to come. I decided to block that last teensy part out and indulge myself in the fantasy that he actually wanted to be there with me, just for today.

I nodded, which made the room spin like one of those old-fashioned carousels Momma used to let me ride on at the fairground.

"Ready to go?"

"Yup."

I got to my feet and clutched at the edge of the table for support when everything tilted sideways. Maybe that wine had gone to my head just a smidgen? Nick held on to my arm as he escorted me through the restaurant, and luckily, I was too busy trying to put one foot in front of the other for it to properly register that he was touching me, because I'd have had palpitations if I'd thought about it.

It was only when we got outside that I realised I had a problem. How was I going to get home? On foot? By bus? I was musing over that when Nick stopped next to a black sports car and opened the passenger door. Ooh, shiny. I stood there, gawping at it.

"Are you getting in?" he asked.

"Why?"

He rolled his eyes and spoke slowly as if I was a small child. "So I can take you home."

"Oh. Okay then."

That was easy. Problem solved.

If only I'd known...

At that point, my problems were just beginning. It was a good thing Nick drove and not Emmy, because there was no way my guts would have survived her attempts to become a racing driver without puking up their contents.

I barely recalled most of the trip, only Nick half lifting me out of the car in the grimy parking lot outside my apartment.

Inside, the out-of-order sign on the elevator made me groan. I lived on the third floor out of six, and the stairs moved alarmingly when I stumbled towards them.

"Wait," Nick said.

I turned in his direction, wobbled, and the floor got closer. That was the last thing I remembered.

# 15

## LARA

A conga line danced through my head as I woke the next morning, my temples throbbing in time to the imaginary beat. Where had I left the aspirin? Looking down, I found I was fully dressed, lying in bed with the covers over me. What? How? I fought through the sludge clogging up my thoughts. Something about a restaurant? With a really hot guy in it? Horror overcame me as I pieced the jigsaw together, and I slumped back against the pillow and groaned.

I'd done it again, hadn't I? Committed another crime against common sense. This time, I'd drunk so much I couldn't even walk in front of my new boss. My extremely good-looking new boss who I'd known for less than a day. *Way to go, Lara*. No wonder Billy had always grumbled about my behaviour when we went out. I wasn't even capable of acting like a lady on a simple lunch date.

No, *not* a date.

Just lunch.

I rolled over, considering whether to drag myself out of bed and get ready for work or simply die quietly. A glass of water on the nightstand caught my eye, and as I propped myself up on one elbow, I saw a bottle of painkillers next to it. And a note. A note written in an unfamiliar scrawl in black ballpoint.

> *Lara,*
> *Take the Tylenol—it'll help. When you feel better, come over and we can sort out arrangements for the next few weeks.*
> *Nick.*

Why did he have to be so nice? It made me feel even worse. How many men would bother to leave pills out like that? I couldn't remember Billy so much as asking if I was okay in all the years I spent with him.

I hauled myself out of bed, ignoring the slosh of nausea churning around my stomach, and swallowed the pills as instructed. My arms ached as I filled the kettle. Surely an extra-strong cup of coffee and a shower would help?

"Ohhhh, fudge."

I caught sight of myself in the cracked mirror above the tiny sink. If my reflection was to be believed, I'd spent the night with my finger stuck in an electric socket before rubbing my eyes with soot. Did the pharmacy at the end of the block sell make-up? Or possibly a replacement head? I'd bet my last dollar Emmy didn't look a mess in the mornings. She probably woke up fresh as a daisy, all perky and ready to start the day. With Nick next to her, the lucky thing.

How upset was Nick going to be with me about my little performance yesterday? I'd hardly created a good impression, had I? Next time, I'd make triple sure to limit myself to one glass of wine, a small portion of something healthy for my main course, and no dessert. Actually, who was I kidding? It was highly unlikely there'd be a next time.

Once I'd got dressed in my black housekeeping dress and put together a hasty lunch to eat at work, I felt halfway human again, helped in no small part by the Tylenol and caffeine. It was almost midday when I got to Nick's, but at least I'd still be in time to make him some food.

I got to the door, key in hand, then hesitated. Probably I shouldn't let myself in if he was home. I'd feel like an intruder, and we'd already had that whole discussion at gunpoint two days ago. I reached out and rang the bell instead, hearing it echo inside the house as I fidgeted on the top step. A few minutes ticked by with no answer. Had Nick gone out? I looked back at the shiny black car parked behind me in the driveway—a Porsche, the writing on the back told me. A silver badge with the words *911 turbo* gleamed beneath the rear spoiler. No, Nick was definitely in.

I was debating whether to risk unlocking the door when it swung open. Holy hell! Nick's tanned body greeted me in all its glory, and the only barrier between me and the best bits was a fluffy white towel wrapped around his hips. I watched, frozen, as a bead of water dripped from his hair and rolled down his torso, skating over his pecs and leaving a wet trail on his sculpted six-pack before it disappeared. Or maybe it was an eight-pack. I was just trying to count when Nick's voice interrupted me.

"Did you lose your key?"

"What?" I snapped my eyes up to his face and saw the corner of his mouth curve into a smile. Shit! I mean, shoot! He knew I'd been looking. "Uh, no, I have my key. I just didn't know if I should let myself in when you were home."

"Yes, you should let yourself in. You can come and go as you please."

Nick opened the door wider, and I followed him inside,

confronted by a back view that was almost as good as the front. Golden skin, thick cords of muscle either side of his spine, and that ass...

*Please, somebody help me.*

He disappeared, presumably to put clothes on, which was a terrible shame. My cheeks burned with embarrassment as I meandered through to the kitchen.

Embarrassment.

It wasn't a word I'd had to use much in the past, but I seemed to be making up for that this week.

I tied on my white apron, something I'd made myself out of a scrap of fabric over a year ago. Without much of a social life, I'd had time to sew little frills around the edge for decoration. Moment of truth—how much mess had Nick managed to make overnight? When I couldn't put it off any longer, I peeped around the kitchen door. Phew. Apart from an empty coffee cup on the counter, everything was as I'd left it, so I busied myself turning on the dishwasher and folding the laundry from the drying rack. I was neatly arranging the last T-shirt on the pile when I felt a presence behind me.

Nick was watching, leaning on the doorjamb. He'd put on a pair of well-worn jeans and a T-shirt from a rock group's tour a couple of years ago, something I remembered putting in his closet last week. He was obviously finding his way around.

The fancy silver clock above the breakfast bar told me it was after one o'clock. "Do you want some lunch?"

He perched on one of the high stools. "Please. How are you feeling? Headache?"

I could hardly bring myself to look at him. "Oh gosh, I'm so sorry. I didn't realise how tipsy I was until I tried to stand up. I hardly ever drink anything, honestly."

"Forget it. I've seen worse. At least you didn't puke in my car."

Thank goodness for the small things, eh? "What do you like to eat?"

"Anything." He wrinkled his nose. "Except tinned sardines."

"I think I can manage to avoid those."

I pulled together a grilled chicken breast with an avocado and tomato salad, and set it out on the counter for him with a napkin and a glass of sparkling water. My murky memory recalled that was what he'd drunk in the restaurant yesterday.

"Aren't you eating?" he asked. "Or did you have something before you came in?"

"You mean eat with you?"

"Unless I've offended you in some way, that was the general idea."

I remembered what Sylvia told me about homeowners not even knowing the names of their staff unless it was to yell at them. "I didn't think it was the appropriate thing for household staff to eat with their employer."

"We had lunch yesterday."

"That was different."

"How?"

"Uh, I don't really know. I guess because it was in a restaurant?"

"So you can sit at the same table with me in a restaurant but not in my house?"

Put that way, it did seem kind of silly. "No, I mean, I can. Okay. I'll just get my food."

I fetched my package of peanut butter sandwiches out of my bag, set them on a plate, and hopped up on a stool opposite him.

"Are you on some sort of weird diet or something?" he asked.

"Er, no?"

"Then why are you eating those tragic-looking sandwiches?"

"I meant to buy groceries on my way home last night, but I, well..." I wasn't about to get into a discussion of my finances or the strict budget I'd set for myself, especially when I still had three more days before I could afford to go to the store again.

"What's wrong with the food in there?" He waved at the giant refrigerator.

"Well, it's your food."

He sighed, then put down his knife and fork. "Lara, while you're here, it's your food too. If you don't like it, buy something else. Make yourself at home. As long as your job gets completed, I don't care what else you do. Use the pool. Watch a movie. The house might as well get lived in."

That was so far from how Sylvia said things worked around here I checked his face for signs that he was joking.

"Really?"

"Yes, Lara, really. And you can lose the little black dress/apron combo. It's like being on the set of a porno flick. Unless that sort of thing does it for you, in which case leave it on, by all means."

Holy fuck, I mean, holy fudge. Did he just say that? "C-c-can I wear jeans?"

"Jeans would work. So, are you gonna eat some proper food now?"

I got off my stool and tugged my dress down as I stood up. As the hem got lower, so did the neckline. Okay, so the dress was perhaps a size too small, but buying second-hand, I couldn't afford to be fussy, and Nick's porn comment was surely an exaggeration. None of the other men I'd worked with had ever complained about it.

I glanced over at Nick. His eyes flicked to his lunch, but I was sure he'd been watching me. Why did he have that little smile on his lips? Was it due to a fondness for avocado, or something else?

As he shovelled food into his mouth, I fixed myself a ham and pasta salad and re-took my seat across from him.

He checked out my plate. "Better."

Nick left after lunch, calling out a goodbye as he slammed the door behind him, and I relaxed a little once I was alone in the house. The afternoon flew by as I cleaned up the dishes then vacuumed, dusted, and did some laundry. Considering he'd been away on a business trip for over a month, there was remarkably little that needed washing. Where had it all gone? Emmy's house?

Nick still hadn't returned by the time I went home at six. Since he hadn't said when or even if he'd be back, I put together a casserole for his dinner and left a note on the counter telling him it was in the fridge. As an afterthought, I added heating instructions, just in case.

Sitting on the bus, I felt my lips twitch and gave in to the smile. Nick seemed like a decent man to work for, even if our first meeting had been horrendous and the distraction of spending time around a living god meant I'd vacuumed the same spot four times today. And, when I saw him half naked this morning, I think I might actually have drooled.

I phoned Tori that evening to give her an update, and she couldn't believe what a strange turn events had taken either. When I got to the comment about the black dress, she choked with laughter.

"He really said that?"

"Word for word, I swear."

"That's hilarious. He's clearly been taking a good look at your assets, then."

"Don't be ridiculous. I'm sure he was just trying to save me from any embarrassment." There was that word again. Could Tori sense me blushing down the phone?

"Whatever you say." She was still laughing.

"He even said I can use his pool. Isn't that amazing?" I tried to change the subject, and Tori gleefully went along with it.

"Sure is. I bet he'd love to see you in a bikini."

"Shut up. I don't even own a bikini."

"I know, but I'm thinking you should buy one." She sighed. "What I wouldn't give to have my own pool. It's so hot here I'm melting just lying in bed."

"In September? In England?"

"We're having an Indian summer. Either that, or it's global warming,"

"Maybe one day you could come over to Virginia. Nick might let us both use the pool if he was out."

"Wouldn't that be awesome? A girl can dream, can't she?"

The next morning, I got dressed in jeans and a loose top. In light of Nick's comment about my outfit yesterday, I thought he'd be happy with that. As it turned out, it didn't matter anyway, because when I arrived for work, he'd already gone. My note about the casserole had been replaced by one from him, telling me he wouldn't be back until late and could I please get some more toothpaste?

No problem.

A week passed with no sign of him. Our only

communication consisted of written words, his in a slanted scrawl and mine printed in my neatest handwriting. He left me his number "just in case," and although I wrote mine back, he didn't call.

I felt strangely disappointed about that.

## 16

## LARA

When I walked into Adler House the following Sunday, Nick was standing in the kitchen wearing a pair of jeans. *Only* a pair of jeans. Soft, washed-out grey denim, frayed around the edges and sitting delightfully low on his hips. I could have stared for the rest of the day, but thankfully he was engrossed in watching something cook in the microwave so he didn't notice me lick my lips.

"I can make breakfast for you," I offered.

He turned around. A chiselled V ran down the muscles on either side of his abs and disappeared into his waistband, but the dark circles smudged under his eyes spoiled the image. The drooping eyelids. The slumped shoulders. I didn't know what I wanted to do more—give him a hug or lick him. The stubble flecking his jaw would undoubtedly be rough on my tongue, but who cared?

"I didn't think you'd be here on a Sunday," he rasped, tiredness turning his silken voice hoarse.

"We never really discussed my hours. I didn't want to assume I could take a day off."

"You pick your own hours. If I want you for anything specific, I'll ask."

"Well, I'm here now, and if you don't mind my saying, you don't look great. How many hours' sleep have you had?"

"About none."

"Then you should be in bed."

"Wish that were the case, but I have a meeting in an hour."

"Can't you move it?"

"No. I'll be fine. I just need something to eat and a jug of coffee."

He leaned back against the counter and yawned. My mouth started to open in sympathy even though I wasn't tired, but I stopped it in time and clamped my teeth together.

"Let me take care of breakfast. You go and get changed. I'm guessing you're not going to your meeting dressed in jeans?"

He looked down at himself and chuckled. "Don't suppose my client would appreciate me turning up like this."

"If your client was a woman, she probably would." Oh, holy fudging mother of Gollum, did I say that out loud? Judging by the way Nick was staring at me, I think I probably did.

He let out a bark of laughter. "My client is a sixty-year-old man. I'll change."

Face burning up once again, I retrieved the scrambled eggs Nick had been trying to cook from the microwave and poked them. Solid. How long had he nuked them for? An hour? I'd need a scouring pad for that bowl later. I started from scratch with a couple of fresh eggs, made him some toast, and brewed a strong pot of coffee.

Fifteen minutes later, he came back, and my jaw dropped. *Okay, breathe. It's just a suit.* A dark charcoal, custom-made suit that only served to emphasise his broad chest and well-muscled legs. *Darn it, Lara, shut your mouth.* He collapsed onto a stool and drained the coffee before digging into the eggs.

"You want another cup?" I asked.

"Wouldn't say no."

Thankfully, I'd used the big cafetière, and the rich smell of arabica had me craving a mugful myself.

"You look exhausted. I'd offer to drive you, but I don't have a car."

"You can drive? I thought you couldn't. I see you walking down to the road at the end of the day."

"Yes, I have a licence."

"Then why do you take cabs? Why not buy a car?"

"I don't take cabs. I ride the bus. It's cheaper than running my own vehicle."

His eyebrows scrunched together, and he put down his fork. "Lara, you live in a sh...in a not so nice area. How far is the bus stop from your apartment?"

"Maybe a ten-minute walk."

"You're not doing that anymore. The garage is full of cars. Take one of them."

He made it sound so straightforward. What was the catch?

"I can't take one of your cars. It's not fair."

"Why isn't it?"

"Well, because."

"That's not an answer. Look, call it a company car."

"Housekeepers don't generally get company cars."

"You run errands and shit, don't you? Take the damn car." He shovelled in another mouthful of eggs, then glanced at his watch. "That's not optional, and I don't have time to argue."

We could finish discussing the matter when he wasn't shoving his stubbornness in my face.

"Okay, fine."

He showed me the lockbox on the wall in the hallway and

gave me the code so I could get the key to the garage and whatever car I wanted out of it.

"Do you want me to drive you to your meeting?" I asked.

"Emmy's picking me up."

Oh, okay then. I instructed my hormones to stand down as he headed for the door, but...

"Hang on. Your tie's not straight."

He stood still while I fixed it for him, so conscious of the heat of his chest under my hands. As I tightened the knot, I could see the pulse beating in his neck, strong and steady while mine raced twice as fast. I tried to calm my breathing as the roar of Emmy's Corvette sounded in the driveway.

"Thanks," Nick called as he dashed out of the door.

I waited until the sound of the engine receded, then fanned myself. Whew. I had to stop getting hot and bothered like that, although I challenged any woman to stand in the vicinity of Nick Goldman for longer than twenty seconds and not lose a teeny bit of her mind.

Now, about the car. I had no intention of taking Nick up on his offer, but out of curiosity, I decided to take a walk out to the garage. What did he have in there? I'd only ever seen him drive the Porsche, so surely he had something more practical for chores? Maybe a station wagon? You couldn't fit much shopping in the trunk of a Porsche.

Key in hand, I hurried across the yard. Billy loved cars, and he'd spent so long yammering on about his beloved Dodge Charger I could recite its statistics in my sleep. His daddy had bought it for him, of course, something to use as a penis extension which, let's be honest, he desperately needed.

The lights flickered on automatically as I pulled open the garage door, and I gasped at the scene before me. So much for practicality. Surprisingly, there was no hint of junk in the garage—the cavernous space was pristine, painted a crisp white with a black stripe running around the walls at chest height. I took a step into the empty slot at the end—left for the Porsche, no doubt—and stared at the array of vehicles gleaming in front of me.

A metallic black Dodge Ram stood closest, intimidating even before the engine growled. What type of engine did it have? A V8? A V10? Next up was a fancy Ford in midnight blue, with silver go-faster stripes running over the roof. I trailed my fingers over the hood as my feet carried me to the last car in line. A shiny red Ferrari. Frick, its curves were a thing of beauty. Billy would have a wet dream if he ever set foot in here.

I leaned against the wall, hearing Nick's voice in my head. He expected me to drive one of these? Was he nuts? I couldn't do that! What if I crashed? The only car I'd driven recently was Missy's Chrysler minivan, and that was ten years old. I doubted I even had the know-how to start any of these up.

Shaking my head, I backed outside and closed the door behind me, shutting the overpowering stench of testosterone back into the garage and pausing to make sure it was securely locked. When I got back into the house, I typed out a quick text to Nick. I didn't want to disturb him with a call at work.

ME

> Thank you for your kind offer, but I've looked in the garage and there isn't anything suitable for me to drive. I've made sure to lock the keys back up. Lara.

Five seconds later, my phone rang. Literally five seconds. Either Nick had me on speed dial, or his reflexes rivalled a teenage gamer's.

"What do you mean there's nothing suitable?"

Uh-oh. Nick didn't sound happy.

"Well, all of your cars are far too nice for me to drive."

"Why?"

"What do you mean, why? Because you choose to have nice cars, I guess?"

"No, I mean why shouldn't you drive a nice car?"

"Because I'm just a housekeeper."

"So? Bradley's 'just' a personal assistant, but Emmy gave him a fucking Lamborghini. Although don't tell him I said that. He thinks he rules the world." Nick sighed, and I heard the Corvette's engine screaming in the background as Emmy put her foot to the floor. "I'll buy you something different next week if you want, but for today, you're picking one of those because I won't be back until tomorrow and you're not, I repeat NOT, taking the fucking bus home."

"I'll borrow the Ferrari," I said hastily. I hated arguing.

"Good plan."

The line went dead. What the heck happened? Did my bossy boss just force me to drive his supercar?

If that was his attitude then fine, I'd take the damn car. What was the worst that could happen? I could crash, and he'd fire me. Well, I'd already tried to quit once, and look how that went.

## 17

## LARA

Since Nick said he wasn't coming back, I had a quick tidy up, and then left. Where was he going to stay? With Emmy? I couldn't help feeling slightly jealous until I recalled how pushy he'd been on the phone.

With a little experimentation, I found the black box on the car keys worked the garage doors and the main gates. Back in the garage, the engine on the Ferrari started with a roar that echoed off the walls and did funny things to my insides. Shivers ran through my veins as I inched the car forward, but despite having all those horses under me, I'd have won the prize for the slowest driver on the road as I followed the winding bus route home. Probably there was a shortcut, but after one look at the satnav and its confusing array of options, I shut it off and took the only way I knew.

I found my allocated parking spot at the back of the apartment building and moved an abandoned shopping cart out of it. It took me four tries to get the bright red beast wedged in between a rusting Toyota and a minivan like Missy's, and even then it was wonky. Would it be okay there?

With its sleek lines, the Ferrari stuck out like a cheetah in a herd of cattle. It had an alarm, right?

I glanced up to see the gang members Emmy had spoken to watching me, and I shuddered even though the biggest guy gave me a gap-toothed grin. What if they decided the car made a good target? Darn it, why had I listened to Nick and brought it home?

Morning came, and the car was fine and dandy. Which was better than me. I'd tossed and turned all night worrying about it and gotten up at one thirty, a quarter to three, and twenty past five to check it was okay.

I rolled out of bed properly at seven thirty, giving myself an extra thirty minutes snuggled under the quilt since I didn't have to take the bus or make lunch. A real treat, not to mention the money I'd save on travel expenses and food. Even though I'd need to buy gas for the car—assuming, of course, I could work out how to open the fuel cap—I'd still be able to tuck some extra into my savings.

There was no sign of Nick at the house, and since he hadn't been home, I had little to do. Once I'd taken the trash out, I put a load of laundry on and headed out to the supermarket. Having the car made shopping so much easier, and I didn't have to suffer the indignity of carrying an economy-sized package of toilet paper on the bus either.

Now what? I'd finished the chores, and it wasn't even midday. Would Sylvia be free for lunch? Yes, it turned out she was. I agreed to meet her at a less swanky café than the last one and caught the bus into town because I didn't dare to take the Ferrari. Quite apart from the trouble I'd have trying to park the darn thing, what would Sylvia say if I turned up in a fancy car? Following Tori's logic, she'd assume sexual favours were involved, and her love of gossiping hadn't escaped me.

"Did you hear about Mr. Mathers?" she asked the moment my butt hit the seat. "He lives three doors down from the house you're at."

I shook my head. "What happened?"

"His wife caught him at it with the au pair in the pool cabana."

"No way! She must have been furious."

"Apparently she fired the au pair on the spot, and he's been giving her all manner of gifts to placate her. The wife, not the au pair. The au pair got sent back to France. Rumour has it that Mrs. Mathers is holding out for a vacation home on Mustique."

"That's it? He's buying his way out of it?"

Sylvia shrugged. "That's how it works in Rybridge, at least with spouses. The lawyer around the corner didn't get so lucky with the cops when they caught him driving back from the golf club three times over the limit. He offered them cash, but they still revoked his licence."

Where did she hear all this stuff? "That's awful."

"No, that's tame. You wait until they come back from their summer vacations—then you'll have some tales to tell."

Spreading rumours about Mr. Goldman? That didn't sit well with me, so I just nodded and finished my coffee. Nice though Sylvia was, I didn't feel the same connection with her that I did with Tori and Missy. If anything, I was lonelier than ever when I got back to my apartment in the afternoon, so I kicked back on the bed and gave Missy a call.

After a quick catch up on life in Virginia versus life in Baysville, I told her about the Ferrari.

"So he handed the keys over, just like that?"

"Kind of. He gave me the keys to all his cars and told me to pick one."

"What were the others?"

"A Dodge Ram and a Ford. A GT? That's the expensive one, isn't it?"

"What does he get out of the deal?"

I knew exactly what she was thinking.

"He's not like that. At least I don't think so. I haven't even seen him since yesterday morning."

"You be careful. Rich men are all the same—they think money can buy anything."

I thought back to Sylvia's story about Mr. Mathers. Could Missy be right? Surely not? I was hardly a catch.

"Well, I tried to take the bus, but he insisted I use a car, so unless I want to make him angry, I don't have any choice but to drive it."

"Don't suppose there's a chance you feel like popping back to Baysville to take your best buddy out for a ride?"

"If it wasn't a ten-hour drive, I would."

Her tone grew more serious. "How about my dress fitting? Will you be able to come? Clyde's mother's trying to make me buy the most boring dress ever made, and I need some moral support."

"When is it?"

"Next Tuesday."

Nadia said I could take time off. Surely Nick could manage for a day if I travelled overnight on Monday, spent Tuesday with Missy, then got back in time to make his lunch on Wednesday?

"I'll need to double check, but I should be able to. I'll come on the bus, though."

"Ooh, fabulous! Let's make a day of it—I'll think of something fun."

"Okay, but nothing too crazy."

"Promise."

There was a long pause, and I knew she had something

more to say. Something I wouldn't like. I stayed quiet so she'd come out with it.

"Lara, you're not gonna like this..." See? "But I need to warn you..."

"Yes?"

"Billy's back in town."

The sandwich I'd eaten with Sylvia began to rise up my throat. Sheer willpower kept it down. Even though I hadn't been friends with Missy when I was with Billy, she knew who he was. Everybody did. When he scored the winning touchdown in the state championship, he became the town hero.

"H-h-how long? Why has he come back?"

"Just this past week. Clyde saw him in the sports bar on Main, drinking with the football crowd. I asked around, and he's moved into one of the houses his dad owns." Her voice quieted. "If you don't want to visit, I understand."

I didn't want to set foot in the whole state with him in it, but where would that leave me? He'd still be in control.

"I appreciate you telling me, really I do, but I'm coming. Maybe we could give the evening out a miss? As long as I only go to your house and the bridal shop, the chances of running into him are pretty slim, right?"

She laughed, and I heard her relief. "No way would he go to the dress shop. From what you've said, I couldn't imagine him making any sort of commitment. I'll see you next week then. Bye, chicky."

Wow. Only a couple of weeks ago, I'd wondered if I'd been right to leave Baysville, and now I knew I absolutely had. Although it wasn't the smallest town in the world, no place would ever be big enough for me and Billy Cooper. I sighed, feeling the weight of a dubious decision lift from my shoulders. My life was in Virginia now, no turning back.

I didn't see Nick at all for the rest of the week, but I knew he was around. A miracle happened, and he learned how to use the dishwasher and the laundry hamper.

And I saw Emmy.

She walked out of Nick's room on Wednesday morning, covering her mouth as she yawned. Hair mussed. No make-up, and yes, she still looked stunning. She'd borrowed one of his T-shirts, a faded black one advertising Jack Riley's Auto Parts, and it didn't appear as if she was wearing anything underneath either.

"Hey, Lara."

"Good morning. Would you like me to make breakfast?"

"Wholemeal toast with honey, if you don't mind. There should be a jar of manuka in the pantry. And some orange juice, with bits if you've got it?"

Oh, so the honey belonged to her. I'd thought it was an odd thing for Nick to have.

"Nick likes his OJ that way too. I'll have it ready in ten minutes."

"You're a legend."

"Do you know what Nick wants to eat?"

"What? Oh, he's not here. He's gone to work."

She padded barefoot along the hallway and let herself into Nick's study. I'd still never been in there, and curiosity niggled at me, but I made myself turn away. If nothing else, Emmy's appearance threw a bucket of cold water over my daydreams of Nick. Okay, and my night dreams too. I'll admit I woke a little hot and bothered when his towel-clad body paraded through my sleep. And what did he have under the towel? Oh, I was so not going there.

While Emmy munched her toast, I puttered around in the

kitchen in case she needed anything else. I didn't risk sitting down with her the way I did with Nick because what was okay with him might not be acceptable to a guest. She ate in silence, tapping away at her laptop with her face a mask of concentration until she headed back to Nick's bedroom.

Why did I grit my teeth when she went in there? I had no right to feel jealous of her relationship with Nick. Was it due to my own failures in that department? Or simply because Nick made my heart, and indeed other parts of me, clench every time I saw him? I slammed the dishwasher closed too hard, and the glassware rattled. Maybe I should find a hobby? Yes, that was it. I'd spent too much time cooped up on my own, and it was starting to make me crazy.

Hmm, a hobby. How about a yoga class? Sylvia went every Tuesday and raved about it. I glanced at my breasts, barely contained in the T-shirt I'd treated myself to last week, then at the swell of my stomach in my old jeans. Sure, they'd gotten looser since I started working here, but compared to the other girls in the neighbourhood, I was enormous. Nobody wanted to see a Christmas pudding bent over in a pair of spandex workout pants. Perhaps I could try jogging? Although I'd need to buy a sports bra for that.

"See you later." Emmy poked her head around the door, making me jump.

I forced a smile. "Goodbye."

She'd used Nick's shower and left her clothes in the laundry hamper. Clearly, she'd decided to spend more time here now that the house was habitable, and while I should have been happy to have the company, that feeling was tempered with dread.

Nick finally reappeared on Saturday morning. When I got to work, he was sitting at the kitchen counter, as gorgeous as ever, wearing a scruffy T-shirt and a day's worth of stubble.

"How are you?" I asked. "Do you want something to eat?"

"Not too bad. Eggs would be good if it's not too much trouble." He put his newspaper down. "And how are you?"

"Good, thank you."

Not much of a conversation, but he still left me tongue-tied.

As I set about making the eggs. I wondered if he'd be around much today. Thanks to a cruel twist of fate, I'd planned to do some work in the garden, so I was wearing my oldest, tattiest clothes. *Think positive*. At least he couldn't complain I looked like a porn star.

The moment Nick pushed his plate away, I loaded it into the dishwasher and beat a hasty retreat outside. The grumpy gardener turned up once a week to cut the lawns and pull up weeds, but the whole two acres was devoid of any personality. Well, no more. I'd picked up half a dozen cheap terracotta pots and packages of seeds to start a herb garden. Fresh herbs were so much tastier than dried. When I lived with Billy, I'd had my own planters out on the balcony, full of chives and parsley and cilantro, but I hadn't had any outdoor space since or even a suitable windowsill.

After lunch, I knelt beside the back steps, sprinkling basil seeds into the fresh compost. The pots looked so plain, lined up along the side of the house, but they'd soon fill with leaves. Maybe I could add some flowers next?

"Lara?"

I jumped at Nick's voice and spilled seeds all over the patio. When I turned, he was standing behind me, phone in hand.

"Yes?"

He dragged a hand through his hair. He hadn't had it cut

since he got back, and now it curled over his collar, making him look younger than his thirty-five years.

"I need to ask a favour."

"Do you need me to run an errand?"

He cleared his throat. "Nice pots."

"Thanks. I thought they'd make the place look a bit cosier when the seeds start growing. What's the favour?"

He hadn't asked for much at all yet. Surely he'd be reasonable?

"What's in them?"

"The pots? Herbs. Mint, chives, basil, and sage. I thought if these work out, I could try lavender and some of those giant daisies to pretty things up. And arugula and a tomato plant or two. And there's a perfect spot for a rosemary bush over..." Now I was rambling. "Uh, what's the favour?" I asked again.

Catering a dinner party? Taking his car for a service? Picking up a gift for Emmy?

"I'm due to attend a benefit tonight, and Emmy's had to fly out of the country unexpectedly. Is there any chance you're free?"

I dropped the rest of the seeds, and they rolled between the cracks in the paving. Oh, shoot—now there'd be basil everywhere.

"I know it's short notice," he continued, "but we wouldn't need to stay late, and you could take as much time off as you want next week."

I glanced down at myself, smudged with dirt. "I'm sure any number of beautiful women would be only too happy to go with you. Why don't you ask one of them?"

"I did. Nobody else on my list can make it."

So I was right at the bottom? That made sense, but it still stung to hear him say it.

"Just walk into the nearest bar and smile. You'll pick

somebody up, no problem." A touch of snarkiness may have crept into my voice, but I didn't care.

He leaned back against the house wall and sighed. "I know, but that's not what I'm looking for. Those women come with strings attached. I don't want any...expectations. I just want to go out for the evening, come back home, and go to bed. On my own."

"Oh." That was novel. If my experience at Buck's was any indication, most red-blooded men wouldn't turn down "expectations." I had to admire Nick for being faithful to Emmy.

"And going alone isn't an option either. Five minutes after I walked in the door, women would be flocking around me like flies on shit. I tried it once and ended up acting as referee in a catfight. One girl ended up bawling because she broke a nail. It wasn't pretty."

I rocked back on my heels. "I'm hardly benefit material."

"You're kidding, right? Have you ever looked in a mirror?"

"I try to avoid them. In any case, I don't have anything to wear."

"That's no problem. I can sort out a dress. Will you do it? Please?"

My head said no, while my libido screamed, fainted, and threw itself at his feet. Common sense, what little of it I had, packed her sensible shoes into a suitcase and headed for Alaska. Before I knew it, I'd nodded. The full force of Nick's smile hit me like a hurricane, and I was glad I'd stayed sitting down.

"I really appreciate it." Oh, that smile was lethal. "Leave everything to me."

What the hell had I done?

## 18

## LARA

Nick wasn't kidding when he said he could sort out a dress. An hour and a half later, Bradley arrived, followed by a pair of assistants each carrying an armful of garment bags. They were followed by two other women, who he introduced as the nail technician and the masseuse.

The masseuse?

The remainder of the afternoon passed in a blur. I was poked, prodded, primped, and pampered until not an inch of me remained untouched. Bradley did my hair himself, chopping layers into it until it sat just below my shoulders and adding some golden highlights to my natural mousey brown. It sure beat my usual visit to student night at a local salon.

Next came the gown. Bradley had the two assistants zip me into dress after dress, and I was beginning to despair of ever leaving the house when he held up a hand.

"Perfect. That's the one."

He turned me around to face the mirror. Yes, he was right.

The strappy yellow dress had a tight bodice that did wonders for my cleavage, and the silk skirt fell in soft gathers to the floor. I'd always hated my curves, but this dress made me feel elegant in a way I never thought I could.

Bradley flicked his wrist at an assistant. "Shoes."

A pair of fancy red-soled pumps appeared as if by magic and found their way onto my feet. They were high. Really high. I loved my heels, but I was used to low-rise apartment buildings as opposed to skyscrapers.

Bradley squeezed my arm and smiled. "Yes, they work. Only your make-up to sort out now."

"They're lovely, but I'm not sure I can walk in them."

"Nonsense, you'll be fine. You can't wear that dress without killer heels. Just hang onto Nick."

I gulped. An evening "hanging onto Nick" would do crazy things to my insides, which felt like the spin cycle of a washing machine as it was. Not only that, I couldn't help thinking back to my previous dining experience with my overly sexy boss, and indeed with Emmy—if this followed the same pattern, I'd die of embarrassment, fancy dress or not.

But I couldn't back out now.

Bradley pinned my hair into an elegant up-do and did my make-up. Nothing too heavy, but when he'd finished, I both looked and felt like a different person. Nick walked in as Bradley spritzed me with perfume.

"Chanel No.5," Bradley said. "We'll stick with something classic. What do you usually wear?"

I couldn't answer because my mouth had gone dry. The sight of Nick in a perfectly cut tuxedo ran a close second to Nick fresh out of the shower. He'd had a trim, too—his dark hair was shorter and spiked up. He looked...edible. I'd have to sit on my hands tonight because I could see them doing their own thing if I didn't. And Nick was my *employer*. This was *work*.

"Limo's here in ten," he said, then paused in front of me. "Lara, you look beautiful. Great job, Bradley."

Bradley grinned at me as Nick vanished out the door. "You're gonna knock them dead."

"I hope not."

Beautiful? Nick thought I looked beautiful?

"Just one last thing." Bradley picked up a plush, red velvet box. "You need jewellery."

I gaped at the necklace he held up. Deep red rubies, each as large as a dime, nestled in a twinkly explosion of yellow diamonds. Except they had to be fake, didn't they? If they weren't, they'd be worth a small fortune. He fastened it around my neck, and I turned this way and that in front of the mirror, watching the stones flash under the lights. I could barely take my eyes off them.

"Hold still." He popped a pair of matching earrings into my ears.

"This is gorgeous."

"Isn't it? It's only on loan, I'm afraid. Do me a favour and remind Nick it needs to go into the safe at the end of the night, would you?"

"You mean it's real?"

"Of course it's real. You don't get that sparkle with paste."

Holy moly!

What if I broke it?

Or lost it?

Or got robbed?

"I can't wear this! Something might happen to it."

"Of course you can. You *are* wearing it. Nick won't let anything happen to you, so don't worry. Now, enjoy the evening."

Bradley kissed me on both cheeks, carefully so as not to disturb my make-up, then he and the entire entourage disappeared.

Nick rematerialised beside me and held out his elbow. "Shall we?"

"I guess."

*Deep breaths, Lara.* My heart hammered against my ribcage as I linked my arm through his. None of this felt real.

I tiptoed my way out the front door, trying not to lean on Nick too much. Thankfully, the driver had pulled right up to the edge of the steps so I didn't have to walk on the gravel driveway, and Nick helped me into the car before scooting around to get in the other side. Then we were off.

A... What was the collective noun for butterflies? Flock? Swarm? Well, anyway, there were a lot of them, and they were having a party in my belly. Partly because I didn't know what to expect at the benefit, but mostly because Nick was sitting next to me. Sure, there was an empty seat between us, but he still sat close enough to make my breath hitch.

I couldn't help hoping tonight would go a little smoother than the last event I went to that required formal wear. Billy had driven us to our senior prom, but then he'd insisted on leaving early because he was horny and drunk. It was easier to go with him than cause a scene. We ended up having sex in the back of his car in the parking lot, and my dress got ripped before he got arrested for DUI on the way home. His daddy made the charges disappear, the same way as he always did, but it still made for an unpleasant evening.

Back then, I'd been flattered Billy wanted me so much, but hindsight was a wonderful thing. As prom queen runner-up, I'd felt like a princess in the tiara he'd bought for me—cubic zirconia of course—but now I cringed at the memories.

*Don't let him get to you. Not tonight.*

I clenched my fists, then made myself loosen my grip on the dress. Thoughts of Billy would *not* ruin this evening with Nick. Nick, who was the perfect gentleman. I hadn't seen him stare at my chest once, although I couldn't say I'd mind if he did.

"So what's the event tonight for?" I asked.

"It's a fundraiser for the American Cancer Society. Which basically translates as a bunch of rich people throwing money around, but it does raise a healthy amount for charity."

"So you've been before?"

Duh, of course he would have been before.

"They have this event every year. I go if I'm in the country."

"I'm not sure I'll know what to do." Words spilled out as nerves got the better of me. "Are the people all refined? What should I talk about? What if they realise I'm not like them? What should I say?"

Nick only laughed. "Not being like them isn't a bad thing. There's a limit to the amount of time I want to spend talking about golf or the stock market, and as for the women, you could make better conversation with a store mannequin. When Emmy goes, she just makes shit up to amuse herself. Did anyone tell you about the pickled egg thing?"

"What pickled egg thing?" I recalled the disastrous interview at Claude's. "I do remember her having a jar of eggs in her purse once."

"When we went to one of these dinners a couple of years back, I ended up stuck in a discussion on the NASDAQ, and Emmy got cornered by the country club set. They started yacking on about weird and wonderful ways of losing weight, so Emmy thought she'd tell them all about her new diet."

"What kind of diet?"

"The Siberian pickled egg diet. She could eat anything she wanted as long as she had a pickled egg before every meal and swam ten laps of the pool backwards before breakfast."

"Backwards? How do you swim backwards?"

"With great difficulty, trust me. A bunch of us tried the next morning, and it's almost impossible. But those women ate it up. Literally. High society ladies were buying pickled eggs by the caseload. The Richmond pickled egg shortage made the New York Times."

"I'm guessing there wasn't really a pickled egg diet?"

"Hell no. Emmy looks the way she does because she works out for three hours a day, but now people keep buying her pickled eggs as a joke. You ever try pickled eggs? They're disgusting. When she ran out of kitchen space last year, we lined them up out the back and used them for target practice."

I sucked back my laughter, praying I didn't split the seams of my dress. "I don't think I've ever tried a pickled egg. I'm not sure I even want to."

"Good call. Anyway, my point is that it doesn't matter what you say. If you want to be yourself, be yourself. If you want to pretend to be a different person, do that instead. Everybody stands around talking bullshit no matter what."

"If that's the case, why do you need to go? Why not just donate some money?"

He grimaced. "Business networking. See and be seen and all that. It's a necessary evil, unfortunately."

"What do you do for a living?"

It was something I'd been curious about for a while. Nick was obviously well off, but I had no idea how he'd gotten that way.

"I invest in various companies. Sometimes I hold onto the investments and receive income in the form of dividends, and other times I sell my shares at a profit." He grimaced. "Or sometimes a loss, if I fuck up."

"That sounds interesting."

"Occasionally, it can be. Day to day, it gets kind of dull."

Nick's phone rang, and he talked into it quietly for most of the journey. I watched out the window, seeing the world through different eyes on my first journey in a limousine. The car was a bubble, insulating me from everything I wanted to forget about.

Time sped by, then the limo drew up outside the Black Diamond hotel. Sylvia had told me this place should have six stars, and there was—I kid you not—an honest-to-goodness red carpet out front. As Nick helped me from the car, I felt like a movie star.

"Over here, sir," a man called from beside the front door.

"Official photographer," Nick whispered. "Smile."

I paused, blinking as the camera flashed.

"Closer," the man said.

Nick unlinked his arm from mine and wrapped it around my waist instead. His touch made me break out in goosebumps, although I wasn't chilly. No, definitely not.

"Great," the photographer said. "Enjoy your evening."

Nick left his arm where it was as he steered me inside. Each time his fingers brushed my waist, a fresh wave of nervousness washed through me, plus something else I didn't want to think about.

A statuesque redhead by the bar waved at Nick, and we headed in her direction. The blond man with her was handsome, but not a patch on Nick. He stopped next to the pair of them, and two more couples broke off their conversations and joined us. Uh-oh, too many people. My throat felt parched as my words dried up.

Nick made the introductions. "Everyone, this is Lara. Lara, meet Luke and Mack, Nate and Carmen, and Sloane and Jed." He indicated each pair in turn.

Oh gosh, I'd forgotten half of their names already. Mack was the redhead, and she was with Luke, I remembered that much. Up close, her eyes matched her emerald gown, and she looked too beautiful for a boy's name. Was it short for Mackenzie? And the slightly scruffy one was Jed—I wouldn't forget that cheeky smile in a hurry. He confirmed my assessment of his character by placing a hand on his date's bottom then laughing as she swatted it away.

"You want a drink?" Nick asked.

"I'd better stick with water. I plan on walking out to the car tonight." Not to mention I'd break an ankle if I got tipsy in these shoes.

"I'll carry you, babe," Jed offered.

Nick glared at him. "No, you fucking won't."

Jed's date rolled her eyes. "He's like this all the time. Just ignore him." She leaned forward. "I love your outfit. Is the necklace one of Emmy's?"

One of Emmy's? "Bradley brought it for me. He said it was on loan."

Mack took a step closer. "Yes, it's definitely Emmy's. I borrowed it last year." Her eyes turned wistful. "So pretty."

Bradley had lent me Emmy's jewellery? I was out to dinner with her boyfriend and her friends, wearing her diamonds? This was too weird. Did she even know? How could anyone lend something so expensive out so casually?

Around me, the conversation moved onto other topics, and I got lost as they discussed people I didn't know and places I'd never been. I half-listened while I took in the atmosphere. The vast ballroom had been decked out in a black and silver theme, and up above, the ceiling twinkled like the night sky. I almost overbalanced staring at it, then embarrassed myself by clutching at Nick's arm. From wall to wall, hordes of beautiful people laughed and chatted. At least Bradley had made sure I was suitably dressed. The women here wore so much jewellery between them that they could have paid off the debt of a third-world country.

"It's time for dinner," Nick said, making me jump as he took my hand. "Are you hungry?"

"Yes."

But not just for food, unfortunately.

In the dining room, Nick pulled out the chair between himself and Luke then motioned for me to sit down. He certainly knew how to charm a lady, even if it was only his housekeeper.

"Have you been to one of these events before?" Luke asked.

I shook my head. At least between him and Nick, I felt safe. The older guy came across as intimidating, and I wasn't sure how to take Jed's outrageous flirting.

"Lucky you. I have to attend far too many of them."

The appetiser of red pepper mousse tasted delicious, and the white wine I sipped was crisp and no doubt expensive. Tempting though it was to knock it back, I declined when the waiter offered to top off my glass.

"Ooh, look at these chocolates," Jed's date said, waving the auction catalogue at us. "Each truffle's flavoured with a different fruit."

Mack grabbed it from her. "Hey, they've got salsa lessons. Luke, you have to bid for those."

"On one condition."

"What?"

"You don't expect me to go with you."

"Oh, come on, I'll need a partner."

"I'll go," Jed offered.

Luke narrowed his eyes. "No, you won't." He turned back to Mack. "Fine, but don't complain when your toes hurt."

"Carmen?" the scary man asked.

"Dinner at La Gallerie. Lot six," the dark-haired lady replied. I loved her Spanish accent.

"Good thing I brought my chequebook, isn't it?"

"What do you like, Lara?" Mack asked.

I shrugged. What did it matter? But she kept looking at me. "The cakes, I guess."

Lot ten was a box of hand-decorated cupcakes, arranged to look like a bouquet of flowers, although eating something so beautiful would be a crime.

Thankfully, the arrival of the main course meant they put the catalogues away, and I dug into the salmon and vegetables arranged on my plate like an abstract work of art. I copied the fork Nick used and ate the lot, pleasantly full even though dessert was still to come. As I shifted on the chair, the water I'd been drinking with my wine made its effects known.

"Do you know where the bathroom is?" I whispered to Mack.

"Sure, it's over behind those drapes." She pointed to the far corner of the room.

Gosh, so far away. I set off, trying not to fall off my pumps. How did all these women walk so elegantly? I wasn't the only girl wearing five-inch heels, but for sure I was the only one waddling like a duck.

# 19

## LARA

I'd just locked myself into a stall when the outer door to the bathroom opened. The click of footsteps on tile headed for the mirrors on the far side of the room, and I heard a zipper being undone followed by a woman's nasal voice.

"Who is she?"

"I've got no idea. I've never seen her around before. Maybe she's from LA? He has a house there, doesn't he?"

"Don't worry, Katya. I'm sure she won't last long. They never do. Except for Emerson, obviously. I wonder where she is tonight."

"Hopefully she's jumped off a bridge, the annoying bitch." The woman sighed, but it came out as more of a hiss. "You're right. The new girl's probably a five-minute fancy. Her face hardly fits, does it? Nick's normally got better taste than that."

Oh hell, they were talking about me, weren't they?

And that meant *I* was the one whose face didn't fit. I held my breath and sank down onto the closed toilet lid, drawing my feet up. I doubted they'd take too kindly to me eavesdropping, but I could hardly walk out in front of them.

The other girl, the one with the saccharine voice, laughed. "I can't believe how short she is. And she's hardly the sample size either. I'm sure the novelty of dating a little round dumpling will wear off soon."

"And I'll be there when it does." I heard the determination in Katya's tone. "I don't understand why he didn't call me when he needed company rather than scraping the bottom of the barrel for something like that."

"Does he have your new number? Maybe he couldn't get ahold of you?"

"I'm positive I sent it to him, but I guess he could've forgotten. I'll make damn sure he's got it before he leaves." There was a pause, and a make-up compact snapped shut. "Or perhaps I'll leave with him if I can convince him to ditch the troll."

The door clicked as they left, cackles hanging in the air behind them. A tear leaked down my cheek. Why on earth had I agreed to come? I should have listened to my instincts and spent the evening curled up with a novel. Even in the most expensive dress and the flashiest jewellery, it was still apparent I didn't belong.

I dabbed at the corners of my eyes with a piece of toilet paper, trying not to smudge my mascara. But it didn't work. As I washed my hands, I caught sight of myself in the mirror, looking like a charcoal portrait of a panda.

And I still had to get through dessert.

"Don't you like crème brûlée, Lara?" Mack asked.

I'd made it back to my seat with only one small stumble to find the most calorific dessert imaginable set out on the table. Normally, it *was* my favourite after tiramisu, but not tonight. I was already a warthog in a room of gazelles, a jellyfish swimming with sharks, and I didn't want to make things worse. Billy had always told me I should cut back on the sweeter things in life, but I'd stuck my head in the sand. I should have buried the rest of me instead. But no more. My diet would start right now.

"I'm not really hungry," I mumbled.

Nick started to say something, but the compère on stage interrupted him. "Ladies and gentlemen. It's time for the highlight of the evening—the charity auction. Are you ready to open your wallets?"

I could open mine, but there wasn't much available for ten dollars and a piece of lint. Nobody else seemed to share that problem, though, and the bidding for a weekend in Aspen soon reached five figures.

Carmen nudged Nate as the dinner she wanted came up, and he opened the bidding at six hundred dollars. Six *hundred* dollars. It seemed a man on the other side of the room was hungry too, but a minute later, Carmen sat back with a self-satisfied smile as Nate jumped from one thousand to five thousand dollars and the competitor gave up.

"Five thousand dollars for a meal?" I said faintly.

Nate flashed the first grin I'd seen from him. "Not just the meal. I also get my wife's undying appreciation, and that's priceless. Right, *querida*?"

Carmen smacked him across the chest and he pretended to wince, but she was smiling too. Luke didn't look quite so happy when he won the salsa lessons.

"Next up, we have a selection of cupcakes from Gilbert's bakery," the compère boomed. "Who'll start the bidding at a hundred dollars?"

Nick stuck his hand up, and a vice clenched around

my heart. Was he bidding because he thought I wanted them? With every increment, the guilt weighed heavier until the hammer came down at two hundred and twenty dollars.

Nick reached over and squeezed my hand. "I hope you enjoy them."

"You didn't need to spend all that money."

"I had to bid on something or it would look bad."

"But I can't even eat them."

"Why not? I thought you liked cakes."

"I'm on a diet."

He looked me up and down. "Since when?"

That was it. I burst into tears. Every eye followed me as I half ran, half tripped back to the ladies' room and locked myself in a stall again.

I just wanted to be on my own.

Except I couldn't even manage that.

The door crashed against the wall, and Nick's voice sounded far too close. Normally, he spoke softly, his voice calm and measured, but now I heard a hint of panic in his tone.

"Lara, open the door."

"No."

I heard him back up, his leather-soled shoes soft on the tile, then Mack spoke.

"Nick, what are you doing?"

"Breaking the door down, what do you think?"

"Oh, don't be ridiculous. All you need is a bobby pin." Twenty seconds later, the door swung open. "Flipping men," she muttered.

Nick crouched in front of me as our entire table watched me make a fool of myself.

"I didn't mean that the way it came out," he said. "I just... You were eating chocolates while you got ready to go out tonight. I was surprised when you said you were dieting, that's all. You don't need to lose weight."

"Yes, I do."

"You're perfect as you are."

"No, I'm not." I swiped at my eyes with manicured fingertips that belonged on somebody else. "A woman in the bathroom said I'm fat."

Oh heck, I sounded like an eighth-grader the way I was whining. I was never touching alcohol again. But promises didn't help at that moment, so I closed my eyes and wished I could flush myself down the toilet I was sitting on. Anything to get away from the people staring at me.

"Are you sure you didn't mishear her?"

"There were two women, and they were talking about you and Emmy. And me. They said I looked like a dumpling."

I opened my eyes in time to see Nick's narrow. "Who were they?"

"One of them was called Katya."

He sat back. "That conniving little witch. Lara, your curves are in exactly the right places, believe me."

Mack laid a hand on my knee. "Oh, honey, nothing but spite and lies ever comes out of Katya's mouth. What else did she say?"

"She called Emmy a bitch and said she'd make sure Nick had her new number so he could call her."

Nick laughed. "She was right about Emmy."

Huh? Why would he say that? Did they have a falling out?

"She called me a broomstick once when she was trying to get her claws into Luke," Mack said. "It'd be good to have her new number though. She had to change it after we signed her up online as an escort with the last one. I believe she was getting a lot of calls."

Jed grinned from his position against the sink. "She got a

lot of calls because you put on the ad that she was offering a group discount. What man wouldn't go for that?"

"Wow. Did you really?" I asked.

"Yeah," Nick said. "They really did. Now forget about Katya. You look stunning. Let's go talk to a few people and then we can head home."

Mack fussed around fixing my make-up then Nick took my hand, keeping me close to him as we made our way across the ballroom. He acted like nothing had happened, but as he introduced me to everybody from a Hollywood actor to a senator, I fought back tears. I had nothing in common with these people, and no matter what Emmy might do, I couldn't pretend to belong.

"Lara, meet Raymond Steppey and his brother," Nick said.

I stuck my hand out again. At least I hadn't screwed up that part. Raymond shook and began talking to Nick, and I was left with...

"Sh-Sh-Sherman."

"Pleased to meet you, Sherman. I'm Lara." The poor man looked almost as nervous as me. He opened his mouth as if to say something, then thought the better of it, so I helped him out. "What do you do for work?"

"I'm a m-m-math professor. At St-Stanford."

Finally! Someone I understood how to talk to. While Nick and Raymond spoke about business, Sherman and I held an interesting discussion on string theory. Although we disagreed on several minor points, I relaxed enough to smile as I bid him goodbye.

"Are you ready to go?" Nick asked.

I tried not to sound too eager. "Whenever you are."

Nick rounded up the others, and we all headed for the exit. It had just turned midnight, and I'd managed not to do anything stupid for oh, at least two hours—a minor miracle.

The door was within touching distance when a sour-faced woman in a fire-engine-red dress blocked our way. Nick tugged my hand, and I lost my balance, falling into him and catching onto his waist to steady myself. Before I could take a step back, he wrapped an arm around my back, plastering me against his side.

"Hello, Nick," the woman cooed.

"Katya."

I studied her, trying not to be obvious about it. Her face was a juxtaposition of sharp angles, and her too-white teeth made her fake smile seem even more predatory. She stroked her fingers down Nick's arm, and he released me for a second to peel them off. Then he held me tightly again.

"What do you want?" he asked.

"I was wondering if you'd like to take me out for a drink this week? I'm free Tuesday and Thursday."

Before Nick could reply, Mack did it for him. "Katya, do you even have eyes? Nick's with Lara, and it's just plain rude to ask him out in front of her. Now, get lost because not one of us is interested in anything you have to say."

She stomped past Katya, and we all followed her.

"Nice," said Jed.

"Just channelling my inner Emmy."

"Emmy wouldn't say that. She'd say 'Fuck off, don't you have to go and throw up?'"

I snorted. "No way. Nobody would dare to say that!"

Although I really wished I could.

"Emmy would," Nick said. "And indeed she did. Her brain to mouth filter could sometimes use work."

Wow. I liked Emmy more and more.

Nick dropped my hand as soon as we got in the car, leaving me strangely bereft. I had to keep reminding myself that this evening was for show, and me being there didn't mean a whole lot to him. I was just a body in a dress to keep the likes of Katya away, and I hadn't even managed to do much of a job of that. In fact, I'd messed up everything.

Nick interrupted my thoughts. "What were you talking about with that guy?"

"What guy?"

"Raymond's brother. The professor."

"Oh, him? We were discussing string theory."

"What's that? Like rope and stuff?"

I laughed. "It's a theory of quantum gravity, where particles are replaced by these one-dimensional objects called strings. Except it's not just a single theory; there are lots of different ones at the moment. Sherman's working on the HE theory, which means there's supersymmetry between forces and matter, and it only uses closed strings, and left and right moving strings differ."

"I'm not even going to pretend I understood any of what you just said. How on earth do you know all that stuff?"

"I went to college at Brown for a few years."

"Brown? What was your major?"

"A double in math and physics. String theory wasn't really my thing, but I had to do a project on it in my second year."

"Without wanting to sound rude, how did you go from studying math and physics at an Ivy League school to cleaning my house?"

How could I avoid discussing my past? While I was in Virginia, far away from Billy Cooper and Baysville, I could block it out and pretend it never happened. Why had I even mentioned stupid string theory? I should have just wittered on about fashion or spa days or something. Not that I knew a thing about either of those topics, but Sherman probably didn't either, so I could have taken a leaf out of Emmy's book and made something up. But it was too late to turn back the clock.

"I didn't manage to graduate. And there aren't many

openings for physicists or mathematicians if you don't have that piece of paper."

Believe me, I'd tried looking and long since given up.

"Why didn't you finish? You certainly sounded like you knew what you were talking about earlier."

"I had an accident at the beginning of my final year, and after that, things happened that meant I couldn't go back. Please, can we just forget this?"

"I'm sorry. I didn't mean to pry."

"And I'm sorry for my behaviour tonight."

"It doesn't matter."

We lapsed into silence, and I focused on the world outside, watching the lights of the city glide by. It must be weird to travel like this your whole life, sitting in air-conditioned luxury, not having to soil yourself by stepping out onto the street. I figured Nick rode this way all the time, unless he was in his Porsche, of course. Had he always been rich? Did he make his own money or was he born into it? I knew so little about him, just his name, age, and the fact that he was obviously wealthy.

He spoke as little about his past as I did about mine. Did he have secrets he wanted to hide too? Curiosity ate away at me, but I could hardly ask questions when I didn't want to answer any.

When the car pulled up outside my apartment building, I couldn't wait to get inside because I needed a good cry. The instant the driver opened the door, I jumped out.

"Wait a second," Nick said.

I turned to find he'd followed me. "What?"

"I'll come up with you."

"I'll be fine."

He ignored my words and fell into step beside me. The elevator hadn't worked since the week after I moved in, and now someone had drawn a crude picture in one corner of the hand-scrawled out-of-order sign and decorated the end with a blob of chewing gum. Lovely. I looked away as we walked past.

We'd climbed halfway up the stairs before Nick spoke again. "Do I not pay you enough?"

"Of course you do."

Michelle had told me I was getting way above market rate, although I'd have needed to be an idiot not to realise that fact for myself. Surely Nick must know it too?

"Then why are you living in a place like this?" There was no judgement in his tone, just worry.

"I have some debts to pay off. After they're settled, I'll be able to move somewhere nicer." In, say, five or six years' time.

"It's not safe here."

"It's fine. I've lived in far worse." He didn't look happy when I said that. "I do worry about leaving your car outside, though."

"The car's fine. The locals know it's mine, so nobody'll touch it. I'm more worried about you."

"Honestly, I'm good here. I'll see you tomorrow, okay?"

*Please, just go.*

"I'd better take your necklace with me."

"Oh, of course."

Because if someone broke in and murdered me overnight, Emmy would still want her rubies back. I turned around as Nick gently released the clasp, his warm breath on the back of my neck giving me goosebumps.

"I'll bring the dress and shoes back tomorrow if that's okay?" I said as I took the earrings out as well.

"Why? They're yours."

"What? I can't keep them. They're far too expensive. And it's not as if I'll go anywhere I have to dress up so fancy again."

At first, I thought he was going to start arguing, but in the end, he simply shrugged.

"We'll see."

# 20

# LARA

Nick wasn't there when I got to Adler House the next morning. In the kitchen, the only signs he'd been home were a half-empty coffee cup on the breakfast bar and a note propped up on the counter.

*Lara,*
*Something urgent came up at work. Back in a few days.*
*Nick*

That was almost good. Good because it meant I could go and visit Missy earlier than I'd planned to. Almost, because I'd miss him. *Dammit, Lara. You shouldn't be thinking that way.* I needed to remember Nick was my employer, not my friend. If the job turned sour, feelings would lead to hurt, and I'd already had enough of that to last a lifetime.

The tuxedo he'd worn last night was draped over a chair in his bedroom, and his socks were on the floor along with a pair of freaking boxer briefs. Nick might have made progress with his dirty plates, but clearly, there was still a way to go with regard to his use of hangers and the laundry hamper. I shook the tuxedo out, ready to drop it at the dry cleaner on my way home, and resisted the urge to take the boxers with me as a souvenir. Nick would never notice a pair missing, and... *Good Grief, Lara, get a grip.* What was wrong with me? I'd never had these thoughts about Billy. No, Nick's underwear needed to go in the wash, not in my purse.

By one o'clock, the house sparkled under its chandeliers, and I couldn't help smiling with satisfaction as I prepared to leave. From dump to model home, the place shone enough for me to take Monday off and head to Missy's a day early.

When I left Baysville, the journey to Virginia had passed quickly while my nerves fluttered with a sense of adventure. The trip back to the town I'd once called home seemed to take twice as long, and I realised that apart from seeing Missy, I'd be glad never to go there again. The place held a few good memories, but more bad ones, and those were magnified by the knowledge that Billy was living there again.

Things only got worse when an electrical goods salesman sat next to me after our ninth stop. He spent the rest of the journey telling my cleavage which vacuum cleaner sucked best, and I thought wistfully of the peace and quiet of Nick's limo as I tried to block out my new friend's overpowering body odour.

I was first off the bus at the terminal, and Missy's squeal pierced the air as soon as my feet hit the concrete. From the hug she gave me, you'd think I'd been gone for years, not months.

"I've got Clyde's truck out back. My minivan's in the shop. Do you have a case?"

I held up my duffel bag. "Just this."

"Really?"

I nodded. Missy couldn't do a weekend away without taking her entire wardrobe along.

Her fiancé still had the same tired Ford pickup as when I left, complete with its collection of empty soda cups and fast food wrappers. If Missy didn't pick up after him, their house would rival Nick's.

"I keep telling Clyde to clear this mess out," she said. "But he hasn't gotten around to it, and I'm not gonna do it for him."

"Well, I'm not doing it either. I've spent enough time cleaning up after Nick."

"Too right! We're going to have a nice, relaxing few days. I've booked us in for mani-pedis tomorrow morning—my treat. My friend Margie works at the salon, so we get a discount."

"I can't wait."

I'd missed hanging out with Missy. Life in Virginia was good, but at times it was like being on a different planet. In Rybridge, the manicures came with real diamonds.

"Then in the afternoon, we've got an appointment at Theresa's Bridal Shoppe. And in the evening, I thought we'd go see a movie. Clyde said he'd play cab driver. I know you said you didn't want to go out, but Billy's never gonna watch a romcom."

"As long as he's not there, I'm good with that."

At the salon, Missy convinced me to go patriotic. I had to admit, the tiny stars and stripes on my toenails were cute.

"You should get them on your fingers as well," she said.

I shook my head. "Too much."

Missy didn't understand the concept of moderation. She went with neon-green for her toes, and her candy-floss-pink fingernails were even more girly than usual, covered in sparkly crystals. After a bite to eat in our favourite café, she led me into a shiny, puffy, lace-and-satin-induced hell. The hundreds of bridal gowns hanging all around left her on the verge of a nervous breakdown.

"I can't decide! There's just so many. Do you prefer the cream one with the rhinestones? Or the white strapless one? Or the one with the train? Ooh, what about this one with the little butterflies? Oh my gosh, they light up! Lara, look at this!"

Now don't get me wrong, Missy was one of my two best friends in the whole world, but one thing I'd never understood was her sense of style. How did I tactfully tell her that if she chose the rhinestone dress the guests would have to bring sunglasses? And the strapless one was a wardrobe malfunction waiting to happen.

Missy tried on six more dresses, and I forced myself not to grimace. Finally, she had a shortlist of three—the butterfly affair; one with a back made entirely of lace, which on Missy, who described herself as "Rubenesque," was unfortunate; and another with a train so long I wasn't sure it would fit into the church at all. I'd be left standing outside, holding the end of it.

"You know what, Lara? I'm gonna sleep on it. Maybe I'll be able to decide more easily in the morning. Now let's look for your dress."

Oh heck, this was the moment I'd been dreading. Missy pulled dresses from the racks, piling them up one after another on the poor sales assistant trailing behind. A bead of sweat dripped down the girl's face, and I feared she'd collapse under the weight.

"Why don't I start trying these on?" I suggested.

"I guess we can always come back for more."

Dresses one through four ranged from bad to terrible, and I cringed inwardly at my reflection as I plastered on a smile. Then when Theresa fastened me into the fifth, Missy's face lit up.

"That's it! That's the dress! Sweet sugar, you look fantastic! We'll take it!"

"It" was a hot-pink strapless number with a tight bodice and frilly skirt. If you want a visual, picture one of those dolls that people of a certain age used to cover up the spare rolls of toilet paper. But it was Missy's special day, and she liked the awful frock, therefore I'd wear it. I barely knew anybody who'd be going to the wedding, anyway. Most of the guests were from Clyde's extended family. On the few occasions I'd met them, every second dragged into an hour.

Worst was Clyde's brother. Clyde may have been a sweetheart, but his brother got held up in the idiot line when God dished the genes out. He was one of those slimy men who kept touching your arm while they talked to you. Or in his case, talked to my chest. If anyone asked him to describe what I actually looked like, he'd be out of answers beyond "G cup." Hmm. Perhaps Missy's choice of dress would be a blessing in disguise—the skirt was so enormous he wouldn't be able to get near me. I mulled that over as I stared absentmindedly out of the window. Should I get Missy to go for something even pouffier?

Then I saw him.

Billy marched past on the sidewalk opposite, a blonde trailing along behind him. Her eyes focused on the ground as her shoulders slumped forward, defeated. I glanced up at the sky where grey clouds gathered overhead, threatening rain. So why was she wearing sunglasses?

Missy must have heard my gasp because she flew to my side in an instant. We skulked behind a mannequin, watching as they carried on along the street.

"When you said he'd come back, I thought you meant alone."

She threw up her hands. "I didn't know he had a new girlfriend, I swear."

"She looks like me."

"She's the same height, but her hair's different."

"I meant her posture. The way she walks. She's given up."

Missy stared after them as they disappeared around the corner. "You might be right."

"I know I am. He's doing the same thing to her as he did to me. Breaking her. We have to do something to help."

"Like what? He's Billy Cooper. His dad owns half the town."

"I don't know. But we can't just ignore it."

My mouth was dry, and I wanted to be sick. The world turned black, despite the array of garish dresses Theresa held in her arms.

"Ladies, I have some more gowns you may prefer," she said.

I couldn't bring myself to try on anything else.

Thankfully, Missy picked up on my mood. "No need, we'll go with the pink one."

"Excellent! Now we just have shoes to select. We can dye them to match the dress."

I shoved my feet into the closest pair, saying a silent prayer that they'd fit. Close enough. I'd get a blister if I tried to walk too far, but since I never danced at weddings or anywhere else, I'd get away with them. I tried to smile.

"These are good."

"Are you sure?" Missy asked, worry lines crinkling her forehead.

I nodded. "Can we leave now?"

Missy still insisted on going to the movie in the evening. She said a nice comedy would take my mind off things. It didn't. All it did was give me more time to agonise over what I'd seen earlier. When that girl walked down the street, it was a flashback to my times with Billy, and I had to fight from being sick in the middle of the theatre. How many times had I done the exact same thing? When I moved back to Momma's, I'd thrown my sunglasses against the wall in a fit of anger when I found them in my bag.

While I may not have known Billy's new girl, I sure as heck knew him. Her life would only go downhill from here. I'd barely avoided dying at Billy's hands—what if she wasn't so lucky?

By the time Clyde drove us back to Missy's, I'd made a decision. I needed to try and help her.

"I'm going to write her a letter," I told Missy. "Will you help me to deliver it?"

"Who?"

"Billy's girlfriend."

"What? Are you crazy? You've never even met the girl."

"I know that, but I can hardly waltz up and introduce myself. If Billy treats her the way he treated me, she won't be allowed out by herself, anyway."

"If she's in that deep with him, what good will a letter do?"

"Probably nothing, but I've got to try. I want to let her know she's not alone. When I lived with him, he made me feel as if everything was my fault, that he was always right and I was wrong. I need to tell her that's not how it is. That if she does leave him, I'll be there for her in any way I can. Please will you help me?"

Missy kept staring.

"I know it might be a bad idea."

"That's not a bad idea. Deciding to walk the three miles home from Manny Stenson's barbecue one night while we were drunk and wearing high-heeled pumps, that was a bad idea. This is a stupid freaking crazy nuts idea."

"I know. But please, Missy. If he sees me in the neighbourhood, he'll throw a fit."

"Fine, I'll deliver the damn letter. But I still think you're insane."

The Billy episode put a dampener on the remainder of my visit. I was scared to leave the house in case I saw him again, and to make matters worse, it rained. Not just a little drizzle, but those big fat plops of water that soaked you through in the time it took to put up an umbrella. Missy and I stayed in, filling in the hours by playing Scrabble and Monopoly. Missy claimed victory in both, even though I tried to argue that "defluff" wasn't a word.

I wrote my letter six times over until I managed something I was happy with. I still shared some of Missy's reservations about sending it, but I'd been there. If the poor girl got hurt, I couldn't live with knowing that I'd stood by and done nothing.

At the bus station, I gave Missy a big hug. "I'll call you, I promise. Maybe you could come and visit?"

"I'd love to, but this wedding won't organise itself."

"After that?"

"Try and keep me away. I'm dying to see this house I've heard so much about. You really think your boss will let us use the pool?"

"He said it was okay."

"You struck gold with that job, Lara."

"I guess."

Although the roller coaster of emotions every time I saw Nick played havoc with my sanity.

But crazy or not, as I boarded the bus for the return journey, I felt relief to be heading back to Virginia. That only served to confirm I'd made the right decision to move there. Hopefully in time, I'd be able to stand in the same room as my employer without a herd of wild mustangs galloping through my chest.

A couple of hours had passed when my ringing phone dragged me out of a delicious dream about... No. That didn't happen. Denial was a wonderful thing. The old lady knitting in the seat next to me gave me a dirty look as I snatched the phone out of my pocket and checked the screen. *Unknown caller*. Probably a wrong number, but I answered it anyway to make the noise stop.

"Lara?" a woman's voice asked.

"Yes?" She sounded familiar, but I couldn't place her. "Who's this?"

"Nadia. Nick's assistant. He's not going to be back in Virginia for a few weeks, so he wants you to go and sort out the house in LA."

LA? He seriously wanted me to go to LA?

# 21

## LARA

Yes, Nadia had said I might need to clean Nick's other houses, but I still found it hard to believe this was actually happening. Just pop over to LA? Nadia made it sound so...so normal.

"Really? Wow. Okay." What else could I say?

"Great, what's your email address? I'll send an e-ticket."

"I don't have one."

"I'm sorry?"

"I don't have an email address. Or a computer."

"But... But..." Nadia clearly found life without email too tough to contemplate. "What about your phone?"

"My phone only makes calls."

"Are you sure?"

"Positive."

"Damn, it should be in a museum or something. Okay, okay, how's this? I'll print out the ticket for a Saturday flight and drop it off at Nick's beforehand. Does that suit you?"

"Yes, perfect." Then I had an awful thought. "Uh, I might have a bit of a problem at the airport."

"In what way?"

"With the metal detector. I have plates in my leg. What if it goes off and they won't let me board?" Panic caused my voice to rise. "I've only flown once before, and that was before my... my accident."

Accident. Right. My parting gift from Billy.

Things had come to a head at the beginning of my senior year. I'd promised Momma I'd visit for a weekend, and we had the time all planned out—first we'd assemble her new bed, then she'd gotten us second-row tickets to the local theatre group's new play. On Sunday, we were going to have a movie marathon. Billy hadn't been keen on the idea of me going, but he'd grudgingly agreed to drop me off at the train station.

Except when Saturday morning rolled around, I found him slumped on the landing, snoring. He hadn't even made it as far as our bed. Not only that, his inevitable hangover meant he'd be in a foul mood. I considered getting the bus, but since the walk to the stop would have made me miss my train, I gave his shoulder a gentle shake.

Biggest mistake of my life.

Torrents of abuse flowed from his mouth as he lumbered to his feet like a bear rising from hibernation. I backed away, but he kept coming, pushing me in the chest with every step.

"You only ever think of yourself, bitch... You want to go to the station? You can fucking walk... Now get me an aspirin."

One last shove, and I flew backwards down the stairs.

I woke in the hospital two days later. Machines beeped and chattered away beside me while Momma remained silent as she clutched my hand.

"Momma, I'm sorry," I croaked.

Her mouth tightened into a thin line. "Never apologise for something that's not your fault."

"Where's Billy?" I whispered.

"You don't mention that boy's name again."

When Momma went for a bathroom break, the nurse told

me Momma had had a stand-up fight with Billy in reception. Momma told him if he came near me again, it would be over her dead body. Either she must have been pretty scary or he didn't consider me to be worth the effort, because he never did come back.

I needed two operations to repair my shattered tibia, and the concussion meant I couldn't think straight for a week. Billy's father paid my medical bills on the understanding that I didn't make a fuss, and when the police came to visit, I told them I'd tripped. Momma was furious with me for letting Billy off.

Maybe I'd have acted differently with more time to consider things, but I didn't have that luxury. Besides, when it came to Billy's word against mine, who would a jury have believed? The son of a man everyone looked up to and who'd offered to cover the cost of my surgery out of "the goodness of his heart" or a penniless student? The thought of dragging myself through a court case was more than I could bear. It was bad enough that I knew what Billy did without all and sundry in the public gallery, and especially Momma, hearing the sordid details.

All I wanted to do was move on.

I did that by moving back to Baysville. Momma helped me through months of physio, and by the time my headaches stopped and I learned to walk again, I'd missed most of a semester. Even if I'd found the money to repeat a year at Brown, there was still the small matter of Billy attending the same school.

I couldn't face him.

Instead, I formed plan B. I'd work at my waitressing job for the rest of the year, get some money saved up to cover my living expenses, and then go back to finish my degree once Billy graduated and left. He always said he wouldn't stick around in Providence after he finished his education.

Only it didn't quite work out that way. Momma got sick, and the book of my life flipped to a new chapter. Destination: NoHo.

The sound of Nadia's nails clicking on a keyboard brought me back to the present.

"Right, I've checked the staff schedules, and if you want to fly tomorrow instead, you can go with Dan, who's more than capable of dealing with the airport staff. Do you have a letter from your doctor about your medical history?"

"I think I can find something."

"In that case, I'll get Dan to pick you up from Nick's place tomorrow at eleven."

"Uh, who's Dan?"

"A colleague of Nick's. Does that work for you?"

"I'll be there."

Nadia hung up with a click, and then it suddenly hit me. I was going to LA! Tomorrow! I needed to pack. What should I take? The weather would be warmer than in Virginia, so I could leave my sweaters behind. I had a pair of denim cut-offs in my meagre wardrobe—I could take those. Beyond that, I doubted I'd need much. I wouldn't have time to do anything but work, anyhow.

A night of little sleep followed. Things churned over and over in my mind—Momma, Billy, the way my life was changing so much with this job.

And Nick.

I thought about Nick way more than I should. It was hard not to. I mean, if I had to describe the most perfect man imaginable, I could have saved words by pushing Nick forward and saying "him." Not just because of his looks, but his kindness too. Billy spent so many years tearing me down that I'd believed I was nothing. Nick made me feel like something again.

And that scared me.

The next morning, I was sitting out on Nick's front steps with my bag when a black Ford Explorer pulled up. A woman hopped out, her glossy dark brown hair pulled up in a ponytail, and when she grinned, her dimples rivalled Nick's.

"Ready to go?"

"Who are you? I was expecting Dan."

"I'm Dan."

"But you're..."

"Female? Yeah, I get that a lot. I brought you a latte." She pointed at the cup holder in the centre console. "I wasn't sure what you normally drink."

"A latte's perfect."

I'd pictured Dan as a middle-aged businessman in a suit, not a twenty-something girl in biker boots, a leather jacket, and a studded black choker. Nadia said she was Nick's colleague, but what did she do? She hardly looked like a typical secretary.

I put my bag in the trunk and climbed into the passenger seat beside her, the smell of the mocha she sipped drifting across and tantalising my taste buds. Then she put the cup back in its holder and gestured at the back seat.

"Nadia sent a phone, an iPad, and a laptop for you. She said you didn't even have email." Dan's eye roll told me what she thought of my technological incompetence.

"What? I don't need all that."

Dan shrugged. "Well, you're getting it."

She cranked the music up, and that was the end of the conversation. I was kind of glad she didn't speak because she'd clearly been to the Emmy school of driving and needed to watch the road. We may have arrived at Dulles International quickly, but it took a few seconds for my brain to convince my fingers to loosen their grip on the seat.

Despite the ride, I was glad to have Dan with me, because when a security guard held me up at the metal detectors, she did the talking. She may have been small, but she spoke with such authority that he didn't dare to question her. In no time at all, we were sipping champagne and nibbling on snacks in the business-class lounge.

I cringed back into the plush sofa as a suited man looked me up and down, his nose crinkling in disgust. Guess my Walmart jeans and second-hand sweater didn't cut it in the land of the rich and beautiful. Still, Dan earned a bemused headshake for her outfit, and she didn't seem to care a hoot. I needed to take a leaf out of her book.

"More champagne, ma'am?" the concierge asked.

"Just one more glass."

I know I said I'd quit alcohol, but nerves got the better of me, okay? I hated flying. I'd studied enough at college to understand the fundamentals of lift and the Bernoulli effect, but there was still a tiny, irrational part of me that was amazed aeroplanes didn't just drop out of the sky.

"Worried?" Dan asked as we walked down the jetway.

"A little," I admitted.

"Don't be. Everybody dies sometime."

Oh, that was comforting. "Do you fly often?"

"About once a week for the last decade, and I'm still alive."

"Wow. That's a lot of flying."

"I know. I'm saving up my air miles to go into space."

# 22

## LARA

The late afternoon sun beat down on me as I lay on a lounge chair by Nick's pool in my shorts, with my T-shirt tied in a knot under my breasts and the sleeves pushed up onto my shoulders. A gentle breeze from the sea provided welcome relief from the heat. It may have been October, but the temperature was in the mid-seventies, and there wasn't a cloud in the sky. For a brief moment, I cursed the fact that I didn't have a bikini, but then I shook my head at myself. Even if I did, I wouldn't dare to wear it. Somebody might see.

The taunts in high school had made me overly sensitive about the size of my chest, and the rumours when I got to college didn't help. It went from pictures of porn stars pasted all over my locker to whispers that I'd paid for my breasts. As if I could afford to do that. My hips matched my chest, and my legs weren't exactly slim either. I was perfectly in proportion, just the wrong type of proportion. I'd never make a cheerleader. No, the only way I'd dress in a swimming costume was if everyone in a ten-mile radius was blindfolded. In the dark.

But here at Nick's place, with its eight-foot-high walls and private beach, I didn't mind lying out in shorts.

Just like the house in Virginia, his LA home was incredible. Not quite as big, but the entire apartment I'd shared with Momma would fit in his living room. It felt sterile, though, and so perfectly put together I almost didn't want to touch anything.

At least Nick hadn't been fibbing about the mess, or rather the lack of it. Apart from dirty dishes that looked as if they'd been there since Clinton left office and a thick layer of dust covering everything, the place was in remarkably good shape.

Tired from the flight, I allowed myself a few hours by the pool before I started my chores. An ornate bookcase in the living room held shelf after shelf of classics, each bound in pristine white leather and embossed in gold. Fifty bucks said none of them had ever been opened. I picked out Jane Austen's *Emma* and settled back in the sun to read, dreaming of England.

All I needed now was a shirtless butler, and the illusion of a life of luxury would be complete.

Three days later, I climbed down from the stepladder in Nick's atrium. I'd found the ladder in the garage and used it to help me clean the ridiculous chandelier that formed the focal point of the entrance. Shaped like an upside-down tree, each branch bore a variety of glass fruit, and after an hour of careful dusting, I was cursing the genius who thought it would be a good idea to include so many pineapples.

My arms ached as I lugged the ladder back to its home, careful not to scratch the black Porsche parked in there, a twin of Nick's car in Virginia. Beside it was a Harley Davidson. Billy always wrote bikers off as savages, but up close, I couldn't help running my fingers over the gleaming chrome.

What would it feel like to sit on? After a quick glance behind me, silly because I'd been alone for days, I swung my leg over and settled onto the leather seat. Wow. The only thing missing was...

No. I refused to let my mind go there.

Instead, I forced myself to dismount and go back to the house where folding the last basket of laundry was the only chore left. Six packages of dusters, fifteen vacuum cleaner bags, and a bottle of dish soap later, the house was done.

Now what?

I sent Nadia a text message asking if she wanted to book me a flight home, but when she didn't reply, I couldn't resist the lure of the pool. So there I was, in the last of the afternoon sun, wearing my one and only pair of shorts again.

On any other weekend, I might have felt relaxed, but two years to the day since Momma died, all I could think of was what I'd lost. I wished I'd had the chance to visit her grave, but making a special trip to Baysville for an hour in the cemetery was out of the question. Missy had promised to lay fresh freesias, Momma's favourite, and I vowed to add my own tribute as soon as I could.

I hated to think of Momma lying in the ground, anyway. No, I preferred to imagine her looking down, a twinkling star, seeing that I was finally starting to keep my promise to her. While I couldn't claim to be happy, I was definitely less miserable than two years ago. Things were gradually slotting into place. I liked my job, my new apartment was habitable, two great friends cared about me, and my debts were slowly, slowly decreasing.

And I had a nice employer.

No, no, nice didn't cut it. I had an employer who treated

me like a human being, even if I wasn't convinced of his own mortality. If gods walked on Earth, Nick was surely one of them. My nipples hardened at the thought of him in a towel. The image of him opening the door to me that memorable morning may as well have been tattooed across the inside of my eyelids.

How I wished Momma really could see me now. She was the one person who'd always believed in me. She'd be smiling as I got my life back on track, but even as I thought of her face, tears leaked down my cheeks and I gave a decidedly unladylike sniff.

"What's wrong?"

I jumped so violently I nearly fell off the lounge chair. Twisting around, I found Nick towering above me, concern etched across his face. Despite his size, he'd crept up on me as quietly as the sun in the morning. I hadn't heard a single footstep.

"Freaking fudge, you nearly gave me a heart attack!"

His eyes softened as he offered a tentative smile. "Sorry, baby. Didn't mean to scare you."

Baby?

"What's wrong?" he asked again.

"It's nothing." My nose started running, and I gave another sniff, trying to make it quieter this time.

"Crying on a sunlounger in the middle of the day isn't nothing."

"My momma died two years ago today." I stared off into the distance, listening to the waves crashing against the shore. If I looked straight at him, the floodgates would open.

Nick perched on the edge of the seat and took my hand in his, squeezing it. "Lara, I'm so sorry. Were you close?"

"Very much. She was my best friend as well as my mom."

He didn't say anything, and I was grateful for that. Words would have been inadequate. He just held my hand, his thumb stroking slowly over my knuckles while I bit back tears. It was so soothing, so comforting sitting there with him. Nick made me feel safe, and for some reason I couldn't consciously fathom, I started talking.

"She had cancer. She fought it for years, but eventually it won, and on the day she died, a part of me did too. I miss her so, so much."

He simply sat there, squeezing, stroking, listening.

"She found a lump in her breast. First, she had chemotherapy. Seven sessions, each a fortnight apart. She'd come home tired, then the day after, she'd be in so much pain she could barely move, but she'd crawl to the bathroom on her hands and knees to be sick, and all that came up was bile because she couldn't eat. She got so thin she didn't even look like my momma anymore. Most of her hair came out, and she had to wear a wig. She joked about it being easier to style, but when her curls started falling out in clumps, I heard her crying at night. Then, one evening, she got really angry and shaved it all off."

Squeezing, stroking, listening.

"Next she had radiotherapy for two months, and after that, she had a double mastectomy. She cried for weeks, and she couldn't even bear to look at herself. I told her she was still beautiful, but she didn't believe me. 'You're sweet, but I've got eyes you know'—that's what she used to say. Then a couple of months later, she got a swelling under her arm, and it turned out the cancer had spread. It reached her bones, and there was nothing they could do. Goodness knows, they tried everything. I made them. But it was pointless."

When I finished my rambling monologue, I burst into tears. I couldn't help it. On a lounge chair, in LA, in front of my insanely good-looking boss. If I'd been capable of coherent thought at that point, I'd have wanted to die of embarrassment. But I wasn't, so instead I bawled my eyes out as Nick pulled me onto his lap and wrapped me up in his arms. I clutched onto his shirt as sobs shook my body. A minute passed, two, and slowly my senses returned.

"I-I-I'm sorry. So sorry. Honestly, I don't know what happened. I've never broken down like this before." Not even right after Momma died. "Really, I don't know what's come over me. Oh my gosh, your shirt—it's soaked! I'll get you a fresh one." I tried to scrabble away, but he held fast.

"My shirt doesn't matter. You're what matters. Crying's part of the grieving process. It helps to let things out."

"But not all over you. That was so unprofessional of me. You're my employer."

"And also your friend, if you want me to be."

Was he serious? Oh goodness, he was so freaking sweet I burst into tears again. He didn't speak, just scooped me up and carried me inside.

"Put me down! You'll hurt yourself trying to carry me. I'm far too heavy."

"Do I look as if I'm struggling?"

"Well...no."

He'd carried me all the way upstairs, and he wasn't even breathing hard.

"And where on earth did you get the idea you were heavy?"

Billy. Billy had told me I was heavy. In the beginning, it was just snide little comments. *Wouldn't you rather have the salad? Did that dress shrink in the wash?* But towards the end, he didn't try to hide his contempt, like the time he told me I looked like the back end of a buffalo. Strangely, it was easier to deal with when he was straight up about it. At least I wasn't left second-guessing, wondering if I'd misinterpreted something.

"Someone I used to date," I said quietly. "And those girls at the dance."

"Your ex must have been blind, not to mention stupid for letting you go. And as for the girls, it was pure jealousy. Surely you must have seen the men looking at you when you walked into that ballroom?"

I couldn't say I had. Mainly because I'd only had eyes for Nick.

"If anyone was looking, it was probably only to wonder what the frick I was doing there. I felt like an impostor."

I had the sniffles again. What was wrong with me? I never got all emotional like this.

"Trust me, Lara, that's not what they were thinking. And you belonged there as much as anybody else."

Nick lowered me onto my bed then sat on the edge of it, holding my hand again. I turned onto my side to hide my blotchy face, because what girl wanted the man she liked to see her in that state? He let go of my hand and stroked my hair. Nobody but Momma had ever done that, which set me off bawling again, but still Nick didn't leave. No, he plucked a tissue from the box sitting in a sheep-shaped holder on the nightstand and passed it over so I could wipe my eyes.

"Where was your father in all this?" he asked.

"I don't know. He left when I was nine, and I haven't seen him since."

"So who was there for you?"

"My friend Victoria. Well, sort of. She lives in England, but she phoned almost every day to see how I was. I couldn't have gotten through it without her."

"But nobody in the States?"

"I met Missy at the hospital when Momma got sick—her brother was having chemo too. Before then, it was just me and Momma. And now it's just me."

We lapsed into silence, punctuated by the occasional snuffle. Nick kept brushing my hair with his fingers, and it felt so calming I started to drift off. As darkness crept in like a fog over the sea, I dreamed I heard Nick whispering to me.

"It's not just you anymore, Lara."

An imagined brush of his lips against my temple sent me into a deep sleep, disturbed only by my yearning for a man I could never have.

# 23

## LARA

A pit of dread yawned in my stomach as I went downstairs the next morning. How could I have broken down on Nick? I was prepared for awkwardness over breakfast, but Nick didn't mention my meltdown, and I certainly wasn't about to bring it up.

As was our custom in Virginia, I made him scrambled eggs, three slices of toast, and a glass of orange juice, just the way he liked it. Apart from the occasional comment about the state of the economy, he barely said a word as he ate.

It wasn't until I bustled around the kitchen afterwards, cleaning away pans, that he asked me what my plans were for the day.

"Tidy a few bits here, pick up some fresh veggies, then I thought I'd go for a walk. Unless there's anything else you want me to do?"

"Yeah, there is. I've got one meeting this morning, and then we can do something fun. You deserve it."

Wow, really? He wanted to spend the day with me?

"Why?"

"You've had a rough time lately. I want to see you smile."

His kindness made my eyes prickle, but I didn't want him to give up his day for me out of pity. "It's okay. You don't have to take me out. Honestly, I'll be fine here. You've got a whole shelf full of books."

"I know I don't have to. I want to. You can read a book another time."

Guilt faced off with my inner hussy. Guess which won?

"Only if you're sure."

"I'll be back in two hours. Make sure you're ready."

What on earth should I wear? I'd only brought casual clothes. No way did I think I'd have to go out anywhere but the grocery store. I took a shower, dried my hair as tidily as I could, and eventually settled on a pair of jeans that fit reasonably well and a pink V-neck top. Shoes were a problem—my beat-up Converse would have to do.

True to his word, Nick arrived back in the Porsche almost exactly two hours later, and I hopped into the passenger side.

"Where are we off to?"

"I thought we'd get some lunch first." He grinned at me, and my heart skipped. "Then I've got a surprise planned for afterwards."

A surprise?

Uh-oh. I wasn't so keen on those. Last time Billy decided to surprise me, he'd taken me to a party at an all-you-can-eat barbecue place then forced himself on me in the parking lot. What would Nick come up with?

We ate lunch in a little restaurant overlooking the sea, sitting outside on the terrace. As I settled back onto the squashy cushions, I felt strangely relaxed, with nothing to do but watch the boats sailing by on the horizon as Nick quickly checked his emails. Then a lady walking to the next table got distracted as she stared at Nick, tripped, and spilled a glass of wine down my top.

"Oh my goodness, I'm so sorry!" She leapt for a napkin and knocked into a glass of water, which sloshed over Nick. "I-I-I..."

She stared at his wet crotch, clearly unsure whether to blot or run.

"How about helping my friend?" He grabbed the napkin from her and passed it to me.

"I'm fine, really."

Quite honestly, the less she tried to assist, the better.

The woman backed away and was swiftly replaced by waiters bearing towels and fresh drinks. My top hadn't gone see-through, thank goodness, although Nick's stain was in a slightly embarrassing place.

"So much for a quiet lunch," he muttered when things calmed down.

"Do you want to leave?"

"No, it'll dry."

"At least it was only white wine that ended up over me. If it had been red, people might have thought you were having lunch with an assassin or something."

His eyes flicked up at me. "Yeah, crazy thought. What do you want to eat?"

I chose fresh tilapia while Nick had the chicken. We managed to get through the meal without further incident, and the waiter even brought us a complimentary dessert. Not that I ate much of mine. My size had weighed on my mind a lot lately, and I didn't want my waistline to expand.

I snuck a look at the front of Nick's pants as we walked out to the car, purely to check on the stain, you understand. Okay, so I may have made a quick estimation of size, but what girl wouldn't? Wow. Anyhow, the damp patch had faded to a dull grey, barely noticeable on the denim.

"Almost dry," Nick said.

Dammit! He'd caught me looking.

"Uh, the same. Where are we going?"

"You'll find out when we get there."

"Will there be other people around? I smell like an alcoholic."

"Only one other guy, and he won't care."

One other guy? I wasn't sure whether to be relieved or apprehensive.

Half an hour later, we pulled into a parking garage underneath an office building. I caught a glimpse of the sign on the outside: Blackwood Security. Why were we here?

"The elevator's in the far corner," Nick said after he helped me out of the car, one hand on the small of my back as he guided me in the right direction.

I shivered at the contact. Why had he brought me to an office? Did he know someone who worked here? As the elevator doors closed, he inserted a key-card into a slot and pressed the button for the roof.

"The roof?"

He smiled, and those killer dimples popped out. "Wait and see."

Twenty seconds ticked by slowly until the doors opened again.

"A helicopter?" I gasped.

It sat just a few feet away, a uniformed pilot standing by its side.

Nick grinned at me. "Surprise."

He paused to shake the pilot's hand.

"Afternoon, Mr. Goldman. She's all fuelled up and ready to go."

I'd only been on a plane three times before, and never in a helicopter. Those rotor blades looked awfully thin.

"Is this thing safe?"

"Believe me, I wouldn't ask you to get in it if it wasn't."

I still had reservations, but I didn't want to act like a coward in front of Nick. My stupid heart hammered against my ribcage as he strapped me in, although that wasn't all because of my fear of flying.

"Ready?" the pilot asked.

Nick nodded. "Good to go."

He settled a pair of headphones over my ears as the pilot fired up the engine, then followed suit with his own. When he spoke, his voice sounded clear but distant.

"Have you ever flown in a helicopter before?"

I quickly shook my head, desperately resisting the urge to close my eyes.

"Just relax and enjoy the ride."

As we lurched skywards, I squeaked and grabbed Nick's hand. He chuckled as he squeezed mine back. How could he be enjoying this?

"It's better if you open your eyes, baby."

"I'll open them when we're back on the ground."

"You're missing the Hollywood sign. It's just over there."

I cracked one lid open. "Where?"

"On the left."

Fear momentarily forgotten, I leaned across him and stared out the window.

"Oh, wow. I need to get a picture of this."

Tori and Missy would never believe it otherwise. I used my new phone to snap photos of everything from Universal Studios to the Sunset Strip, then the pilot turned towards the coast.

"I thought we'd watch the sun go down from the air," Nick said.

"Sounds goo...eew!"

Wind buffeted the helicopter, and I grabbed Nick's hand again. If I died, at least I'd do it with the man I...was developing feelings for. I knew it was wrong, but I couldn't help it. Where his palm touched mine, crackles of electricity ran through my veins, and every time he smiled at me, I went weak inside. I treasured every glance he gave me. *Stop thinking about it, Lara*! He was with Emmy, for goodness' sake, and not only could I never compete, I actually liked her. There was no way I wanted to hurt anyone.

By some miracle, we survived the flight, and I was still babbling about it as Nick pushed open the door to an Italian restaurant on a quiet side street. I'd learned Italian was his favourite, and luckily, he knew all the good places to go. The food tasted divine, and I put my diet plans temporarily on hold as I worked my way through a bowl of spaghetti. I was only human, okay? We'd almost finished our main courses when Nick's phone rang.

"What do you want?"

I tried not to eavesdrop, but I heard the high pitch of a woman's voice on the other end. Not her words, though. I only had Nick's side of the conversation to go on.

"No, we'll pass... No, we're out for dinner... Look, it's been a long day... Okay, okay, I'll ask her."

He put the phone down on the table and rolled his eyes. "Dan's asking if we want to go out to Black's with her tonight. If you don't, that's fine."

"Black's?"

"It's a club."

"Like, the famous one? Where there's one in London and another in New York?"

"Yes."

I'd heard of Black's. Who hadn't? It was the nightclub of the rich and famous. All the A-listers hung out there. Tori had been to the one in London once when a friend of a friend managed to get her onto the guest list, and she'd raved about it for weeks afterwards.

"Do you reckon we'd be able to get in?"

"Trust me, getting in isn't a problem."

Of course it wouldn't be. I'd forgotten who I was talking to. "I'd love to go, but I only brought jeans with me."

Nick picked up the phone again. "Dan, can you sort out something for Lara to wear?"

The answer must have been yes, because he sighed. "Okay, we'll see you in an hour."

"Dan's staying with a friend," Nick explained, as we headed to the limousine waiting outside after dessert. "His house is in Malibu."

House turned out to be a bit of an understatement. Mansion was more like it, complete with eight-foot-high white walls and a uniformed guard standing outside. He gave us a careful once-over before allowing us to proceed through the gates.

"A guard?" I asked.

"Armand's had problems with people trying to get in. Mostly girls. They don't mean any harm, but it got pretty irritating for him."

The door swung open as we approached, and I did a double take as Dan appeared in the entrance. Gone was the biker outfit, replaced by a fuchsia-pink cocktail dress and a pair of delicate black pumps, her hair tumbling around her shoulders in soft waves. She caught me by surprise when she threw her arms around me and dragged me inside.

"This is going to be so much fun! I've got half a dozen dresses for us to pick from, then I'll put your hair up."

"Just go with it," Nick whispered from behind. "It's easier that way."

Dan strode off along the hallway, and I hurried to keep up. So focused was I on her disappearing back, I didn't notice the man pop out of a side room until I walked into him. As I tried to keep my balance, strong arms held me up, and I cursed myself once again for being a total klutz.

"Shoot, I'm so sorry." My eyes were level with his chest, so I looked up. "Holy fudge, you're Armand Taylor."

As in Armand Taylor, highest-grossing movie star of last year, Hollywood A-lister, and general all-around Adonis. Oh my gosh, I was in his house! And not only that, I was currently plastered against his chest.

He chuckled as I sprang back like he'd burned me. "I was last time I looked."

I could have given a goldfish a run for its money with my choice of facial expression, but before I managed to form words, Dan interrupted me.

"Armand, we're late. Lara needs to get ready. If you're not doing anything constructive, get out of the way."

How could she speak so casually to him? I peered through my eyelashes to see his reaction, but he simply stepped to the side as Dan herded me up the stairs into a bedroom scattered with make-up.

I sagged into the nearest chair. "That was Armand Taylor."

"Yeah, and?"

"He's, like, the king of Hollywood. Women go nuts over him." Me included, if I was honest. I'd watched every single one of his movies with Missy.

"I know. It's hilarious."

"Why are you here? Fudging frick, are you dating him?"

She laughed. "When you signed your contract with Nick, it had a confidentiality clause, right?"

I nodded.

"I'm not dating him. He's gay. Tonight, I'm his cover story."

My jaw dropped. "Are you serious? But he's always in the paper with some actress or model on his arm."

"That's all arranged by the studios. Armand's been with his boyfriend for three years. Hans pretends he's the butler."

I was back to goldfish. "Oh, my goodness."

"The general consensus is that it would hurt Armand's career if he came out right now, and Hans is supportive enough to keep things quiet. He's staying in to watch the football game tonight while Armand charms the ladies at Black's." Dan shrugged. "Armand hates football anyway."

Another fantasy shattered, although I had to admit that Nick had usurped Armand since he came onto the scene. And Dan was right—screaming women the world over would weep into their hair extensions if Armand's sexual preferences became front-page news. Just last week, he'd made the papers when a wealthy heiress from New York paid a hundred thousand dollars at a charity auction for a "date" with him. She'd no doubt be disappointed not to get a second.

So busy was I digesting that revelation, I didn't notice what Dan was up to. It wasn't until she stepped back and said, "Ta da," that I looked in the mirror. The girl staring back definitely wasn't me. My eyes were smoky, my lips scarlet, and my hair had expanded to twice its normal size.

"Now for the outfit." She handed me a scrap of slinky red material and a pair of shoes that matched hers. "I think this'll suit you best."

I wasn't sure I shared her sentiment, but I scuttled into the en-suite bathroom to change. *Just go with it*, Nick had said. The knee-length dress was every bit as bad as I'd imagined.

"I can't go out looking like this," I hissed, peering around the door.

Dan yanked it all the way open. "Why not? You look amazing."

"Because I'll fall out of it. And it's way too revealing."

The top had something built into it that made my boobs grow in line with my hair.

"Everything's secure." She grabbed the neckline and gave it a jiggle. "See? Come on, let's go."

I dug my heels into the carpet. "It's too bright. People might notice me."

I was happiest flying under the radar. Being noticed only got me sniggers and nasty comments.

"That's kind of the point." She paused, and her face softened. "Don't worry. Nick'll beat all the men off with a stick. Now we have to get going—we're running late."

I gave in. The club would be dark anyway, wouldn't it? I could just hide in a corner.

But Nick nearly choked on his drink when he saw me.

"Oh, no. No way."

Great, he hated it. "I know. It's far too bright, right?"

"It's not the fucking colour I'm worried about. Dan, put her in something else."

"Piss off, Nicky. That dress looks great on her, and she's wearing it."

Dan pushed me out of the door while Nick looked at her with murder in his eyes.

I gave him an apologetic shrug. "Like you said, it's easier just to go with it."

## 24

## LARA

The line outside the club stretched right down the block, but the limo dropped us off at the front, and the bouncer didn't even check his clipboard before he moved the hallowed velvet rope.

"Armand! Armand! This way!"

Before we could get inside, the waiting paparazzi descended in a pack. Armand took a few steps forward with Dan, happy to oblige as they hollered at him for pictures. After all, I guess that was the point of the night.

"Lara, get on the other side." Dan grabbed my elbow and hauled me towards them.

A wall of camera flashes blinded me as Armand wrapped his spare arm around my waist, pinning me against his side. Until that moment, I'd never truly understood the expression "deer in headlights," but that was how I felt, all gawky and uncoordinated.

"Smile," Armand whispered.

Oh, that was easy for him to say. He dazzled with his million-dollar grin and two-million-dollar dimples with Dan looking gorgeous by his side, while I attempted a grimace that made Elmer Fudd look photogenic.

As Armand manoeuvred us into the club, I fell against Nick, breathing hard. I'd never seen him get annoyed, but now his eyes burned with anger. He grabbed Dan's arm and stopped her in her tracks.

"What the fuck was that for?"

She shook her arm free and grinned. "Lara looks hot. It was just a bit of fun."

"I know she looks hot, but does she look as if she had fun?"

Nick took a step towards Dan, and I put a hand on his biceps. Too late, I recalled Billy slapping me for doing the same thing, but Nick stopped instantly, and I let out a long breath. This was Nick, not Billy, and yes, the experience with the photographers had been terrifying, but with it came a rush the likes of which I'd never felt before. I could understand how people got addicted to fame.

"It's okay, really. It's over."

"No, it's not okay. Dan, if you ever do that again, I'll throw you out of the fuckin' helicopter."

"Like to see you try, wiseass."

"You'd better believe it, shrimp."

"Stop bickering you two, for goodness' sake," Armand interrupted, the voice of reason.

Dan huffed, linked her arm through his, and stomped off into the club.

"Should have stayed home with a nice bottle of wine," Nick muttered as we followed.

Bass thumped through my soul as he led me through the crowd, and even without having a drink, the atmosphere left me buzzing. The music, the lights, the sheer energy of the place... Wow. We caught the other pair up in the VIP area where Dan was already halfway through a glass of bubbly.

Nick motioned at a seat, and I climbed up onto it, relieved to take the weight off my feet. These shoes were an inch higher than I'd normally choose.

"What can I get you?" asked a perky brunette in a waitress outfit. Traci, according to her name badge, and she'd replaced the dot over the "i" with a little heart.

Nick opened his mouth, but Dan got in first. "More champagne. And nibbles. Do you guys want wine as well?"

Nick shook his head. "Water. For fuck's sake bring some water."

Yes, that was probably for the best. I still hadn't forgotten my mortifying outing to the first Italian restaurant.

From our position on the mezzanine level, we could look out over the people below, drinking and dancing to a DJ I recognised from the television, and then I happened to glance to the side.

"Holy fudge—is that Scott Lowes?" I mouthed.

A face I'd drooled over in movies was now only feet away.

Dan leapt up and gave him a hug. "Scott!"

To his credit, he only rolled his eyes once. After he'd managed to extricate himself from Dan's clutches, he shook hands with the guys, then Nick introduced me.

"This is Lara."

Scott leaned forward and kissed me on the cheek. That was it—I was never washing that side of my face again.

"Have you seen my brother?" he asked Armand.

"Not tonight. Is he causing havoc again?"

"Same old. Do me a favour and call if you spot him?"

"Sure."

As Scott walked off, I sat down before my legs gave way.

"He touched me!" I whispered to Dan.

"I noticed," she giggled. "Did you see Nick's face? He looked as if he wanted to punch him."

"What? Why?"

"Dan!" A shout came from nearby, and a pair of blondes rushed up. "Come and dance."

She gave me an apologetic smile as they dragged her off. "Laters."

Armand followed, leaving me alone with Nick and a magnum of champagne.

"Do you want to dance?" he asked.

"I'm not really much of a dancer."

"Did he tell you that?"

"Who?"

"Your ex."

Of course he did. Apparently, I cramped his style, which was somewhere between dad dancing and the funky chicken. It got worse as he got drunker.

"He might have mentioned it a time or two."

"Well, since everything else that seems to have come out of his mouth is complete bullshit, I bet you're a great dancer."

I shook my head no.

Nick leaned over, so close his lips brushed against my ear when he spoke. Flashes of fire travelled down every nerve fibre in my body at the sound of his voice, low and throaty.

"Baby, that asshole did a number on your head. You're easily the most beautiful woman in here tonight, and I want you beside me on the dance floor. Come on." He held out a hand. "Come with me."

Nick thought I was the most beautiful woman there? How much champagne had he drunk? Did he need his eyes tested? This was Hollywood, where cosmetic surgery was as common as cough syrup and the fad diet changed weekly. I didn't even own a lipstick.

The touch of his fingers on mine made me jump, and the timbre of his voice still vibrated through me long after he stopped speaking. Dazed, I let him pull me forward. Apparently, my feet *did* want to dance.

Nick, unsurprisingly, moved like Patrick Swayze, and he stuck close as we made it to the lower level of the club. Seriously close. My breasts squashed against him, their pebbled tips pressing into his chest. Could he feel that? Please tell me the answer was no. My brain reminded me this was far from a good idea, but I couldn't take my eyes or my hands off him, and apart from the odd glare at other men, his gaze stayed firmly fixed on me. As we moved in sync with the music, a tightness started in my belly, followed by a wild fluttering. When Nick said he wanted me to come with him, I doubted he meant literally. I tried to take a step back, to put some space between us, but he held me tightly. I was in trouble. Big trouble. Huge trouble, going by what I felt pressed against my hip.

"You okay?" he asked.

Darn it, he must have noticed me squirming. "Uh, I need to use the bathroom."

Dan was flinging her arms in the air close by, and Nick waved at her to come over.

"What?"

"Can you show Lara where the bathroom is?"

"Sure."

Dan led the way as we threaded through the writhing bodies packed in front of the bar, heading towards the back of the club. With every step, the butterflies in my stomach settled, replaced by a sense of loss. What on earth was wrong with me? In all my years with Billy, I'd never experienced anything so...so *intense*. Two layers of clothing between me and Nick, and still I'd nearly orgasmed on the dance floor for crying out loud. Inappropriate didn't even begin to cover it.

The line for the ladies' room rivalled the line outside the club, but Dan bypassed it and tugged me through an unmarked door beside the fire exit instead, nodding to the security guard as she went past. My ears thanked me as the decibels dropped to a level where we could talk without shouting.

"Why are we in here?" I asked.

"This bathroom's nicer." She motioned at a door ahead as if that answered everything. "And I'm sorry about earlier. I shouldn't have dragged you in front of the cameras."

"It doesn't matter." I'd gotten over the shock now. "Actually, it would be nice to borrow Armand sometimes, that way I could get into Black's whenever I wanted."

She looked puzzled for a second. "But you don't need Armand. Just call Emmy and ask her to put you on the guest list."

"She can do that?"

"Didn't Nick tell you? They're Emmy's clubs."

"What, all of them?"

"She likes dancing, and when her favourite club in London closed down, she bought it. Too much of the profits had been going up the old owner's nose. She rebranded, and she's been expanding ever since. This chain makes her a packet."

Whoa. I'd assumed Emmy was a trophy girlfriend, but I'd been dead wrong on that, hadn't I? And I'd just been dancing with her man! I stepped into the nearest bathroom stall and sagged back against the wall, disgusted with myself. What had I been thinking?

And what had Nick been thinking? He hadn't exactly objected, had he? Was I reading too much into things? I mean, we'd been pressed against each other, but with the number of people in the club, what other choice did we have? Maybe Nick behaved like that with other girls too? It was a possibility. After all, I barely knew him.

Dan flushed the toilet next to me, so I got a move on and joined her as she washed her hands. For the rest of the evening, I vowed to act like a lady and not a wanton hussy.

At least, that was the plan.

"Oh, shit," Dan said, as we wove our way back to the others. "We leave them alone for ten minutes and they get into trouble. I'll rescue Armand, you help Nick out."

A mob of girls elbowed each other out of the way in a bid to get closer to Armand Taylor, and I had a feeling his terrified expression wasn't down to his acting skills. On the opposite side of the table, Nick stared at an approaching female with similar trepidation.

Dan nudged me forward. "Quick! Selina has Nick in her sights, and he can't stand the woman. Emmy normally gets rid of her, but you'll have to step in instead."

I looked again, and this time I recognised Selina May, number one on last year's list of the world's sexiest women. A bouffant of blonde hair bounced around her shoulders, and she tossed it back into some poor guy's face as she passed. Step in, Dan had said. What did she mean by that? I shuffled closer, and Selina gave me a glare that could melt steel.

But Nick didn't share her sentiment. "There you are, baby," he cooed. "What took you so long?"

He tugged my hand, and I overbalanced into his lap. I'd barely processed where I'd landed when he wrapped his arms around my waist and gave me a chaste kiss on the lips.

"Uh, I..." Words failed me as my lips burned. "I, uh, there was a line for the bathroom."

I wasn't lying about the line; I just hadn't been in it.

"Lara, this is Selina. Selina, meet Lara."

"New girlfriend?" Selina asked, her famously smooth Southern accent tinged with spite. "You finally got sick of that nasty blonde?"

"Something like that." His hand took up residence on my thigh, and I forced myself to stay calm. "You look tired, baby. Want to go home?"

I sensed he was looking for a yes. "I wouldn't mind."

Selina didn't give up. "We'll be out for hours yet, Nick. Why don't you drop her off and join us?"

Gosh, that woman was so brazen! Not to mention rude.

"I'll pass on that. We've got an early start tomorrow."

"Well, you have my number." She twirled a lock of hair around her fingers, looking coy. Were those extensions? Her hair had always fascinated Missy, who was determined to emulate her style for the wedding.

"Definitely fake," Dan said into my ear. "Along with her tits, her nose, and most of her biography. Did you know she was born in Queens?"

She'd freed Armand from the mob, and he looked as if he wouldn't mind leaving, either.

"Queens? No way. What about that story she always tells? How her ancestors owned a plantation in South Carolina?"

"Her family ran a hardware store in Hollis."

Nick stood me up, then got to his feet. "I'm well aware I have your number, Selina. If you'll excuse us."

We all went through the same door Dan had used earlier, except this time we headed along a different hallway and emerged in a service alley behind the club where our car was waiting. Only once I'd slumped back on the leather seat did I realise I'd been telling the truth—I was exhausted. By the time we reached Armand's house, I could barely keep my eyes open.

"You staying here?" Nick asked Dan.

"Too damn right. I'm not missing Hans's breakfast pancakes." She leaned over and gave him a peck on the cheek. "I'll see you back in Virginia."

Alone in the car together as it purred its way back to Nick's, the sound of my heart racing drowned out the engine. At least that's how it sounded to me.

"Sorry we cut out early," he said, yawning. "I didn't feel like sticking around when Selina turned up. Thanks for helping me out there, by the way."

"It's fine. I didn't lie about being tired, and my feet hurt from all the dancing."

"Sit back."

"What?"

"Sit back."

I did as instructed, then squealed as Nick swung my feet up onto his lap. What on earth was he doing? He took off my right shoe and dropped it onto the floor, followed by the left. Oh. Oh! He was massaging my feet. I tried to snatch them away.

"Lara, relax."

"But my feet are icky."

"They're not icky. They're perfect, just like the rest of you. Stop wriggling."

My bones liquefied, and when Nick's thumbs dug into exactly the right spot, I couldn't have moved if I'd wanted to. Was it possible to have an orgasm from a foot massage? Because I was in serious danger of finding out. My head dropped back, and I'm pretty sure I let out a moan.

Then we were back at the house. Too fast. Far too fast. The driver opened the door, and Nick scooped me up, carrying me towards the front door with my shoes in one hand.

"I can walk."

"Yes, I know, but tonight you're not."

He lugged me all the way up the stairs and deposited me gently outside my bedroom door. Although the last time he'd done that, he made it look easy, tonight his breathing seemed laboured. Had I eaten too much in the last few days?

Thoughts of the diet I should have been on vanished as he leaned in. Our foreheads touched, and his warm breath washed over me, smelling slightly of whisky I hadn't noticed him drinking. Me? I froze.

Close. Nick was so close. Just half an inch away, and if I

moved a fraction, his lips would be on mine. His eyes opened, and there was a depth to them I'd never seen before. An abyss I could fall into and never again see the light of day. Then the shutters came down, and the moment was lost. He kissed me softly on the cheek before pulling back.

"Good night, Lara."

"Good night," I whispered as he disappeared along the hallway.

The slam of his bedroom door echoed through the house as I quietly closed my own.

# 25

## LARA

I n Adler House, I'd almost finished setting the table for lunch. Nick had complimented my fajitas last time I made them, and this time, I made sure to buy extra guacamole because he'd covered them in it. I held a tea towel, ready to take the chicken and vegetables out of the oven as soon as he got downstairs.

I'd flown back to reality a few days earlier. Or, should I say, my new reality, which was still so unbelievable I pinched myself every day. Nick had acted like the perfect gentleman on the trip, carrying my bag at the airport and stopping me from going through the wrong gate, but now things had changed. There were no more massages and no more dances. It was as if I'd dreamed that night, but I sure wasn't imagining the distance between us since our return to Virginia.

Still, it was for the best. I mean, nothing would ever happen between Nick and me, and I found it easier to hide my feelings when he wasn't nearby. Not only that, Emmy was around. She'd picked him up in her Corvette on two mornings this week.

He sauntered into the kitchen, free of his suit, wearing

jeans and another of the washed out T-shirts I'd grown accustomed to seeing him in. I glanced down at his bare feet then quickly looked up again. What was it about seeing him with no shoes on? It made me want to fan myself.

"Do you want something to drink?" I asked as I laid out his food.

With the weirdness between us this week, I'd stopped setting an extra place for myself, and he hadn't commented on that.

"Just water."

I went to the fridge, and from the corner of my eye, I noticed him put his iPad next to his plate. Thank goodness. A little of the tension in my chest eased because he clearly wasn't expecting conversation. While he ate, I'd pop outside and water the pots. The basil had started sprouting already, and I'd bought mint seeds to plant.

Except I'd barely gotten halfway to the door when my phone rang. Not the smartphone from Nick, but the one I'd brought from Baysville. Missy and Tori already had my new number, so who was calling?

The screen flashed with Paul's name. What did Tori's husband want? Or had she lost her phone and borrowed his? Considering she'd left two phones in cabs and dropped one down the toilet in the last year alone, my money was on the latter option.

"Hello?"

"Lara? Thank goodness you answered." Paul's voice sounded shaky. Scared, even, and that tension came back twofold.

"What's wrong?"

"I-I-I don't know how to... I mean... Tori's had an accident. She's in the hospital."

"What happened? How bad is it?"

"Nobody'll tell me what's happening. She's in surgery, and

they've put me in this room, and no one'll answer any questions."

"What happened?" I asked again.

"A car. She was on a crossing, and the driver couldn't have seen the red light because he drove right into her. The boys said she went right over the bonnet."

"The boys were there? Are they okay?"

"Fin's got a broken leg, but Robbie wasn't touched."

I clutched at the counter for support, but it didn't help. My knees gave way, and the floor came rapidly closer.

"Hey, what's wrong?" Nick caught me a second before I hit the tile.

"My friend Victoria," I whispered. "She's had an accident."

Paul's voice crackled from my phone, muffled and distant. *Don't freak out, Lara.* The last thing he needed was me getting hysterical.

"She's got to be okay," I told him as Nick helped me to a chair. "She's just got to be."

"I don't know what to do. Her parents are on a cruise in the Balearics, and I can't get hold of them. Robbie won't stop crying, and Fin...he hasn't said a word since the nurse put his cast on."

Quite honestly, Paul didn't sound as if he was in a much better state than the children. His gulping breaths said he was struggling to keep it together.

"Uh, hang on. I'm not sure..." I put my hand over the mouthpiece and turned to Nick. "Could I take a few days off? I promise I'll make the time up, work evenings, weekends, anything."

"Of course. You don't even have to ask."

I squeezed his hand in a silent thank you as I spoke to Paul. "I'm on my way to help, okay? Just hang in there."

It shocked me to hear him sobbing. "What if she doesn't make it?"

"She will. Stay positive. I'll be there as soon as I can."

I hung up the phone, then stared into space. For years, I'd been the weak one, and Tori had always been there when I needed support. Now the roles were reversed. How could I help her best? My mind was too numb to think straight, but I definitely needed to get on a plane because I sure couldn't do much from Virginia.

How did I book a flight? Thanks to Nick, I had enough money in my bank account to pay for one, but I'd never had to deal with the logistics of international travel before. At least I'd been through an airport recently.

"Nick, how do I buy a plane ticket?"

"Where do you need to go?"

"London."

"I'll sort it out. Just turn off anything that's still cooking and get in the car while I lock up the house. We can stop at your place for you to collect some clothes on the way to the airport."

"You'll drive me to the airport?"

"You're hardly in a fit state to drive yourself at the moment."

I hugged him. Boss or not, I couldn't help it.

"You're the best. I really mean that."

# 26

## NICK

Nick gunned the engine of his Ferrari and took off down the road. He rarely tested the limits of his vehicles, but today was an exception, at least until he hit traffic. There should have been a fucking law against people taking cars on the road if they insisted on driving at half the speed allowed.

He blew past a station wagon, ignoring a horn blast from the truck driver coming in the other direction. What was the guy's problem? Nick had gotten in front of the startled old lady peering over the steering wheel with at least a foot to spare.

A squeak next to him caught his attention, and he glanced at Lara, staring wide-eyed out of the windshield. Aw, shit. The news about her friend had really upset her. He leaned over and squeezed her white knuckles.

"Don't worry, baby. It'll be okay. We'll get you to England in no time."

"Right now, I'm worried about getting there at all."

"What? Why?"

The car in front slowed to make a left turn, so Nick put

two wheels up on the sidewalk to drive around it. Emmy had taught him that manoeuvre a few years ago—she swore it saved at least half an hour of her life every year.

"Because... Freaking fudge, you're heading straight for that car!"

"The road's plenty wide enough for three." Nick flashed his headlights just to make sure the other car moved over. "What were you saying?"

"Never mind. Could you at least put your other hand back on the wheel?"

They pulled into the parking lot behind Lara's apartment in record time, and she climbed stiffly from the car. Nick caught himself staring at her ass and gave himself a mental slap. *Now isn't the time, Goldman.* No, he had more important things to do. As soon as Lara disappeared inside, he pulled out his phone.

"Emmy, is the big jet still at Dulles?"

"Yeah, unless someone else took it. Why? Do you need to borrow it?"

"Please. And Brett if possible." Brett was Emmy's pilot.

"Where are you going?"

"London. RAF Northolt. I need a car waiting there as well."

"Hang on."

Nick heard her instructing Sloane, her office assistant, to call the airport and ask them to get the plane ready while Brett hustled over there to file a flight plan. It might have been short notice, but Blackwood paid Brett well over the going rate to be on standby for emergencies just like this one. Today, he'd be earning his salary.

"Okay, sorted. Now tell me what's happened."

"Lara's got a friend who lives in London, and she's had an accident. I don't have all the details, but Lara needs to get there ASAP."

"Are you going with her?"

"Planning to. Can you cover for me?"

"If you'll pick up my shit in Europe. I was due to fly to London myself the day after tomorrow."

"What shit?"

"A bunch of meetings in King's Cross, another one in Paris, plus a teensy weensy little job in Ukraine."

Nick's stomach dropped when he heard the last part. "I take it the Ukraine thing is hands-on?"

"Intelligence gathering on a suspected arms dealer."

Nick sighed. "Fuck. Yeah, whatever, I'll do it. I just want to be around for Lara as much as I can. She looks pretty shaky."

"You really like her, huh?"

Nick had carefully avoided asking himself that question for weeks, but now he had to face up to his feelings.

"I think so. I don't know. She does things to me, and I can't stop thinking about her. I almost kissed her the other night. Dammit, I was so fucking close. It almost killed me not to."

"Well, why didn't you? She likes you too. Dan said she looked like she wanted to lick you all over in the club the other night."

"She did?"

"Apparently so. You know, for a smart guy you can be really dumb sometimes."

"Thanks. I love you too."

"Doesn't everybody?" Nick visualised Emmy shrugging as she sat in her office. "And you're avoiding the question. Why didn't you kiss her?"

"You know why."

Her voice quieted and lost a little of its brashness. "Nicky, it's been seven years. She's not coming back."

"You think I don't get that? I spend every damn day wishing I'd done something different."

Except in the last few weeks, Jana had drifted further and further from his thoughts as he rehashed every moment spent with Lara, pondering his next move. Guilt weighed heavy in his chest because Jana deserved to be more than a distant memory, a tragic footnote in the story of his life.

"And what else would you have done?"

"Stayed with her. Sent her somewhere else. Put guards on her. Anything but leave her home alone."

"You couldn't have foreseen what happened. Stop beating yourself up about it."

But it *had* happened.

Six years ago, in the depths of a miserable winter, Nick had travelled to Berlin to oversee the opening of a new Blackwood office in the city. The shareholders took it in turns to make those sort of trips, given that they could last a month or more, and that time, Nick had drawn the short straw. Or so he thought until he stopped in a bar after work on his third day there.

"What can I offer you?" the waitress asked.

*Your phone number and your company tomorrow night*, his heart screamed. *Your mouth*, another part of his anatomy put in. Luckily, his brain overruled them both.

"A beer and a menu, please." He hadn't planned to eat, but at the thought of spending more time watching her delectable *Hintern*, he suddenly developed an appetite.

Never a fan of German cuisine, Nick developed an insatiable taste for Bratwurst and Schnitzel over the next week. Or at least, he forced it down while snatching every moment of conversation with Jana that he could. She laughed at his mangled attempts to talk about cars and scuba diving, then sang the praises of her own passion: history. The romantic era, specifically—the first half of the nineteenth century.

Beethoven and Chopin, Goya and Delacroix, her obsession with Grimm's fairy tales.

At work, he made sure to practice his German with colleagues and contractors in a desperate attempt to improve his grasp of a language he'd barely spoken since his time in the Navy SEALs. Back then, he'd spent three months seconded to GSG 9, the German government's counterterrorism unit, and his translation skills were more suited to the battlefield than the bedroom. That didn't help him much now. He watched German movies at night, old black-and-white romances and those modern chick flicks women were supposed to love, because sweet talk was what he needed.

Then the following Saturday, he learned the meaning of the word disappointment. A sour-faced matron dumped his dinner on the table and stomped off without a word.

"Hey!"

She turned and glowered at him.

"Where's Jana?"

"Day off."

Shit. He was about to leave and find something edible when the object of his desire slid into the seat opposite.

"I thought you weren't working today?"

She gave him a shy smile. "I'm not. Why do you always eat here? The food's terrible."

Okay, time to man up. "I'm not here for the menu."

Another smile, followed by a glance under her eyelashes. "And I'm not here for the ambience."

"Do you want to go somewhere else?"

"With you?"

He nodded. "Anywhere you like."

She took the arm he offered, and he threw a fifty euro note on the table, keeping his fingers crossed it would be the last time he had to look at their sauerkraut. A cab passed as they left the bar, and he flagged it down.

"Where to?" the driver asked.

Jana shrugged. "I don't eat out much. I'm on a student budget."

"I've only eaten two other meals in this city, and they were both in the hotel restaurant."

"Is it good?"

For the amount it cost, Nick would have been pissed if it wasn't. "Yeah, it's good."

"Then let's go there."

They made it through the appetiser and main course, and Nick reckoned he'd done a good job of pretending to be interested in Jana's history degree when really all he'd done was watch her lips and listen to the sweet timbre of her voice. He'd never thought of German as a sexy language, but her words caused him to rethink.

"Are we having dessert?" she asked.

"Do you want to?"

"I'm full." She fell silent and Nick waited, sensing she had something else to say. "But I don't want to go home."

Thank goodness. His heart leapt, swiftly followed by a tightening sensation across his chest and the front of his pants. *Do not fuck this up.*

"We can stay as long as you like. We don't have to eat."

Jana motioned to the waitress hovering in the corner. "I think she wants to leave. I've given that look many times before."

"There's a lounge. Why don't we head there? It'll be more comfortable as well."

Nick scribbled for the check as fast as the waitress could bring the pen, looking forward to a cosy sofa rather than the stiff-backed leather chairs in the dining room. Except when they got to the Schumann Lounge, they found a private function in full swing. A gaggle of drunk businessmen clustered around a microphone, murdering something by Britney Spears.

"I doubt they'd notice if we went in..." Nick trailed off as he took in Jana's disappointment.

"It's so noisy."

"My room's quiet." Her eyes widened, and he hurriedly backpedalled, cursing his inability to think straight around her. "Sorry, that sounded bad. I meant I've got a suite. It has its own lounge, and we could get drinks from room service."

"Okay."

"Okay? Really?"

A little nod, and Nick's spirits soared.

Half a dozen partygoers followed them into the elevator, and an overzealous bald dude shoved Jana into Nick. He wasn't sure whether to punch the asshole or thank him as Jana squashed against his chest. In the end, he settled for sliding an arm around her waist to shield her from the imbeciles.

The rabble got off on the fourth floor as the elevator continued to the penthouse. Far too quickly for Nick's liking, and it seemed Jana felt the same way because when the doors opened, neither made a move to get out. Instead, they stood frozen, and Nick felt her heart hammering along with his own.

"What are you thinking?" he whispered.

"That I want you to kiss me."

Birthdays, Christmas, Thanksgiving—they all paled into insignificance beside that moment. Nick forgot he was in an elevator in a hotel—hell, he forgot his own name as his lips touched Jana's. Soft and sweet, yet burning with a fire he'd never felt before, she tasted of hope and happiness. Lost in the moment, he surrendered his soul to her, only coming back to earth at the sound of a throat clearing behind him.

"Excuse me? Are you going down?" An elderly lady stood in the doorway, clearly unsure where to look.

Where the hell were they? Not on Nick's floor, anyway. "No, I'm going up."

And not just in the elevator either. Luckily, Jana's body shielded his groin from view, and as they once again rode to the top floor, she took a step forward and rubbed against him.

"Gotta stop that, babe," he murmured in her ear.

"Why?"

He didn't have an answer.

As it turned out, words weren't necessary. Room service and the sofa were quickly forgotten as they tore at each other's clothes and stumbled towards the bedroom, and Nick got his first look at what he'd been dreaming of since the day he laid eyes on the woman he'd fallen for.

Jana didn't disappoint.

Nick didn't go into work the next day. Or the one after that.

"I'm sick," he told Emmy, doing his best to cough.

"Bloody lovesick, more like."

How did she know? "I can't help it. I don't understand what's wrong with me." Nick meandered onto the balcony and stared out at a grey sky, but the dreary weather couldn't dampen his mood. "I can't think of anything but Jana. I don't even know what day it is."

"I'm glad you've finally found her," Emmy said softly. "I'll sort out the office. Take a week. Take two. Just don't mess it up."

Two weeks turned into a month, and with the German office up and running, Nick needed to get back to his day job. Only he couldn't. He lived to see Jana's smile first thing in the morning and to fall asleep with her at his side. The idea of flying back to Virginia alone filled him with sadness, but what else could he do? Was moving to Germany a viable option?

Of course, Jana picked up on it. "Why so sad, Nick?"

"Just thinking about the future."

"Our future?"

"Yes." Was there another?

"I know you have to go home. The people at work need you."

Nick had told her about Blackwood, and she'd been nothing but proud of all he'd achieved there.

"Not as much as I need you. I'm thinking of moving here."

She dropped her arms from around his waist and stepped back. "No. I can't see you living in Berlin forever. Your home's in America."

"My home's with you."

"Then I'll move. I have five months left to study, and after that, I'm free. I've always wanted to travel, and I've heard so much about Virginia I feel I belong there already."

"Are you serious?"

"Of course. I've been considering this since the eighth of January."

Nick did some rapid calculations. "That was two days after we met."

Jana simply smiled, and that was when Nick knew what he had to do.

Fuck it. "Marry me."

Her smile slipped. "What?"

Nick asked again, this time more hesitantly. "Will you marry me?"

She threw herself into his arms and clung on like a limpet, then the tears started. What the hell did that mean? Was she happy or upset?

"Er, babe? What's your answer?"

"Yes. Of course yes."

The weight of the ocean rushed off Nick's shoulders. "You want to travel? I'll give you the world."

Only it didn't quite work out that way, did it? One fucked-up job, and he'd lost Jana forever.

As he watched her casket disappear into the ground, he swore he'd never get close enough to care like that again. He'd even thought about ending it, of taking the pain away with a single bullet, but the need to avenge her death overrode the lure of numbness.

Two months passed before they found the man who'd killed his fiancée living rough in a barn near Düsseldorf. Nick rarely took pleasure in killing, but for that fucker, he'd made an exception. With Emmy at his side, he drew the man's death out for eight long hours, one for each minute Jana lived in agony after he shot her.

She never got to see the house Nick had bought for them, the one she'd named for the eagle that lived up on the bluff behind it; or the wedding she'd spent every evening planning; or the world he'd promised her. All she saw was an early grave, and for years, Nick lived in that darkness with her.

But since Lara fell asleep on his sofa, he'd seen colours again. The trouble was, his work would always be risky, and he didn't know if he could bring that hell into a woman's life for a second time. Emmy was well aware of that.

"You know why. Lara's sweet and innocent and beautiful. She's real. She wears her heart on her sleeve and shows her emotions rather than hiding behind a mask. I'm a former Special Forces commando, and I always will be. Work already got one girl I cared for killed, and I can't let it happen to another."

"Look, Lara knows you've got a dangerous job, and she's still crazy about you. Why don't you let her make the choice?"

"Uh, she doesn't exactly know what I do for a living."

Emmy laughed. "Shit. You haven't told her? Why don't you just come clean?"

"She hasn't had the best life so far, and I don't want to put her in a position where she could get hurt again. Her mom died of cancer a couple of years ago, and it hit her hard, plus her dad left when she was a kid. There's also an ex who screwed with her head. Can you believe she thinks she's fat?"

"Fuck me, I'd kill for her tits. Most women would."

"So would most men. Me included, obviously." He'd certainly spent enough time staring at them when she wasn't looking. Imagining what they felt like, tasted like, whether she'd scream if he sucked on them. If he ran the tip of his tongue around one hard nipple... Dammit! He needed to stop thinking like that. "Anyway, I want her to be happy, and I'm going to do whatever I can to make her that way. I don't think dropping her into the middle of our lifestyle is the answer."

"I still say you should tell her. Being together could be good for you both. Have you ever stopped to consider your own happiness?"

Nick remained silent.

"Why do you think we hired her? Bradley didn't pick her out because of her unique ability to vacuum."

"I should have known."

"You need someone like her. She's sweet and straightforward. Look on the bright side, she's about as different from me as you could get." Emmy referred to her own failed relationship with Nick, which hadn't so much fizzled as gone out with a bang when she accidentally landed him in the hospital almost a decade previously.

Nick's turn to laugh. "That *is* a definite plus."

"Look, I hope everything goes okay over there. If you send me her friend's details and the name of the hospital, I can try to find out what's happening."

"Thanks, Ems."

"No problem. Just let me know if there's anything else you need. And Nick?"

"Yeah?"

"Tell Lara the truth."

Emmy hung up, leaving Nick agonising over feelings he didn't understand.

## 27

## LARA

**B**ack in Nick's Porsche, I hugged the bag of clothes I'd packed on my lap as he took off for the airport. The way he was driving, it would be faster travelling to England by car.

"You've got everything you need?" he asked.

"I hope so."

In truth, I had no idea. Probably I'd get to London and find I'd forgotten my clean socks and brought toothpaste but no toothbrush, but who cared? The only thing that mattered was getting to Tori.

How was she? Paul had barely told me anything. And the boys? Oh hell, what about the baby? How was the baby? She'd been so excited about having another little one. Last time we spoke, she was wishing for a girl because she'd been outnumbered by boys for years. Paul had said she was in surgery, but what for? A broken bone? Or something much worse?

As well as being a true friend, Tori was one of the few people left who'd known my momma before she got sick. Who knew how things used to be. Losing her would be like losing Momma all over again.

My eyes prickled, and I tried to hold back the sniffles. Tried and failed. The tears came thick and fast, and I turned towards the window so Nick wouldn't see. The streets flew by, homes and warehouses and out-of-town superstores, but the buildings got blurrier as my eyes filled. Wiping at them with my sleeve didn't help one bit.

Then the car stopped, and Nick hopped out to open my door. "Can you walk or shall I carry you again?"

Talk about making me feel inadequate. "No, I can walk."

He took my bag and held out an arm, and though I wished I didn't need it, my wobbly gait meant I needed to hang on tight as we walked into—

"Hang on, where are we?"

"The airport?" Nick seemed confused by my confusion.

"What on earth is that?"

"A plane?"

Well, obviously, but I'd expected to be at the drop-off point outside the terminal, or maybe in a parking lot. Almost anywhere but where we were, which was on the tarmac beside a freaking jet.

"I know it's a plane, but why are we next to it?"

"So we can get on board and fly to London."

"You hired a private plane?" I whispered. "Nick, I can't afford that."

"Not hired, I borrowed it from a friend. And you're not expected to pay anything."

"This is crazy."

Actually, crazy would be an upgrade to business class. This...this was freaking insane, at least to any normal person. But Nick had different thoughts.

"No, crazy would be waiting around for a commercial flight, then spending another hour at Heathrow getting out of the terminal when there's a perfectly good plane sitting here. Now, can you walk up the steps?"

I could hardly refuse, could I? I managed the climb, although my legs felt weirdly detached from my body. Nick sat me down in a cream leather armchair and buckled a safety belt around my waist before taking the seat next to me.

"Good to go, Brett," he called out.

Five minutes later, we thundered along the runway, taking off on my third flight in two weeks.

"You should get some rest," Nick said.

"I don't think I can. I keep worrying about Tori."

"Try." He handed me a glass of wine. "You'll need your strength on the other end."

Next thing I knew, he was shaking me gently awake, and the first thing I heard was silence. "Have we landed?"

"Five minutes ago."

How had I slept all the way? That must have been some wine.

"We're in England?"

He chuckled. "London." Then his face grew more serious. "Tori's got a broken leg and a lot of bruising. They're not worried about that, but she also hit her head."

I clutched at the arms of my seat. A head injury? "Is it bad?"

"She's in a coma. They want her to sleep until the swelling in her brain goes down." He reached out and unpeeled one of my hands, clasping it in his. "Did you know she was pregnant?"

"She told me a few weeks ago." But he'd used the past tense. "Did she lose the baby?"

"I'm so sorry."

Numbness overcame me, starting at my toes and rapidly working upwards. Tori would be devastated. How did a girl get over losing a child like that?

"You spoke to the hospital?"

"Emmy found out. I don't know how. I've long since given up asking."

"What else did they say about Tori? When do they think she'll wake up?" Because the prospect of her not waking up was something I couldn't even contemplate.

"They couldn't say. Hopefully, they'll have more news when we get there."

I hated hospitals. I'd spent so much time in them, first with my leg and then with Momma, that I never wanted to set foot in one again. All the whispered voices, the feeling that if news was delivered quietly, it somehow wouldn't be as bad. The beeping of machines and the rattle of gurneys. The unique smell of sterilising fluid and vomit and death. And worst, the hollow-eyed stare of patients who knew that the inside of the hospital was the last thing they'd ever see. I shuddered.

"Come here, baby."

Then I was in Nick's arms, and the comfort he offered overruled my feelings of guilt at being so close to him. I stayed there all the way to the hospital, and Nick's arm only left my shoulders when I rushed forward to hug Paul in the waiting room. Five years had passed since he and Tori last visited me, but he'd aged fifteen. I suspected most of that had happened during the last day.

The boys huddled next to him, seven-year-old Robbie and five-year-old Fin, both looking as scared as I felt.

"Is there any news?"

"She's out of surgery, but our baby died." Paul let out a choking sob, and Fin started crying. "Tori's still asleep. They don't know when she'll wake up. What if she never does, Lara? What if she never does?"

I tried to hide my fears for his sake. "She'll wake up. This is Tori we're talking about, and she's always been a fighter.

Remember the time she battled through Hamleys on Christmas Eve because Robbie wanted the latest Lego set? You have to think positive." I dropped my voice to a whisper and gripped one of his hands in both of mine. "And don't speak like that in front of the children. Have you seen her?"

"Not yet. The doctor said I'll be able to sit with her soon. Is there any chance you could take the boys home? The hospital isn't any place for them."

"Sure I can."

"They got a couple of hours sleep here last night, but they're still tired and hungry."

"I'll get them something to eat then put them to bed. Just stay with Tori."

Paul eyed up Nick, who stood silently on the other side of the room, giving us space.

"That's Nick, my boss. He flew over with me."

"Your boss?"

"Yes."

"And he dropped everything to fly halfway around the world with you?"

"Well, yes. He knew someone who had a plane, so he borrowed it. He's a really nice guy."

"Lara, nice would be if he'd organised a cab to the airport for you. Flying here with you, that's something else."

I bit my lip. "No, it's not. That's just how he is."

"When I first met Tori, her car was broken down at the side of the road. If I was being nice, I'd have called her a tow truck. I called her a tow truck, then I arranged for her car to go to a garage to get fixed. Then I gave her a lift home. Then later on, I married her."

"I'd better get going. Boys, I'll take you home."

I held my hands out to them, trying to block out Paul's words. What he'd suggested was too preposterous to even think about.

"You can run, Lara, but you can't escape. Love's got a funny way of catching up with you."

The doctor came out and tapped him on the shoulder. "Sir? You can go through now."

Paul gave me one last sad smile over his shoulder as he went to be with his wife.

# 28

## LARA

"What can I do to help?" Nick asked.

He looked totally out-of-place standing in the cramped living room of Tori and Paul's three-bedroom duplex. Nick belonged on a calendar, not next to a half-size model of a Dalek made out of cardboard.

"Uh..." What should I say? It felt wrong to ask my boss to assist around the house.

"Lara, I'll do whatever you need. Just tell me. You want me to help with the boys?"

"Okay, sure. That would be good. And could you feed Gordon?"

"Who's Gordon?"

"Tori's cockapoo."

"Her what?"

"Her dog."

The boys were already as smitten with Nick as I was. He'd carried Fin out to the car at the hospital, helping him to forget his troubles for a moment while he balanced him on his shoulders. They disappeared outside, leaving me to tidy up the house as best I could and make SpaghettiOs on toast for supper. I'd forgotten Tori's reliance on convenience food—tomorrow, I'd go to the nearest grocery store and do some vegetable shopping.

Dinner didn't take long to prepare, and once I'd got the plates on the table, I stuck my head out the back door to call the boys inside.

Then I stopped.

Nick was running around the lawn with a shrieking Fin on his back while Robbie chased them, brandishing a toy sword. That wasn't the Nick I knew. American Nick usually wore worry lines like they were going out of fashion, and his eyes lacked sparkle. As he set Fin down on the bench and pretended to die on the patio, he looked ten years younger. Not that Robbie cared. He was focused on the task at hand, namely whacking Nick around the legs with the sword.

"Robbie! Stop that."

Nick rolled over. "It's okay. He's just playing."

"Yes, but violence is never acceptable."

Robbie hung his head. "Sorry."

Nick did the same, looking guilty but so darn cute, then ruffled Robbie's hair. "Better do what she says. Is dinner ready?"

"On the table."

The boys must have been tired after all the drama of the last couple of days because I had no trouble getting them off to bed. Well, a little. Robbie fell asleep on the couch, and I had to get Nick to carry him upstairs. He was getting heavy.

And he wasn't the only one who was tired. I collapsed onto the couch myself just as the doorbell rang.

I groaned. "Who's that?"

"It's for me."

Huh?

Nick came back a minute later carrying a bottle of wine, a couple of glasses, and a fancy box of chocolates.

"Where did those come from?"

"I called Bradley. There didn't seem to be much in the kitchen cupboards, and I figured you could use a pick-me-up."

What? "Isn't Bradley in Virginia?"

Nick shrugged. "Bradley's a global presence." He pulled a penknife from his pocket and made use of the corkscrew. "Cheers. Wonder what tomorrow will bring?"

"More of the same, I guess. You're good with children."

"Probably because I'm just a big kid myself."

"What's your family like?"

He grimaced, and at first, I thought he wasn't going to answer. "Dysfunctional is the best description. My parents divorced when I was ten, and my father died when I was twenty. Mom lives in Seattle with her second husband and my half-brother. That's it for biological family."

"I'm so sorry about your dad."

"Don't be. He wasn't much of one."

"You lived with your mom, then?"

"No, I lived at boarding school. Or rather boarding schools. I managed to get expelled from six of them. Eventually, Father sent me to stay in Switzerland and told me not to bother coming back until I got my act together. Mom's new husband wasn't interested in having me around either."

Wow. I thought my upbringing had been tough, but I'd had Momma, and there was never any doubt how much she loved me. Nick didn't seem to have had anyone.

"That's awful. What happened in Switzerland?"

"I did a lot of growing up. As well as learning how to ski." He cracked a smile for a second, but his expression quickly grew serious again. "Then Father decided he'd had enough of paying for me to have fun and decreed that I'd come back to the US and go to college. I had a place at Stanford. The plan was for me to get my MBA and take over his business."

"Oh my gosh, Stanford? It's so tough to get into. I bet an MBA from there opened plenty of doors."

"Probably would have if I'd gone. That life wasn't for me, and needless to say, Father was furious. We barely said two more words to each other before he died. Anyway, enough about me. Want to watch a movie?"

There was absolutely nothing subtle about that change of subject. I didn't push it. Nick clearly wasn't happy discussing himself, and I could understand that. Maybe he'd open up more in the future?

"A movie sounds great."

I raided Tori's DVD collection and found a copy of *The Spy Who Loved Me*. Surely that would be acceptable? I held it up, and Nick nodded his agreement, but that didn't stop us both from falling asleep halfway through.

I never found out how the movie ended, and I didn't care. All that mattered was being wrapped up in Nick's arms again, which was how we woke at almost one in the morning. Nick's eyes popped open as I stirred, and we quickly untangled ourselves. What was I thinking?

"I'm so sorry. I didn't mean..."

He stretched his arms above his head. "Yeah. Probably not a good idea. Where are you going to sleep?"

"I'll borrow Paul and Tori's bedroom. Uh, are you going to a hotel or something?"

"I was planning to take the couch."

My boss on the couch? "I can sleep down here."

His mouth set in a firm line. "No, you can't."

"But—"

A shake of his head sent me on my way, and I didn't have the energy to argue. But I chided myself as I climbed the stairs. How could I have left Nick to sleep on a pull-out bed with Gordon snoring next to him? He may have been super-rich, but in some ways, he was so incredibly normal.

In the morning, Nick dropped me and the boys off at the hospital. By limo, no less. I was getting dangerously comfortable with that mode of transport, but the boys were more used to riding in the back of Paul's cab and bounced around like lunatics. I kind of preferred them tired.

The chauffeur opened the door when we arrived, and Nick hung up from his phone call. "Good luck. I'll send the car and driver back for you—they're yours for the time you're here."

By the time I opened my mouth to thank him, he was gone.

Inside, I swapped with Paul, and he went home with the boys for the shower I insisted he take.

"Thank you," one of the nurses murmured as she showed me to Tori's bedside in the intensive care unit. "He needed a break."

I'd tried to prepare myself for what Tori might look like, but I'd done a woefully inadequate job. IV lines ran into both of her arms, and a tube helped her to breathe. The huge cast on her left leg dwarfed her, and part of her hair had been shaved off where they'd operated to relieve the pressure on her brain. And she was pale, so pale. If not for the sign with her name above the bed, I'd never have recognised her. The sight reminded me of my last days with Momma, and I shuddered.

Hours passed as I talked to Tori, starting with stories of our childhood. Those memories of Baysville were my best ones. Then I told her how much the boys missed her, and how Fin broke Robbie's Lego model this morning and Robbie threw what was left of it at him. Finally, I told her my secrets.

"Nick makes me come alive, Tori. I fall asleep thinking about him, and he's the first thing on my mind in the morning. I can't concentrate, and I can't even breathe when I'm around him. All those years with Billy, and I never felt a flicker of what I feel for Nick now. And the worst of it is, he's got a girlfriend, even if he wasn't a hundred miles out of my league."

Through my monologue, the machines kept up their monotonous beeping, the rhythmic hissing of the ventilator the background music to my words. Tori didn't stir.

Paul returned as dusk fell, and I took the boys back home. What sort of life was this for them, shuttling back and forth to the hospital morning and evening? They'd begun to look bored, but Nick's suggestion of going out for burgers cheered them up. Two hours later, he had to carry Fin to the car while I took Robbie's hand.

"I think we wore them out," he said as they slept between us on the back seat.

"You're good with them."

"I had no idea what to do when Fin wouldn't let go of the waitress's skirt."

"Do you ever want kids?" I blurted, then immediately regretted it.

Nick said so little about himself, and I'd just crossed the line, big time. Would he be angry?

"My lifestyle's not really compatible with kids. I work too much, and I'd never want to be the kind of father my dad was to me."

"What about Emmy?"

He looked at me strangely. "What *about* Emmy?"

"Does she want kids?"

He laughed. "Emmy hasn't got a maternal bone in her body. She was at the birth of her nephew a few months ago, and it's the only time I've seen her truly panic-stricken."

"That's a shame. I think you'd make a great dad."

Nick went quiet after that, and the next morning, I found

the spare blankets folded neatly at one end of the couch with a note propped on top of them.

> *Lara,*
> *I've had to go to Paris. Back in a week or so. Call Nadia if you need anything.*
> *N*

I had an awful feeling I'd scared him off.

# 29

## LARA

"She's awake! She just opened her eyes." Jubilation and relief came through loud and clear as Paul more-or-less shouted down the phone line three days later.

"How is she? Is she speaking? Does she...? Does she remember?"

The doctors' main fear was that Tori would suffer from memory loss after her head injury.

"She told me off for letting Fin eat a lollipop and grumbled because she'd missed her appointment at the hair salon." His voice dropped. "But I think she was only trying to put a brave face on things."

"You told her about the baby?"

"She already knew. As soon as she woke up, she knew."

"I'm so sorry." Words were always inadequate in these situations.

"We'll get through it. At least Tori's going to be okay."

I shared his relief. For days I'd been dreaming of darkness and death, but that night, I went back to visions of topless Nick relaxing on a lounge chair. I knew which I preferred. And I tried to stay upbeat when I visited Tori in the hospital.

She spent two more days in the intensive care unit before they moved her to a regular ward, and she hated every second of it.

"I'm so bored." She tossed down one of the magazines I'd brought her and stared straight ahead. "There's nothing to do except think, and I hate that too."

She'd never been one for sitting around, and doing so only made her more melancholy.

"Do you want me to bring you anything? Books? Something to eat?"

"A book might help. Something juicy. And could you pick up a big bar of Dairy Milk?"

"Of course."

"Don't tell Paul about the chocolate, though. I always moan at him for eating too much of the stuff."

I giggled. "Scout's honour."

"You weren't in the Scouts."

"Yes, but you know, if I was..."

I returned that afternoon, laden with a couple of board games, half a candy store, and a stack of raunchy romances. I flicked through the top one, and the heroine...she sure wasn't shy.

"Do people really do that stuff?" I whispered.

"If you get lucky. Nobody's ever tied you up?"

"No! I mean, how would you...? I don't even...?"

She rolled her eyes. "You need to be more adventurous. Just don't do what Paul did. He couldn't get the knots undone, and Robbie had hidden the scissors. Paul had to nip down to Tesco's for another pair, and his mother was due round any second."

"No way."

"Yes way."

We dissolved into laughter, earning a dirty look from the old lady in the next bed. Then Tori burst into tears.

By day four on the ward, Tori was good friends with all the nurses, and by day five, she'd organised a Scrabble tournament for everyone. She still had bad moments, but not quite so many. On day six, I found her whizzing around on a pair of crutches, and she tried to convince me to help her make a run for it but I wasn't that brave. And on day seven, the doctors gave in and let her go.

Day eight? On day eight, Nick came back.

I hadn't heard a peep from him since he left, even when I tried to call and give him the good news about Tori. He'd diverted his phone to Nadia, who informed me he was working and couldn't be disturbed.

"Could you pass the message to him?"

"Sure. Is there anything else?"

Yes. I missed him. "No, nothing else."

The next day I'd received a single text message:

NICK

Great to hear about Tori. Don't forget to call Nadia if you need anything. N.

That was it. Nothing to say where he was or when he planned to come back. Or even *if* he planned to come back.

I couldn't deny I was a little miffed, but when I thought about it logically, why should he call me? He had no obligation to keep me informed of his plans. If he wanted to jet off to the moon for three months without a word, he was perfectly entitled to do so.

He was just my boss.

And a kind boss at that.

Then he turned up at Tori's door that evening. She

answered it, hobbling on crutches while I stirred the spaghetti sauce.

"You must be Tori."

Nick's smooth voice drifted through to the kitchen, and I promptly dropped the spoon. *Well done, Lara.* I got into the living room as he kissed Tori on the cheek, and she went redder than the tomatoes I'd just chopped. Uh-oh. From the look on her face, I was in trouble.

"Want a beer, mate?" Paul asked.

"Sure. And I brought these for your wife."

A huge bouquet of flowers and a box of expensive chocolates—the same brand as he'd bought me the other day with the gold-embossed box and a velvet ribbon tied around the outside. Tori accepted them graciously then prodded me back into the kitchen with her crutch.

"You little minx," she hissed. "You said he was easy on the eye, but you didn't say he was, well, *that*."

"That's because there aren't words for it."

She picked up a magazine and started fanning herself with it. "I can't believe you work for him. And he pays you! I'd do it for free."

"Calm down. He's just a normal person when you get to know him. Apart from being obscenely rich, obviously."

"Lara, he's Prince freaking Charming. And he's here to see you. You!"

"*You* were the one who got the chocolates. Now let me out before he wonders what on earth I'm doing in here."

"Wait, your hair's coming loose at the back. Do you need to borrow mascara?"

"No! Just let me out."

I found Nick sitting on the couch, drinking beer out of the can and chatting with Paul about soccer like they were old friends rather than two guys who'd met a handful of times under less than ideal circumstances. Yet another thing I'd noticed about Nick—he had no airs and graces, no arrogance. He fitted in anywhere.

He motioned for me to come and sit next to him, and like an obedient little puppy, I did. I'd have humped his leg too if it wouldn't have been wildly inappropriate.

"I didn't know you were coming back today."

"Neither did I until a couple of hours ago, so I figured I'd surprise you. Sorry I was away for so long. I had to do a favour for a friend, and it took longer than I thought."

"It doesn't matter." *He's the boss, remember.* "And it's a nice surprise. Do you want dinner? I'm making spaghetti bolognese."

"Sounds good."

Fin and Robbie came barrelling down the stairs. Well, Fin skip-hopped as fast as he could with his leg still in plaster, and Robbie sprinted past and threw himself at Nick. *Oof.* As Robbie landed, Nick's face screwed up in pain.

"Robbie! Be careful." I pulled him away and parked him on the couch. "Sit over here, little one."

"I'm not little anymore. Fin's little."

"Okay then, not so little one."

"Can I play with Nick?"

I glanced across and saw Nick standing stiffly by the sideboard, and he didn't look comfortable. Had Robbie hurt him?

"Not right now, okay?" I hustled over to Nick. "Are you all right?"

"Yeah, I'm fine. Don't worry about it."

Really? He gave me a grimace-like smile, so I had to let it go, but I kept an eye on him as I served up the food. What were those pills he swallowed? Painkillers? I'd have to keep a closer watch on Robbie. He didn't realise his own strength sometimes.

A game of Monopoly followed dinner, and I'd been sent

to jail four times and gone bankrupt twice by the time we decided to call it a night.

"What time is it?" I asked as Paul helped Tori up the stairs.

Nick glanced at his fancy watch. "Almost midnight. Are you still staying here?"

"On the couch. Do you want to take it? I can always sleep on the floor."

"I'm sleeping at a friend's place. Want to join me? I know from experience that the couch is as comfortable as a bag of rocks."

True, but the worst part was five people trying to share one bathroom, especially when two of them were in plaster. It had been a logistical nightmare for the last few mornings. We needed one of those numbered ticket machines that delis had, not to mention a bigger hot water tank. Tori's only did two-and-a-half showers no matter how quick you were.

"Are you sure your friend won't mind?"

"Not one bit. It's only me there tonight, anyway."

"In that case, yes please. I could do with catching up on some rest."

## 30

## LARA

When Nick said he was staying at a friend's place, I'd imagined an apartment somewhere, albeit a reasonably upscale one. But twenty minutes later, the cab pulled up outside a freaking mansion. I didn't know a whole lot about London property prices, but it had to be worth millions.

The entrance hall was bigger than my whole home and done out in cream with a huge multi-coloured glass chandelier hanging in the middle. That was a work of art in its own right. Staircases swept up both sides, and Nick took the right-hand one, leading me to the third floor.

"My room's this one. All the others on this landing are empty, so pick whichever you prefer."

I opened each door in turn. This was voyeurism meets HGTV—property porn at its finest.

Did people actually use these bedrooms? They looked more like movie sets or those fancy mock-up boudoirs they had in furniture showrooms that nobody ever slept in. Mint green, earth tones, fifty shades of grey, something futuristic with hot pink feathers everywhere. In the end, I settled on a pretty room done out in pink, mainly because of the antique claw-foot tub in the centre of the bathroom. It was fit for a princess, although I fell far short of that.

The mattress felt like a cushion of air, and even though my eyes popped open at six the next morning, I felt re-energised and ready to start the day. Was Nick up yet? I listened carefully, but the only sound was the occasional car on the road outside. Good. Because I had a plan—I'd try to find the kitchen in this place, then make him breakfast.

Nick said we were the only people there, so I just threw on the robe I found hanging on the back of the bathroom door and headed downstairs. Where was the kitchen? Several false starts led me to three separate living rooms, a music room with a grand piano, a dining room that would seat at least twenty, and—I'm not even kidding—a freaking ballroom. The kitchen itself was huge, fitted with the kind of equipment that could easily be used to cater a banquet. Actually, having seen the ballroom, I had no doubt that was exactly what the owner used it for.

Hmm, what to make… I selected a pan from the rack and found a stack of plates in a warming drawer. Opening the giant fridge was like taking a step into the Arctic, and I half expected to see a family of Eskimos and a couple of polar bears camping out at the back. Bread… Where was the bread? Wow, I had the choice of wholemeal, bloomer, sourdough, or soda bread. Or…what was that? It looked like a loaf, but when I tapped it on the corner of the counter, it felt more like a brick. I settled on plain wholemeal, then moved onto the eggs. Quail, duck, or hen? Or… Hang on? I picked out something the size of my head. Pterodactyl?

The door clicked open behind me, and I cursed under my breath. Darn it! I'd hoped to make breakfast before Nick got up.

"Good morning. I'm just…"

I screamed and dropped the giant egg at the sight of the stranger. The thing shattered across the floor, and the slimy yolk landed on my foot.

"Sorry! I'm so sorry."

"These things happen." The grey-haired lady reached for a roll of paper towel and began blotting. "I'm guessing from your reaction that Nick didn't tell you I'd be coming in?"

"No, he said it was just us. I'm sorry I dropped... I don't even know what it was."

"An ostrich egg, dear. But don't worry—I need to mop the floor later today in any case. You must be Nick's friend Lara?"

"Housekeeper. I'm his housekeeper."

"When you're here, you're his friend. I'm the housekeeper for this place." She wiped one hand on her apron and held it out for me to shake. "Ruth."

I cringed at my sweaty palms. "Hi."

"Emmy was right. You're a pretty little thing."

She said that? "You know Emmy?"

"Well, of course, dear. This is her home."

Holy fudge! She owned this place? I'd guessed she had money, but this was a whole other league. Those clubs must be doing really, really well. No wonder she was dating Nick— she was exactly the type of person I'd expect him to be with.

Not me. Never a person like me. Even though when I was alone with him, the way he treated me, the way he looked after me, I could almost believe differently.

*Lara, stop it*! Nick wasn't mine and never would be. I needed to give myself a mental kick up the bottom and stop wishing.

And I also needed to finish making Nick's breakfast. Ruth waved me away when I tried to help her clean up, so I grabbed two normal eggs from the fridge and whipped up an omelette. Once I'd added toast, coffee, and fresh orange juice to the tray, I carried the whole lot towards the stairs.

Ruth stopped me in my tracks. "Hold on, Lara, has nobody shown you where the lift is?"

An elevator? Of course there was an elevator. Silly me.

Upstairs, I balanced the tray in one hand and tapped on Nick's door. No answer. I knocked again, a bit louder, and was rewarded with a muffled, "What's up?"

"I brought you breakfast."

"Door's unlocked."

It turned out I'd been missing a trick. If I'd known Nick slept without a shirt on, I'd have made sure to bring him breakfast in bed every single day, just to enjoy the view.

When I hesitated in the doorway, he motioned me forward, and as I walked closer, he straightened and the sheet slipped down towards his waist. What the...? The dishes shifted dangerously close to one side as the tray wobbled, and coffee slopped over the edge of the mug.

"What happened to you?" I whispered. Nick's entire left side was a mass of bruises. No wonder he'd winced when Robbie landed on him yesterday.

"Oh, that? It's nothing. Probably just a cracked rib. It'll heal up in a couple of weeks. Are those eggs?"

How could he brush off a cracked rib like that? I knew how painful they could be—from experience, unfortunately. Billy had busted mine on two separate occasions. The first when he was drunk for no apparent reason other than I happened to be there, and the second when I accidentally burned his dinner.

"Yes, eggs. But surely that must hurt?"

"I've had worse. I wouldn't say no to some Advil, though."

"Of course. I'll be right back."

"And where's your breakfast? Or are you expecting me to eat up here on my own?"

Downstairs, I fetched myself a slice of toast and a juice,

although in truth the only thing I wanted to eat was Nick. Although very gently, what with all those bruises. How the frick did he hurt himself like that? Ruth hunted out a package of painkillers, and I hurried back upstairs, only to find Nick had put a shirt on. Darn it. I perched on the edge of the armchair opposite the bed while he propped himself up against the pillow.

"D'you know, I don't think anyone's ever brought me breakfast in bed before. Feels strange. Like I'm an invalid or something."

"Well, you kind of are. Even if I didn't know that before I started cooking."

"Nah, this isn't much. If I had bones sticking through skin, maybe."

"How did you do it, anyway?"

Billy had made me watch the second Terminator movie once, and there was a part at the end where the creepy liquid robot morphed through all the people he'd killed. Nick's face reminded me of that, except with emotions. He went through nonchalance, panic, guilt, and finally settled on resolve.

"Do you really want to know?"

"Yes."

"Okay then." He took a deep breath. "I was in Eastern Europe, parachuting into the compound of a suspected arms dealer at two in the morning, when I had a coming together with a tree that was bigger and uglier than I am."

For a moment, I stared at him in confusion. Then I realised he must be joking. I threw a pillow at him, aiming carefully to avoid his sore bits.

"Nick, stop messing around! How did you really do it?"

He held his hands up. "Okay, you got me. I was trying to get something down from a high shelf, and the ladder slipped."

"Oh gosh, that's awful. You should've asked somebody to hold the bottom."

"I'll remember that for next time. So, enough about my lack of balance. What are your plans for today?"

"I promised to help Tori with the boys. Fin and Robbie are going back to school, and she's anticipating a fuss. They're normally so good, but the past few weeks have been hard on them."

"So are you free for lunch? Tori too, if she wants to come."

"I'm sure we could be." And Tori would probably faint at the idea of going for lunch with Nick, who she'd taken to calling Mr. Hot Stuff. "Don't you need to work today?"

"I haven't got much going on. Just a video call with the US that I can do from here." He took a sip of coffee and sighed. "I'm gonna have to think about heading back home at some point in the near future."

"You should've said so. I didn't mean to keep you away from work. Or Emmy."

"Emmy's happy to have me out of her hair, I'm sure. And I'm good to stay for a few more days. But there're meetings at the office next week that I need to be around for."

"The funeral's tomorrow. Tori wants to say a proper goodbye, and I think planning it helped her grieve." That and interrogating me about my love life, or rather, the lack of it. "I promised to help with the food, but I could leave the day after that? She's mobile now, and with the boys at school, she'll be okay."

"You don't have to come back with me. You can stay if you want."

"Uh, I kind of do need to go home. I have a wedding to attend next week."

Which I totally should have mentioned before. Shoot.

"A wedding?"

"Yes. A friend in my hometown's getting married, and I'm

a bridesmaid, so I really have to go even though I don't want to. But I promise I'll make up all the missed days when I get back." I put my head in my hands. "I'm the worst housekeeper in the history of the world."

"Are you crazy? I'm not even in the damn house right now. And you saw how I used to live. You honestly think I'm gonna be worried by a layer of dust? Tell me, why don't you want to go to the wedding? I thought women loved weddings?"

"Not this one. I have to wear a shocking pink dress so wide it can be seen from space, Missy's mother-in-law moonlights as a dominatrix, and the best man turns being a pervert into an art form and smells like old socks."

Nick started laughing, but to me, it wasn't funny. It was my life.

"I'll spend the entire reception having to fend him off. He's already told me his favourite wedding tradition is the one where the best man gets to have his wicked way with the bridesmaid."

"Wicked way? Which century was he born in?"

"Clearly the wrong one."

"Does your invitation have a plus one?"

"Yes, but I don't."

"You do now. I'll save your virtue from the wicked scoundrel, fair lady. Plus I've got to see this dress."

# 31

## LARA

I almost couldn't believe it—this was really happening. Nick was coming to Missy's wedding with me. Not only that, he'd promised to take care of the travel arrangements, which meant no trip on the bus.

L... Dare I say it? Lucky me.

I'd already finished packing. It only took me half an hour, mainly because I didn't own much. Other girls might have agonised over what to take, but I simply stuffed my entire life into a suitcase.

Nick hadn't said which car we'd be riding in, so I wheeled my case into the hallway and left it beside the door. The tiny bag looked ridiculously out of place. Adler House called for a matching set of monogrammed leather luggage, preferably filled with designer clothes and a hundred pairs of shoes.

When Nick ran out of the house after an early breakfast, he'd said he wouldn't be back until lunchtime, so when the front door flew open mid-morning, I nearly jumped out of my skin.

"Right, I've come to help. Sorry I'm late. One of the designers promised my order would arrive yesterday, and it didn't. Some pathetic excuse about the plane breaking down on the runway in Milan." Bradley dumped a mountain of garment bags on the chair in the hallway and headed for the door again. "Can you give me a hand with the rest of this stuff?"

"Uh, sure."

Me and a small army of mules. Bradley had packed so much into his Ford Explorer he could have opened his own boutique and had enough left over for New York fashion week.

"Bradley, what *is* all this stuff?"

"Clothes." He rolled his eyes. "Duh. Here, take this bag inside."

"Doesn't Nick have enough already?"

It'd taken me ages to wash and iron everything. *Weeks*. He could have worn a different outfit every day for a year and still not gotten through them all.

"Oh, I've only brought a few things for Nick. A new suit, more T-shirts, and a bundle of stuff he left at Emmy's that needed to be brought home. The rest is yours. Whatever fits, anyway. Anything that doesn't, I can exchange. Now, get a move-on. You've got to try it all on so I can pack for you both."

"But I've already packed." I pointed at my case.

"What's that?"

"My luggage?"

"Where's the rest?"

"That's it. I've only got one suitcase."

Bradley laughed like it was the funniest thing he'd ever heard. "But how can you do a wedding with one suitcase? It's logistically impossible." He ticked off on his fingers. "You need an outfit for before the wedding, one for the church, and another for the reception. Plus backups in case someone's worn something similar. Then there are shoes and a bag for each, coordinating wraps, and an umbrella in case it rains. And you can't go without jewellery and the right make-up."

Was he serious?

"I'm helping to organise things, so I'll wear jeans beforehand. Then I'm a bridesmaid, and Missy's picked out the most hideous dress in the world for me. I'm hoping to change for the reception, but I already have a dress for that." A dress that I'd bought on eBay for seven dollars with the tag still on, but best not to mention that to Bradley. "Also, I can't afford to buy new clothes."

And speaking of money... Darn it. With Tori's drama and then the wedding, I'd clean forgotten to pay the most recent instalment of Momma's medical bill. Visions of interest charges danced in front of my eyes like glittering daggers.

"Bradley, I need to make a phone call."

"Well, hurry up, sweet cheeks. We've got far too much to do already."

I slipped out to the kitchen and dialled. How could I have let something so important fall between the cracks? Maybe Nick could show me how to set the alarm on this fancy phone so it wouldn't happen again.

"How can I help?" the lady asked.

I launched into a lengthy explanation, followed by an apology. "So can I send you a cheque today? Will that be okay?"

"Miss Reynolds, I don't understand what you're saying. The balance on your account is nil. Why would you want to send a cheque?"

"Because my account balance definitely isn't nil, and I don't want to get more penalty charges. I can pay a thousand dollars off now."

"Ma'am, there's definitely no balance. Your account was paid in full over a month ago."

"There's been a mistake, because there's no way I paid all that. I don't have that kind of money."

"Well, someone's paid it, that's for sure."

"Can you tell me who?"

"Sorry, data protection rules say I can't give you that information."

"But it's my account."

"Yes, but if it wasn't you who made the payment, I'm not authorised to discuss the details of it."

"This is crazy. I didn't make the payment, and when you realise you've made a mistake, you'll hit me with extra charges, won't you?"

"Ma'am, we most certainly won't. You don't owe us anything. I'll send you a statement in the mail to confirm."

What the heck should I say? It was like arguing with a robot, and I could hear Bradley muttering in the hallway.

"Okay, fine."

"Is there anything else I can help you with today, ma'am?"

"No."

Great, just great. Something had clearly gone wrong with their system, and now I had the nightmare of sorting it out to look forward to when I got back.

"Are you done now?" Bradley grabbed my arm and dragged me up to a spare bedroom. Wow. It looked as if the Unabomber had been on a rampage through Bergdorf Goodman. "You need to start trying these on."

"I already told you I can't afford all this."

"Well, it's a good thing you don't have to, isn't it? Nick's playing fairy godfather. And he told me to ignore any protests you might make, so there's no point in even bothering to start."

"But, Bradley..."

"Shhh! Get undressed, woman!" He fanned himself. "Ooh, now that's something I'd never normally say."

"No, really—"

"Don't waste time arguing. Nick likes his girlfriends to dress nicely. This little lot won't even put a wrinkle in his finances, so just take the clothes, look pretty, and enjoy yourself. If I was going out with that delicious piece of man candy, I know I would."

"But I'm not Nick's girlfriend! I'm just his housekeeper. And what about Emmy?"

"What *about* Emmy? Hey, it's not as if she's together with Nick anymore. And the whole girlfriend thing? Only a matter of time. We're running a pool at work, so if you could hold off for two more weeks, I'd be grateful."

What was Bradley talking about? Had Nick really split up with Emmy? On Monday, I'd seen her walk out of his bedroom dressed in a silk robe with her hair wet from the shower.

"Is everything okay?" I'd asked. "Would you like some breakfast?"

She'd laughed her deep, dirty laugh. "Excuse the attire. Me and Nick got a bit hot and sweaty this morning. And yes, I'd love a coffee."

That was hardly what I'd expect from an ex. How could so much have changed in two days? Bradley must have made a mistake.

"I'm definitely not—"

He threw a silky pink dress at me. "Try. It. On."

I attempted to protest again, but Bradley cut me off every time. What was I supposed to do? A lump came into my throat because the clothes really were beautiful, and the part of me that thought of Nick every time I went to sleep or woke up or closed my eyes or breathed wanted to look worthy of standing next to him.

Bradley's description of him being a delicious piece of man candy was right on the money, and in my old clothes, I was just one of those squidgy candies you found covered in lint, long forgotten in the bottom of a pocket.

So I tried the things on. How did Bradley choose clothes that fitted so well without having me with him? Even the shoes slipped on like they'd been made for me. As I took each item off and passed it around the bathroom door to Bradley, he packed, and by the time we'd finished, I had four bulging suitcases. He'd thrown almost everything from my original bag into an empty closet, looking disgusted as he did so.

Nick's needs didn't escape his attention either, and we'd just dragged all six suitcases down to the hallway when a strange *whomp-whomp-whomp* came from outside.

"Oh good, he's finally back," Bradley said.

"Do you mean Nick? What's that noise?"

"Nick's helicopter," he said, giving me an "isn't it obvious?" look.

A helicopter? Nick had a freaking helicopter? Of course he did.

# 32

## LARA

Not only was there a silver and black helicopter settling onto the lawn, but Nick was sitting in the pilot's seat. Next thing I knew, he'd be donning his underwear on the outside of his freaking pants.

"Did you pack Nick's cape?" I muttered to Bradley.

"Huh?"

Two minutes later, Nick strode into the hallway and eyed up the luggage.

"Bradley, you know we're going away for four days, right?"

The smaller man scratched his chin. "You're right. Maybe I should have packed more."

"No!" Nick and I shouted at the exact same time.

"I'm sure we can manage with what we've got," I added hastily. "Thank you for all your help."

The cases took up the entire rear cabin of the helicopter, and the door only just closed. Missy was gonna have a cow.

"Good thing there's only two of us," Nick said.

Bradley ignored him. "I'll lock up. Don't be late."

Nick settled himself behind the controls while I fumbled

with my safety harness in the passenger side. My second helicopter ride, but I still hadn't gotten over my nerves.

"Need a hand?" Nick asked.

"I'm fine."

I wasn't. The stupid buckle wouldn't go in the stupid hole, and Nick leaned across to help me despite my protest.

"Stop biting your lip."

"Sorry. How long have you been flying?"

"I'm not gonna crash."

"I didn't mean..." Okay, I did. "It's just that I've only been in a helicopter that one time before, and..."

He reached over to squeeze my hand. "I'm sorry too. I keep forgetting you haven't flown much." He started the engine. "Twelve years. I've been flying helicopters for twelve years, and conditions today are good. It should be a smooth trip."

I forced myself to breathe. "How long will it take to get there?"

"We're not going all the way in this. It's too far, and we'd have to refuel."

"Then what...?"

"We'll switch to a plane at Silver Springs Airfield, then land near Indianapolis. Should take about two hours in total. Bradley's arranged a car for us at the other end."

How did Nick make that sound so normal? Missy would totally freak. Like me, she'd barely travelled, and she and Clyde couldn't even afford a honeymoon yet. Wedding this year, take a trip next year—that was what they'd decided. Missy had spent months talking about the Caribbean, so my wedding gift to them was a set of matching luggage monogrammed with their new initials. I'd arranged for it to be delivered after the wedding, but I'd stuck a picture of it in a card to give them on the big day.

Down below, tiny buildings and a patchwork of trees and

fields rushed by, and I couldn't help smiling. This might not have been LA, but I still had Nick next to me, and I was *in a freaking helicopter*. And before I knew it, we'd landed.

"Okay?" Nick asked as he helped me down to the ground.

"I think I'm starting to like flying."

"Glad to hear it. Your next chariot awaits." He pointed to the jet parked nearby.

"Is that the same plane as last time? It looks smaller."

"No, this is a Learjet 85. The last one was a Bombardier Global 8000. This one doesn't have the same range."

"Is it yours?"

"No, I borrowed it."

So there were some limits to his wealth. Still, owning a helicopter was quite enough.

"Boy, you must know a lot of people with planes."

"This one and the last one actually belong to the same person, believe it or not. He's pretty generous. I've got a twin-prop, but it's in LA."

What was a twin-prop? I didn't want to admit I didn't know, so I just nodded. Mental note: look it up on the internet later.

Not the same plane, but the same pilot. He smiled and nodded as we climbed on board, and a flight attendant handed me a glass of bubbly. This was too much.

"I'm surprised you're not flying this too," I said to Nick.

"Sometimes I do, but it's easier to use a pilot."

"I was joking. You mean you *do* know how to fly this?"

He nodded. "But I usually work on flights. Not enough hours in the day and all that."

"Do you get much time off?"

"This is the first proper break I've taken in five years." His grin was more dangerous than his smile. "Normally, I end up answering emails, but this weekend I'm off-limits unless there's an emergency."

I held up my champagne. "Here's to your first relaxing break in ages. I might even fetch you breakfast in bed again."

Nick picked up his own glass and clinked it against mine. "I'm gonna hold you to that, baby."

The vehicle waiting for us turned out to be a two-seater Mercedes sports car. I looked at the tiny trunk, then back at the luggage Brett had stacked on the tarmac, and one into the other didn't compute.

"Uh, how...?"

Nick pointed past me.

Problem solved. A cargo van pulled up, two men hopped out and picked up all the suitcases, then poof—they vanished. That was actually quite embarrassing.

"Forget I asked."

"Bradley's a master of organisation."

He'd also booked us into a ridiculously extravagant hotel, in a suite, no less. It had two bedrooms, a sitting room, a dining room, and a small kitchenette, not to mention its own bar and a giant TV. There was even a roof terrace and a hot tub with a jungle's worth of foliage arranged around it, all designed to shield the occupants from people like me. An expensive paradise and one usually out of my reach unless I was pushing a vacuum cleaner.

"What's the plan?" Nick looked longingly at the hot tub. "Should I order lunch?"

"I promised Missy I'd help, but you can stay here."

"If you're helping, I'm helping. What do we need to do?"

I checked the list of instructions she'd sent me earlier. "First, we have to pick up the dresses. Actually, that's second. You need to meet Missy before we do that."

"Sure."

"If she tries to interrogate you, just let me do the talking."

"Okay."

"And if she offers you any homemade appetisers, say you're allergic."

He sucked in a breath. "Got it."

When we drew up outside her house in the Mercedes, the drapes twitched, and before we could walk up the path, Missy flung the front door open.

"Should've brought earplugs," Nick whispered as she squealed loud enough to wake the dead three counties over.

A group of small children on bicycles paused, and a man watering his garden two houses along stared as I put a finger to my lips.

"Shhh."

But Missy was having none of it. "Ohmigosh! He's hotter than all his cars. And speaking of hot, how the heck did you get on celebgossip.com with Armand Taylor? His arm was touching you! Tell me you haven't taken a shower since?"

"I had to. I got all sweaty dancing." What a lovely picture to put in Nick's mind. "Wait a second—I was on the internet?"

"Don't worry, you looked real pretty." She turned to Nick. "As do you, stud muffin. And the pair of you make a lovely couple."

"Missy, we're not—"

"Look at the time! We're late. Theresa hates it when people turn up late."

Theresa herself was waiting at the door of the bridal shop when we drew up in Missy's minivan. Nick had taken the front seat while I got wedged in the back beside Missy's nephew's car seat and six boxes of fairy lights, and even though she drove sedately, I still felt sick by the time we arrived. Which dress had Missy chosen? When I asked, she wouldn't tell me. It would be a surprise, she said. I'd love it.

Would I? *Would I?* If she'd picked the one with the giant train, I'd end up with a hernia trying to get Missy to the altar.

My heart hammered as I climbed out of the van and trudged inside. Missy's fashion sense wasn't the only reason I was nervous. The only thing more awkward than going to a bridal shop with a man I really, really liked but couldn't have was doing so while keeping one eye out for the ex who'd tried to kill me.

Then it got worse. Two assistants struggled in with the mother of all garment bags, knees buckling under the strain, and the true horror of the situation became clear.

The butterfly dress. Missy had chosen the butterfly dress, but that wasn't where the nightmare ended.

"Theresa added a train and rhinestones as well. It's like three dresses in one. Isn't it something else?" Missy reached out and touched it reverently.

Oh, it was something else all right. Nick let out a snort of laughter and hurriedly turned it into a cough while I tried to wipe the look of shock from my face and plaster on a smile.

"It's lovely. Uh, what's that?"

Another giant garment bag, another monstrosity of a dress, and this one was mine. It was even more hideous than I remembered because Missy had convinced Theresa to cover it in rhinestones as well.

Please, somebody kill me now. Where was Billy when I needed him?

"Now we match!" Missy clapped her hands in glee. "Isn't it great?"

"Fantastic."

Beside me, Nick was struggling. I elbowed him in the side, but his lips kept twitching like he had a tic disorder.

"Stop it!"

Missy looked at him, and he took a hasty step back. "Excuse me. I have to make a call to, uh, to my stockbroker. Really important."

He hightailed it out of the store, leaving me to get stuffed into my dress by Theresa. Was it too late to send Nick back to Virginia? I'd happily take the bus home if it meant he didn't have to see me looking like an extra from *My Big Fat American Gypsy Wedding*.

"How does it fit?" Theresa asked.

"It's a little loose."

Running around after Fin and Robbie had helped me to lose a few pounds.

"Don't worry about that, hun. I'll be at the church tomorrow morning to make some quick adjustments. I can't wait to see you two princesses walk down the aisle."

Great, yet another witness to my impending humiliation. Would we even *fit* down the aisle?

"And you can make the top tighter?"

"Sure I can. Don't look so worried, hun—you'll remember the day for the rest of your life."

That's what I was afraid of.

After the dresses, we picked up the cake. Missy had gone for a four-tier sponge, pink and covered in glitter. The bride and groom figures on the top tier must have been custom made, because the bride wore a tiny replica of the butterfly dress, complete with a train that flowed all the way down the top three layers, and the groom bore a remarkable resemblance to the Michelin Man.

Next, we stopped off at the church hall to check on the reception preparations, and the place looked more like a carnival. Basically, if it was pink or sparkly, Missy had bought it. All of it, probably within a four-state radius. It was just...well, really I had no words. Even Bradley would have been speechless.

When Nick and I finally got into the Mercedes at the end of the day, he calmly put the car in gear, drove around the corner, and then pulled over. We looked at each other. Then the laughter came. I'd never laughed so much in my whole freaking life. Tears streamed down my face as Nick doubled over the steering wheel.

"Tell me, did this day really happen? Do women actually like that stuff?"

"Most women, no. Missy, yes."

"Fucking hell, it's a good thing Bradley isn't here. We'd be giving him CPR. Those dresses..."

"It's okay for *you* to laugh. You don't have to wear one of them tomorrow. Everyone's gonna be staring at me."

"Hey, don't worry. If it helps, I'll just imagine you without it."

"I'm not sure you visualising my wobbly bits would be an improvement."

"Shit, that came out totally wrong." He put his head in his hands. "And you've got curves, not wobbly bits." He turned back to me, and his dimples popped out again. "Did you see the figurines on that abomination of a cake? Does the groom really look like the Stay Puft Marshmallow Man?"

I nodded and dissolved into laughter again. Maybe our trip out hadn't been so awkward after all.

# 33

## LARA

The morning of the wedding dawned bright and clear. Which was good, because Missy was determined to release two doves outside after the ceremony, and rain would spoil the effect.

The plan called for us to get ready at Missy's house, and right now, I was standing very, very still as Theresa made some last-minute adjustments to my dress involving a needle, which she waved around alarmingly as she talked to Missy. I held my breath as the sharp tip narrowly missed my arm.

"Uh, Theresa? Does it need to be this tight?"

"You want it to stay up, don't you, hun? Best not to take any chances."

Of course I wanted it to freaking stay up. The only thing worse than wearing this dress would be not wearing it, so I sucked in my stomach and lived with the discomfort.

Once we were dressed, the next challenge was getting into the wedding car. Missy had pushed the boat out and rented a stretch Hummer—in pink—but no matter how big the car was, the door still wasn't very wide and the dresses were. To add to the problem, Missy's bodice was decidedly lower cut than I remembered it being, which didn't lend itself to careless tugging.

"Did Theresa make adjustments to the top of that dress as well?" I asked.

Missy grinned and pointed at her boobs. "God wouldn't have given me these if he intended for me to keep them covered up the whole time."

I wasn't sure that falling out of her wedding dress in church was exactly what he'd had in mind, but as Missy always told me, God moved in mysterious ways.

In the end, Missy's mom climbed into the Hummer and pulled, and I shoved from behind, just like Rabbit did that time Winnie the Pooh got stuck in his house.

"Push harder, Lara," Missy begged as she tried to wriggle through the door.

"I'm pushing as hard as I can."

All at once, the dress gave way and Missy landed inside. I almost pitched onto my knees, but Nick caught me and half lifted, half shoved me into the car as well.

So far, so good.

Missy's mom snapped away with her camera, capturing our heads and arms sticking out of miles and miles of satin and chiffon for posterity, and all too soon, it was time for our trip down the aisle. The train weighed a ton, and bending forwards to pick it up was impossible. I had to do an awkward little curtsey and pray nothing ripped. My own dress was so tight I could barely breathe, and when we reached the altar, my face must have been as pink as my outfit.

Still, the way Missy's face lit up when she saw Clyde standing at the top of the steps, looking slightly uncomfortable in an ill-fitting white suit with half a florist's display stuck in his buttonhole, made all the effort worth it.

"Will the bride and groom step forward?" the pastor asked.

Oh, thank goodness. That was my cue to sit down. I stumbled over to my allotted space on the front pew and tried to sink gracefully onto the seat. *Tried*. The dress was so big I slid off the edge, and only Nick's quick thinking kept me from landing on the floor. He clung onto my waist for the whole ceremony, smirking on occasion, while I willed myself not to melt into a gooey puddle at the feel of his arms around me.

Then Clyde and Missy were husband and wife, and everyone breathed a collective sigh of happiness. Well, everyone apart from me, because inhaling was a problem, but the sentiment was there.

The reception didn't start for an hour, and after I'd grimaced for the official photographer, desperation set in. I had to get out of this freaking dress. Quite apart from the breathing issue, I needed to use the bathroom. Where the heck was Theresa?

"Nick, have you seen Theresa anywhere?"

"Theresa?"

"From the bridal shop. In her forties, blonde hair, and a dark suntan."

"You mean the peroxide blonde with skin like leather and an indecently short skirt?"

"That's the one."

"She got in a convertible and drove off ten minutes ago."

"Did she say when she was coming back?"

"No, she didn't say a thing. Why? Is there a problem?"

"I need to get out of this dress. Like, I *really* need to get out of this dress. And I really, really need to find the little girls' room."

"Can't one of the other ladies unzip you?"

"Theresa sewed me into it. It's a nightmare! I'm gonna be stuck in it forever. When I die, they'll have to give me a super-sized casket so it'll all fit in."

"What about scissors? Someone must have a pair. Most of these women are carrying purses so heavy it could be an Olympic sport."

"They were handing out free champagne before the ceremony. Half of them can hardly stand. If I let them near me with scissors, I'll end up scarred for life."

As if on cue, a lady wearing a rather adventurous pair of heels tripped over and narrowly missed landing in the font.

"*Shit*. Okay, wait here."

He hurried out of the church, then came back a few minutes later carrying a small bag.

"What's in there?"

"A spare dress. Somehow I couldn't see you making it through the reception in that one, so I thought we'd better have a backup plan."

Wow! The man was officially a saint. Or a genius. No, both.

Nick found a tiny storage room at the side of the church and led me in there, locking the door behind us.

"Turn around," he whispered.

I tried, but I was stuck. "I think I'm caught on something."

Nick unhooked my dress from a sack truck and helped with a hand on my waist. I swivelled to face a stack of dusty chairs and a table that had seen better days, and now I had more butterflies than Missy's dress.

"Hold still. I've got a penknife in my hand."

I suppressed a shiver as Nick's warm breath touched my bare neck.

He got to work, and the stitching soon gave way with a quiet *pop*. Slowly, slowly, he slid the zipper down, and I clutched the front of the dress against myself as his fingertips caressed my skin, tracing across my shoulder blades. He dipped his head and his lips fluttered against the back of my neck then moved slowly, slowly up to my jaw. The trail of kisses was so soft, yet my skin was on fire everywhere he touched.

My legs trembled as one arm snaked around my waist, holding me steady and pulling me closer at the same time. His chest pressed into my back, and even through his suit, his body heat seared into me.

He paused his kisses to whisper in my ear. "So fucking beautiful."

Crude, yes, but heat pooled between my legs, and when he nibbled on my earlobe, I felt it right *there*. How was that even possible? Nick was a contradiction—solid and tough, yet gentle and sweet at the same time. If heaven came in human form, I'd found it.

But I needed to see his face. I needed to remind myself how beautiful he was, and more than anything, check it wasn't a dream. My dress loosened as I twisted in his arms, but I was beyond caring. Honestly, at that moment, if he'd stripped me naked and bent me over the battered table, I'd have been helpless to do anything about it.

I looked into his deep brown eyes, the irises flecked with gold, pupils dilated. Then a look of panic appeared in them, and he released me instantly.

"What the...?" I started.

He pushed me back onto my feet, I tripped over my dress, and my damn boobs fell out. *Freaking hell*. I made a grab for the bodice and yanked it up again, but honestly, what did it matter? I couldn't have gotten any more embarrassed if I tried.

There I was, half-dressed, with the man I'd been lusting after for months staring at me in abject horror.

What the heck just happened?

Did I have a pimple? Or food in my teeth?

Had I suddenly grown a pair of horns?

What?

# 34

## LARA

I wanted to run away, but I didn't stand a chance in that awful outfit. Since we were in church, I thought it was worth a quick prayer for the ground to open up and swallow me, but did anybody listen? No. Instead, my knees gave out and I fell to the grubby stone floor, drowning in a sea of pink chiffon. Tears prickled my eyelids, and I blinked them back, willing myself to hold it together in front of Nick.

"Lara, I'm so sorry... I don't know what came over me... I wasn't thinking."

Of course he wasn't. No way would a man like him ever want a girl like me if he was.

"It's okay. I understand."

I was half telling the truth. I *did* understand, but it wasn't okay. At that moment, I wasn't sure things would ever be okay again.

"It's not okay. I shouldn't have touched you. I should have kept my hands off." He seemed angry, but was he annoyed with himself? Or me? "I'm no good for you. You need a man who can keep you safe. A man who can give you more than I ever could."

Why would he think that? Sure, I didn't know much about him, but I knew enough to fall in love. I closed my eyes and groaned. Because that was what had happened, wasn't it? Why else would I feel as if he'd torn my heart out and shoved it into the garbage disposal?

Missy's voice echoed in the hallway outside. "Lara, where are you? We need to go to the reception now."

"I'll tell her you're getting changed," Nick said as he slipped out the door.

I had the presence of mind to lock it behind him. Then I cried. Big, horrible, ugly tears. It was times like this I missed my momma more than anything. I needed her to hold me and tell me everything would be okay, that I could find my way back from this. But I was on my own, lost without a map.

And I still had a wedding reception to attend. However bad things were, I couldn't ruin Missy and Clyde's big day. I used the pink monstrosity to wipe away my tears, and when I'd caught my breath, I tossed it aside. What had Bradley picked out for me? I unzipped the duffel and pulled out a pale lilac shift dress with a matching jacket and dainty cream pumps. There was even a make-up compact and a cream flower to clip in my hair.

My mascara claimed it was waterproof, but it was safe to say the manufacturer had bent the truth on that. Ugly, black smears ran down my face, reminding me of my days with Billy. I had another rummage in the bag. Did Bradley put in any tissues? The answer was no, but I did find a jewellery box right at the bottom. A beautiful necklace nestled inside, sparkling stones surrounding a lilac cabochon that matched the dress. Diamonds? I ran a finger over a couple and found them cool to the touch. Surely not? But they looked too flashy to be paste.

Where had it come from? It looked too expensive for a gift. Part of Emmy's collection? Although with a huge question mark over her relationship with Nick, I wasn't sure whether she'd have lent it to me either.

Was she part of the reason he'd stopped what he was doing with me? Did he want her back? Perhaps he wasn't over her, and if that was true, I sure couldn't compete.

I wiped my eyes again, then put my ear to the door. Was Nick still out there? If so, attending this wedding reception would be more awkward than the time Billy made me go to a family dinner with two black eyes. An accident on the squash court, he told everyone.

But if Nick had gone? Missy would ask so many questions my ears would bleed.

And I'd miss him. Despite everything, I'd miss him.

I cracked open the heavy door and checked the hallway. Empty. No Missy, no Nick. I took a deep breath, gathered up what was left of my dignity, and headed for the church hall next door. Only when I stepped outside, I saw Nick sitting in the car, watching me from the driver's seat. Did he expect me to stay or go?

Well, it wasn't his decision, was it? I gritted my teeth and kept walking. Maybe I should have tried talking to him, but after the way he took off, what the hell was I supposed to say?

A car door slammed behind me, and footsteps ran across the parking lot. Nick caught up as I climbed the steps and hurried ahead to open the door for me. Ever the gentleman, even if he had just shredded my soul.

Inside, Missy and Clyde sat at the top table with their families, leaving Nick and me two rows back with three couples I'd never met before, much to my relief. If Missy was nearby, she'd have noticed the frostiness between us and an interrogation would soon have followed.

"Wine?" Nick asked.

"Yes."

I tried not to fidget as the appetisers were served—red

onion puff pastry tarts cut into heart shapes accompanied by bright pink sauce. I'd completely lost my appetite, but I picked at mine until I'd forced half of it down.

Next to me, Nick seemed unperturbed as he debated the merits of cars versus motorbikes with the other men. The women started talking about their kids, happily comparing the best indoor play centres and discussing the easiest way to clean yoghurt off the carpet. How could Nick be so sociable? I felt as though I'd taken a one-way trip to Awkwardsville, population: me.

I'd still barely said two words when the main course arrived, a bizarre arrangement of heart-shaped steaks with heart-shaped potatoes and vegetables set out in heart-shaped dishes. Why hadn't Missy gotten married on St. Valentine's Day and been done with it?

I pushed my food around until a waiter removed the sorry remains and replaced it with a heart-shaped strawberry mousse. On a different day I might have found the theme sweet, but today it made me feel ill. It may as well have been my heart sitting on the plate, being cut up then stabbed with a fork.

And worst of all, Nick didn't seem to care as he got involved in a long-winded discussion over the benefits of winter tyres. Did he do this often? Wind a woman up to the point of orgasm then walk away? His heart must be made of granite.

It was almost more than I could take when the speeches started. Missy's father's heartfelt tale about true love and how there was one special person out there for everybody nearly had me in tears again. As soon as it was over, I excused myself to the bathroom where I was free to weep in peace.

And weep I did. Between the wedding and Nick, I was on a roller coaster of emotions today. All I wanted to do was get off, but the ride was still going and I was stuck on it until the end. Which meant going back outside. I checked my make-up in the mirror, but there wasn't an awful lot left of it. With my bloodshot eyes and blotchy face, I looked more like an alcoholic than a bridesmaid. *Way to go, Lara*. At least Missy was drunk enough not to notice now.

I paused at the door to the restroom, wishing I could be someplace else. But where? The hotel suite? Adler House? Everywhere in my life right now was associated with Nick.

He was sitting alone at the table, but as soon as I left the safety of the crowd, his eyes fixed on me, following until I sat down.

"You okay?" he asked.

"Fine."

"Do you want to leave?"

"I can't. Not until Missy does."

"She snuck out the side door with Clyde while you were in the bathroom. I think they were hoping nobody would see."

Well, at least someone would be having an enjoyable night tonight. Clyde had whispered to me earlier that he'd be surprising Missy with a night in the honeymoon suite at the best hotel in the area, and I also knew Missy had stocked up on trashy lingerie, chocolate body paint, and even a pair of furry pink handcuffs. The two of them wouldn't be coming back.

"In that case, please could we go? I'm not feeling so good."

Heartsick, lovesick, sick, sick.

The silence in the car was like a physical thing, creeping into my chest and squeezing, smothering me and making me choke. How could things have changed so quickly? On this morning's ride, we'd been laughing and joking, and I was the happiest I'd been in as long as I could remember. Now, I just felt hollow inside.

Nick parked at the hotel without a word, then got out and opened my door.

"Do you want me to stay somewhere else?"

After his performance at the reception, I'd thought he was unaffected by what happened at the church, but the quake in his voice told me otherwise. I met his eyes and found a sadness there I'd never seen before. For some reason, that made me feel a little better.

"You're in a separate bedroom as it is. There's no point in wasting money."

Besides, if I was going to keep my job, which I really needed to do because of the salary, I'd have to see him occasionally.

When we got upstairs, I went straight to my room. I wanted to change into my pyjamas, then eat something comforting. Like a pint of ice cream, a bowl of chocolate brownies with hot chocolate sauce, and a couple of cream cakes.

Only I forgot Bradley had repacked my bags. The only sleepwear I could find was a satin nightgown that probably cost more than my entire wardrobe and barely covered anything. It would have to be jeans. Designer jeans, it turned out, and they fitted perfectly.

Now, where was the room service menu? I checked the dressing table but only found a spa price list. Darn it. The menu must be outside.

Along with Nick.

When I stepped into the living room, he was sitting at the bar, tie off and top button undone, contemplating the glass of whisky sitting in front of him.

"Have you seen the room service menu?"

He turned his head slowly, his reactions dulled. "What do you want?"

"Something sweet. I need sugar."

He picked up the phone and instructed the person at the other end to send up one of everything on the dessert menu.

"Done."

"I can't eat all that. Well, not and still be able to fit into my clothes."

"Just leave what you don't want. It doesn't matter." His words were already slurred, but he took another mouthful of whisky.

"Nick, what happened?" I whispered, taking the stool next to him. It hurt, but I still wanted to know.

"I lost control, that's what happened. I did something I've wanted to do for a long time, and I should have stopped myself before it got as far as it did."

"Why?" I leaned forward and rested my head on my folded hands. I couldn't bring myself to look at him. "I thought it was obvious I wanted it as much as you did."

"My life's complicated, and you don't understand the half of it. If you knew the real me, your feelings would be very different."

"You don't know that. Show me the real you and let me make up my own mind."

"It's not that simple. There are other people involved in that side of my life, and I have to consider them as well."

"Is Emmy one of them?"

"Yes. With her...well, it's complicated." He took a slug of whisky and wiped his chin.

"Oh."

"Lara, you're...you're..." He paused, contemplating. "You're special. Believe me when I say if circumstances were different, nothing could have dragged me out of that room this morning."

"So what now?"

"I don't know. I've never been in this situation before."

"Me neither." He laid a hand on my back, and I jumped. "What?"

"Could we try to go back to how things were before? Although I'll understand if you want to leave. I'll keep paying you whatever you get paid for as long as you want."

Wow. Talk about generous. Which path should I take? The easy one? Leave and ride the bus into the sunset to find my next disaster? Or should I stay? I didn't have many friends, and even though Nick had hurt me today, I couldn't deny he had a good heart. Could I salvage a friendship?

I needed to try. *Wanted* to try.

"I'll stay. At least for the moment."

"Thank you. That means more to me than you'll ever know." He took a couple of steps towards his bedroom, paused, then reached back for the whisky bottle. "I'll see you in the morning."

"Sweet dreams, Nick."

Before he wobbled off, he reached out and ran his fingertips down my cheek. "I'm sorry, baby."

Him and me both.

I rummaged in the minibar for a bottle of something, anything. Vodka would do. I twisted the cap off and swallowed half of it neat, choking as it burned my throat.

Had I done the right thing by agreeing to stay? Only time would tell.

A few minutes later, a cart arrived with nine different desserts on it, but it was too late; my appetite had deserted me. I left the dishes where they were and went to bed.

# 35

# LARA

First I couldn't sleep, and then I overslept. When I dragged myself out of bed on Sunday morning, it was almost ten o'clock. I'd spent hours lying awake in the night, analysing Nick's words, but nothing made sense, and I wasn't sure it was all because of the vodka. He'd said there was a lot about him I didn't understand, and that I wouldn't like it if I did. But what could be so bad that it would change the way I felt?

He was a good man at heart; I knew that.

I absolutely knew it.

Before everything turned to poop yesterday, we'd promised to help Missy clean up the church hall in the afternoon, and even if I had to walk there, I refused to let her down. Especially since Clyde's boss wouldn't give him the day off work. Apparently, his fly-fishing was far more important than Clyde's post-marital bliss. When Missy heard that, she'd threatened to chop his tackle into little pieces, so if nothing else, I needed to make sure she didn't follow through. Having to bail someone I cared about out of jail would be the perfect end to this trip.

When I slunk out of my room, Nick was already up, eating a bowl of granola at the table with his laptop in front of him.

"I thought you said no work this weekend?" I said in an attempt to break the ice.

"Okay, you caught me." He shut the laptop. "Are we still helping Missy this afternoon?"

"I wasn't sure you'd want to."

His sigh settled over the room like a veil. "I said I would, so I will."

Despite the discomfort between us, I was grateful Nick came. He made light work of carrying the stacks of chairs, and he didn't need to stand on a ladder to pull Missy's glittery garlands down from the walls. Luckily, Missy was so busy telling me in excruciating detail about her wedding night that she didn't realise anything was amiss.

Six times we filled up the minivan and drove it to her parents' house, and by the time we finished, the door hardly shut on their single-car garage.

"Why are you keeping it all?" I asked Missy.

"We can reuse it at our first child's christening."

"What if it's a boy?"

"Oh dearie, I didn't think of that." A crinkle appeared on her forehead. "I guess we'll have to buy another set in blue."

And her parents would need to buy a bigger house.

I collapsed on the couch in their front room as her mom served up bottles of ginger beer. Nick settled in an armchair opposite, although he didn't look tired in the least. I needed his kind of stamina. Maybe I should take up his offer of using the gym when we got back after all? We only had one more night here. I could start tomorrow.

"Thanks so much for your help," Missy said. "We couldn't have done it without you. The wedding went great, don't you think?"

Except for the parts she was blissfully unaware of. "Sure did. You and Clyde looked so happy together."

"We will be. I'm sure of it. And as a thank-you for all your help, I want to take you guys out to dinner. My treat."

Oh, great. Another dinner with Nick to get through.

"What about Clyde? Won't he miss you?"

"He won't be back until late. The asshole's making him work overtime. Say, I never did find those scissors..."

No, not the scissors. "Dinner sounds lovely. Where did you have in mind?"

As well as saving Clyde's boss's valuables, maybe going out in public with Nick would be less awkward than a private dinner in our suite. At least I wouldn't be tempted to throw myself at him and beg if there were others around.

"Buck's? I just love those steak sandwiches, and Becky's created a new cocktail menu, or so I've heard."

Buck's? I didn't particularly relish the thought of being leered at by my ex-boss, but I couldn't help being curious as to how he was managing without me.

"Becky's still there?"

"Not because Buck hasn't tried to find a replacement. That woman's thicker than a bowl of oatmeal. Buck wanted you back, but I told him you'd had a better offer." She leaned close and whispered into my ear. "Which you did. Nick is one fine piece of ass."

"Missy!"

She shrugged. "Truth."

I peeked at Nick, but he was busy fiddling with his phone, thank goodness.

"It may be the truth, but he's also unavailable, so don't you dare get any ideas. Shall we meet you at Buck's at seven?"

"Sure thing, sugar plum."

Buck had always chided me for wearing jeans, so I picked out a dark blue boot-cut pair from Bradley's selection. Let him dare to say anything now that I didn't work there anymore. Plus they fitted really, really well. I teamed them up with a white camisole and a checked shirt—Buck's was that kind of bar.

Nick wore jeans too, but he'd gone for the calendar model look of black biker boots and a plain white T-shirt. Bradley deserved a raise for his packing skills. In the car, I couldn't help sneaking little glances at what would never be mine. I tried not to, but my eyes seemed to have a mind of their own and disobeyed my brain's instructions to focus elsewhere.

"So, this bar we're going to, you used to work there?" Nick asked.

"For about a year until I moved to Virginia."

"What made you move? I don't think I've ever asked you, have I?"

And I'd been hoping he never would. "Buck cut my shifts, and I knew it wouldn't be easy to find a new job. I'm not really qualified for much. So I thought I'd have a fresh start instead."

"Why'd he cut your shifts? Business wasn't good?"

"It was more that he found a younger, prettier waitress and thought she'd sell more drinks."

"Prettier? Is Buck blind?"

Why did Nick have to say things like that? "Well, it was kind of my fault. I started wearing jeans rather than skirts, and he said the customers didn't like it so much. My tips went down too, so he was probably telling the truth."

Why was I defending him? Habit, I guess. I'd stood by Billy for years, and those old habits died hard. And Buck hadn't been the worst boss I'd ever had. That was the guy before him who pinched my ass rather than just staring at it.

"Why'd you start wearing jeans? Did something happen?"

Oh, me and my big mouth. "Nothing serious, just a few nights when I thought someone might have followed me home. I felt safer in jeans and a pair of sneakers, plus I didn't want to attract unwanted attention at the bar."

In the dim glow from the streetlights, Nick's expression turned grave. "Did you report this?"

"I tried, but the cops weren't interested since I didn't see anyone for sure. Please can we just forget about it? Everything's been fine since I moved, and it creeps me out."

"As long as you promise to tell me if you ever feel that way again. I don't care whether you're sure or not. I want to know, because I'm not having you scared."

"I promise."

*That* was why I needed to keep Nick as a friend. He cared, regardless of whatever there wasn't between us.

We arrived at Buck's at the same time as Missy, and she almost broke a rib hugging me before we walked in together. Buck's eyes went wide when he looked up from behind the bar.

"Lara! You've come back! Are you here to stay or just visiting? Missy said you'd moved away."

Buck never moved faster than an amble, and tonight was no different as he came over to greet us.

"Just visiting, Buck."

"No chance I could tempt you to stick around? I'll give you as many shifts as you want."

"I don't even live in the same state anymore."

He turned to Nick, shaking his head. "I was a stupid man to let her go, and I'm suffering now, believe me."

"I get where you're coming from."

Buck clapped both of us on the back. "Well, I'll make sure

you have a good meal tonight. Becky's got a new cocktail menu you ladies might like to try."

Missy led the way to a booth and slid in first. I sat next to her, and Nick took the other side. Barely a minute passed before Buck came back with the menus. There was no change in the offering, and I still knew it by heart.

"What's good?" Nick asked.

"Everything, to be honest. The cook must be at least seventy, and he's been here forever. I don't think the regulars'll ever let him retire. Some of them come here every night. Buck tried to mess with the food once, and there was almost a mutiny."

"In that case, I'll have a burger with everything. Got to keep my strength up."

"I'll have the same, except I can only ever eat half of it."

Nick picked up the cocktail menu and skimmed through it. Then he did a double take and choked back a laugh.

"Holy fuck, have you read this? There's a cocktail on here called 'Becky's Bukkake Special.'"

Now I may not have been worldly wise, but Billy went through a phase of forcing me to watch porn with him, which left me well aware of what bukkake was. Had Becky gone mad?

Missy let out a whoop of laughter. "Where, where? Show me!"

Nick waved the menu, and that good-natured smirk came back. "It's halfway down, between 'Morning Glory' and 'Golden Shower.' Fuck me."

Missy snatched the list from him. "Apparently it's Becky's special recipe of coconut cream, peach schnapps, and cider. Is that even drinkable?"

Just then, Becky came over, all bleached blonde hair, silicone-enhanced boobs, and minuscule skirt. Nick got her full attention, but he seemed to be having trouble looking her in the eye.

"What can I get for you, sweetie pie?" She teetered on impossible heels and stuck her chest straight into his face as he fixed his gaze on the table.

"A burger with everything, and Lara'll have the same. Missy?"

"A steak sandwich for me."

Becky dragged her gaze away from Nick to acknowledge our existence, then smiled as she saw what Missy was holding. "Oh, I see you've found my new cocktail menu. Would you like to try one? I created them all special myself."

I kicked Missy under the table, but she totally ignored me.

"Sure. Gimme a Morning Glory."

How did she say that without laughing?

"One Morning Glory. Got it. Lara?"

"How did you come up with the names?"

"Oh, I was having trouble with that, so a couple of the regulars helped me out. Some of them sound real exotic, don't you think?"

"Uh, I guess so. I'll just have a lemonade, though."

"Sure." Her smile faded, but she quickly perked up when she turned back to Nick. "What can I get you to drink, honey bear?"

"Just a beer, thanks."

"Honey bear?" Missy asked after Becky had sashayed away.

Nick rolled his eyes. "I guess that's why the 'dumb blonde' stereotype is alive and kicking."

Becky quickly returned with the drinks and made a beeline for him. Totally predictable.

"So that's a root beer for you, Coke for Lara, and a Bukkake Special for Missy."

"Definitely alive and kicking," Nick muttered.

Thankfully when our food orders turned up, they were

more or less right. More or less. Nick's portion of fries looked twice the size of mine, even though they were supposed to be the same. Obviously he warranted special treatment. Becky had probably shoved half of my fries onto his plate before she left the kitchen, and I noticed she'd also fluffed up her hair and refreshed her lipstick.

But the food hadn't lost its appeal, and as we ate, the strained atmosphere eased a little. Nick chatted away, mostly to Missy, pausing occasionally to nod at Becky on the six occasions she stopped by to check that everything was all right with his meal.

I'd worried he might turn his nose up at Buck's, considering the restaurants he normally ate at, but he seemed quite comfortable there. To me, the place looked even seedier than I remembered—a few more chips out of the scarred wooden tables, paint peeling from the wall by the restrooms. Had that window always had a crack in it?

But being in the bar sure beat the suite, where I'd have been at a loss for conversation. Missy more than made up for my lack of words. Yes, we'd made the right decision to come out to eat.

Hadn't we?

Wait a second... Why had Missy gone white? That was impressive, seeing as she'd had a spray tan for the wedding. A piece of steak fell out her mouth as she stopped chewing, her eyes fixed on a point to the side of me, and I slowly turned around to see what she was looking at.

Only it wasn't a what; it was a who. And when I saw him, the blood drained from my face as well.

## 36

## LARA

"Billy, what do you want?" I whispered.

"Heard you were in town tonight, so I stopped by to ask what the hell you think you're doing." He spat the words, and his eyes flashed with a rage I knew all too well.

"I don't know what you're talking about. I'm just having dinner."

"Interfering in my life, that's what."

He took a step closer, and I shrank back, pressing into the cheap vinyl seat as if it could swallow me up. How many times had I'd been in that position before? I usually ended up with bruises at best, broken bones at worst. Sometimes a bit of blood thrown into the mix for kicks.

But then Nick spoke. "Don't take another fuckin' step."

"Stay out of this, pretty boy."

Pretty? Nick didn't look pretty. He looked furious. I'd never seen his eyes hard like that before, two chips of onyx, and he managed to be both rigid and relaxed at the same time.

Not that Billy cared. He turned back to me with an ugly

smirk on his face, and I knew something bad was coming my way.

"You wrote to Jeanie and told her to leave me." He drew a piece of paper out of his pocket, and I recognised my writing as he ripped it into pieces and threw it at me. "Page after page of bullshit. All lies."

"They weren't lies. Everything in that letter was true."

"You filled her head with garbage. She started acting funny, sneaking around. It wasn't until I went through her stuff I found out what you'd done, you stupid bitch."

Movement caught my eye as Nick stood up, and I prayed he'd stay out of this. If Billy blew his fuse, he'd lash out at anyone.

But Nick didn't back down. "You don't speak to Lara like that. Now get out before I throw you out."

"Butt out, man, this is between me and my girlfriend."

"Ex. *Ex*-girlfriend," I said. No way did I want Nick thinking I was still in any way associated with Billy.

"The moment you stepped up to this table, you made it my problem too. Last chance."

Nick radiated confidence, which gave me confidence too. I'd never had anybody stick up for me that way before. But what would happen next? Billy and Nick weighed about the same, but Nick was four inches taller, and he got his bulk from the gym while Billy's came from beer and pizza. Billy was mean as a snake, though, and I knew firsthand that he'd had plenty of practice at hurting people.

Luckily, I was saved from finding out because Buck sidled up to the table.

"We got a problem here, gentlemen?"

Buck wasn't small either, and I knew darn well he kept a baseball bat stashed behind the bar for emergencies. I guess Billy knew that too because he held up his hands and took a step back.

"No problem. I'm leaving."

As soon as the door closed behind Billy, my tears came. I couldn't help it. The relief that Nick and Buck had stopped Billy from hurting me again caused my eyes to overflow. I picked up my napkin and dabbed at my cheeks, rueing my decision to wear mascara. You'd think I'd have learned by now, wouldn't you?

Nick crouched down beside me. "Baby, what the fuck was all that about?"

"That was Billy."

"I gathered that. What was he talking about? What was in that letter?"

Where did I start? My stupidity in the beginning? With the dramatic end? Luckily, Missy jumped in and helped me out.

"Billy's her ex, and he's an asshole. No, scratch that. He's herpes on an asshole."

"I got that."

"Yeah, well, Lara finally left him after he almost killed her. Then when she came to visit me a few weeks back, she saw his new girlfriend and got worried he'd do the same to her, so she wrote a letter to the girl telling her what he did."

Nick raised my chin so I was looking at him. "Is this true?"

I tried to speak but ended up sniffling instead. Missy passed me a tissue, and I wiped my nose before I tried again.

"Y-y-yes."

"He hurt you?"

"Yes."

"And the new girlfriend?"

"She looks just like I used to. Defeated."

"Fuck. Why didn't you tell me this?"

"I thought it was all in the past. Honestly I did. I left Billy five years ago, and I didn't see him again until my last trip here. I just wanted to block it all out and pretend it never happened."

"He's the reason you didn't go back to college, isn't he?"

I nodded at the reminder of my past failures.

"And the accident you had?"

"It wasn't so much of an accident. Billy pushed me down the stairs, and I broke my leg."

Nick leaned his forehead onto mine, and the smell of root beer washed over me as he exhaled.

"You should have told me."

"Why? He's my problem, not yours. Why would I want to admit I was stupid enough to waste nearly six years of my life with him? I was crazy about you. I didn't want you to think less of me because I let Billy treat me like a doormat."

A second passed, and my addled brain processed what I'd just said. Diners from nearby tables stared as I clapped a hand over my mouth. Telling my hot boss I was crazy for him—how inappropriate could I get?

Nick reached out and squeezed my trembling hand. "Lara, nothing could make me love you any less than I do."

Huh?

Did he just say the "L" word?

I guess so, because his eyes saucered and he looked as horrified as I felt. He didn't mean it, right?

Or... Or...

Missy flipped the bird at the couple sitting at the next table who'd started whispering behind their hands, and Nick dropped a couple of bills on the table as he stood.

"Are we leaving?" I whispered.

"I've lost my appetite. Haven't you?"

"I feel sick."

My legs shook as I tried to stand, and I clutched at the edge of the table for support. Nick didn't wait for me to get my balance back; he simply scooped me up and headed for the door. I clung to his neck as Missy scuttled along behind.

Despite my best efforts, I couldn't stop sobbing as Nick strode across the parking lot. This entire trip had been a disaster. Before we left, my biggest worry had been looking awful in the pink dress, but the debacle with Nick and now Billy's appearance made the dress incident seem positively tame.

How could I carry on working for Nick after this latest chapter in the horror story?

The answer was I couldn't, but the thought of never seeing him again brought even more tears.

We'd almost gotten to the car when Nick stopped short.

"Why...?"

I trailed off as I followed Nick's gaze to a blurry-looking Billy blocking our path. And he wasn't alone.

I recognised two of his old high-school friends, Bart and Corey, standing on either side of him, and a shiver of fear ran through me. Corey had been captain of the wrestling team until he got kicked off for knocking out a teammate in a locker room brawl, and Bart got suspended after homecoming when a cheerleader accused him of assault. Of course, his daddy's money made the charges go away, so he and Billy had something else in common besides being jerks. Why were the three of them there? I didn't know, but I'd bet my last dollar it wasn't because Billy wanted to beg for my forgiveness.

And now his arrogant voice came out of the darkness. "Oh, I get it now, man. You wanna fuck her. Let me save you the trouble. She might look all right, but she's a lousy lay, and she doesn't get better with time."

Right then, I wished Billy *had* killed me when he shoved me down the stairs. He was still ruining my life, even now.

Nick lowered me to my feet, one arm still around my waist, and tossed the car keys to Missy.

"You sit Lara in the car, you lock the doors, and neither of you gets out until I say so. Understand?"

Missy's eyes were wide. "Y-y-es."

She took my hand and pulled me towards the Mercedes, but I didn't want to leave Nick. This was all my fault, and the idea of him getting hurt was far worse than the prospect of being injured myself. I clung to him as he bent to whisper in my ear. His lips brushing against me only served to increase my fears.

"Go, baby. It's okay."

"It's not okay. They're gonna hurt you."

He pressed a soft kiss to my jaw. "Get in the car. Trust me."

I wanted to throw up as Missy tugged my arm again, bundling me into the passenger seat before she ran around to the other side. A second later, she hit the locks, cocooning us in safety while Nick faced three monsters outside. The logical part of my brain told me to call the cops, but fear left me frozen.

Billy's lips moved, and his stance was pure aggression. Nick had his back to me, and his hands hung open at his sides —a sharp contrast to my own, which clutched at the hem of my shirt so hard they went numb.

Five seconds passed...ten...and I strained to hear what they were saying. Then it didn't matter anymore because Billy's roar could have been heard in the next county as he put his head down and charged at Nick.

I closed my eyes. Yes, I fully admit to being a coward, but I couldn't bear to watch Nick get hurt. Three against one. It would be no contest.

Missy gasped next to me, and my eyes flew open again of their own accord, just in time to see Billy sail through the air and land head first on the hood of the car with a sickening crunch. He slid off in slow motion and crumpled into a heap at the side.

Missy moved to open the door, and I grabbed her arm. "Don't go. Billy's not worth it."

"I wasn't going to help. I was gonna kick him in the balls."

"Just wait. Please."

Nick turned as Corey rushed at him, hefting a tyre iron in his hands. I didn't want to watch, but I couldn't look away this time. Missy had no such problems. She squealed and buried her face in her sweater.

Nick leapt back, ducked into a crouch, and swept Corey's legs out from under him. As Corey fell, Nick snatched the weapon and straightened up, just in time to face Bart.

Something glinted in his hand. What was it? A car swept by on the road outside, its headlights momentarily showing the detail.

"Knife!" I screamed, but Nick showed no signs of hearing.

Bart's feet pounded on the tarmac as he hurtled towards his prey, and still Nick didn't move. It wasn't until the last second that he sidestepped, and as Bart's momentum carried him past, Nick grabbed his arm and twisted it up behind him. The knife flew into the bushes. Even inside the car, I heard the crack as Bart's arm broke, and everyone in Baysville surely heard his howl of pain.

Bart stumbled back, cradling his arm, but another blood-curdling yell came as Corey scrambled to his feet and ran at Nick again.

"Turn around. Please, turn around," I pleaded, but Corey was fast and fuelled by anger.

He reached out for Nick, biceps bulging. But then Nick's head snapped back and blood sprayed everywhere as Corey's nose disintegrated.

"Please let all that blood be Corey's," Missy muttered from beside me.

"I think it is. I hope it is."

A shadow rose to the left as Bart made it to his feet again. The pain must have fed his fury, because he mustered up some energy and flew at Nick, attempting a high-kick, martial-arts style. Nick simply grabbed Bart's leg and upended him. Wow. I wasn't sure whether to be awed or nervous.

Bart must have cracked his head as he fell because he didn't get up again. Nick was standing in the midst of the three motionless bodies, still holding the tyre iron, when a siren whooped and the first police car rolled into the lot.

Uh-oh.

The two cops took one look at Nick and drew their guns.

"Drop your weapon."

Nick let go of the tyre iron, and it clattered to the ground. As the policemen stalked towards him, he slowly raised his hands above his head.

A chill seeped through me. I tried to swallow, but my throat muscles didn't seem to be working properly. Thanks to me, the man I'd fallen for was being held at gunpoint. I brought disaster with me wherever I went.

I unfroze, half falling out of the car as I wrenched the door open. *Don't fall on your face, Lara. Not now.* My knees threatened to give way as I stumbled across the lot and threw myself in front of Nick.

"Don't shoot! He was only defending himself."

"Ma'am, move out of the way."

"Not until you put your guns down."

The shorter of the two cops glared at me. "We're not going to shoot him unless he acts threatening."

Nick bent his head and spoke softly into my ear. "Angle your body so they can't see your hand, then take my phone out of my right front pocket."

I shifted my feet and reached behind me, feeling for it. Oh freaking fudge, too far left. That wasn't his damn phone! After two attempts, I got it and transferred it to my own pocket.

Nick reassured me as my heart hammered. "Now, move away and call Emmy. There're two numbers in there. Use the one with an 'R' after it. PIN number's the same as the house alarm."

"What if they shoot you?"

"They won't; don't worry. Trust me, baby."

Again, he asked me to trust him, and again, I had no choice. I stepped to the side, and the cops swooped in with handcuffs. My stomach churned as I tried to keep from losing my dinner.

A second police car arrived, then a third, and one of the newcomers motioned for Missy to get out of the car and stand next to me. I started to explain what happened, that Billy and his buddies had attacked unprovoked, but he wouldn't listen. Four cops surrounded Nick on the other side of the lot. I recognised most of them from my time working at Buck's, but they were all business tonight.

"Why aren't they letting him go?" Missy asked the officer standing next to us, but she was met with a stony silence.

We could only watch as Nick was led to a squad car and pushed into the back. I averted my gaze as his head turned in my direction because, coward that I was, I couldn't face him.

Three ambulances arrived, and Billy, Corey, and Bart were soon strapped onto stretchers. An EMT patted Billy's arm in a gesture of sympathy, and I wanted to scream at him to stop. Billy didn't deserve kindness. He deserved to rot.

And why hadn't they let Nick go?

I didn't understand it.

# 37

# LARA

As the car holding Nick drove away, I fumbled in my pocket for his phone. Call Emmy, he'd said. It made sense that he'd turn to her in a time like this—I hadn't exactly been much help, had I?

"Now what?" Missy asked.

"I need to call Nick's friend."

When the screen lit up, I found it wasn't his usual phone. That one had a picture of his Ferrari in the background, and this one was all black. Since when did Nick have two phones? As he said, there was a lot I didn't know about him.

The cop next to me stepped forward before I could dial, and he didn't look happy. "What are you doing?"

"Making a phone call."

"Ma'am, I'm going to have to ask you to refrain from doing that." Using "ma'am" gave the illusion of politeness, but he made it sound like an insult.

"I'm allowed a phone call. I've seen cop shows on the TV. Everybody's allowed a phone call."

"That's if you've been arrested. You haven't been arrested."

Missy cut in, hands on hips. "Well, if she hasn't been arrested, why can't she make a call?"

"Because I'd rather she didn't."

"You can rather whatever you like. She can make a damn phone call if she wants to."

He glowered at me as I typed in the PIN code, but I was beyond caring. I scrolled through Nick's contact list, and just as he'd said, there were two entries for Emmy. What did the R mean? Now wasn't the time to wonder, so I hit dial.

Two rings, and then, "Nicky, I knew you wouldn't get through a whole weekend without calling me."

"It's Lara."

"Oh. Where's Nick?"

I fought back tears as I imagined Emmy calm and composed at the other end of the line. "My ex-boyfriend showed up, and there was a fight. It was h-h-horrible, and then the police came."

"And I presume Nick was involved in this, given the fact that you're talking to me on his phone and he isn't."

"They arrested him. I tried to tell them he acted in self-defence, but they wouldn't listen. What can I do? He's been taken to jail, and it's completely my fault. I was the one who wanted to come here."

"You can calm down, for starters. You're no help if you're hysterical. Now, have you got someone there with you?"

"Missy. My friend."

"Good. Get Missy to go with you to the police station, and I'll send someone to meet you there. Can you do that?"

"We have to go to the police station," I told Missy.

But the cop had other ideas. "You can't leave. Ma'am." This time, the "ma'am" was a definite afterthought.

Great. I went back to Emmy. "The police say we can't."

"Are you under arrest?"

"I don't think so."

"Then they can't keep you there. Let me speak to the cop."

I passed the phone over, and his face went from a delicate shade of pink, through tomato, and all the way to beetroot at whatever Emmy said to him. Just as I thought steam would start coming out of his ears, he handed the phone back.

"I need your names and addresses as witnesses, and then you're free to go."

Ouch. I bet it hurt him to say that. I sent a silent thank you to Emmy as Missy and I scribbled down our contact details in his notepad, then waited as Missy rooted through her purse for the car keys.

"You want me to drive?" she offered.

"Better not after that cocktail."

She eyed up the gaggle of cops watching us. "I guess you're right. It was awful, by the way."

Just like the entire evening.

We'd only been at the police station for a few minutes when two men walked in, one in a suit, the other in jeans.

The suit ignored the desk sergeant and held out his hand to me. "Conrad. I'm part of Nick's legal team." He gestured to his companion. "This is Dominic."

Nick had a legal team? What for? His investment deals? I only hoped Conrad knew his way around assault and battery laws as well as corporate jargon. Still, he'd come to help, and goodness knows we needed it.

"Thank you for coming."

"What happened?"

We snagged a group of chairs in the corner of the room, as far away from the desk sergeant's ears as possible, then I explained what had happened. When I got to the parts about Billy and how he came to be there, Missy had to take over while I fought down the bile rising in my throat.

Conrad asked the occasional question while Dominic simply listened, expressionless. Why was he there? He didn't look like a lawyer. Once we'd finished, Conrad nodded to himself.

"Seems straightforward. Let's get this sorted out."

I wished I shared his confidence.

Dominic stepped outside, and through the glass doors, I saw him put his phone to his ear. I didn't know what he was doing, and to be honest, I was glad he'd gone elsewhere to do it. He scared me a little. Conrad, meanwhile, strode up to the desk sergeant and demanded access to his client. The cop obviously realised Conrad wasn't a man to be messed with and led him off into the bowels of the building.

Left alone with Missy, my imagination ran wild. I had Nick eating his last meal on death row by the time Conrad came back and told us not to worry.

"Everything's in hand. It just takes a while."

"How long?"

He shrugged. "Hard to say with this lot. They don't seem to possess a brain between them."

Waiting became unbearable. I alternated between sitting on the hard plastic seat, fidgeting, and pacing up and down as one hour passed, then two. Dominic came back inside and sat opposite me, barely moving a muscle.

Then things got worse.

A shadow fell like dawn in the freaking underworld as Billy's father loomed over me, sneering as he looked down.

"Well, you've really gone and done it this time, haven't you?"

I'd never gotten on with the man, mainly because he thought I wasn't good enough for his son and I found him rude, arrogant, and condescending. Now we could add angry into the mix.

"I didn't do anything. Billy turned up and started a fight."

"You know as well as I do that Billy would never do that. You're a bitter woman, trying to ruin his good name because he finally came to his senses and realised he could do better than you. My son's suffered enough from your lies."

"I haven't told any lies."

"You almost ruined his reputation at college. People were actually suggesting that he had something to do with you falling down the stairs."

"That's because he did. He pushed me."

"You're nothing but a vindictive little bitch. I'm going to make sure your boyfriend gets the book thrown at him. Did you hear Billy's got a fractured neck? He could've been paralysed. You'll both be sorry this ever happened."

Dominic stepped in front of me and stared Mr. Cooper down. "Sir, that sounded like a threat to me, and should anything happen to Mr. Goldman or Miss Reynolds, I'll be only too happy to stand up in court and tell a jury all about it."

"Who the hell are you?"

"Mr. Goldman's representative."

"You obviously don't know who I am."

"I know exactly who you are, Mr. Cooper. What I don't do is share in the sense of self-importance you so obviously have."

"Why, you little..."

Mr. Cooper took a step towards Dominic, but he didn't budge.

"I should probably remind you we're in a police station."

Mr. Cooper looked as if his head was about to explode, but instead of arguing, he turned and marched through a door marked private, ignoring the desk sergeant's shouts to stop.

Dominic settled back into his vigil. "Apple didn't fall far from the tree, did it?"

Almost an hour later, another man arrived, and he and Dominic huddled in the corner, muttering. Then a couple of cops came through, and the four of them disappeared into the back of the police station.

"What do you think's happening?" I whispered to Missy.

"I don't know, but the new guy was hot."

"You just got married."

"A girl can look."

Fifteen agonising minutes later, Dominic came back with Conrad and the mysterious third man in tow.

"What's happening? Are they gonna let Nick go?"

Conrad's mouth set in a hard line. "They should have done that already. Buck's had some problems with vandalism recently, so he got security cameras installed. The whole fight's on video. Then there are Bart's fingerprints on the knife and Corey's on the tyre iron. That evidence speaks for itself."

"So why is Nick still back there?"

"Because so far, the cops have refused to watch the camera footage or test either of the weapons for prints. And they've said they'll get around to interviewing the witnesses 'at some point.'" He used little finger quotes. "They're stalling on everything."

"So now what? Is Nick okay?"

"Nick's fine. Trust me, he can take care of himself. We've got our own investigators on the case, and they're going to start gathering witness statements in the morning."

"Tomorrow? But—"

He laid a hand on my shoulder. "Don't sweat it. The

police don't have a case, and Nick'll be out in no time. He didn't have a weapon nor did he use excessive force under the circumstances."

"I thought he'd get badly hurt. There were three of them."

"It'd take a lot more than those three jerks to hurt Nick."

"What do you mean? He's only a businessman."

Conrad laughed. "Nick's always been good at taking care of business." His phone rang, and he glanced at the screen. "Better get this."

The mystery man went outside with him, and Dominic resumed his silent watch in the corner. Why couldn't they do something more? Surely it must be obvious this wasn't Nick's fault?

As the minutes ticked by, I grabbed a passing detective out of desperation and begged him to tell me what was going on.

"Look, ma'am, being honest, you might as well go home. He won't be getting out tonight."

"But why? He didn't do anything except defend himself."

"It's more complicated than that. Three men are in the hospital, and one of them is the son of a prominent local businessman. The mayor's been in contact with the chief and insisted a full investigation be undertaken before the suspect can be released. That'll take a week at least. So, as I said, you should go home and get some rest."

I felt like kicking something. Preferably Billy Cooper or his father. Then it hit me—the detective had said the mayor was involved. And Billy's dad and the mayor were golfing buddies. They played a four-ball every Thursday morning, or at least they had the whole time I was with Billy. And if memory served me right, Mr. Cooper also contributed heavily to the mayor's campaign.

So this was what he meant about making sure Nick got the book thrown at him. I cursed the day I'd ever met Billy Cooper.

My phone vibrated, and I fished it out of my pocket. Except I realised it wasn't my phone ringing at all, it was Nick's. Emmy calling. Great. This night kept getting better and better. What the heck should I say to her? *Oh hey, Emmy, your maybe-boyfriend, complicated or not, is still locked up, and they won't let him go. It's my fault, but I'm really sorry.* I could only imagine how well that would go down.

The phone stopped ringing but began again two seconds later. I couldn't leave Emmy hanging. That wouldn't be fair.

*Deep breaths, Lara.*

"Emmy? It's Lara again."

"Yeah, that's kind of obvious. Nick's still locked up?"

"It's awful. They won't let him go. I'm so worried about him."

"Don't be. He's a big boy, and he can look after himself. This isn't the first night he's spent in a jail cell, and it probably won't be the last. But what I don't understand is why he's still in there? Dom said they had crystal clear footage of three assholes attacking him."

I told her the whole sorry story about Billy, Billy's father, and the mayor, and almost died of embarrassment. Having to admit how messed up my life was to somebody so impossibly perfect hurt.

But weirdly, Emmy didn't get judgemental. "So Cooper wants to play the political game, huh?"

"It looks like it. I'm so sorry."

"Well, he picked the wrong fucking person to play it with, didn't he?"

"What do you...?" I started, but I was speaking to empty air.

Conrad had meandered in while I was speaking to Emmy, and now Dominic rose to join him.

"Was that Emmy?" Dominic asked.

"Yes."

"What did she say?"

I repeated the conversation, short though it was.

Dominic shrugged and turned to Conrad. "Fifty bucks says he's out of there in less than an hour."

"No way I'm taking that bet."

What were they talking about?

Twenty-seven minutes later, I found out. The police chief looked nothing like he did on TV as he stormed past, face white and fists clenched. Mr. Cooper followed, and in contrast, he'd gone the colour of a cheap merlot.

Six minutes after that, Nick joined us at the door.

# 38

## LARA

When I saw Nick, I was so relieved I threw my arms around him before I realised what I was doing. He didn't seem to share my sentiment as he looked down, tight-lipped.

"We're leaving."

He shifted me to his side, slung an arm around my waist, and half carried me outside. Missy trotted after us with Dominic and Conrad bringing up the rear.

When we reached the car, Nick stuck out his hand. "Keys."

Where had I put them?

I fumbled through my purse until I found them lurking under a scarf and passed them over, hand shaking. Nick threw them to Conrad and told him to drive Missy home.

"You two need a ride?" Dominic asked Nick.

"To the airport."

Oh heck, he was furious, and I had no idea what to say or do to make things better.

"I'm sor—"

"Not now, Lara, okay?"

Nick channelled Dominic as we drove to the airport, staring out the window in silence. His frown lines had turned into furrows. The plane was already on the tarmac, and Nick herded me up the steps.

"Strap yourself in." He pointed at a seat in the middle.

"What about our things at the hotel?"

It probably seemed trivial to him, but I didn't have many belongings, and I'd taken most of my toiletries with me.

"Someone'll deliver it all."

"Do we have long to wait for the pilot?"

"You're looking at him."

"Oh."

The jet soon roared along the runway, and I gripped the edges of the seat, not so much from a fear of flying anymore, but because I was terrified of what would happen with Nick when we got back. The lights were dim and the sun hadn't risen yet, but despite having been awake for almost twenty-four hours, I couldn't sleep. Worse, I still felt quite sick. The only time I ventured from my seat was to fetch one of those paper bags from the galley, just in case.

Not only was my life a complete mess, now Nick had been dragged into it. I couldn't blame him for acting cold towards me. In fact, if he never spoke to me again, I'd completely understand. Oh, how I longed to hurt Billy and Mr. Cooper. I spent most of the trip dreaming up awful things to do to them, from throwing Mr. Cooper's golf clubs off a bridge to covering Billy's beloved Dodge Charger in paint. Pink paint. Or maybe lime green.

But I knew I'd never be brave enough to actually go through with any of my plans, and I hated myself even more for that.

*Once a coward, always a coward.*

When we landed, a car was already waiting to pick us up.

The driver opened my door while Nick climbed into the other side.

"Drop Lara at home, then take me to Emmy's."

Of course, he would turn to her. She'd stayed calm through the whole crisis, and if Dominic and Conrad were to be believed, she'd had a hand in getting him out of jail too. Although I couldn't imagine how she'd done that, seeing as she wasn't even there.

It was only natural that Nick should go back to Emmy, looking for what I couldn't give him. He deserved a beautiful, clever woman who could come through for him in his time of need, not a screw-up with more baggage than a lost property office.

He needed Emmy, not me.

# 39

## NICK

Nick stormed through Emmy's front door, pausing as an afterthought to slam it behind him.

"Don't worry," she called out. "I never liked that door much anyway. You want a beer?"

"Fuckin' need a beer after the night I've had."

Emmy found him in the kitchen, rummaging in the fridge. "I spoke to Lara and Dom. I gather there was a small hiccup with Lara's ex?"

"Yeah, there was." He pulled out a bottle and popped the top. "I'm gonna need a favour."

"You mean you want me to do what you didn't manage yourself?"

"Hey, I was in front of Lara and her friend. I'd already plastered the asshole over the hood of the car she was sitting in."

"Nice. So why'd you stop?"

"Going back to finish the job would hardly have endeared me to her, would it? Not to mention the other two fuckers I had to take care of."

"Calm down, I'm kidding. I'll deal with it, Nicky."

He gave her hand a squeeze. "Thank you."

"Only the son? The father seems like a cunt too."

"We'll have to watch the body count."

Two dead Coopers in a short space of time might arouse suspicions, even from the dumb pricks in Baysville.

"I'm nothing if not professional about these things."

Of course she was. She always had been. "Sorry. It's just this one's personal."

"I promise I'll sort it."

No, Emmy wouldn't let him down. She never let him down.

"And I'll owe you one. What happened with the father, anyway? Con said he was stalling the investigation?"

"He was. Lara figured it out, actually. Cooper senior's a golfing buddy of the mayor, so he had him call the police chief and tell him to hold things up. But nobody plays that game better than me." Emmy grinned. "I pissed all over their bonfire."

Nick dropped onto a stool at the breakfast bar. "Go on then, what did you do?"

"Got Senator Wilmslow to phone the police chief and ask him to explain why he was holding a gentleman who'd selflessly acted to protect two women from a man who'd already threatened one of them earlier in the evening, and why he was refusing to consider any of the evidence in front of him. The chief now has a meeting with the good senator next week, in which he will be reminded of the need to make the wheels of justice turn, well, a little more justly."

"I didn't realise you knew Senator Wilmslow. Isn't he a new appointment?"

"I don't, personally. But James knows him, and I know James, so I woke James up and asked him to make the introductions."

She did what? "You called James in the middle of the night?"

"Yeah. He's always been a light sleeper."

"Shit. How many favours do I owe him?"

"Relax. I sorted that too. While James tracked down the senator, he passed me over to his wife. You're expected at her fundraiser in six weeks' time, and Lara too. Diana's intrigued to meet the woman who's finally stolen your heart, as is James."

"Fuck. I keep telling you, I'm not *with* Lara. That's not gonna happen."

"It is."

"No, it isn't, especially since I managed to screw things up twice while we were away."

"For fuck's sake, Nicky. What did you do?"

Nick took a long pull on his beer then slammed the bottle onto the counter. "I need something stronger."

"Scotch? Patrón? Grey Goose?"

"Scotch'll do to start."

Emmy fetched a bottle and poured Nick a generous measure, and he knocked half back before he spoke again. Talking about the debacle in Baysville was the last thing he wanted to do.

"Okay, so we were in the church after the wedding. Lara got stuck in her dress, and I was helping her out of it."

"Smooth. So what went wrong?"

"Stop laughing. It wasn't funny. I might have kissed her shoulders, but she turned around and I panicked."

"Oh, but it's hilarious. You don't balk in a gunfight, but you freak when the woman you love looks at you."

Love? He didn't love Lara, did he? Even if he had accidentally told her that. Shit. This situation couldn't get much messier, and even now, Nick couldn't stop thinking of the way that ridiculous pink dress had slid down her body, exposing those sweet, firm... Enough!

"She looked so fuckin' perfect. How can I bring her into our world? I'd spend every day worrying in case something happened to her."

"She could get hit by a car tomorrow. Or slip in the shower. Or choke on a grape."

"Would you mind not talking about death?"

"Sorry, but you've got to stop thinking like that. Sure, it happened once, and that was devastating, but the odds are you've had your bad luck now. I still think you should let Lara make that decision. She might surprise you."

"You didn't see the horror on her face after I laid those three bastards out." She'd refused to look at Nick as the cops arrived, and that had nearly brought him to his knees. "I'd give anything to turn the clock back and deal with things differently."

"What would you have done? Asked Billy nicely if he'd mind lying on the nearest set of train tracks?"

"I don't know. But something."

"You need to talk to Lara about it."

"Yeah," he muttered. "But what the hell do I say?"

"Just explain why you did what you did."

"Last week, she said violence is never acceptable."

"Under what context?"

"One of her friend's kids was hitting me with a plastic sword."

"Good thing she never sees what we do in the gym." Emmy snorted. "But that's completely different. Even a saint would have knocked Billy Cooper's teeth out."

"While we're on the subject of Cooper, what do you know about him? And Lara's accident? Don't pretend you didn't do a full background check before you hired her."

Emmy found a box of chocolates in a cupboard and popped one into her mouth. "Caramel?"

She seriously thought he could eat at a time like this? Nick shook his head, and Emmy took a seat next to him.

"Lara met Billy at sixteen in high school. According to her former teacher, they sat together in math, and Lara did Billy's homework for him the whole time they dated. Then they went to college together. Brown. Billy's father paid for their apartment, and Lara was on a math scholarship. Billy's thing was football, except he got injured. I didn't look into him much. Just her."

"I can't believe she lived with that dick."

Emmy shrugged. "He wasn't even a pretty face. Lara kept to herself, mostly, but her grades stayed up. Then she had an accident when she was twenty-one, or at least that's what she claimed. The apartment was split-level, and she fell downstairs and broke her leg. It was a compound fracture, and let's put it this way, when she goes through the airport, she's gonna set off all the metal detectors."

"She says Billy pushed her."

"Quite possibly he did. She never went back to him. She moved home with her mother instead and worked a series of dead-end jobs while her mom got treated for breast cancer. That was a nice gesture, by the way, paying off her medical bills."

"How do you know about that?"

"I know everything."

"Emmy..."

"Okay, okay. Nadia left your bank account open on her computer. You should tell her to be more careful."

"Noted."

"So, Mommy popped her clogs, and Lara's been on her own ever since. No boyfriend since Billy. Phone records show her only regular contact is with Missy and the girl you went to see in London, Victoria. Job at Buck's bar, no other income. Lived in a shitty one-room apartment in the worst part of Baysville until she upped and moved out here. No idea why she moved, but everything else came back clear, so we took a chance and hired her."

"She said Buck cut her shifts at the bar because he favoured some airhead blonde with plastic tits who doesn't know the difference between beer and root beer, and also thinks a bukkake special's a kind of cocktail."

Emmy let out a snort of laughter. "Bloody hell, us blondes work our arses off trying to improve our image, then someone like that comes along and undoes decades of work."

"Lara also mentioned she thought someone had been following her."

"She didn't file a police report."

"She said she tried, but they didn't take her seriously. Which, having had the pleasure of meeting Baysville's finest tonight, I can certainly believe."

"We can look into it if you want. Does Lara have a description?"

Nick shook his head. "She didn't see anyone for definite, and she reckons it's stopped since she moved here."

"Probably not a hell of a lot we can do then, to be honest. Now what are you doing? Bed, food, or heading for the gym?"

"I can't sleep, and I'm not hungry. Plus I still feel like killing somebody. You up for some sparring?"

"A fight? Bring it on, tough guy."

# 40

## LARA

Three days later, I still hadn't left my apartment. I'd cleaned it six times, and with every surface sparkling, it was hard to justify picking up a cloth for a seventh go. When I wasn't wiping or vacuuming, I'd alternated between staring at the wall and eating my emergency ice cream stash.

I hadn't called Nick, and he hadn't called me. Did I still have a job? Even if I did, how would I be able to face Nick if I returned to Adler House? What do you say to a boss you almost kissed, accidentally told you were crazy about, and indirectly landed up in jail? "Sorry" wouldn't cut it. Besides, I'd tried that already, and it hadn't gone down well.

I returned to staring at the wall.

Mid-afternoon, somebody knocked on the door, and I ignored it. I had nothing to say to anyone. Another knock. What if it was Nick? No, he'd fire me by phone, not make a special trip all the way out here. I stayed on the bed.

A scraping noise came from the door, it flew open, and I jerked upright just in time to see Bradley dragging one of my suitcases into the room.

"Oh, you are here. Why didn't you open the door?"

"Maybe because I didn't feel like speaking to anyone? How did you get in? I'm sure I locked it."

"You did. But I've been working for Emmy for years now, and I've learned a few things along the way. Your lock's a piece of junk, by the way. You should get a new one."

Why would working for Emmy necessitate picking locks? Was she always losing her keys or something?

"The whole apartment's junk. The lock's the least of my problems."

"Well, stay at Nick's house. I'm sure he won't mind. It's not like he's there, anyway. He's been making his mess at Emmy's all week. Her housekeeper's already grumbling about it."

"Haven't you heard what happened?"

"You mean the jail thing?"

"Yes, the jail thing. How can I go back to working for Nick after that?"

Bradley patted my hand. "It was a minor mishap, that's all. Nick's dealt with far worse."

"What could possibly be worse than getting arrested?"

"Let's see... How about the time he went over for pizza at Emmy's and the place got stormed by a gang of commandos armed with machine guns and rocket-propelled grenades?"

I couldn't help laughing. "Trust you to make up some outrageous story to try and make me feel better."

"It's true, I swear. Anyway, you need to come back to work. Nobody else would put up with Nick and his disgusting habits."

True? Yeah, right, and I was a Victoria's Secret model.

"Are you positive Nick's not home?"

If I could wangle another week's pay, it sure would come in handy.

"I've just come from his place. There wasn't a soul there."

We hauled my other suitcases inside then Bradley gave me a ride to Nick's, seeing as I didn't have a car at my apartment. With nobody in Adler House, the only damage was a layer of dust. I whizzed around with a duster, desperate to get the cleaning over with.

Should I take a car home? I thought back to Nick's insistence that I drive the Ferrari, and I couldn't resist one last trip in it.

Before I left, I propped a note against the vase on the kitchen table.

*I'm sorry.*
*Lara*

I wanted to write more, but I didn't know what else to say.

When I returned the next morning, the house was silent. Was Nick still at Emmy's? I thought so until I got to the kitchen. My note had disappeared, and a new one lay in its place. I recognised Nick's untidy scrawl.

*You have nothing to be sorry for.*
*N*

And that was it. I didn't see Nick for the rest of the week. His bed remained unslept in, and the food in the fridge gradually spoiled. On Friday, I threw most of it out. Was he avoiding me? Or did he stay away for the simple reason that Emmy had made him a better offer? Or both?

I couldn't carry on like this. Every time I set foot in Adler House, the ragged ends of my nerves frazzled a little more, wondering whether today would be the day I'd cross paths with Nick. So much strife had passed between us by now, I doubted we'd ever get past it.

As soon as I got home on Friday, I called Michelle at the agency.

"I've decided to move on."

"What, from Mr. Goldman?"

"I need a change."

"Has he been unreasonable?"

"No, not at all. But I'm on my own at the house so often, and I've been getting lonely. I'd prefer a job with more people around. Perhaps with a family? I was wondering if you've got anything available?"

"Oh, I'm so sorry it's not working out." She sounded genuinely apologetic. "There's not much around at the moment unless you want to go back to hotel work?"

The thought of cleaning up behind drunk, deranged businessmen again made me groan. After the initial clear up, looking after Nick was hardly taxing.

"Is it okay if I think about it? I can hold out here for a few more weeks."

"Absolutely, and I'll call you if anything better comes up."

I hadn't totally lied to Michelle. I *was* lonely. My whole time with Billy, one of the things that had kept me from leaving was the thought of coming home at night to nobody. The reality hadn't turned out to be quite as bad as I thought, but I longed to meet someone who cared for me.

The problem was, I'd measure every man against Nick from now on, and they'd all be found wanting.

Maybe I should settle for somebody safe? Somebody who might not make my heart beat like crazy but who'd keep me company? The trouble was, the stubborn part of me still wanted the whole darn fairy tale.

In the past week, I'd cycled through the whole spectrum of emotions: sadness, hurt, love, anger, depression, loneliness, confusion, misery, and hope. But until Wednesday evening, the one thing I hadn't felt was fear.

I opened my apartment door, and it took a long second to register. My brain went for denial first. No way. The room couldn't possibly smell of cigarette smoke mixed with cheap cologne, hanging in the air over the faint lemon scent of polish.

*I must be imagining it.* There was no other explanation. I forced myself to take another step forward, trying to decide whether to leave the door open for a quick escape or close it to intruders and potentially trap myself inside with a stalker.

In the end, I opted to push it almost shut, then I grabbed a knife from the drawer in the kitchenette. Brandishing it in front of me, I stepped into the bedroom.

Empty, thank goodness.

The bathroom came next, and I whipped back the shower curtain as that horrible scene in *Psycho* played through my mind.

Nothing.

My knees gave way, and I perched on the edge of the bath. Was this a nightmare? I pinched myself, studying the red mark left on my skin. Nope, I was definitely awake.

I reached out to straighten my toothbrush, realising too late that I'd never have left it wonky in the first place. A drop of water fell off the end. I always blotted my toothbrush on my towel when I'd finished using it because I hated leaving watermarks on the shelf. *Always.*

How did it get wet? Had somebody used it? I hurled it across the room as bile rose up my throat, then vomited into the toilet.

This couldn't be happening. Not again. I'd moved to another state, for goodness' sake! How could my stalker have found me here? And what on earth was I going to do?

Staying in my apartment was out of the question, that was for sure. I ran from room to room, throwing essentials into a bag. I needed to find a hotel.

Where would have vacancies? And more importantly, where could I afford?

I yanked the front door open, slammed it behind me, and ran to the Ferrari, letting out a long breath when I locked myself inside without anybody grabbing me.

Now what?

Ah, yes, a hotel. I needed a bed for the night. I switched the satnav unit on and the screen blinked, a bright yellow line showing me the way to Adler House.

Did I dare?

I thought of Nick's six empty bedrooms and state-of-the-art alarm system and decided I was scared enough that I did.

I nearly chickened out a dozen times on the way to Nick's, but then I drove through the gates, and it was too late to turn around. The lights on the outside of the house blinked on, welcoming me in.

To safety.

I parked in the garage, then scurried inside and dropped my bag in the smallest guest bedroom. I'd re-armed the perimeter sensors on my way in, and now I headed for the control panel at the top of the stairs and activated the motion sensors on the first floor. Only when all the LEDs turned green did my breathing begin to slow.

Back in the bedroom, I flopped down on the covers, exhausted. Just when I thought life couldn't deal me any more blows, it got up and punched me in the face.

How was I supposed to get over this? What should...?

My brain gave up mid-thought and led me into darkness.

I woke in the early hours, desperate to use the bathroom. My mouth tasted like day-old pizza, and of course, I didn't have a toothbrush. I'd need to borrow a spare from the vanity and replace it tomorrow.

Sleeping in jeans had given me stripy legs from the seams, and my polo neck left me sweating. Once my mouth was minty fresh again, I stripped down to my underwear, flushed the toilet, and headed back to bed.

Everything else would have to wait until morning.

Or so I thought. Fate had other ideas.

I'd only gotten one toe under the quilt when the door flew open. In a near repeat of our first meeting, I stared down the black barrel of the gun Nick pointed at me.

What was a girl to do? Well, I took the only sensible option and screamed.

Unlike last time, Nick lowered the weapon right away, and with the gun out of my face, I realised there *was* one significant difference to last time.

Nick wasn't wearing black.

In fact, he wasn't wearing anything. Holy hell!

"Baby, what the fuck are you doing here?"

Oh, crap. I dragged my eyes up to his face. "Uh, someone's been in my apartment, and I was scared."

"What do you mean, someone's been in your apartment?"

"They used my toothbrush," I squeaked. "And I panicked and threw up. And do you think you could put some clothes on because I'm having trouble looking at your face?"

Hell, did I just say that last bit out loud? Please, just raise the gun again and shoot me. It'd save me from having to do it myself.

Nick merely smirked as he nodded in my direction. "That's hardly fair. You're not exactly dressed yourself."

Oh freaking fudge, I wasn't! I snatched up the quilt and wrapped it around myself, then squeezed my eyes closed so everything would go away.

"Why are you here?" I mumbled.

"I live here."

"But you haven't been here all week. I didn't think you'd be back."

"I wanted to talk to you. I thought I'd wait for you to arrive in the morning."

This was it. He was going to fire me, wasn't he?

"Well, we're both here now. So if you don't want me to be your housekeeper anymore, you can just say it."

The pause was so long I cracked an eyelid open to check he hadn't disappeared. Although if it turned out I was dreaming, that would have solved a lot of problems.

But Nick was still there, natural as life and twice as large. And then he shrugged. "I don't want you to be my housekeeper anymore."

# 41

## LARA

Something inside me broke. No, not something. My heart, or what was left of it. Pieces pierced every atom in me as it shattered into a thousand tiny pieces. I closed my eyes again. They say the eyes are the window to a person's soul, and I didn't want Nick to know mine was bleeding.

So I didn't see him move. Or hear him. I only felt his lips on mine, gently caressing as his tongue coaxed my mouth open. When I allowed him in, he kissed me deeply with the sweetness of a fresh apple pie. Delicious, moreish, and if you tried hard enough, you could almost believe it was good for you.

I almost didn't want to open my eyes, but I had to. I needed to look at him. When I did, he pulled back.

"Baby, if you want me to leave, tell me now and I'll go. But if I stay, I'm not stopping for anything. Time could end and the world could fall apart, but that wouldn't stop me from making love to you tonight."

"Stay."

Emmy popped briefly into my head, but I trusted Nick.

Bradley must have been right about their romance being over. Nick wouldn't cheat on her, would he? He was far too much of a gentleman.

Although there was nothing gentle about his next kiss. Fire burst through my veins as he pulled me against him, and the quilt slithered to the floor. Then we were skin on skin. Nick hardened against me as he ravaged my mouth, and I wrapped my arms around him. The results of his hours in the gym rippled as I ran my fingertips up his back. Wow.

We fell back on the bed, and his weight pressed onto me, sending my pulse on a crazy gallop. I wanted him more than I wanted to breathe. No, not wanted. I *needed* him, more than I needed air. At least he'd come in naked—clothes would only have slowed things down.

Slow had its time and place, but tonight wasn't it. No, if Nick didn't make good on his promise, and quickly, I'd burst into flames.

I wanted a whole different kind of hot.

Nick popped my bra open, and my breasts spilled out into his hands. Heat blazed across my skin as he kneaded them gently and stroked the tips of my nipples with feather-soft fingers, then went to town with his tongue. Surely I'd wake up any moment? This couldn't be real.

But my body sure thought so. Slickness seeped around the edges of my panties as he fluttered kisses down my stomach, and the blush searing my cheeks gave away my lust. I lay back and let the sensations overtake me. Was it normal to be soaking like that?

A finger snuck under the elastic, and Nick paused to smile at me.

"Someone's happy."

I tried to form words, but all that came out was a moan. Then a gasp as Nick slid a finger inside, followed by a second.

"I've dreamed of having you underneath me for a long

time," he whispered. "And of feeling you come on my fingers. But I know it'll be even better in real life."

"You dreamed of me?"

"Every fuckin' night."

"I dreamed of you too."

He brushed soft kisses over my temples. "So in your dreams, what did I do to you?"

My cheeks heated again. How could I possibly tell him that?

"Baby, if you tell me, I can make those dreams come true."

Ohhhhhh. I paused, torn between totally embarrassing myself and having the mother of all orgasms. Guess which won?

"First you touched me."

"Where?"

"Uh... Down there."

He brushed his fingers along my thigh, leaving a cool trail. "Here?"

"No."

He traced up my hip to my stomach, softly circling my belly button. Billy had always complained about my size, not to mention my lack of muscle tone, but Nick made me feel sexy for the first time in my life.

"How about here?"

"Not exactly."

"Then tell me."

I closed my eyes and whispered, "Between my legs."

He pushed my panties aside and stroked, hitting the perfect spot. My back arched off the bed as I pressed against him.

"Baby, in my dreams you screamed my name."

Ten seconds later, I did precisely that.

The rush was so intense that when I came back into my own body, it had melted into the mattress like a crayon left out in the sun. I still hadn't recovered when Nick's mouth found my nipples again, teasing first one and then the other into stiff little peaks. And they weren't the only things that were hard. I could feel a certain part of his anatomy resting on my thigh.

He shuddered as I reached out and stroked his cock, root to tip. Hang on, what the...? My fingers shot back like they'd been burned.

"What the hell is that?"

"An apadravya."

"An apa-what?"

"An apadravya—a piercing. It makes things more pleasurable."

Oh, holy fudge! He had a pierced freaking cock. I brushed one of the smooth metal balls, and it felt cool to the touch.

"Doesn't it hurt?"

"Not now. If it worries you, I can take it out, but I promise it'll be good for both of us."

I wasn't sure what to say. I mean, I'd never had a lump of metal inside me before. But I trusted Nick, and the spark of the girl who'd existed before Billy Cooper came into my life told me to take the risk.

I ran my fingertips over it again. "Leave it in."

"Okay, but you're going to have to stop touching it that way because right now, I feel like a horny sixteen-year-old fumbling in the back seat. And I want to come inside you rather than all over the upholstery."

"Then what are you waiting for?"

"Nothing anymore. Are you on the pill?"

"Yes."

"I'm clean, I swear. But I'll use a condom if you want me to."

"Just get inside me. Please. I need you."

My panties vanished as if by magic, but when the tip of his cock slipped between my lips, I had a sudden panic.

"What if it doesn't fit?"

His smirk ratcheted all the way up to cocky. "Baby, it'll fit. You're soaked, and I'll go slow."

And he did. A low moan escaped my lips as he slid inside oh-so-gently, although I was stretched more than ever before. If I'd had a lust-induced heart attack at that moment, I'd have died happy, but then Nick started to move. And oh boy, was he right about the piercing. It hit exactly the right spot inside me, one Billy had never managed to find in five and a half long years. Another orgasm built, and before I could prepare for it, I saw stars. My scream barely registered in my own ears, but I did have the vague thought that it was good none of Nick's neighbours lived nearby.

Now I knew how ice cream felt on a hot summer's day— all soft and gooey, but at the same time delicious and a little bit decadent. With one of those chocolate flakes stuck into me. Nick flexed his hips, and a shiver ran through every inch of my body, but then I fluttered back to earth and landed with a bump.

"Oh my gosh, you didn't..."

He hadn't come. I'd messed up again. When Billy didn't get off fast enough, he never hesitated to push harder, and fear gripped me as memories of him thrusting, taking, and tearing hit.

Nick's fingers skimmed over my hip as he began to move again with agonising slowness.

"Don't bring that man into our bed, baby."

What? How did he know? "I wasn't..."

"You were. I saw it in your eyes." He leaned down and kissed each eyelid. "Forget him. He doesn't exist anymore. And you're gonna come twice more before I do, so you'd better hurry up because I can't hold on much longer."

"I don't think I can, I mean, I've never..." I didn't even finish the sentence before I detonated again.

Nick grinned at me. "Sorry, you were saying?"

This time, he didn't wait for me to get my breath back, and my hungry gasps punctuated every thrust. Nick managed to be hard and soft at the same time, tender yet rugged. A river of desire flowed through me, carrying away all my bad memories, and then the dam broke. Nick spilled into me, and I floated off to a happier place.

I'd finally found it. Found *him*. My own little slice of heaven wrapped up in a sinfully sexy package.

Nick peppered my face and neck with hundreds of tiny kisses, supporting his weight on his forearms. What should I say to him? "Thank you," hardly seemed adequate. I'd never come with a man inside me before, and now Nick had given me that three times. He was a magician. No other explanation.

"Best I've ever had," he whispered. "But I knew you would be."

"It was... I just... Wow."

"Exactly. Are you ready to go again?"

What? He couldn't. Could he? He wasn't? I raised my head an inch or two off the pillow, which took a momentous effort. He was. He was hard again. Just wow. I think I nodded.

His teeth nipped at the skin on my shoulders as he slid into me, and I arched up against him, needing to get closer to this man who made me feel like no other. My legs wrapped around him of their own accord, which created a whole new type of friction. And mess, a few minutes later.

We both collapsed in a pool of sweat and lust and bodily fluids. Old Lara would have changed the sheets right away and put on the washing machine. New Lara didn't care.

After Nick blew my mind, I collapsed into his arms and slept. I didn't dream. How could I when they'd already come true? I woke still wrapped up in a hot mess of a man, with a tangle of sheets around our ankles and his gun lying next to us on the nightstand.

For a moment, I wondered whether my imagination was working overtime, some weird hallucination brought on by stress and unruly hormones. But when I reached out and poked Nick, his eyes popped open.

"Ouch. What was that for?"

"Just checking you're real."

His deep chuckle vibrated through me. "If you dreamed last night, we had the same dream."

I reached under the sheets, finding his cock and fingering the piercing at the end of it. It started to harden under my touch.

"You like the apa then, baby?"

"I wasn't sure I would, but just, well...wow. And you're sure it doesn't hurt?"

"Not for a long time."

"Why did you get it? For a woman?"

"Yes, but not in the way you think. It was the result of an impulsive bet that went horribly wrong." He nuzzled my shoulder. "Or so I thought. To see you smile like you did last night, I'd turn myself into a fuckin' pincushion."

The metal felt smooth under my fingers as I stroked. "No, this is plenty."

A phone rang somewhere in the house, disturbing our moment. Nick let out a low groan.

"Give me a minute. I'll call in sick."

"But you're not ill."

He stood and walked towards the door, and I got a view of him from the back, minus the towel. His ass surpassed even my wildest dreams. Then he paused in the doorway and looked over his shoulder.

"I'm fuckin' lovesick, baby."

Oh. My. Gosh. Inside, I wanted to get up and dance around the room, but there was no way my legs would have cooperated. Could I have a future with Nick? For a moment, I dared to hope.

Then I remembered what he'd said the night before.

*I don't want you to be my housekeeper anymore.*

By the time he slipped back into the bedroom minutes later, little beads of sweat had popped out on the back of my neck. I needed to work, and despite my recent misgivings, I wanted this job. The view of oh-so-perfect abs and slick, golden skin distracted me for a moment, but I gave my head a shake to make myself focus on the important things. I'd never tire of looking at Nick—*never*—but I needed to clarify where I stood.

"Last night, you said you didn't want me to be your housekeeper anymore. Are you firing me?"

"Whatever." He laid back down on the bed and arranged my leg over his hip so I rolled into him. "I want you to be my girlfriend instead. We can hire another housekeeper."

"Oh. Wow."

"Is that your word for today? Wow?"

"I guess so, yes. I can't really think of another one."

"You can say it as many times as you want. In the shower, to start with. We need to get clean. Well, first we need to get dirty, then we need to get clean. What do you say?"

"Wait. Wait! I need a job. The money..."

"I make plenty of money for the two of us. I'll give you a credit card."

Become a kept woman again? The idea made me nervous, but Nick was already halfway out of bed.

"I'm not sure—"

"If you want to work, then work, but don't feel as if you have to pick up after another asshole like me because you're worried about not pulling your weight. I enjoy my job, and it makes me a stack of cash, but money's just a facilitator to get me more of what I want. And right now, that's you."

"Wow."

"I'll have Nadia arrange the credit card."

Nick's bathroom had the best shower, and he carried me into it, bridal-style. Jets hit us from all sides and took what little breath I had left away.

"Maybe not," he muttered and pressed a few buttons on the console at the side. The jets eased, and water rained from the top showerhead instead. "Better."

I expected him to pick up the bottle of shower gel, but no. He dropped to his knees and parted my legs, and I didn't know where to look or what to think as he tasted me. No man had ever ventured down there before. What if it was icky?

I tried to pull Nick up, but he clasped my hands in his and kept going.

"I need this, baby."

What could I do but surrender?

"Best," I whispered.

Nick carried me out of the shower half an hour later, which was a good thing because I couldn't walk. I lay on his bed in a crumpled heap while he sat beside me and stroked my hair.

"You look tired."

I stifled a yawn. "You've worn me out."

"I'd apologise, but I'm not sorry."

"Neither am I, but I am hungry. I didn't eat dinner yesterday."

He reached for the phone on his nightstand. "I'll get food delivered."

"I can make something."

"Not today. I want to spoil you."

I took his hand and peeled the phone out of his fingers. "You already have, and now it's time for me to repay the favour. I love cooking for you. What do you want to eat?"

Wrong question. His eyes roved down my naked body with the hunger of a rabid wolf.

"From the kitchen, Nick. From the kitchen."

"Anything. I don't care as long as I'm sitting next to you when I eat it."

## 42

### LARA

Today, I got a different Nick to the one I used to know. This Nick didn't bother to hide his desire as he sat at the breakfast bar, watching my every move. He didn't bother to put a shirt on either, and I had to remake the pancake batter after I got distracted and added too many eggs.

"You want bacon?"

He nodded, and I felt his eyes on my behind as I bent to fetch the package from the bottom shelf in the refrigerator. Like a laser, they heated my blood to the boiling point. The atmosphere in the room sizzled more than the frying pan.

As we ate, I was free to ogle him in a way I couldn't before, and after three-quarters of a pancake, temptation got the better of me. I reached out and traced each solid square of his six-pack with a finger, fascinated by the way his muscles rippled at my touch.

"Don't do that if you want to finish your breakfast."

I looked at the food, then looked at Nick. "I've lost my appetite."

Nick's California king was larger than the bed in the guest

room, and we made use of every last inch as he showed me positions I'd never even thought of. By the time he'd finished, I'd turned into a wet spaghetti noodle. Even Nick looked sleepy.

"You want to try eating again?" he asked. "Food, I mean."

"My mouth's tired."

He laughed. "Not surprised, baby. I'll feed you."

This time, I didn't try to stop him when he ordered in. Not a pizza or Chinese. No, Nick called Rhodium, the best restaurant in town, and had them send a fancy dinner in a cab.

"That's too much," I whispered.

"Nothing's too much for you."

We'd got as far as dessert when Nick broached the subject I'd hoped to avoid.

"Open." He slid a forkful of chocolate orange-mousse between my lips. "What were you talking about last night? When you said someone had been in your apartment?"

All the good vibes slithered away, leaving me with the memory of my wild dash across town.

"You remember in Baysville I thought someone had been following me? I've got an awful feeling he might have come here. You probably think I'm crazy, don't you?"

"You're lots of things, but crazy isn't one of them. Tell me what makes you think that. Start at the beginning, and don't leave anything out."

So I did. I told Nick how I'd smelled tobacco smoke and cheap cologne, about the objects that moved around, and the warm patch on my bed. I expected him to laugh it off, but his face stayed solemn. Concerned, even. "And last night when I got home, my apartment had that same smell, and I swear someone had used my toothbrush. I always dry it after I've used it, and it was wet."

"You dry your toothbrush?"

"Nick! I'm being serious."

"Sorry, baby. I know. I'll get it looked into, I promise. We can get cameras set up in your apartment. Until then, you're staying with me."

"Really? I can stay here?"

"Too fuckin' right. Your apartment's got no security whatsoever."

"Bradley said the lock isn't very good. He picked it."

"If Bradley managed to pick the lock, you might as well not have one. This place is connected to a central monitoring station, and I'll warn them to stay extra vigilant. The glass in the windows is bulletproof, and the doors are reinforced with steel. There's a panic room upstairs you won't have seen yet, and another in the basement."

"What basement?"

"Exactly."

Once I'd stacked the plates into the dishwasher, Nick led me out to the hallway and stopped in front of an alcove. When I arrived, it had been hidden behind a dead yucca, but once the hideous plant found its rightful place in the dumpster, a stunning stone eagle had been revealed. Someone with talent had sculpted that bird. Almost five feet high as it perched on a branch, every detail was perfect, from the way its talons gripped the wood to the textured feathers to the gleam in its eyes. Now, Nick reached out and twisted its beak.

"What the...?"

The mirror next to it slid back, revealing a set of concrete steps leading downwards.

"Basement," Nick said. He flicked on a light and led me down.

"Wow. It's...empty."

The cavernous room stretched the length of the house, and apart from a desk and what looked like a safe in one corner, it was completely bare. Basement? It was more like a bunker. Presumably, the single closed door at the far end was the panic room.

He tipped his head to one side, sheepish. "I never got around to doing much with it."

"Thank goodness. If it looked like upstairs used to, I'd have cried."

Strong arms wrapped around me as he rested his chin on top of my head. He sure knew how to make a girl feel short.

"How about we furnish it? Put in a movie theatre or something? Or a game room? You ever play pool?"

I barely heard most of what he said because the third word made my heart skip. We. How about *we* furnish it. The life I'd craved with the man of my dreams—might it come true?

My imagination ran wild as I followed him upstairs to his bedroom. Nick cuddling me as we watched a movie. Nick lying in the garden next to me on a blanket while the sun shone. Nick coming home and eating dinner with me every night. *We*. Nick wanted a future with me.

"Baby, are you watching this?"

"Huh?"

He chuckled. "Earth to Lara. You need to twist the whole light switch clockwise."

When he did so, the painting next to his closet slid to the side. I peered into the gloom. The house was full of secrets, although the biggest enigma so far was Nick himself.

"It's not big. More of a cupboard, really. But it's got a reinforced steel door, a phone installed on a separate line, plus a screen linked to the cameras so you can see what's going on. If anything happens, get inside and press speed dial one for help."

"Shouldn't I phone the police?"

"The monitoring service will do that. Call them first."

The thought of having to call anyone made me shudder, but I appreciated Nick's concern over my stalker. And he was probably right about the cops. It wasn't as if they'd taken me seriously the first time. Right now, I felt safe. Not only because Adler House was like a fortress, but because Nick believed me.

His phone rang, and he glanced at the screen. "Now what?" He jabbed it with a finger. "This had better be good."

His face clouded over as whoever it was spoke to him. "Tonight? You're kidding... No, I'm busy... You know why... Fine... Two hours, and if I'm not back by ten, I'll turn you into a fuckin' pumpkin."

I didn't hear the words, but I got the gist of them. "You have to work this evening, don't you?"

"I'm sorry, baby." He grimaced. "Dinner with a couple of Russian businessmen. A colleague was gonna go, but he had to pull out at the last minute, and nobody else knows enough about the deal." Nick dipped his head and brushed his lips across mine. "I'll make it up to you, I promise."

"It's okay, really. I'll have a snack and watch a movie. Are you going somewhere nice?"

"That new Lebanese place, Levante. But I'd rather stay home with you."

"Maybe when you get back, we could..." Oh gosh, I was blushing. Heat spread up my cheeks, mirrored by the warmth between my legs. What was wrong with me? "Can we...?"

"Can we fuck?"

I nodded quickly.

"You'd better believe it, baby." He kissed me on the forehead. "It's so damn sweet that you can't even say the word."

330

Nick roared off in his truck at seven, leaving me alone to fix an omelette and salad. Cheese, ham, no onions because Nick wouldn't appreciate my stinky breath in the bedroom. Being alone in the house felt different to all the other times—no loneliness, just a delicious sense of anticipation.

Although if this was going to be a regular thing, which I sure hoped it would, I'd need to pick up some clothes. I'd been wearing a robe the whole day, which was decadent but hardly practical.

But in the meantime, I decided to watch a movie. And where better to do that than in Nick's bed? He had a massive TV on the wall opposite, a mattress so comfortable it was like floating on puffs of cloud, and thousand-thread-count Egyptian cotton sheets. Best of all, the bed smelled just like him. And I borrowed one of his T-shirts to wear. He wouldn't mind, would he?

Now, where did he leave the remote? I hunted around, then spotted it on the nightstand. Right next to... Oh, shoot! Nick's wallet. He'd forgotten it.

And worse, he said he'd be entertaining clients. How embarrassing would it be if he went to pay for dinner and didn't have his credit card?

I hurried through to the guest room and retrieved my phone. If I warned him before the check came, maybe he could make other arrangements? Except when I called his number, I heard the muffled tune of Whitney Houston's "I Will Always Love You" coming from his bedroom. I'd never pegged him for a Whitney fan, but it was nice when a man got in touch with his feminine side.

I shook that thought out of my head because I still had the darn wallet. And I felt a little guilty about that. After all, if he hadn't gotten distracted and made out with me for fifteen minutes before he left, he'd have probably remembered to take it.

What should I do?

Right now, he'd be sitting down to eat, running up a bill with no means to pay. That had happened to Billy once, and steam came out of his ears when he realised. I'd paid the price for it later. Nick wouldn't use his fists, I knew that, but he'd be mortified in Levante, and with such a distinguished audience too. Hang on! Levante. I knew where he was. I could drive there with the wallet, hand it over, and be gone before his dining companions even noticed. Perfect.

I tugged on yesterday's clothes and armed the security system. The Ferrari was waiting in the garage, beautiful as always, and five minutes later, I was on my way with the wallet tucked securely in my pocket. How long would it take to get to the restaurant? Twenty minutes? Thirty?

It took twenty-five, with another ten minutes of circling to find a parking space halfway along the block. Oh, please tell me I'd made it in time?

The lights of Levante spilled onto the sidewalk, reds and golds and blues from the ornate lanterns that decked the window. Pretty. Two months ago, I'd never have hoped to set foot inside, but now? Maybe Nick would take me to dinner there one day if we had something to celebrate? I quickly shook my head to clear away the thought. *Lara, you're getting way ahead of yourself, girl. You have a job to do here.* Gentle sitar music drifted from the doorway as I peered through the glass, trying to spot Nick's handsome face.

And I did.

Except he wasn't at a work dinner with Russian businessmen. He was sitting at a table for two with Emmy. Her hand was firmly clasped in his as they gazed at each other, an empty bowl with two spoons in between them. I recognised that look in his eyes. Why? Because I'd seen it last night. I couldn't read lips, but when he spoke, I was fairly sure he wasn't giving her tips on the latest mergers and acquisitions.

My heart shattered all over again. Why did he have to lie to me? Although technically he hadn't lied, had he? He'd never said it was over between Emmy and him. After what Bradley told me, and then Nick's actions, I'd just assumed. And I didn't know what was worse—that the man I'd fallen for had cheated or that I'd accidentally turned myself into the other woman.

What would Emmy do if she found out? She'd have every right to be furious. I deserved nothing less.

Tears leaked onto the sidewalk along with my wounded soul as I ran to the car. My life was just one freaking disaster after another, and I'd had enough. I slammed the door of the Ferrari as I slid into the driver's seat. Who cared if it broke? Not me. Not anymore. I wiped my eyes as I fired up the sexy red beast, trying to clear my blurry vision. I didn't even know where I was going. Not back to Adler House, that was for sure. Never again.

Anger flooded through me as I did a U-turn and headed for my apartment. I didn't have much choice but to sleep there tonight, and I didn't even care if my stalker was waiting. Life couldn't get much worse, could it? And the way I felt about men at that moment, I'd kick him where it hurt if he dared to come near me. In fact, I almost hoped he did.

That way I'd get closure. The end of my old life before I moved on with the new, somewhere far away from dangerous men, dreamy houses, and beautiful girls. Tomorrow, I'd leave for good.

## 43

## NICK

"Nick, for fuck's sake, at least try to look like you're in love with me," Emmy hissed.

"It'd be easier if you weren't so damned annoying," Nick murmured back. "Why did you just kick me, anyway?"

"Because you weren't concentrating. You need to listen to what arsehole number two is saying. You're closer than I am, and I can't quite hear. Shit, he's looking this way again. Gaze into my eyes, will you? Just imagine I'm Lara. That should do it."

Nick clasped Emmy's hand over the table and squeezed, harder than was necessary, then covered up a grunt as she kicked him again. Bitch.

"Will you stop doing that? Your shoes are really pointy."

"Well, play nice then."

"I'm trying, but I can't help feeling this is a waste of time. I'm not convinced that second guy's trying to buy arms."

"And I'm beginning to think you're right. The intel must have been dodgy." She trailed a finger along his arm. "But look on the bright side—that new guy at the NSA owes us a favour now."

The waiter brought over dessert as Nick made a real effort to look besotted with his dining companion, but all he could think of was the curvy brunette waiting for him at home.

Emmy giggled, smiling at the waiter. "Ooh, sweetheart, look! Two spoons, isn't that lovely?"

"Yeah, sure is, my little pumpkin."

Nick gave Emmy a soppy smile and carefully fed her a spoonful of chocolate cake. The Russians at the next table glanced over, and one of them said something in his mother tongue.

"Aw, how sweet. Asshole one just told asshole two he wishes his wife would look at him the way I'm looking at you," Emmy told Nick. "Maybe he's a romantic at heart."

"Not sure about that."

Emmy tilted her head and listened to the first asshole again. "Actually, you're right. He reckons it's time for a new one, and he'll get shot of the old *suka* when he gets home. Oh, and I think he's talking literally about the 'shot' part."

"Heartless bastard."

"He's an arms dealer. They're not exactly famed for their compassion."

One last spoonful of cake, and Nick and Emmy settled back to listen while the arms dealer and his companion discussed Spartak Moscow's chances in the Russian Premier League over a bottle of vodka. They weren't good, apparently.

"I hate soccer," Nick said, stifling a yawn as asshole one clicked his fingers at the waitress and ordered another drink.

In many ways, soccer players were worse than arms dealers. Blackwood had been hired to provide close protection for a highly paid pussy in France's Ligue 1 recently, and it was like babysitting an oversized toddler—tantrums, messes, and a complete refusal to take responsibility for his own actions.

"Keeping you up?" Emmy asked.

Nick's yawn turned into a smile. He couldn't help it, not with Lara's naked body front and centre in his mind. Soft, curvy, and spread out underneath him.

"That's Lara's job now."

"Well, these dicks look like they're almost done. You'll be back in your little love nest before you know it."

Nick hadn't told Emmy that things had progressed with Lara, but she'd guessed the second she saw him. Not surprising when his face ached from smiling so much. He felt different inside too. Lighter. He'd even go so far as to say happy. And he hadn't felt that way in years. Not since...since Jana.

His phone vibrated against his thigh, snapping him out of his reverie. He'd only brought his emergency phone with him, designated R for red because if somebody called him on it, there was a good chance blood was being spilled. Like seven years ago when it rang for his fiancée.

Dammit, his fingers shook as he answered. "What?"

"Are you okay?"

Nick recognised the voice of Matt, the control room supervisor at Blackwood and a man who could stay calm through a nuclear blast.

"Why wouldn't I be?"

"Because your Ferrari just went from sixty to zero in less than a second?"

His Ferrari? The Ferrari he'd left safely tucked up in his garage at home?

"I'm sitting in a restaurant. Who the hell is in my car?"

"An excellent question."

"Check the camera in my garage."

"Give me a minute."

Even as he waited for Matt to call up the video feed, the serpent of fear coiling through Nick's gut told him who must have been driving.

"Don't bother with the camera. Tell me where the car is."

Matt read out the coordinates, and Nick scribbled them onto a napkin then repeated them back.

Matt confirmed. "Want me to call the emergency services?"

"Get an ambulance on its way."

When Nick hung up, Emmy already had her jacket on. She raised an eyebrow as she dropped three hundred-dollar bills onto the table.

Nick didn't answer her unasked question. He didn't need to. They'd worked together for long enough that words weren't necessary. His palm was clammy against hers as he grabbed the hand she held out and led her from the restaurant, plastering on a smile for the benefit of their Russian friends.

Emmy had illegally parked her Dodge Viper half a block away, and Nick broke into a jog as soon as they got out of Levante. Emmy kept up, looking remarkably comfortable in pumps.

"You think Lara took your car?"

"Nobody else had access."

"Did she say anything about going out?"

"She said she was gonna watch a movie."

Emmy bleeped open the Viper and jumped into the driver's seat. For a brief moment, Nick considered snatching the keys, but although he hated to admit it, he knew she was the faster driver. As Emmy gunned the engine and peeled off down the road, he punched the target location into her GPS unit.

Three miles to go, and the speedometer crept over a hundred miles per hour.

Two miles, and Emmy missed an SUV by inches as she overtook a semi. Nick leaned his head back against the seat and prayed for his own safety as well as Lara's.

One mile, and the smell of burnt rubber permeated throughout the cabin.

Then Emmy skidded to a halt. "It says we're here."

"Then where the hell's the car?"

The wooded road was deserted, with no streetlights, no traffic, and no fucking Ferrari.

"What's that?" Emmy pointed ahead.

Nick squinted into the gloom. "Looks like a car, but it's not mine."

Emmy reached under her seat to retrieve her gun of choice, a Walther P88, and stuffed it into her waistband.

"Let's take a closer look."

The engine growled as the Viper rolled forward, and Nick focused on the light-coloured sedan ahead. A Nissan Sentra, maybe? He couldn't see a driver, and all its lights were off.

Emmy slammed on the brakes as both of them caught movement from the tree line. "What the...?"

Nick didn't bother to reply. He leapt out of the car and ran for the man scrambling out of the trees, cradling a woman in his arms.

Oh fuck. No! It couldn't be.

It was.

Lara's head lolled to the side, and the trickle of blood running down her temple glistened in the Viper's headlights.

"Her car went off the road right in front of me!"

"Is she alive?"

The stranger glanced up at Nick but didn't stop walking. "She has a pulse. I'm taking her to the hospital."

Emmy planted herself between the man and the Sentra. "In that?" She jerked her head towards his car, never taking her eyes off him. "You're bloody not. She could have spinal injuries. You shouldn't even have got her out of the car."

He looked back towards the trees. "I couldn't just leave her there. It might have caught fire."

"Unlikely. Put her down."

"Trust me, I'm a cop. It'll be okay."

"Oh, really? You're a cop? Then you should know better than to move an unconscious woman like that. Now put her the *fuck* down."

In her heels, Emmy stood an inch taller than the guy, and he took a step backwards. Nick added his six-foot-two frame into the mix as well as his voice.

"Do exactly as the lady says. Put the girl on the ground. Gently. Then do something useful and flag down the ambulance that's on its way."

No doubt realising his idea of driving an injured girl to the hospital himself wasn't a sensible one, the man lowered Lara to the damp asphalt and stepped back. Nick and Emmy dropped to their knees in an instant, and Nick said a thousand silent thank-yous for the medical training he and Emmy had undergone over the past couple of decades.

"Pulse?" Emmy asked.

"Faint, but there."

"Good. She's breathing, but she's hit her head and fuck knows what else. She needs medical attention, and quickly."

Emmy rocked back on her heels and pulled out her phone. For once she'd managed to keep it intact, and for that Nick had to be grateful. A few seconds later, she spoke to the control room.

"Matt? The ambulance—where is it?" A brief pause. "Tell them to hurry the hell up."

She tossed the phone to the side and got to her feet. "They're two minutes out. And our buddy isn't sticking around."

Nick glanced up to see the wannabe hero's car careering off along the road. A second later, the tail lights rounded the bend up ahead at speed.

"Fuck. So much for helping."

"Don't think about him right now—Lara's our priority. I'll get the first aid kit out of the trunk."

Nick's hands shook as he grabbed the blanket Emmy brought back and tucked it around Lara. Not again. Please, not again. One woman he loved had already died in his arms. What kind of cruelty would it be if it happened a second time? All the fears that had gnawed at him since he met Lara came to life on a deserted roadside in Richmond.

Emmy took over, checking Lara's injuries while Nick knelt helplessly at her side. The metallic tang of blood brought a lump to his throat. So much blood. On her arms, in her hair, on her chest.

"This cut on her left arm needs attention. Hold."

Emmy straightened Lara's elbow, and Nick took her arm as Emmy applied a QuikClot trauma pad over the oozing wound and bandaged it on.

"No arterial damage, I don't think," Emmy muttered.

Jana's face swam into view. Not her beautiful, smiling face. No, the one with blood running from the strangely neat bullet hole in her cheek. But that wasn't what killed her. She'd bled out from her brachial artery seconds after she told Nick she loved him one last time. And he'd told her he loved her right back. Did she hear him? He had to believe she did.

But he'd never told Lara, had he? Not properly. He leaned over and whispered close against her ear.

"I love you, baby. You hear that? I love you."

"Nicky, stop thinking that way."

"I can't help it." A tear trickled down his cheek and splashed onto Lara's. "She's everything."

It seemed like forever before the faint sounds of a siren reached his ears.

"Thank goodness," he barely got the words out.

"She'll be okay, Nicky. She's still breathing, and that wound's clotting nicely."

He clung to Lara's hand as the medics leapt out of the ambulance and took over, and when they asked him to let go of her, Emmy had to peel his fingers away. Numbness spread through him as a second ambulance arrived, and the teams strapped Lara onto a spinal board and then lifted her onto a stretcher. A Rorschach of her blood stained the dirt at the side of the road. When Nick squinted at it, it turned into an eagle. A fucking eagle. Jana's fucking eagle.

"Nicky..." Emmy's voice held a warning.

"What?"

"Pack it the fuck in. She's still alive. Are you coming with me or in the ambulance?"

"Ambulance."

The cops had joined the party, and one of them tried to stop Nick as he left the scene. "Sir? We have some questions."

"They can wait."

"Uh..."

Emmy took pity on the guy. "Ride with me. We'll answer them at the hospital."

## 44

## NICK

The cop looked remarkably unruffled as he trailed Emmy into the waiting room.

"Most boring drive of my life," she muttered as she dropped into the seat next to Nick. "Anything?"

"They've taken her for tests."

"Still unconscious?"

"Yeah." Nick rubbed his hands over his eyes as he remembered his trip to the hospital with Jana all those years ago. Back then, the thin thread of hope had snapped twenty minutes after they arrived, but Lara was still hanging on.

The cop cleared his throat. "Did either of you witness what happened?"

Nick let Emmy take the lead. He didn't trust the Richmond police, and he didn't want them poking their noses into Blackwood's business either. But tonight he was too tired to lie. Luckily, Emmy was the master.

"Yeah. We were driving back to my place in convoy. Lara was ahead, and something ran out in front of her. A fox, I think. Or maybe a small deer."

"And she swerved?"

"Right into the trees."

"What speed was she going?"

"Something sedate."

"In a Ferrari?"

"Not everyone drives like they're in a race."

Nick choked back a laugh. Emmy treated the whole of life as a race, and she always had to be in pole position.

The cop raised an eyebrow and scribbled in his notepad. "So, an accident then?"

"Sure looked that way. You want a coffee?"

The cop nodded.

"Nick?"

He didn't even bother to answer.

Emmy brought him a cup anyway, shitty stuff from the vending machine, and he ignored it as the cop asked more questions about Lara and the car. Once he'd established she was insured, he went back to his donuts at the station.

Emmy, who'd been pacing in her customary habit, paused in front of Nick.

"So, something was off about that dude..."

"The cop?"

"No, idiot. The guy carrying Lara."

Nick had blocked everything except Lara's broken body from his mind, but now he thought back to the scene.

"Yeah, it was."

"I mean, what kind of arsehole drags an injured woman out of a vehicle like that? He said the car was at risk of exploding, but that sort of thing only happens in the movies. I should know. I've tried it enough times."

"Too many people believe what they see on TV."

"He also claimed to be a cop. If he really was, he should have known better. And if he wasn't, he lied. Why would he lie?"

"I don't know." Only with a sickening feeling, Nick did.

"Or I might. That guy Lara thought was bothering her in Baysville, she reckons he's followed her to Richmond."

"She's seen him?"

"No, but she's sure he's been in her apartment. I was gonna look into it, but she only told me yesterday, and then I got distracted."

"And you reckon the crash is connected? That she had help leaving the road?"

"Maybe." Nick punched the seat beside him and would have done it again if Emmy hadn't grabbed his hand. "Fuck. I thought she'd be safe in my house."

"Well, she would have been if she'd stayed in it. Why'd she leave?"

"I don't know. I don't know anything anymore."

Emmy gave his hand a squeeze, which fucking hurt. "I'm gonna make some calls. Don't hit anything else, yeah? I don't want to deal with any more injuries tonight."

Nick tried to blank everything out as he waited, but all he could think of was last night with Lara. One night. One fucking night was all he got. Heaven help the man who pulled Lara out of the car if he'd had something to do with this, because Nick wasn't about to let him walk away.

Emmy came back half an hour later and curled into his side in a silent show of support.

"Things are happening," she whispered.

"Good."

Seconds turned into minutes, and almost an hour passed before a doctor pushed through the double doors leading to the ER. Nick tried to read the expression on his face but got nothing.

"Family of Lara Reynolds?"

"That's me." He struggled to his feet. "How is she?"

"Not as bad as we first feared. We've scanned her brain, Xrayed her, and stitched up a couple of cuts, but the worst damage appears to be a broken finger."

"Is she awake?"

"She came round briefly, but now she's asleep again. Best that she rests."

"Thank goodness." Nick sagged back in the chair, relief spreading through him like a new dawn. "Can I see her?"

The doctor gave a small smile. "Just one of you."

Emmy pushed Nick forward. "I'll wait here."

Lara lay in a private room, sleeping. Apart from the cut on her temple and the constant beeping of the machines, she could almost have been resting peacefully after a long day. Nick dragged a chair to her bedside and held her good hand as he explained just how pointless his life would be without her in it. Could she hear him as he poured his heart out?

If not, he'd just have to tell her again later, wouldn't he?

The sun had risen by the time Emmy meandered in with a fresh cup of coffee for him. He grabbed the foul-tasting brew and slugged half of it back.

"How'd you get in here?"

She shrugged. "Got lost on the way to the bathroom. You okay?"

"I'm better than I was a few hours ago."

"I'll be in the corridor if you need anything."

Nick only needed one thing—for Lara to wake up. And an hour later, he got his wish. The beeping from the heart monitor quickened, and her eyelids fluttered open.

"Baby, I missed you."

Her eyes struggled to focus, but he saw the moment they did. And heard it.

"Get out!"

"Huh?"

"Get out! Get away from me!" She snatched her hand from his and wriggled to the other side of the bed. "I never want to see you again."

"What?"

Lara's heart may have been racing, but Nick's had frozen. Why wouldn't she look at him? He tried to reach out for her as she broke down in tears, but she slapped at his hand.

"I hate you."

A nurse ran in, no doubt alerted by the ear-splitting chorus from the monitors. "What happened?"

"I don't know. She just woke up and started yelling at me."

"Please make him go," Lara begged the nurse.

"Baby, don't do this."

The nurse parked herself in front of him. "I think you need to go."

Nick tried to reason with the woman. "She's my girlfriend. I need to make sure she's all right."

"At the moment, you seem to be the reason she isn't all right. I have to ask you to leave."

"But—"

"Now, sir."

With one last look at a sobbing Lara, Nick shuffled out of the room. But he left his heart behind, torn from his chest and clasped in her hands. What had happened in there?

Emmy looked up at him with big violet eyes from her seat in the hallway. "What was all the shouting?"

"I have no idea. The only thing I know is that she doesn't want me there."

"But when you left her at home earlier, I thought everything was going fine?"

"It was better than fine. We were finally where I've wanted

346

to be for months. I'd even begun to think I might have a chance with her."

"Maybe it was the bang on the head. Trauma like that can easily confuse a person. Remember the time Bradley got knocked out by that curling iron, and when he came round he thought he'd died and gone to hell?"

"Emmy, that was different. You were leaning over him wearing a Halloween costume."

"But still, he wasn't thinking straight." She clasped his hand. "It'll be okay, Nicky. I promise."

# 45

## LARA

Beeping broke into my consciousness, grating on my nerves. What was it? An alarm clock? I tried rolling to the side, but something dragged on my hand, and a bolt of pain shot up my arm. It took some effort, but I raised an eyelid. A white room. White blankets. Machines by the bed. Slowly, too slowly, the fog cleared and I remembered. The restaurant, driving away, the accident. Nick. Yelling at Nick. This must be the hospital.

A sharp pain cut into my arm as the blanket dragged across it, but I ignored that and the ache in my neck as I looked around the room. Had Nick gone? I couldn't cope if he'd stayed. One argument was quite enough for today. I caught sight of somebody curled up on a chair in the corner and stifled a groan. Emmy. Of all the people I didn't want to see at the moment, she ran a close second after Nick. Maybe I could just close my eyes and pretend to be asleep until she went away? Yes, that was a good plan.

"Hi," she said.

Okay, perhaps not quite such a good plan.

"Hi." My voice came out as a croak.

"Do you want some water?"

I nodded. My tongue and the sides of my mouth were all stuck together like a mess of papier-mâché.

She brought me over a cup with a straw in it, and I sipped, inwardly cursing her kindness. I didn't deserve it. Not after what I'd done.

"Do you remember what happened?" she asked.

I nodded again.

"Can you tell me?"

What the heck should I say? Should I own up to sleeping with Nick? She'd be upset, but she couldn't kill me in a hospital, right? Not with all the doctors and nurses around. Or should I leave that part out and make up another story about why I was upset enough to crash Nick's car? I remembered it hurtling through a forest.

As usual, my mouth acted before my brain had a chance to catch up.

"I'm so sorry," I blurted. "I ended up in bed with Nick. I didn't mean for it to happen, and I'm so, so sorry."

Of all the looks I'd expected to see on her face, confusion wasn't one of them.

"Why are you sorry? He's not that bad a lay, is he?"

"What? No, of course not. But I thought you'd broken up because Bradley said you weren't together anymore, then I saw you in that restaurant and realised you hadn't, but it was too late because we'd already slept together the night before. If I could turn the clock back, I would. But I can't."

"Night before last?"

"I think so. I wasn't unconscious for that long, was I?"

"Nope. Less than an hour." She checked her phone. "Awesome. I had that day in the pool." One corner of her mouth tugged up in a smile as she tapped away at the screen. "Suck on that, Luther. Now, all the rest of what you just said, can you run that by me again?"

I told her the whole sorry tale, fighting back tears and adding on a thousand more apologies as I went. And at the end, Emmy started laughing.

"So let me get this straight, this whole time, you thought I was dating Nick?"

"Well, yes. Weren't you?"

"Fuck no. Didn't he mention I'm married?"

"You're *married*?"

She waggled a fancy diamond ring at me. "Yeah, but I don't always wear this when I'm working. Nick's one of my husband's best friends. He's also an idiot. I can't believe he didn't tell you."

"But...but what about the time I saw you coming out of his room in the morning? You'd slept in his bed."

"Yes, but he wasn't in it. He was at my house, watching a ball game with my husband and twenty other guys. Those nights always end in carnage, and I wanted to get some sleep, so I borrowed his place."

"And his bed?"

"I didn't want you to have another set of sheets to wash. Plus the other times I've done that, his bed's been the only one that wasn't buried under mountains of shit."

Should I believe her? Could I have been so wrong?

"What about a couple of weeks ago when you came out of his room wearing only a robe? You said you'd been getting hot and sweaty."

"Yeah, we had. In the gym. And then I needed to use his razor and his shower gel. I'd appreciate if you didn't mention the razor. He hates when I borrow it for my legs."

The look on my face must have said I still wasn't convinced.

"Hey, I won't lie to you. Nick and I did have a thing together, but it ended in spectacular style a decade ago. If you really want the sordid details, the last time I slept with him was a year after that and we were both drunk. And to be honest, things were so different between us by then, it was strange and a little bit yucky. Like fucking my brother."

No, I didn't want the details. "But last night, you were on a date. Nick told me he was going out with some Russian businessmen."

"We were working. What's Nick told you about what he does?"

"He said he invests in companies. Buys them, builds them up, sells them, something like that."

"That bloody idiot." Emmy shook her head. "He does invest, but it's more of a hobby. His main job is at a company owned by him, me, my husband, and Nate. You've met Nate?"

Yes, at the charity ball. I nodded. "So what does Nick do there?"

"Security work."

"Like installing burglar alarms and stuff?"

"Not exactly, and I'm afraid that's something I can't say too much more about. But I will tell you that last night, we were in that restaurant because the dudes sitting at the next table are into some seriously fucked up stuff, and we were eavesdropping on their conversation to try and find out more information."

"In a restaurant?"

"They were speaking in Russian and too arrogant to consider that the American couple beside them might actually understand everything they said. Not all bad guys skulk around in abandoned warehouses, you know. Restaurants are good meeting places because they're harder to bug, and there's background noise. But enough said about that."

"Is any of this stuff dangerous?"

"Yes. Which is why he held off getting involved with you for so long, even though it was obvious to everyone he was crazy about you."

Everyone except me, it seemed. "I didn't realise."

"I know. Because that shit of an ex made you doubt your own worth."

She held up a hand when I tried to explain the truth in Billy's views. After all, what had I done with my life?

"Don't. Just don't. I can see we still have work to do. Anyhow, I told Nick to tell you everything and let you make your own mind up whether you wanted to date him, but did he listen? Of course not."

"He hasn't told me anything."

Emmy tucked her legs under her and regarded me through critical eyes. "How well are you feeling?"

A chill ran through me. "Why? What is it?"

"If Nick won't explain things, I probably should. But you won't like it."

"Over the past few days, I've been stalked, stressed out because I thought I'd turned into the other woman, and then crashed Nick's car. How much worse can it be?"

"Much worse. Has anybody mentioned Jana?"

My chill turned into goosebumps, and the heart monitor raced. I turned to watch the green lines tracking across the screen. Even if I told Emmy I felt fine about everything, she'd know the truth.

"No, I don't know who that is."

"Was. She was Nick's fiancée." The machine kicked up a gear, and Emmy glanced across at it. "Breathe deeply. Otherwise you'll have a flock of nurses in here."

I tried, but the revelation shocked me to my core. Nick had been engaged?

"What happened? Why didn't he marry her?"

"Because she died. Seven years ago now, give or take. They were living together in Germany at the time. Nick had just bought Adler House, and they were gonna move in once Jana finished her degree, but it never happened. Adler. Did you know that's German for eagle?"

I shook my head. "The eagle statue in the hallway?"

"Jana chose it."

Words deserted me. All I could do was watch Emmy's lips as she continued with the story I wasn't sure I wanted to hear.

"Nick was working as a bodyguard for an heiress who'd been getting some unwanted attention. Her ex kept following her, and Nick caught him breaking into her home one evening. The cops locked him up for the night, then let him out on bail. One fucking night. And when he got out, he found a new target."

"Jana," I whispered.

"Right. He wanted Nick to feel his pain. Phoned and told him exactly that. By the time Nick got to Jana, it was too late."

"Oh..." I had no words. Poor Nick. Poor Jana. "I don't... I can't..."

"It broke him. Not in every way, but in here." She pressed her palm against her chest. "Until you came along. You stuck him back together. Now you hold his heart, and it's up to you whether you want to keep it."

"Does he still do the same job?"

"Yes, and he'll never quit. He's gonna go to work, and when he comes home, he won't tell you about his day. He's gonna turn up with dings, dents, and scratches and maybe worse, and he won't be able to say where he got them. Some nights he won't come home at all. There's a lot of women who couldn't cope with that. The question is, are you one of them?"

"But what if he gets badly hurt?" My voice rose in line with that darn machine and its squealing. I recalled the bruises on his chest in England, and how he'd joked about getting them. Could he have been telling the truth? "He got injured in England. His chest."

"Ah, yes, the tree and the parachute. It happens, but getting hurt is a risk he takes. A risk we all take. It's a calculated risk, though, and he's well trained."

So he *had* tried to be honest with me, and I'd brushed it off. I thought back to our last night in Baysville. The way he'd met Billy head-on without any hesitation, so calm and assured. How many similar situations had he faced? And where the heck did he learn to fight?

"You said on the night he was in jail that it wasn't the first time he'd been there. Was he a criminal?"

Emmy laughed. "He spent a couple of nights in a cell when he was fifteen because he stole a truck and his arsehole of a father decided to teach him a lesson. Then he got put in the brig for a week when he and his platoon stripped down their commanding officer's car and reassembled it on the roof of the mess hall. The captain didn't see the funny side. Oh, and he got held hostage in Iraq for two days before he escaped. I think that's it."

"He was in Iraq? And what's a brig?"

"Yes, he was in Iraq. We have an office over there. A brig is a Navy prison."

"So Nick was in the Navy?"

"For a few years. He joined up to piss off his dad, then found it actually suited him quite well."

"This is all...it's so much to take in. I wasn't expecting any of this."

"Take some time to think it through. Lara, he's a good man."

"I know. I know he is. But Jana... His job... And I don't understand why he's even interested in me. I mean, why isn't he with someone like you? You seem like you'd be perfect for each other."

"Nicky needs sweet, and he needs straightforward. I'm neither of those things, and I never will be."

"I wasn't sweet earlier. I shouted and told him I never wanted to see him again."

"He'll get over it."

"Do you really think so?"

"I'm certain of it."

I wasn't so sure. When I closed my eyes, I could still see the hurt on his face. I'd done that to him. Me.

"Where is he now?"

"Out working. Looking for your stalker. How much do you recall about the car crash?"

"Hardly anything." The road, the dark... Then nothing. "I wrecked Nick's Ferrari."

"He doesn't give a fuck about the car. Only you. Now, tell me what you remember."

I racked my brain, but most of the journey was hazy. "He forgot his wallet, so I went to take it to him, then I left the restaurant, and there were headlights... Trees. I remember trees."

"Did you see another car behind you?"

"I don't think so. Why?"

"Because there was white paint on the back of the Ferrari, and we suspect you might have had some assistance leaving the road. The car has a tracking device and sensors on it, so as soon as you crashed, Nick got a call. When we arrived on the scene, a man was carrying you along the road."

Now the darn machine really went wild. I'd barely swallowed the lump rising in my throat before the door burst open and a nurse ran in.

"Is everything okay?"

"Uh, fine?" I needed answers, not a medical exam. Please, just go away.

The nurse narrowed her eyes at me. "Are you sure?"

Emmy cut in. "We're fine. Your machine sounds like it's

on the blink, though. Every time Lara inhales funny, it goes haywire."

I forced myself to stay calm as Emmy stared down the nurse, who didn't seem convinced. "Those monitors are normally very reliable."

"You should get that one checked. But don't worry, I'll call you if Lara needs help."

I smiled and nodded, and the nurse backed out of the room. As soon as the door closed behind her, I uncurled my fingers from the blanket and turned back to Emmy.

"Man? What man? Where was he taking me?"

"He claimed to the hospital, but he hadn't bothered calling 911, and he took off after we made him put you down. He also had a light-coloured car that would match the paint we found. Nick said you've had trouble with a stalker, and we're trying to find out if the two are connected."

"How close did you get to him?"

"Pretty much toe to toe."

"Do you remember what he smelled like?"

"What he smelled like?"

"I've never seen him, but I can tell when he's been in my apartment because it smells funny afterwards."

Emmy flicked her gaze towards the window as she pondered. "Cigarettes. Not just his clothes. His breath too, so a smoker. And there was something else. Aftershave. Not sure I could pick out which one, though."

"It's him. Tobacco smoke and cheap cologne."

My pulse sped up again as I realised how close he'd come to abducting me, and I glared at the monitor screen. Emmy reached out, unclipped the sensor from my thumb, and stuck it on her own instead. The machine slowed right away. Forty-seven beats a minute. How did she do that?

Free of technology's watchful eyes, I gripped the sheets in

panic again. "My life's getting worse and worse. Sometimes I wonder why I get out of bed in the mornings."

"No, this is good."

"Good? How?"

"Because it means we're working one case instead of two. One stalker. We don't need to split up our team."

"What team?"

"I told you, we run a security company. We'll find the guy. Don't worry."

She sounded far more confident than I felt. "How?"

"Don't sweat the details." She reached over and checked my pulse, then clipped the sensor back onto me. "Right, I need to speak to our people. There's a guard outside the door, and the only people allowed in are verified medical staff and our team. No stalkers." She threw me a backwards glance as she sauntered out the door. "Relax."

## 46

## LARA

Emmy closed the door behind her, and I thumped my head down on the pillow. Ouch. What she'd said about Nick left my mind spinning, even more than the accident already had.

Nick truly cared for me, or so she said. I wasn't just a convenient fling. If I'd known that a few days ago, not even the apocalypse could have wiped the smile from my face, but today? Finding out Nick was some sort of commando left me unbalanced. And Jana?

Emmy told me she'd died because of Nick's work, and I'd be lying if I said I wasn't worried history might repeat itself. But then again, I'd managed to attract two crazies all by myself, hadn't I? First Billy, and now a stalker. If Emmy's guess about the accident proved correct, they'd both tried to kill me, and twice Nick and his training had gotten me out of nasty situations.

So, did I give Nick my heart? Oh, who was I kidding? He already had it. But did I try to salvage what was left to prevent a bigger heartache in the future?

What if he went off to work one day and never came back?

If that happened now, I'd be devastated. But if it happened a year down the line, after Nick gave me more of the sweetness that turned my insides into spun sugar, I'd break completely.

I longed for Momma's words of wisdom. She'd have known the answer, just as she always did. Like back in the early days of my relationship with Billy when she'd tried to warn me away from him, but I'd been too young and too headstrong to listen.

Would she approve of Nick? I liked to think so.

Voices in the hallway startled me, and seconds later, Emmy returned. Only this time, she wasn't alone. I took in the newcomer—a teenage girl wearing ripped jeans, a pink sweater that hung off one shoulder, and high-heeled boots. She radiated the confidence Billy had knocked out of me at her age.

"Lara, meet Tia. She's going to help us with a sketch of the guy who tried to take you."

"Like a police sketch artist?"

Tia looked as if she'd barely graduated high school.

"Yes, except she's not police."

"What are the police doing? You've reported it, right?"

"Not exactly. Best to keep them out of this for now."

"But—"

Tia dropped onto the chair next to the bed. "Trust her. She knows what she's doing. One time I got kidnapped, and Emmy was the person who found me."

"I'm still not sure—"

Emmy interrupted. "Let's get this drawing done, shall we?"

Tia moved to the chair by the window, and Emmy dragged the other seat over to sit by her side. I wished I could see what was going on, but all I got were snippets of description from Emmy as Tia pulled a pad and pencils out of her leather satchel and started work.

"Pointier chin, and his lips were thinner than that."

Tia's pencil moved over the paper. "Like this?"

"Better. Dark eyes. Brown, I think, although it was pretty dark when I saw him. No glasses."

Tia worked away, her face a mask of concentration. She had a habit of biting her lip, I noticed. A nurse popped in and prodded me as an hour passed, then two.

"And his hair? Long? Short?" Tia asked.

"Collar length. Messy, like it needed a cut. The style might have changed recently, but he had a receding hairline. That's something he couldn't easily hide."

Ten more minutes, and Tia leaned back in the chair and flexed her fingers. "How's that?"

"Pretty damn good. I'd say that's worth a shopping trip with Bradley."

Tia whooped and flung her arms around Emmy. "Awesome!"

I couldn't stay quiet any longer. All the time they'd been talking, curiosity had been eating away inside me.

"Can I see?"

Tia skipped over and sat on the bed. "What do you think? Do you recognise him?"

Holy moly, the girl could draw. The face almost came alive off the page. And... Yes, I'd seen him before. Somewhere.

"He's familiar, but I can't put my finger on where from."

Buck's? I ran through a tableau of the patrons in my mind, but nothing clicked. College?

"He's from Baysville, I reckon," Emmy said. "He had to have followed you back from the wedding. The timing's too much of a coincidence. But he couldn't have followed the plane, so he was connected enough to find out where you or Nick were living."

"I barely spoke to anyone. Just small talk at the wedding.

Only Missy knows where I live, but she's known since I moved here."

"You ever have much involvement with the police there? You and Nick both ended up in the police station, and the dude told me he was a cop." She shrugged. "He could've been lying, but the association fits."

"That's it! That's where I remember him from. Not that night, but I got mugged a few months ago, and he was the guy who came out to interview me." I squinted at the sketch again. "I'm sure of it. But his hair was shorter back then."

"There wasn't any police report filed by you for a mugging."

What? "But I called the station when I got home."

"Not 911?"

"I couldn't see the point. The guy was long gone, and I might have taken cops away from someone who needed them more than me. That detective came the next day and took down all the details."

"If he did, he never turned the report in. Bradley did a thorough background check before I interviewed you. No police reports. Not even when Billy pushed you down the stairs, which, by the way, you should have hauled him into court for. He deserved to be punished, drinking problem or not."

"You know about Billy?" I whispered. "Nick told you?"

"He told me what you told him at the weekend, but I'd already guessed. A girl doesn't turn up at the hospital with a shattered leg, refuse to let her boyfriend of five years see her, then drop out of school to move somewhere that's nowhere near him afterwards if her relationship is a normal, happy, and loving one."

I blinked back the tears threatening to spill out because the last thing I wanted to do was cry in front of Emmy. She had so much poise, so much confidence. I couldn't imagine her ever breaking down.

"I was so weak. I didn't want to burden Momma, and I had nobody else to turn to. Every day, I kept thinking that if I could just get through the last year of school, save up some money and escape, everything would be all right."

Tia dropped the sketchbook onto the wheeled table next to the bed and hugged me. Darn it. Her gentle squeeze released the tears I'd fought to keep in, and I blubbered all over her.

"You weren't weak," Emmy said. "You were stuck in a difficult situation, and the only way you could see out of it took time. If Billy hadn't fucked with your plan, you'd have sorted things out on your own."

If only I truly believed that. Emmy had more confidence in me than I did in myself.

"Is that what you would have done?"

"Honestly? No. But everyone's different, and that's not necessarily a bad thing. The world would be a boring place if people all acted the same."

"What *would* you have done?"

At first, I thought Emmy wasn't going to answer, given the long pause, but then she smiled faintly.

"Billy would have had higher medical bills than you did." She cleared her throat and changed the subject. "I don't suppose you remember the detective's name, do you?"

How I wished I could, but I barely remembered his face, his voice, or anything else about him either. Apart from the chewing. "I don't recall, but he must have gotten through five pieces of gum while we were talking." The squishy sound echoed in my head, and that loosened a memory. "Uh, I think his name began with a J, or maybe a G."

Detective J... Gah! I couldn't quite grasp it.

"No worries. I'll head out and talk to people, and we'll get this sketch circulated. Tia, you stay here, okay? Keep Lara company. Any problems, call me, yeah?"

"Got it."

I lay on the bed when the door closed, drained. How could a policeman be stalking me? Didn't they take an oath to protect people?

"Are you okay?" Tia asked.

"Not really."

Once, I'd have brushed off her question with an "I'm fine," or "Everything's great," but at that particular moment, I was too tired to put on a brave face.

"Emmy'll sort everything out. Don't worry."

"I feel terrible about this. Causing all this trouble. I barely even know Emmy, and she's running around trying to fix up my mess."

Tia shrugged. "It's what she does."

"How do you know her?"

The friendship between Emmy and the young girl seemed an unlikely one.

"She used to date my brother, but now she's more like my sister."

"I wish I had a sister. Or any family, really."

"Emmy says you can choose your own family if you don't like who fate gave you. So I picked her. She's helped me through so much shit in the last year. She's awesome."

"Being able to choose your own family sounds like a lovely idea."

"Do it then. Why not? Emmy always tells me to grab every opportunity with both hands. She wants to die knowing that she's lived."

I wanted that too. More than anything, I didn't want to wake up in fifty years and imagine what might have been. The safe option might help me to avoid heartbreak, but what was the point if I felt nothing at all?

And I wanted Nick. My heart knew it, and now my head knew it.

"I need to talk to Nick," I muttered.

Would he accept my apology? I'd never hoped for anything as much as I hoped for his forgiveness.

"You want to borrow my phone?" Tia offered.

"Could I?" I didn't know where mine was. In the ruins of the Ferrari, most likely. "Do you have Nick's number? Or Emmy's, even?"

She tapped on the screen and passed the phone over. "It's ringing. For Nick."

His voice crackled through seconds later. "Tia?"

"It's Lara."

"Thank fuck. Are you okay?"

"I'm okay. And I'm sorry. So, so sorry."

Silence.

"Nick?"

"I'm here. I've been going out of my mind."

And that was *my* fault.

"I wasn't thinking straight, and this is all so new." A tear rolled down my cheek. "Can we talk? Please?"

Another pause. "On my way. I'll be there in ten."

The phone slipped from my fingers as I desperately planned what to say when he arrived. How did a girl apologise for being stupider than an amoeba?

Tia passed me a tissue. "What's wrong? He's coming, right?"

"Yes, but I don't know what to say to him."

"Just tell him how you feel. Men are terrible at guessing."

"How I feel? Like, 'I'm sorry I yelled at you. I thought Emmy was your girlfriend and you were cheating on her and then me, but now I know I was totally wrong about that. Can we just turn back the clock to the bit before you left for dinner?'"

Tia burst into giggles. "You thought Emmy and Nick were an item?"

"I didn't know they weren't. I kept seeing them together, and she slept at his house, and I just assumed…"

"Never assume. It makes an ass out of u and me. That's another Emmy-ism."

"I'll have to remember that one. How about I tell Nick I had a freak-out?"

"You don't want to sound like an idiot."

"I am an idiot."

"He doesn't think so."

Hmm. Right now, I wasn't convinced. "What about apologising for the car and telling him I don't want to live without him? Too needy?"

"Nah, he'd be happy to hear that."

"You don't think he'll run a mile?"

"Only if it's towards you."

We lapsed into silence as I mulled over the right words. This had to be good. No, perfect. Except things didn't go quite to plan. Because when Tia slipped out of the door a few minutes later, my mind went blank.

And when Nick collapsed to his knees at the side of the bed looking more haggard than I'd ever seen him, took my hand, and kissed it gently, I could only say three words.

"I love you."

# 47

## LARA

A spark lit in Nick's brown eyes as our gazes locked.

"I love you too, baby." He dipped his head and brushed his lips across mine. "And I'll spend the rest of my life showing you that."

"I'm so sorry I yelled at you. I got confused, and—"

He silenced me with another soft kiss. "Shhh. It's in the past. Emmy told me what happened, and it's my fault too. I should have made my relationship with her clear, but I thought she'd already told you."

"It turned into such a mess, didn't it?"

What was that cheeky smile for? Nick squashed onto the bed and wrapped his arms around me.

"There's only one kind of mess I want to make with you."

"We're in a hospital," I hissed.

He glanced over at the door. Closed. Firmly closed.

"In case you haven't realised, I like to take risks."

His two-day-old beard scratched against my chin as he kissed me again, and when our lips met, he took me away from my disaster of a life. One touch of his tongue made me forget my own name. I closed my eyes as warm fingers crept under the thin blanket, caressing my side through the ugly gown.

A whispered sigh escaped my lips. This man was everything. Everything.

Then a commotion outside the hospital door brought me to my senses, and I jerked my head to the side.

"Someone's there!"

Nick didn't remove his hand. In fact, it crept lower. "Don't worry. There's a guard outside, and Tia, and Tia's a tiny little pit bull in designer clothing."

Hushed voices filtered through the door as Nick kissed me once more, and for a moment, I blocked out reality again. Despite being in a hospital bed with a psycho ex-boyfriend wishing me harm and a crazy stalker cop on the loose, I was officially the happiest girl in the world. Or at least, I would be when whoever was outside went away.

But they didn't, and one voice grew louder.

"But I'm a doctor, and I need to check on Miss Reynolds. She could be taking a turn for the worse in there."

"She's fine," the guard outside replied.

"You don't know that."

I tore my lips away from Nick's for a second. "The doctor's just trying to do his job. We probably shouldn't be making out in a hospital bed, anyway."

"I can think of worse places. Ignore him."

Nick kissed a fiery path down my neck, then trailed the tip of his tongue up my jaw. The sensation made me shiver, but in a good way for once. One finger nudged under the edge of my horrible paper panties, and the darn things rustled. Talk about embarrassing.

"Those aren't mine."

"Who cares? They're coming off."

The ripping sound almost covered up the doctor's protests in the hallway outside. Almost, but not quite.

"If you don't let me in, I'll call security."

The guard didn't back down. "I *am* security."

"Nick, why don't we let him in and get it over with? Perhaps he'll say I can be discharged?"

Apart from a few aches and some ugly-looking bruises, I felt pretty darn good.

Nick wadded up the paper panties and stuffed them into his pants pocket. "Let's keep our fingers crossed. Then I can get you into a proper bed."

The doctor poked and prodded, shone a light in my eyes, and asked a whole bunch of questions. Then he told me I had a concussion, and I could go home tomorrow if I felt up to it, but not before. Nick asked if he could stay with me tonight. The doctor said no.

Nick called Emmy, and ten minutes later, two orderlies carried a cot into the room.

"How does she do that?" I asked.

"Emmy's connected like you wouldn't believe. She knows people everywhere, and she treats favours as her own personal currency."

"Is that how she got you out of jail that night?"

"Yeah. She phoned an old friend and got him to call someone else. But in return, she roped me into attending his wife's fundraiser next month. Will you come with me?"

"To a formal dinner?"

He grimaced as he nodded. "We wouldn't have to stay for long."

"I'd love to go."

That got me a kiss on the hand, seemingly out of relief.

"You really don't enjoy those sorts of things?" I asked.

"I can think of a hundred other places I'd rather be, but it won't be so bad if you're there."

"You're too darn sweet, Nick Goldman."

He caught me by surprise when he flicked my earlobe with his tongue. "You're sweeter, baby. I'll let Bradley know you need a dress. Actually, I'll tell him to get several because these events come up far too often."

"You don't have to buy me expensive clothes. I can find something at the mall."

"No, you can't. I want you to have a dress that's as special as you are."

I just about melted into the pillow at that, but I couldn't help remembering what started the conversation.

"Nick, about that night with Billy..."

"It's done, baby. Don't dwell on it."

"But I'm not sure it *is* done. Billy's dad said we'd be sorry it ever happened. He's a mean man, and Billy's got a vindictive streak as wide as the Pacific Ocean."

One time, a kid in high school had reported him for cheating on a test. Billy denied everything, but I knew he'd done it, mainly because he was as good at calculus as a walrus was at ballet. But rather than admit his mistake and take his punishment like a man, Billy got his dad to step in and fix things with the principal, and a month later, the kid who blew the whistle found his car half-submerged in the river. Billy swore it wasn't him, of course, but years later, he admitted what he'd done during one of his drunken rambles.

No way would the Coopers let Nick's punishment go.

But Nick didn't share my fears. "I'm not worried about Billy or his father, and you shouldn't be either."

"I still think we—"

"Baby, you're lying beside me with no underwear on. I've got other things on my mind right now."

"We really shouldn't..."

He dumped the blanket on the floor and shoved the hospital gown up around my waist. I didn't feel self-conscious around him anymore, because how could I when he looked at me like *that*?

"What if we get into trouble?"

"I'll take the blame, baby. All you're doing is lying there."

At the first swipe of his tongue, I arched up off the bed, and the heart monitor went crazy again. Oh, hell. This was gonna be a problem.

"Can you wear the sensor thingy? That's what Emmy did earlier."

Nick held out his thumb, but when I clipped the widget on, his pulse was racing almost as fast as mine.

"Uh-oh."

"Plan B." Nick rolled off the bed and pulled the plug out of the wall. "Problem solved."

Okay, so technically we shouldn't have done that, but apart from a slight headache, I felt amazing. I didn't need a machine or a doctor to tell me that, for the first time in my life, I was truly living.

Nick did that, and he didn't even use words. He circled my clit with his tongue and slid a finger inside me, stroking, and a whole stream of filth flowed from between my lips. I clapped a hand over my mouth.

"Sorry! I never normally talk that way."

"I like the dirt, baby. Keep going."

So I did. And then I kept coming. Once, twice, three times before somebody knocked at the door and I nearly fell off the bed.

Oh, shit. I tried to pull the gown back down and accidentally ripped it. Great. Now everyone could see my boobs. Nick quickly threw the blanket over me, but there was no way he could hide the bulge in his pants.

"Who is it?" he called.

"Dude, are you decent?"

Emmy. Thank goodness. Well, not good exactly, but it could have been worse.

"Just a second."

Nick tucked in the blanket while I finger-combed my hair, but my face was still burning when Emmy walked in. She glanced at the black screen of the heart monitor and tapped the plug with her foot.

"Let me guess... The machine malfunctioned?"

"Something like that."

"Nice move. Just be aware that the shift changed ten minutes ago, and the new nurse supervisor's a real jobsworth. Great if you're sick, not so good if you're horny."

"Is this a social visit?"

"Nope. I came to tell you that Detective Jonas has gone to ground."

Jonas! *That* was his name.

"He stole the Nissan Sentra a couple of days ago," Emmy continued. "Took the keys out of a lady's purse while she was shopping, then just drove the car out of the parking lot. Nobody's seen it since. We've got a team out canvassing low-end motels and guest houses, but I'm not convinced we'll find anything. The guy's a cop, so he knows the places to avoid. I'd put money on him sleeping in the car. That's what I'd be doing in this situation."

"Fuck. I was hoping we'd have something concrete by now."

"Look on the bright side—we're gathering more information about him. Lara's not the first woman he's done this to. There was another one last year, but she was a lot more vocal and put a complaint in."

"What happened? Did he get a disciplinary?"

Emmy's hollow laugh bounced off the walls. "You know what cops are like—they stick together. The woman moved out of state, and it all got swept under the carpet. Then Lara rocked up and Jonas had someone new to fixate on."

"That bastard."

"How can a police officer get away with that?" I asked.

I'd trusted him, and he'd repaid me by making my life a living hell.

"These guys rarely go from nothing to what he did to you. My bet is that we'll find more victims as we look back further. The cops in Baysville aren't being particularly forthcoming, but my new buddy Senator Wilmslow is helping out there. We've also tracked down Jonas's mother. She lives in Indiana, but she hasn't seen him in four years, and she doesn't like him much either. She told us he deserves everything he gets."

"Sounds like there's a good story there."

"And the guys from our Indianapolis office are busy ferreting it out. Jonas didn't seem to have any friends other than his work colleagues. I've pulled everyone spare onto this, and we're doing all we can."

"Thanks, babe. If he's still out there, we need to sort out a guard roster for Lara as well. The doc says she can leave tomorrow."

"Okay. That's soon. Good, but soon." Emmy flopped into the chair beside the bed, sucking on her teeth as she stared straight ahead.

Nick grimaced. "Shit."

"What?" I asked.

"Emmy's thinking. That's not always a good thing."

She sat forward, elbows on her knees. "I do have a bit of an idea."

"Do I even want to hear this?"

"Probably not, but I'm gonna share it anyway."

Nick didn't look thrilled at the prospect. "Go on."

"What does Jonas want?"

"That's obvious. Lara."

"Exactly."

Six feet two of angry Nick leapt up and glowered at Emmy. "Oh no. No, no, no. A million times no."

If he shook his head much harder, he'd have a worse concussion than I did.

"Hey, hear me out."

"We're not using Lara as bait."

Bait?

"It could speed things up. Draw him out."

"No fucking way. I'll build her a fortress and send everyone in the company out to look for that asshole before I put Lara in the line of fire."

"Fine." Emmy leaned back in the seat, tilting her head up to meet Nick's gaze. "Okay, how about we make him believe Lara's running around loose? She can stay locked down in Fortress Riverley."

"Now, that's a better idea. You'll do it?"

Nick got a worrying gleam in his eyes as he looked Emmy up and down, and she nodded.

"Better than going to meetings."

"You're taller and thinner, but with the right clothes it could work, as long as you're not seen together."

"Guys, what are you planning? This is my problem too, and I don't understand what you're talking about."

Nick perched beside me and took my hand. "The quickest way to get Jonas to show himself is to make him come to you. Or think he's coming to you. I'm not risking your safety, so Emmy can take your place."

"Isn't that dangerous? I mean, if he could hurt me, he could hurt her too, right?"

And how would I live with myself if someone else got injured because of my mess? It was bad enough that Nick had spent a night in jail without Emmy being stalked by a man who made my skin crawl with fear every time I thought of him.

"Emmy can look after herself. On a scale of one to ten, this level of danger scores a two."

"But even a two means there's still a risk."

Emmy brushed off my fears with a wave of her hand. "Yeah, yeah, and I could get shot by a terrorist tomorrow. Right, that's decided. I'll get Bradley to go shopping."

# 48

## LARA

The next morning, I pulled on a pair of dark blue boot-cut jeans while Emmy and Bradley turned their backs. Nick did no such thing. He licked his lips, then groaned as I did the zipper up. The pants were cut far too long for me, but that meant they hid the four-inch platform shoes I needed to wear underneath to bring me up to Emmy's height.

Emmy didn't seem to share my embarrassment about getting undressed in front of an audience because she pulled off her loose, floaty top and threw it to me while Bradley stuffed her bra with silicone chicken fillets. After she'd pulled on a long wrap dress, it was onto the hair. Bradley produced wigs for both of us and curled the strands around our faces—all the better to hide them. He'd already worked his magic with make-up, and my bruises were barely noticeable from a quick glance.

I didn't look exactly like Emmy, and it was hard to hide the fact I was a good few pounds heavier. If anyone stood us next to each other, the differences were clear. However, the plan was that Emmy—dressed as me—would leave first with Nick, and if Jonas was watching, he'd have to follow or risk losing them. That meant that when I caught a ride with Bradley afterwards, he'd be long gone.

Emmy stood in front of the mirror and checked herself out from every angle. It was obviously easier to add weight than to take it away, and she'd padded out her hips as well as her bust, giving her a curvy figure rather than her usual athletic one.

"The fake tits are sweaty as hell, but the cleavage would stop traffic, wouldn't it, Nicky?"

"No comment."

"Do I really look like that?" I asked.

"Yeah, baby, but without the hard edges."

Nick wrapped his arm around me and nuzzled my ear. That didn't go down well with Bradley.

"Nick! You're messing up her hair."

The next half hour was the strangest of my life, and that was saying something after the last few months. Emmy chatted with me, and as she did so, she copied my mannerisms and the way I talked. I'd never thought much about my accent or my speech patterns before, but she picked out every nuance.

"Now walk around the room," she instructed.

I did, and she followed, swinging her hips a little more and shortening her stride.

"How's that?" she asked our audience.

Nick nodded, and Bradley gave her two thumbs up.

The way she'd turned into me was uncanny. It was like watching myself in a movie, only she answered back.

"Have you done this sort of thing before?" I asked.

"A few times."

"What's that nose wrinkle thing?"

"You do that when you're thinking."

"Oh, gosh. Do I?"

Nick laughed. "Don't stop. It's cute."

Hard to stop when I didn't even realise I did it. I wiggled my nose, then touched it. Did I really?

Without further delay, Dr. Beech signed my discharge papers, and the time came for us to leave. Sweat trickled down my back as Emmy took Nick's arm and walked out of the room, looking for all the world like she was slightly worse for wear. Bradley plopped back onto the bed beside me.

"Are you okay?" he asked.

"I think so. This all feels so strange."

"Emmy and Nick's whole world is strange, but you get used to it. At least you'll never be bored. Now, I've got one of the company Ford Explorers outside. I figured my Lamborghini would be too difficult for you to get into with your injuries, and because Emmy wouldn't let me help her, I'm afraid I can't help you."

"I'll be okay to get in. I'm just a bit stiff."

To my utter relief, Bradley drove far more sensibly than Emmy. I'd been worried her tendency to speed might have rubbed off on him, but he puttered along like a mom on her way to the grocery store.

"How long until we get to Emmy's house?"

"About thirty minutes. And it's actually her husband's place we're going to. Emmy's home's undergoing a touch of renovation at the moment."

"They live in different houses?"

"No, they share both of them. But Emmy likes modern, and her husband prefers things more traditional, so they compromised and decorated one each. It's an interesting relationship."

"It sure sounds that way. What's her husband like? I don't know anything about him."

"That's probably for the best."

"Why?"

"Sometimes he scares people."

377

"Scares people?"

"He won't do anything to hurt you. But if anyone else does, I wouldn't want to be in their shoes. Don't worry—you'll be safe at Riverley, which is why Nick's sending you there."

Forty minutes later, Bradley drew to a halt outside the tall iron gates of Riverley Hall and honked the horn. A mop of brown hair popped out of the window of a stone cottage built into the wall that surrounded the property, then the gates swung open on silent hinges.

Bradley jerked his head at the funny little building as we passed. "Guardhouse. Two people from the security team are on duty inside."

"Mr. Black has a security team? Is that because of me?"

"No, they're here all the time. He likes to keep the place safe. He also has patrolling teams and a state-of-the-art security system."

"Isn't that expensive?"

"He's loaded."

"Does he have more money than Nick?" A personal question, but I couldn't help asking, and Bradley seemed happy to talk.

"Emmy and her husband make Nick look like a kid with a piggy bank. They're in a whole other league. And don't make the mistake of thinking Emmy lives off him either. She earned her money herself, every cent of it."

The house came into view, and I did a double take. Back in elementary school, Tori and I had done a project on English stately homes, and this place reminded me of one of those, from the turret on the left to the fountain in front of the steps.

The ornate stonework, the big mullioned windows, and the huge columns flanking the front doors. A swath of ivy covered the right-hand corner, and when my eyes followed it upwards, I caught sight of a row of gargoyles staring down from the roofline.

"Do people really live here?"

Bradley chuckled. "Yes, they really do. The house is quite something when you first see it, huh?"

I nodded, speechless.

"Come on, let's go inside."

Bradley helped me out of the car and linked my arm through his as he guided me up the steps. He didn't bother to knock, just stared into a retina scanner hidden in the eye of a stone lion, and I jumped as a muffled *clunk* came from the door. What kind of person had a James-Bond-style security system when a simple key would do? Well, apart from Nick and his eagle-beak lock, which was admittedly very cool.

Going inside was like stepping through a portal to the dark side. Buck's Bar would have fitted in the hallway twice over, and polished wood panelling gave the place an ominous air made all the more foreboding by two full-sized suits of armour flanking the entrance. Blood-red velvet couches butted against the walls, and the only brightness came from a giant chandelier whose lights glinted on the black and white chequerboard tiles. The place was elegant in a gothic way. At least, that's what I thought at first. When I looked closer, I realised the crystals hanging down from each branch were shaped like tiny skulls with gleaming teeth and empty eye sockets, and I couldn't help shuddering. The place gave me the creeps.

Bradley ducked down a passage to the side, and I followed. If I'd hoped for a cheerier theme, I'd run out of luck. The tapestry gracing the wall showed everything from a man being speared to a woman being decapitated.

"It's from the Battle of Gettysburg," Bradley said. "Dates back to 1863. Ugly as hell, isn't it?"

"It's very morbid."

A lady wearing an apron stepped out of the shadows. "It's an heirloom, dear. We've learned to live with it."

Bradley introduced us. "This is Mrs. Fairfax. She takes care of the house."

Mrs. Fairfax ignored my offered hand and pulled me into a hug.

"I'm Lara," I mumbled into her chest. "I'm Nick's housekeeper."

She pulled back and gave me a sympathetic smile. "I don't envy you. That boy leaves a trail of mess wherever he goes."

"I think he's getting better. He puts his plates in the dishwasher now."

"I always said if the right woman came along, he'd change his ways. It very much seems like you're her."

A blush spread up my cheeks. "I sure hope so. That's if this stalker doesn't send him running."

"Nick won't worry about a little thing like that. I know he's got people out hunting for the man, and Logan's here to keep an eye on you. He's waiting in the gallery."

"Gallery?"

Bradley grabbed my hand. "You know, for the art collection?"

He said it like having a gallery was perfectly normal. I was way, way out of my depth here. Mrs. Fairfax gave me a wave as Bradley tugged me deeper into the bowels of the house, talking as if words were going out of fashion.

"So, what do you want to do? There's a movie theatre in the basement and a library on the second floor. I don't imagine you'll want to use the gym, but sitting in the Jacuzzi might help your aches and pains. Or are you hungry?" He glanced at his watch, and diamonds glinted in the glimmer from a flaming sconce high up on the wall. "It's just past noon. Mrs. Fairfax'll serve lunch soon in the Lincoln Room."

It felt like much later. "If it's okay, I'd prefer to rest. All of a sudden I'm exhausted."

"Sure thing, doll. I'll show you where Nick's room is—it's best you sleep in there. I can introduce you to Logan afterwards."

The room was on the third floor and bore a worrying resemblance to Adler House before the dumpster arrived. I tried to ignore the mountain of laundry and peered out the window instead. Beyond the tennis court, three horses grazed in an expanse of fields, and a man worked on the fencing, hunched over with a pair of black dogs playing around his feet. Except one of them moved strangely.

"Bradley, what's wrong with that dog?"

"What dog?"

I pointed. "The one on the right."

"Oh, that's not a dog. It's a jaguar."

"A...a...jaguar?"

"You know, like a big cat. He's Emmy's pet. She inherited him."

I guess I must have as gone pale as I felt because Bradley pushed me down onto a chair.

"Don't worry, Kitty won't hurt you. He likes women."

This truly was a House of Horrors. Nick had promised I'd be safe here, but between the dark atmosphere and the wild animal outside, I didn't feel it. This house had a black heart. If not for Bradley's presence, I'd have run screaming.

But for now, I was stuck here.

After Bradley slipped out, I kicked off my shoes—or rather, Emmy's shoes—then pulled off the wig and climbed under the quilt. I was sure I wouldn't be able to sleep, but the pillow smelled of Nick, and curling up and inhaling deeply were the last things I remembered.

## 49

## LARA

I must have been more tired than I thought because when I opened my eyes, a sliver of moon hung in the dark sky beyond the open drapes. I'd lived in towns my whole life, and the street lamps meant it never got pitch black. Or quiet. There were always people coming and going, plus the constant hum of traffic in the background. Here in the country, the isolation made Riverley Hall seem even eerier.

The glow from a small lamp on the nightstand showed a stack of clothes had appeared on the end of the bed. Did Bradley bring them? Or Mrs. Fairfax? Either way, I was grateful I'd have something to wear. My stomach grumbled as I realised the last thing I'd eaten was a slice of rubbery toast at breakfast. What were the chances of me finding the kitchen in this place without falling into a dungeon?

Bradley must have picked out the clothes because the pair of jeans I pulled on fitted perfectly, and the sweater that went with them was the prettiest shade of deep pink. I slipped out of the room barefoot and found myself in a dimly lit hallway filled with almost identical doors. How would I ever find my way back? I needed to leave a trail of breadcrumbs. Or cake.

Cake trumped bread. Counting the doors, I followed the hallway until I came to some stairs. Were these the ones I'd come up earlier? Portraits of old men in period costume glowered down from the walls, but the faces all looked the same to me.

I crept downstairs and ended up in a hallway I didn't recognise. How big was this place? I figured the kitchen would be towards the rear of the house, but I'd lost my bearings, and I didn't know whether I was at the front, back, or somewhere in the middle. Left or right? I was never right, so I picked left, slipping through a heavy wooden door that belonged in Dracula's castle. The dark walls seemed to close in around me, and I began to fear I'd be stuck there, destined to wander around the maze forever, when the faint strains of piano music drifted through the heavy air.

Where was it coming from?

If I could work that out, maybe I'd find a person. Or a ghost. The haunting melody grew louder as I walked, the tempo changing, speeding up to something almost joyful before slowing again to a tune that tugged at my heartstrings. Beautiful, just beautiful. Whatever song was playing, I wanted to buy my own copy of the recording.

A thin beam of light spilled from a door ahead, beckoning me forward. Thankful I hadn't put on Emmy's noisy heels again, I pushed the door open and found the music wasn't coming from a stereo, but rather from a black grand piano at the far end of the room. A man sat half hidden in shadows, his face impassive as he played. I froze as his fingers danced over the keys.

He seemed to sense rather than see me, because as the piece came to an end, he looked up. Caught, like a kid with my hand in the cookie jar.

I couldn't move as he rose to his feet and walked towards me. Actually, no, that wasn't right. He stalked towards me, his eyes never leaving mine, and I withered under his dark gaze.

As he came closer, I realised how big he was—a heavier build than Nick, and at least four inches taller. They both had dark hair, but there the similarity ended. While Nick was handsome in a boy-next-door kind of way, with twinkling eyes and dimples when he smiled, there was nothing boyish about this man. He was textbook gorgeous, from the outside at least, but his eyes told a different story.

They were almost as black as his hair, two deep pools that brimmed with danger. Goosebumps broke out on my arms as he stopped in front of me. Okay, this was worse than the jaguar and worse than a ghost.

He held out a hand. Oh heck, I was supposed to shake it. I willed myself to stop trembling as I reached my fingers out to his.

"I-I-I'm Lara."

"Yes, I'm aware of that."

Now what? "Uh, you're really good at playing the piano."

"It's a hobby. I play to relax."

"You don't look very relaxed."

Oh shoot! Did I just say that out loud?

He shook his head faintly. "If you were married to Emerson, you'd struggle to relax as well."

So this was her husband. Bradley was right about him being scary. At least he didn't seem mad at my intrusion, and from what I'd seen of Emmy, I could understand his point.

And speaking of Emmy. "Is there any news on the...uh, the situation? You know, with whoever's stalking me?"

"Nothing yet. Logan went back to the office to help with the search while you slept. Nick's just dropped Emmy off at your apartment, and he's on his way over."

Nick was coming here? That revelation raised my spirits

tenfold. Being in this strange house wouldn't be so bad with him at my side.

My happiness must have shown on my face, because the Dark Lord smiled, revealing a set of perfect white teeth. No fangs. I checked.

"I'm glad he's finally found someone who can make him happy, and it's good to see the feeling's reciprocated. You can wait for him in the living room. I'll show you through."

I followed as he glided down the hallway, dressed all in black, another shadow in this house of many. Only when he'd left me in a huge room filled with antique furniture did my pulse slow.

"Baby, I missed you."

Nick strode in ten minutes later and swept me into his arms. I squeezed him as tightly as I could, ignoring the pain from my bruises.

"I missed you too."

"How are you finding Riverley?"

I couldn't help shivering. "Creepy."

"I thought that too when I first came here. But the place grows on you. Wait until you see the pool and the gym."

"Maybe not the gym."

He pressed his lips to my good temple. "Okay, not the gym. I had a different kind of workout in mind, anyway."

"Can we get something to eat first?"

"Nobody's fed you?"

I went a little pink. "I've been asleep."

"Then we'll go and find food."

After a late supper of bread and cheese, with wine for me

and water for Nick because he was on call, I reminded him to put his plate in the dishwasher.

"I always forget that part."

"Then I'll keep reminding you until you remember."

"It'll take forever for me to learn."

"Then I'll remind you forever."

We were both grinning as he picked me up, and unlike me, he knew the way back to his bedroom. Along a hallway, turn left, turn right, through a door...okay, I was lost again. Anyhow, we made it, and as soon as the door closed, he pushed me against it and fisted his hands in my hair.

"I've been waiting all day to get you naked."

I stilled his hand when he started to lift my top. "Should we be doing this? We're guests in somebody else's house."

"I practically lived here for years. It's fine, trust me."

"But Emmy's husband's home. What if he hears?"

"He and Emmy sleep in a different wing. Nobody wants to be anywhere near her. Even if you screamed, he wouldn't hear you." Nick grinned. "And I'm gonna make you scream."

"Hang on. Why doesn't anyone want to be near Emmy?"

"Shit. I probably shouldn't have said that."

"Well, you did, and now I'm curious."

Nick sucked in a deep breath. "Emmy has some issues with sleeping. She acts out without knowing what she's doing, and it can get dangerous."

"Like sleepwalking?"

"Among other things."

"What does she do? Try to jump off the balcony or something?"

"More like tries to throw other people off the balcony."

"Has she ever hurt anyone?"

He gave a sheepish look. "Yeah. Me."

"Seriously? But you're so much bigger than her."

"The devil himself lives in her when she's asleep. She

386

caught me by surprise. Broke my nose and a few ribs, and she didn't even know she was doing it. Took two people to pull her off me."

"But...how? I don't understand how she could do that."

"Don't think about it. I try not to. Just promise me that if you ever see her sleepwalking, you'll get well out of the way."

"I promise."

He pressed against me, and all thoughts of Emmy, her husband, and their freaky house fled from my mind.

"Oooh."

"Exactly. Now, why are you still wearing clothes? I wanted you in bed ten minutes ago."

Put like that, I wasn't about to argue.

# 50

## LARA

Over the next few days, we got into a routine. Nick spent his mornings and afternoons searching for Detective Jonas, then after he'd dropped Emmy off at my apartment each evening, he'd sneak over to Riverley Hall and we'd spend the night together. And every time he made love to me, the memories of Billy receded further into darkness.

Speaking of darkness, Nick was right about the house—it did grow on you. As prisons went, I had to concede it wasn't bad. On the second day, I discovered the library with its floor-to-ceiling shelves and ladders that slid along on rails to reach the high-up books. It was a scholar's paradise, and judging by the number of first editions I found, a very rich scholar's paradise. I spent hours in there, curled up on the old brown leather couch next to the middle balcony with a mug of hot chocolate, tangled in the adventures of a different literary heroine each day.

In between reading and getting lost, I made friends with Mrs. Fairfax, who was often the only person to talk to during the day. Logan was in the house, but he mostly stayed in an office on the first floor, working. Other people flitted in and out, but nobody hung around for long.

"Don't you get lonely?" I asked her, thinking of my own experiences at Adler House.

"It's not always like this, dear. Your Nick's got everyone spare out looking for that awful Detective Jonas."

*My* Nick. I still found that difficult to believe, but with every look, every caress, and each murmur that he loved me, I became a little more convinced. He'd already talked about taking a trip to his villa in Italy when this was over, just the two of us.

"I'm so grateful they're helping. I don't know what I'd have done by myself."

"You're not alone anymore, dear. These people take care of their own, and they've claimed you as one of them. You belong here now whether you like it or not."

"I think I *will* like it, even if those suits of armour still give me the creeps."

"Emmy and Dan hid in them one Halloween. That was something to behold. Bradley took off in his Lamborghini and didn't stop until he reached North Carolina."

"Oh my gosh! Poor Bradley."

"He got his revenge, don't you worry. Emmy was walking around with purple hair for a week."

Yes, I was going to like this place, although I made a mental note not to go anywhere near the hallway at the end of October. And I wanted to fit in.

"Is there anything I can do to help?"

Mrs. Fairfax quickly shook her head. "Oh no. You're a guest, and besides, everything's under control. After thirty years, I've got a system."

"You've worked for the Dark Lord for that long?" I clapped a hand over my mouth. "Oops. I shouldn't call him that."

She chuckled. "It's quite a good name for him, dear. I used to work for his parents, and even as a child he was...intense. Now, what do you want for lunch? Sandwiches? Or I could make soup?"

"I'd prefer soup, but I can make it. I love cooking."

"Young Nick's never going to let you go, I'll tell you that now."

I sure hoped not.

Mrs. Fairfax eventually gave in and let me help out in the kitchen, and she even gave me a file full of her recipes. Her risotto was the best I'd ever tasted. I longed to get back to Adler House and recreate some of the dishes for Nick.

Although it didn't look as if that would be happening any time soon. Every evening I asked how the investigation was going, and every time, Nick grimaced and shook his head.

"There's no sign of the bastard. Emmy's convinced he's out there, though. She says she can feel him."

"Isn't that a bit odd?"

"Yes, but Emmy's gut feelings are usually right on the money. We're just watching and waiting at the moment."

So watch and wait we did. Logan popped in to update me several times a day, and I noticed he always wore an earpiece with a microphone attached. So did Nick when we weren't in the bedroom.

"What's that for?" I asked him, pointing.

"It keeps me in touch with the control room at headquarters and the rest of the team."

"Can you talk to Emmy?"

Nick tapped a button on his ridiculously complicated digital watch. "When I press this, it's like she's standing next to me."

As the days passed, I began to feel guilty for keeping Emmy and her husband apart. After all, this was my mess, not theirs. It should be me sleeping in my pitiful apartment while

Emmy lived in this palace where she belonged. I'd seen her husband with an earpiece too, and when he talked softly into it late at night, it was the only time I saw him smile.

"How much longer will this go on?" I asked Nick one evening as we curled up in the living room. "It's not fair for everyone to keep living like this."

"You're not going home, baby. End of discussion."

I glanced at Emmy's husband on the sofa by the far wall. A movie played on the big-screen TV fixed above the fireplace, but he was more interested in his laptop. From the curve of his lips, I bet Emmy had a webcam with her.

"But look at him. He misses her."

"He's probably enjoying the peace and quiet."

I dug Nick in the ribs. "Be serious. It must be awful for them."

"It's fine. Believe me, they've been in far worse situations."

"Like what?"

"I'll explain later. It's a long story."

How could he say something like that and leave me hanging? "No, I think you should tell—"

A loud, "Fuck," from Emmy's husband stopped me mid-sentence. Nick leapt to his feet in an instant and flew across the room to stare at the laptop screen.

"Whoa. Fuck me."

"What's happening?"

Neither of them answered, so when Logan burst in and ran to watch whatever was happening as well, I snuck over behind him. The screen was divided into four. The top left quadrant displayed a mass of static while the segment next to it showed a rolling grey shadow. Bottom left showed the door to my apartment building, dim because the bulb over the door hadn't worked since I moved in. Then I focused on the bottom right quarter.

"Fuck!" For a moment I forgot Momma brought me up

not to curse. Even if I'd relaxed my rule in the bedroom, I still tried to stick to it in company. "What's going on?" The fourth quarter showed the back of my building, and flames leapt from one of the units. "Is that my apartment?"

"It was, yes," Emmy's husband said.

"But what about Emmy? Wasn't she in there?"

"She was. She isn't now."

"What happened? Where is she?"

"The suspect took out your living room window with a bullet, then followed up with a firebomb. Emmy climbed out the bathroom window."

I'd always hated the lack of windows in my bedroom, as well as the fact that the only entrance to the bathroom was on the far side of my bed, but now it had proven to be a blessing. Still, that didn't entirely explain Emmy's escape.

"But there isn't a fire escape. She can't get down."

"Doesn't matter." Nick pointed to a dim figure scaling the wall, just disappearing out of camera shot.

"But why is she going up?"

"There's a man with a gun on the ground. Up's safer." Logan sounded as if he were discussing the weather. How could he stay so calm?

"What if she falls?"

Logan grinned. "Emmy's a good climber. Isn't she, Nick?"

"I don't need a reminder of that, thanks."

"Reminder of what?" I asked.

"Nick here thought he could out-climb Emmy once. He's got a reminder of the bet he lost in a certain part of his anatomy I believe you're familiar with." Logan winked at me.

Did he mean Nick's apa? I recalled him mentioning he'd lost a bet to get that. If so, I had more than one reason to be grateful for Emmy's climbing skills.

"Enough about that," Nick said. "Look." He pointed at

the screen again, where a second figure was scrambling out of my bathroom window.

"Looks like that's our boy," Logan muttered.

My heart stuttered as he clung to the drainpipe, and I wished he'd lose his grip. At first, I felt guilty for thinking that way, but then I remembered the man had caused nothing but hurt to me and the other women he'd targeted. Blackwood had found five so far.

"Do you think he'll fall?" I whispered to Nick.

"I'm keeping my fingers crossed."

Those fingers dug into my hips, and Logan's foot tapped out a jerky rhythm on the floor. Only the Dark Lord remained impassive as he watched the screen.

And it seemed he was in charge. "No, don't shoot unless he goes for his gun."

"He's talking to the team on the ground," Nick whispered. "He doesn't want this to get messy."

"I'd say it was already messy."

"Messier."

Nick wrapped his arms around me, and I sagged against his chest. I hated the waiting game, and even more so, the feeling of helplessness that came with it. Emmy had given me a chance when nobody else would, and that had led me to the man I loved. Now she was risking her life to solve my problems. I owed her everything, and I hoped with every atom in me that I'd be able to repay her.

*Please, let this turn out okay.*

There was a simultaneous intake of breath from Nick and Logan as a dark figure fell through the camera shot so quickly I wondered if I'd imagined it.

"What was that?" I had a horrible suspicion I already knew. "Did someone fall?"

The Dark Lord grinned, the first time I'd seen him look genuinely pleased. "It seems Detective Jonas lost his grip."

# 51

## LARA

Nick's Porsche sped through the night towards my apartment, or rather, what was left of it. I gripped his hand in my lap as I tried to process the night's events. My stalker was gone, as were most of my belongings and my home. I should have felt devastated, horrified even, but all that spread through me was an overwhelming sense of relief.

It was over.

Everyone I cared about was safe.

"You okay, baby?"

"Yes. I thought I wouldn't be, but I am. And you're sure Emmy's not hurt?"

"She broke a nail on the climb. Bitched like hell about it over the radio."

"A nail? That's it?"

"That's it; I promise."

As we got closer to my apartment building, the sky lit up like a macabre disco, orange from the dying flames with tinges of blue and red from the emergency services vehicles that had rushed to the scene. Nick drew to a halt half a block away and turned to me, his face serious.

"I hate to ask you this, but could you keep Blackwood's involvement quiet? We had some problems with the local cops last year—the chief in particular. Emmy bypassed him on a few matters, and she's not in his good books right now."

After what Emmy had done for me, I'd lie my butt off from here to Baysville if it helped her out. Not to mention the fact that Jonas had tried to kill me twice and nearly succeeded in roasting my friend. Sympathy for the man was in short supply.

"Just tell me what to say."

Nick pressed his lips to mine. "Thank you. I mean that. We all work as a team, and you're one of us now."

"I always will be."

That got me tongue and a whole lot of happiness, until a passing siren reminded us of the reason why we'd come. Nick pulled back but kept his arm around my shoulders.

"We'll say you lent Emmy your apartment after she had a fight with her husband and needed somewhere to crash until emotions simmered down. You don't know anything about Jonas or why he set the place on fire. We kept your name out of any discussions we had with the Baysville PD."

"Got it. I'll play innocent."

Acting clueless came easily to me because most of the time I didn't need to pretend.

"And if anybody mentions the car accident, that's all it was: an accident."

"I don't recall it being anything but."

He gave my hand one last squeeze, then put the car in gear. "I love you, baby. Let's go sort this out."

Nick drove closer to the scene, and I took in the devastation. Flames still licked up the outside of the building from my living room window, resisting the efforts of the firefighters' hoses. I guess my landlady hadn't paid much attention to fire safety as she counted her rent dollars every month. Probably every piece of furniture in the place was flammable. As well as the three fire trucks, I counted six police cars and an ambulance plus any number of uniformed men hanging around, watching the building along with a crowd of residents wearing pyjamas and dressing gowns. Heads turned as the Porsche pulled up.

Nick helped me out of the car and tucked me against his side, and his presence gave me the strength to deal with the situation. I spotted Emmy standing with a cop, a blanket wrapped around her shoulders and her feet firmly on the ground. Somewhere along the way, she'd lost the wig and padding and looked like her normal self again.

We headed in her direction, but before we could reach her, the Dark Lord strode past, eyes fixed on his wife. Emmy flung the blanket at the cop and raced over to him.

"Oh, darling! I'm so sorry. It was such a stupid quarrel, and now look what's happened. Can you ever forgive me?" She wiped an eye and left a sooty streak down her cheek. "I just want to go home."

He pulled her against his chest and glared at a cop who dared to look at him. "Of course I forgive you. I want you home more than anything."

Another policeman stopped beside them, and I noted he didn't make eye contact. He most likely feared being sucked into hell.

"Sir? Are you her husband?"

"I am."

"I understand from your wife that you had a fight recently, which…" He checked his notepad, more out of nervousness, it seemed, than a need to jog his memory. "Which resulted in her temporarily moving out."

"That's correct. She felt she needed some time alone."

"Can you tell us what the argument was about, sir?"

"She wanted to redecorate the living room, but I like it the way it is. Looking back, it all seems so trivial. Diamond, we can paint the damn room pink if it means that much to you."

"It doesn't matter anymore, honey. I overreacted; I can see that now. My life passed before my eyes in there, and it made me realise what's important. Plus it was that time of the month, and I was being a teensy weensy bit touchy."

The two cops exchanged a look of understanding, as every man did at the mention of PMS. The taller of the two took a half step back as the Dark Lord focused on him.

"Sir, do you know of any reason why someone would want to harm your wife?" the cop asked.

"Not unless they've tried her cooking."

The officer gave a nervous laugh as Nick pulled me forward. "This is Lara Reynolds. It was her apartment that got burned out."

I drew on my new-found strength as the cop turned to me, notepad in hand.

"You weren't home tonight?"

"I've been staying with my boyfriend."

"We're trying to work out why the place was targeted. Have you gotten into any arguments recently? Received any threats?"

I was about to shake my head when I thought of Billy. Perhaps I could cause just a tiny bit of trouble for the Cooper family? They sure did deserve it. "I had an argument with my ex-boyfriend a few weeks back, and his father said I'd be sorry. He lives in a whole other state, but it's not difficult to travel, is it?"

Emmy flashed me a grin as the cop scribbled notes.

"Can you give me their details?"

"Sure." Names, addresses, Billy's date of birth—I recited them all. I'd have added his GPA, favourite foods, and shoe size if I thought it would help. It just sucked that my efforts would come to nothing when they found out Billy was still incapacitated and Jonas wasn't Mr. Cooper. Unless... "I can't imagine Mr. Cooper setting a fire like that personally, but he has lots of money. Maybe he hired someone to follow me?"

That was definitely plausible, and judging by the slight curve of the Dark Lord's lips, he thought so too.

The cop looked up again. "That's useful information, Miss Reynolds. We'll certainly check into it. Can you think of anyone else?"

"Well, I haven't lived here long, and I'm only renting the place. What if someone had a grudge against a previous tenant? Or even the landlady?"

Wow, this lying game got easier the more of it you did. I wasn't sure whether that was a good thing or a bad thing, but much to my shame, I kind of enjoyed it. I was racking my brains for something else to say when a man pushed past me and planted himself in front of Emmy.

"Mrs. Black. Once again I arrive at a crime scene to find you right in the middle of it."

"Nice to see you too, Chief. I see you haven't taken on board the memo on tact that Senator Rutherford sent you last year."

The chief's face screwed up in an interesting mix of anger and confusion. "How do you know about that?"

"I know lots of things. But sadly not why that man set fire to my friend's apartment tonight. There I was, sound asleep, when some arsehole decided to shoot out the window and throw a Molotov cocktail through it."

"And yet somehow you survived then climbed up the outside of the building. The unknown male pursued you..." The chief looked at the other officer, who nodded. "And just as he climbed over the edge of the roof, he lost his grip and fell five storeys to his death?"

"That's pretty much it, yeah."

He stared daggers at her. "And you say you were staying in this apartment because you had an argument with your husband?"

"Oh, come on, Chief, last year you thought I had him killed. Why do you find it so hard to believe we had a little tiff?"

"I'm still not convinced by your story from last year, either."

"Give it up, would you? Your lab made a mess of the DNA testing, and the fact that you've got no idea who really did get killed in that incident is hardly my fault. Instead of haranguing me, why don't you focus on tightening your procedures?"

He opened his mouth, but Emmy didn't give him a chance to speak.

"Now, if you've quite finished, I'm going home to get some sleep."

She turned her back on him and stomped off, followed by her husband, who was smiling again. The chief looked as if he wanted to stop her, but after a long moment, he shook his head and disappeared in the other direction.

Well, this new world I'd landed in certainly was exciting.

"Do you want to go home too?" Nick asked.

I looked up at my apartment. The fire was out now, but blackened water still dripped from the windows, and a pervading smell of burnt plastic drifted through the air.

"I don't have a home anymore."

"Yes, you do. It's with me."

"You mean I can stay for a while?"

"I was hoping more like forever."

"Are you asking me to move in with you?"

"That's exactly what I'm asking."

I let out a whoop and leapt into his arms.

"Is that a 'yes'?" he asked.

"Yes, yes, a thousand times yes."

It was soon, but it was right. I felt that in my heart. Sure, we'd had our ups and downs, but I'd learned my lesson on the need to communicate, and judging by Nick's hourly texts and phone calls, he had too. Life had never been so good before, and no matter what the future might bring, I wanted to spend every minute I possibly could with the man in front of me.

He scooped me up in his arms and practically threw me into his car. "It's a good thing most of the cops in town are here."

"Why?"

"Because otherwise I'd get pulled over for speeding on the way home."

# EPILOGUE - LARA

I sat in front of the mirror while Bradley arranged my hair into a perfect chignon. It was a hairstyle I'd tried to do on myself time and time again, but each attempt left me looking as if I'd stuck a hedgehog to the side of my head. There were no such problems tonight, not with Bradley's magic touch.

He'd also chosen my evening gown, a stunning red number I'd never have dared to wear six months ago. It perfectly matched the ruby necklace Emmy had lent me. The hotel suite was a hive of activity as everyone got ready to go out for dinner, with Bradley calling out instructions to a bevy of assistants.

A make-up artist came over and retouched my lipstick. Beige, because Bradley said we shouldn't overpower the dress, and she'd already done the rest of my face so well I looked airbrushed. I wouldn't need to hide from the cameras tonight, that was for sure, and if I was lucky, maybe I'd even get my picture taken with the president?

I still couldn't believe this was happening. Just over a month had passed since the nightmare at my apartment, and each day had been better than the last. And this evening, to top it all, I'd be having dinner with the president of the United States. Well, not with him, exactly, but in the same room. The fundraiser had been organised by the first lady, and she and the president would both be attending.

"I can't believe you're not more excited," I said to Dan, who was having her nails buffed next to me. "I mean, we're about to meet President Harrison!"

At forty-two, he was the youngest ever elected president, beating JFK, and he certainly beat him on looks as well. Last summer, photos of him on a beach vacation had graced the front of every magazine at the grocery store, and the man most definitely worked out.

"We've all met him before."

"Oh my. What's he like?" I glanced around to check Nick wasn't in earshot. "Is he as sexy in person?"

"Hell, yeah."

"Do you think he really has a tattoo?" Rumours had circulated in the gossip mags last year, but nothing got confirmed.

Emmy meandered past, resplendent in a silver dress that shimmered like a waterfall. "It's an eagle on his arse."

"Are you serious?"

But she'd gone, already on the other side of the room where the Dark Lord stood spreading his shadowy aura in a tuxedo.

"Oh, she's serious," Dan said.

"How does she know?"

"Emmy knows everything."

I was about to question her on how Emmy could possibly know the president had a tattoo on his behind when my phone rang. Missy was calling.

Bradley had taken off my watch and replaced it with an elegant silver cuff, saying ladies shouldn't wear watches to events like tonight's dinner. When I pointed out that Emmy had her watch on, he scoffed and told me she wasn't a lady. Still, according to the clock, we only had twenty minutes before we were due to leave, so Missy would have to keep this short. I ducked out into one of the bedrooms in the Washington, DC hotel suite to get out of the way of the chatter.

"Hello?"

"Lara? You sound all refined. Like, British."

Must've been Emmy's influence rubbing off. "It's me."

"Guess what? Actually, no, you'll never guess. But it's good news. Well, it isn't, but it sort of is, really."

"Missy, you're making no sense whatsoever."

"Billy's dead."

"What?" I slumped onto a chair by the window. "How? When?"

"I got it from Bobbie who heard from Mary-Sue who spoke to Ginny whose brother's a cop that he got drunk and fell down the stairs. Clean broke his neck. Nobody found him for a few days, and the central heating was on high in his house so the results weren't pretty."

"Oh my gosh! Who found him?" Please not his girlfriend. She'd had a hard enough time already.

"His father. Jeanie hightailed it back home to Wisconsin while Billy was in the hospital. Hey, this is poetic justice, right? Him falling down the stairs."

It was, and that wasn't lost on me. A tiny part of my brain remembered Nick saying Billy wouldn't be a problem, and I quickly catalogued his whereabouts this week. He'd been around more than usual, and he'd even done some of his work from home so we could eat lunch together every day. Believe me, he was there every night too. The ache between my legs reminded me of that. No way would he have had time to travel to Baysville and back without me noticing. I mentally kicked myself for even thinking he could have had anything to do with Billy's death. It was an accident, and not a tragic one.

"I guess it is, Missy."

"And it gets better."

"How could it possibly get better?"

"Billy's dad's been arrested. Apparently, he got investigated over some fire in Richmond, and when the police confiscated his computer, it was full of kiddie porn. Thousands and thousands of pictures. Really nasty stuff, according to Ginny's brother. People are talking about it all over town. His golf club membership's already been revoked."

"Wow. I had no idea. That's disgusting."

Billy's father had always been a nasty man, but I'd had no clue he was into something quite so vile. Not the slightest hint.

"It's always the men who appear the most respectable that have secrets, isn't it?"

"It certainly seems that way."

"Are you okay about this? I know you were close to Billy, but he was a real asshole."

"I'm more than okay. And it may be wrong, but knowing those two are out of the picture'll help me sleep better at night."

"Karma has a funny way of coming back to bite people in the ass."

When I walked back into the living room, I found Nick waiting, dressed in a made-to-measure tuxedo I wanted to peel him right out of. He crushed me against his chest and kissed me, ignoring the whistles from around the room.

"Stop!" Bradley shrieked. "You're ruining her make-up, and that dress'll crease."

"Get a room, guys," Jed muttered.

I blocked them out. All that mattered was Nick and his

lips, and he didn't step back until I was well and truly breathless.

"Sure you want to go tonight?" he asked.

"Ignore him." Emmy jabbed a finger in his chest. "You're both going. I promised Diana."

"I want to go," I murmured, trying to smile. Inside, I was still reeling from Missy's call.

"What's up, baby?"

"Missy just phoned. Billy's dead. He fell down the stairs and broke his neck. And his father's been arrested for having child pornography."

Nick wrapped me up in a hug. "How do you feel about that?"

"Honestly? Relieved. Nothing else, just relieved."

"Good. Then don't waste another second thinking about either of them. That part of your life's done. Finished. From now on, you're going to enjoy yourself, starting tonight."

He was right. I darn well would have a good time. It wasn't every day a girl got to have dinner in the same room as the president, was it?

I loved my new life. I had Nick, a fabulous new home, friends, and no debt since Nick had admitted he'd paid off Momma's medical bills and refused to take a cent from me. When I'd tried to insist, he told me the price was me naked in his bed every night. Those were repayments I was only too happy to make.

The column of limousines that left the hotel on our way to the dinner venue was something to behold. I no longer felt like a complete impostor, but I was still nervous as all heck.

"If I speak to him, what should I say?" I asked Nick.

"The president?"

"Yes!"

"Just introduce yourself. He'll do most of the talking. He's used to it."

"Does my hair still look okay?"

"It looks beautiful. You look beautiful."

"I'm terrified."

"Don't be. It's just dinner."

That was easy for him to say. He knew what to say and how to act. I settled for clutching his left hand as he circulated with a flute of champagne in his right. I'd quaffed one glass of wine, but I didn't want to get any wobblier than I already was in these pumps.

"This is Senator Rutherford," Nick told me.

The senator shook my hand, and I grimaced at my sweaty palm. "Pleased to meet you, Miss...?"

"Reynolds. Lara Reynolds."

"Miss Reynolds. Are you enjoying the event?"

"Uh, I think so. I mean, yes. It's all a bit overwhelming."

He patted my hand in a fatherly way. "Between you and me, I felt the same at the first few of these dinners I came to."

"Really?"

"Everyone does. They're always a circus."

"As long as I don't end up the clown."

He chuckled. "I doubt Nick will let that happen. Good to have made your acquaintance, Miss Reynolds."

Nick drew me close as the senator moved on to the next person. "See, that wasn't so bad, was it?"

"I sounded like an idiot."

"No, you didn't. You're doing perfectly."

And then came the moment I'd been both hoping for and dreading. We found ourselves standing next to the president. Dan was right about the heat factor—up close, he exuded power, and his emerald eyes were mesmerising. He grinned at Nick as he shook his hand.

"Nick Goldman. It's been a while."

"I've been busy."

"I can see that. Is this the lady I've heard so much about?"

The president knew who I was? My knees went wobbly at the thought. Nick gave me a gentle push, his hand hot on the small of my back, and I tripped forward.

"Yes, this is Lara."

I forgot whether to bow, curtsey or swoon at the president's feet. His outstretched hand reminded me I needed to shake it.

"P-p-pleased to meet you."

"Likewise. We've got a wonderful turnout tonight. Cancer research is a cause close to my heart."

"Mine too. My momma died from breast cancer."

"I lost my grandmother. Science has made a lot of advances over the last few years, but there's always room for more. One of my challenges is to make sure we keep pushing forward."

A man with a camera tapped me on the shoulder. "Ma'am? Would you like a picture?"

With the president? Wow. A second later, I found myself squashed between Nick and the leader of the free world with a big, stupid grin plastered on my face, willing myself not to blink when the flash went off. Apart from meeting Nick, this was the highlight of my year, and now I had plenty of friends to share it with.

"The photos will be on the event website next week," the man informed me before aiming his camera at the next couple.

One final handshake, and the president moved on too. But I'd met him! That would be something to tell my children about. Children. Oh gosh. In my time with Billy, I'd never wanted any, but with Nick? That was another difficult conversation we'd need to have at some point in the future.

But not tonight. Tonight was all about us, fun, and dinner. We were at a table for eight, with Emmy and her husband, Luke and Mack, and Dan and Jed, he of the wandering hands. I spent half the time talking with Mack about her upcoming wedding. I'd offered to help Bradley with some of the planning as he had so much to do right now, what with renovating Emmy's house on top of his usual duties.

Amazingly, I managed not to make a fool of myself through all three courses, despite sitting next to the Dark Lord. He still unsettled me, but I no longer quaked in my shoes when he came close. And at least I could copy what cutlery he used. Nevertheless, I breathed a sigh of relief when he went off to talk to people after dessert.

"You look mighty happy tonight," Emmy said across the now-empty chair.

"How could I not be? I'm with Nick, I just ate chocolate mousse, and I met the freaking president."

"I'm with you on the chocolate mousse."

A body sliding into the seat between us interrupted our conversation, and I found myself looking at neat, light brown hair and the back of a man's tuxedo. His whisper was just loud enough for me to hear.

"Where the fuck are my cigars?"

"In the ugly-arse vase on the sideboard."

The man sighed. "And why are they in there, Emerson? Do you realise I offered the Japanese ambassador a pickled egg?"

Emmy grinned at him. "I did a good job with those. Did you like the little cupcake cases?"

"No, I did not."

"Well, I didn't like having to explain to airport security

why I was carrying a jar of the little fuckers in my handbag. Any idea how they got in there?"

Another sigh. "Can we call a truce?"

"Nope. Because I'm better at this than you are. And you just interrupted a conversation."

The man turned, and I almost fell off my chair when I looked into the face of President Harrison.

"So sorry—Lara, isn't it?" He smiled, but not the practised pose he used for the press. This one reached those mossy eyes. "I'm afraid you've stumbled into the middle of the pickled egg wars."

What did a person say to that? "Uh, it's fine. You carry on."

He leaned towards Emmy. "We'll finish this later."

I watched his departing back as Emmy picked up her wine. "Think I need this. He's plotting something, I know it."

I pushed my own glass far away. With the conversation I'd just imagined, I'd clearly drunk far too much of it.

Half an hour later, the results of my drinking made themselves known in a different way.

"Where's the ladies' room?" I whispered to Nick. He'd come back with a second helping of chocolate mousse for me, and I loved him all the more for it.

"Out that door to the side, and it's the second or third door on the left."

"Back in a minute."

I thought I'd be wobblier on my feet, but I made it to a stall with only one minor stumble and locked myself inside. *Good going, Lara.* I did my business, and then I heard it. Or rather, heard *her*. I'd only listened to Katya's voice that one night, but her nasal tone was imprinted on my mind.

"I can't believe I had to suck that old guy off to get a ticket to this, and it took ages for his Viagra to kick in."

Her whiny friend was back too. "My date's older than my grandfather. I don't understand it—you'd think men would be falling over themselves to ask us out. My father's got his own plane."

"Ridiculous, that's what it is. Half the women here have wrinkles."

"And we didn't get to meet the president. Do you think he really has a tattoo?"

"I doubt it. His publicist probably made that up to get column inches."

Oh, Katya had no idea, did she?

"That's a good plan. Maybe we should try that?"

I stifled a giggle, picturing a pair of tattooed socialites prancing across the cover of the *National Enquirer*.

Then Katya's talons came out. "And Nick Goldman's here with the dumpling girl again. What does he see in her?"

"I have no idea. But Emerson's with a billionaire—at least, that's what my date said. She probably takes it up the ass for that."

Oh, that was the last straw. I'd had quite enough of their rudeness, and I wasn't about to let them insult Emmy either. I quickly checked I hadn't left my dress tucked into my panties then marched out the door.

"Don't mind me, girls. It's just I'm in a hurry to get back to my incredibly handsome boyfriend who has his own helicopter and doesn't need any performance-enhancing drugs." I caught sight of their shocked expressions in the mirror as I washed my hands. "It's been a busy night, what with getting my photo taken with the president and eating two portions of chocolate mousse."

Katya's mouth dropped open, and I couldn't help smiling. Moments like this weren't quite as sweet as Nick, but they were up there. I didn't even wobble as I marched out the door.

And walked right into a member of the Secret Service, complete with earpiece and scowl. Ahead of him, a silver dress swished around the corner, followed by the now-unmistakable profile of President Harrison.

"Sorry," I mumbled, and the bodyguard stood aside to let me past.

"Not a problem, ma'am."

Was that Emmy in the silver dress? Where was she going with the president? I took one last look, but apart from a solitary man in a suit lurking at the corner, the entourage had disappeared.

Oh well. I headed back to the dining room, and Nick smiled as I took my place at his side.

"Everything okay?" he asked.

"Perfect. But what's up with him?" I gestured towards the Dark Lord, who was staring into a tumbler of whisky as if his eyes could shatter the crystal.

"Emmy's left him on his own. He'll be fine; don't worry. Tonight's our night. Do you want to dance?"

"As long as it's with you."

"I'm not planning to let you go. Ever."

And that suited me just fine.

# BLACK CATS AND BULLETS

Did you wonder how on earth Bradley managed to knock himself out with a curling iron? Yes, I did too, so I decided to write a little story explaining things...

## BLACK CATS AND BULLETS

Nothing fancy, just a quiet Halloween dinner at Riverley Hall. What could go wrong?

Everything, when Emmy and Carmen get involved...

Download your FREE copy here:
www.elise-noble.com/GoldBonus

# WANT TO STALK ME?

For updates on my new releases, giveaways, and other random stuff, you can sign up for my newsletter on my website: www.elise-noble.com

If you're on Facebook, you might also like to join Team Blackwood for exclusive giveaways, sneak previews, and book-related chat. Be the first to find out about new stories, and you might even see your name or one of your suggestions make it into print!

And if you'd like to read my books for FREE, you can also find details of how to join my advance review team.

Would you like to join Team Blackwood?

www.elise-noble.com/team-blackwood

facebook.com/EliseNobleAuthor

x.com/EliseANoble

instagram.com/elise_noble

goodreads.com/elisenoble

bookbub.com/authors/elise-noble

tiktok.com/@EliseNobleWrites

# WHAT'S NEXT?

**The Blackwood Security series continues in *Gray Is My Heart...***

Georgia Rutherford-Beaumont has it all.

A wealthy husband.

A powerful father.

A hitman trying to kill her.

Congressman's daughter Georgia longs for a little excitement in her life, at least until it arrives in the form of a high-velocity bullet. With Blackwood Security on the case, Georgia hides out with reclusive artist Mitchell Gray as the team tries to unravel the web of secrets, lies, and worse, actual spiders. Who wants her dead? One of her father's many enemies? Somebody closer to home? Or is it the Horsemen, the elite band of assassins Georgia's not supposed to know about?

Georgia's time away from home leads her to question everything, including herself. Where does the real danger lie? In death? Or in a life not truly lived?

*What's next?*

Find out more here:
www.elise-noble.com/gray

**If you enjoyed *Gold Rush*, please consider leaving a review.**

For an author, every review is incredibly important. Not only do they make us feel warm and fuzzy inside, readers consider them when making their decision whether or not to buy a book. Even a line saying you enjoyed the book or what your favourite part was helps a lot.

# ALSO BY ELISE NOBLE

**Blackwood Security**

For the Love of Animals (Nate & Carmen - Prequel)

Black is My Heart (Diamond & Snow - Prequel)

Pitch Black

Into the Black

Forever Black

Gold Rush

Gray is My Heart

Neon (novella)

Out of the Blue

Ultraviolet

Glitter (novella)

Red Alert

White Hot

Sphere (novella)

The Scarlet Affair

Spirit (novella)

Quicksilver

The Girl with the Emerald Ring

Red After Dark

When the Shadows Fall

Phantom (novella)

Pretties in Pink

Chimera

The Devil and the Deep Blue Sea

Blue Moon

## Blackwood Elements

Oxygen

Lithium

Carbon

Rhodium

Platinum

Lead

Copper

Bronze

Nickel

Hydrogen

Out of Their Elements (novella)

## Blackwood UK

Joker in the Pack

Cherry on Top

Roses are Dead

Shallow Graves

Indigo Rain

Pass the Parcel (TBA)

## Blackwood Casefiles

Stolen Hearts

Burning Love (TBA)

## Baldwin's Shore

Dirty Little Secrets

Secrets, Lies, and Family Ties

Buried Secrets

A Secret to Die For

## Blackwood Security vs. Baldwin's Shore

Secret Weapon

Secrets from the Past

## Blackstone House

Hard Lines

Blurred Lines (novella)

Hard Tide

Hard Limits

Hard Luck (2024)

Hard Code (2025)

Hard Evidence (TBA)

## The Electi

Cursed

Spooked

Possessed

Demented

Judged

## The Planes

A Vampire in Vegas

A Devil in the Dark (2024)

## The Trouble Series

Trouble in Paradise

Nothing but Trouble

24 Hours of Trouble

## The Happy Ever After Series

A Very Happy Christmas

A Very Happy Valentine

A Very Happy Halloween (2024)

A Very Happy Easter (2025)

A Very Happy Thanksgiving (TBA)

## Standalone

Life

Coco du Ciel

Twisted (short stories)

## Books with clean versions available (no swearing and no on-the-page sex)

Pitch Black

Into the Black

Forever Black

Gold Rush

Gray is My Heart

## Audiobooks

Black is My Heart (Diamond & Snow - Prequel)

Pitch Black

Into the Black

Forever Black

Gold Rush

Gray is My Heart

Neon (novella)

A Very Happy Christmas

A Very Happy Valentine

Dirty Little Secrets

Secrets, Lies, and Family Ties (2024)

Buried Secrets (2024)